The Comedienne's GUIDE TO PRIDE

The Comedienne's GUIDE TO PRIDE

HAYLI THOMSON

PAGE STREET
PUBLISHING CO.

For Mum,
who has always loved Lucy

"While we have the gift of life, it seems to me the only tragedy is to allow part of us to die—whether it is our spirit, our creativity or our glorious uniqueness."

—GILDA RADNER, *It's Always Something*

From: Taylor Parker (debbie.downer04@gmail.com)
To: Jane Lincoln (jane.lincoln@nbcunicareers.com)
Subject: Re: Congratulations! Finalist Announcement for the Emerging Writers' Diversity Award
Sent: November 1, 2016, 8:34 p.m.

Hi Jane,

I was really excited to receive your email. This is literally the best thing that has ever happened to me.

I'm sending this reply because I need to ask something of you. It's kind of humiliating. I don't want to come off as ungrateful, but I need to request that you don't include my name on the finalist list on the NBC site. The thing is, I'm not exactly out of the closet. I realize that I should have thought about the consequences before I entered a contest for diverse writers, but when I submitted my entry all those months ago, never in a million years did I think I would actually be selected as a finalist. Now I'm in a bit of a pickle—you've selected me as a finalist for this fantastic opportunity *because* I'm a lesbian, but it's actually something I'm hiding.

All I'm asking is that you keep my nomination on the down-low until the winner is announced. By then, I'll make sure I'm out (not that I think I'll win or anything . . . but just in case). All I need is a little more time. I need the news to come from me, not a social media announcement, you know?

1

Anyway, if you absolutely have to put my name down on the finalist list, that's still cool (well, it's not really cool, but I'm the one who got myself into this situation, and I'll get myself *out* of it—see what I did there?). In no way am I forfeiting my nomination. Seriously, Jane. I was born to be a sketch writer. I mean, I'd rather you come into Gay Narnia and drag me out kicking and screaming than I would give this up.

Whatever you decide to do, I can guarantee that you'll have my finalist submission sketch by Thanksgiving Eve, because if there's anything worth coming out for, it's the chance at winning an internship at *Saturday Night Live*. I need whoever is behind this screen to know that there's a seventeen-year-old girl living in Salem, Massachusetts, who takes her future in comedy as seriously as Trump takes his fake bake.

So, in conclusion . . . thank you.

Kind regards,
Taylor Parker

From: Jane Lincoln (jane.lincoln@nbcunicareers.com)
To: Taylor Parker (debbie.downer04@gmail.com)
Subject: Re: Re: Congratulations! Finalist Announcement for the Emerging Writers' Diversity Award
Received: November 2, 2016, 11:21 a.m.

Hi, Taylor,

Your email made me smile. How about I go ahead and put you down on the finalist list as "Anonymous, Massachusetts"? I assure you that we won't release your name to the public until the winner is announced after Christmas.

I hope these next couple of months aren't too hard on you. You certainly sound like somebody with a fighting spirit, and I wish you nothing but the best.

Good luck writing your finalist submission, and once again, congratulations on your nomination.

Jane Lincoln
NBCUniversal Careers

ONE

$\mathcal{I}$ *hadn't always* lived in Salem. We relocated from Virginia when Mom had the bright idea to open a bed-and-breakfast on Essex Street. Conveniently, since 2010, we'd been direct descendants of Bridget Bishop, the first woman in Salem hanged for witchcraft. The lodgers always ate it up when Mom told them "our story" and "upgraded" them to the Bridget Bishop Suite. Most of the gift shop owners farther down Essex did the same thing, especially the pedestrian street "psychics," who charged two dollars a minute and sold rosemary-filled apothecary bottles for twelve dollars a pop. It was a twisted little thing about Salem, Massachusetts: more than three hundred years after the witch trials took place, most people still claimed some sort of connection to the hysteria.

I was eleven when Mom sat me down and made me watch *The Crucible*. "Taylor," she'd said, "if you're going to grow up in this town, you're going to need to know what Salem is all about." I think my mother actually believed that what went down in Arthur Miller's *The Crucible* was the honest-to-god true story—that seventeen-year-old Abigail Williams had an affair with thirty-year-old John Proctor and that when he dumped her, Abigail tried to send Proctor's poor pregnant wife, Elizabeth, to the gallows for dancing with the devil. Soon after, I found out that in real life Abigail had been *eleven* and John had been *sixty*—most likely, nothing had ever happened between them. The truth was that the hysteria had been ignited by a bunch of bored eleven-year-old girls who'd decided to play a very dangerous game. At eleven, I could sympathize. I knew what it was like to be bored in Salem without electricity—we'd once had a power outage, and without screen time I'd had no option but to keep myself busy by shaving everything from the waist down until I looked like I'd fallen pants-less into a bramble bush.

Out of everyone involved in the witch trials, I always felt kind of bad for Abigail. From my place on our newly delivered leather couch—on my third rewatch of *The Crucible*—the whole thing just seemed like an unfortunate accident to me. I was sure Abigail didn't *mean* to send half the town to the gallows (in hindsight, my judgment *might* have been clouded by Arthur Miller's choice to cast Winona Ryder and her perfect face as Abigail Williams).

There's one scene where Abigail meets Proctor in the woods. It's the first time in the whole movie that the bonnet's gone, her hair's down, and Winona's looking like a goddamn Pantene commercial for the *Mayflower* pilgrims. "You will *never* cry witchery again!" Proctor threatens, and a vengeful Winona just glares up at him with her huge brown eyes and grins seductively. My eleven-year-old body flared up—I was burning at the stake of Desperate Longing right there in my living room. "Isn't he dreamy?" Mom said from the other end of the couch. I think I nodded, but as far as I was concerned, Mom could have Daniel Day-Lewis—watching Winona Ryder claim that Elizabeth Proctor's spirit had come into her bed "in the middle of the night" and "bitted" her breast was the single most exciting thing I'd ever seen.

So even though I didn't really have ancestors of the Puritan kind—of the gallows kind—I could trace the origins of my lesbian proclivities through a single person: Abigail Williams.

For the second time since I'd received the finalist notification, I ventured over to Salem's Museum of Witchcraft. Like a professional stalker, I drifted into the theater on the tail of the line and disguised myself among the November tourists in the back row.

I didn't want to think about how obsessive I was becoming. I didn't want to think about why I kept the museum's flyer hidden in my nightstand drawer. I was so unbelievably tired of thinking. Almost two weeks had passed since I'd been named a finalist, and I hadn't told a soul. What I *had* done was think and stress and think and stress while November ticked by like a time bomb.

The curtain pulled back. The spotlight switched on. There she was. Abigail Williams was fake hyperventilating downstage left and I was low-key *actually* hyperventilating. As Abigail pointed her finger at Elizabeth Proctor and accused her of witchcraft, it all came rushing back—my eleven-year-old theoretical affair with Winona Ryder, my blind sympathy for Abigail, my complete and total disinterest in Daniel Day-Lewis. There was that hot, familiar feeling when Abigail went to slap Elizabeth Proctor in court, but stopped, brushed her fingers over Elizabeth's cheek before recoiling, shrieking that her fingers burned. I wanted it to be *my* skin that burned Abigail's fingers, but in a *good* way, and I still wanted it ten minutes later when Abigail sent another hundred villagers to the gallows. It was happening all over again. Abigail's phantom touch was reaching all the way to the back row of the theater and strangling the lingering breath of heteronormativity right out of me.

But it wasn't Abigail Williams who seemed to have her hands around my neck so tight I couldn't breathe. No. It was Charlotte Grey. Charlotte Grey, head to toe in Puritan costume. Charlotte Grey, who'd lived the first decade of her life in Salem and returned from Maine last year just in time to start her junior year and turn my entire universe upside down. Charlotte Grey, with her heart-shaped face and wide eyes, who was just as alluring as Winona in that bonnet. Charlotte Grey, who was bound for *way* better than the Museum of Witchcraft's Saturday reenactment and walked in and out of every one of my Advanced Placement classes like she knew it. She had the X factor—it was especially radiant when she put seventy-year-old Rebecca Nurse in a dungeon cell so small, the innocent woman couldn't even sit.

I knew what was coming next. Upstage, five dilapidated mannequins were preparing to plunge to their death from the museum's papier-mâché Proctor's Ledge to the tune of Chopin's funeral march, but it might as well have been "Bridal Chorus" because Charlotte Grey was fainting downstage right like the Oscar-caliber actress she was, and I was falling in love all over again for the first time since I was eleven. I wanted Charlotte Grey—I wanted everything about her.

After taking her bows with the rest of the cast, she pushed back her bonnet. Her gaze danced across the sea of wool hats. "Any questions from the audience?"

My fingers curled around the edge of the pew. *Marry me?*

Outside the museum, I checked my phone.

Mom: Just got home from Walgreens and Jen has already checked in. She's asking where you are!! This is the second time in a row you've done this the day she's arrived! Don't be such a 🥒

Really, Mom? An eggplant emoji?

I took the long way home through Salem Common. Snowfall hadn't come yet, and it was colder without a blanketed ground. I really wasn't dressed warmly enough in my leather jacket, but it didn't matter—I was on fire.

As excited as I was to see Jen, I was also a little bit terrified. I felt the same way each time she came back to Salem; I always wanted her to like me more than she had the time before. In every way imaginable, she was exactly the kind of person I wanted to be—sure of myself. The summer I was thirteen, I'd seen her take a woman into the Proctor Suite late one night. I'd known what it meant. I'd only ever heard Jen call herself a lesbian once; she was one of those progressive lesbians who obviously thought their sexuality was the least interesting thing about them, but even though she was quiet about it, you could tell she was really proud, too, because she'd show it in little ways—an extra thumb ring or a fresh undercut or how she'd gesture for our female guests to take the stairs before her like she was an extra on *Downton* fucking *Abbey*. And she loved her community, too—this past summer, the morning after the Orlando gay nightclub shooting, she'd gone out to drink coffee with a guest on the porch, and when she'd come back in, her eyes had been bloodshot.

As for me? I knew there was a *reason* why I dialed the rotary phone at least three nights a week thinking about how pretty Charlotte looked in her sandy-colored sweater, but my sexuality was still Amelia Earhart–themed—I had no idea where it was going to end up. I'd been questioning for a long time. The year before, when I was sixteen, I'd even tried to go to a PFLAG meeting at Prides Crossing Community Hall, but I hadn't been brave enough to push open the door and figure out how I fit in. *You should have it figured out by now. You should be able to feel it in your bones. . . .* I knew there wasn't a single guy at school who'd ever set my heart racing, but it wasn't like I was drooling over every girl who passed my locker, either. Just one. Just one with dark hair and blue eyes and a cleft chin and dimples deeper than the Hoover Dam. What if I was just really, really gay for Charlotte Grey?

Leaves crunched under my Timberlands. What if Jen took one look at me and saw the uncertainty written all over my face? What if she *pitied* me? After what had gone down between us last summer, this time the rumbling low in my chest was a whole lot more intense. . . .

I followed Jen out onto the balcony of the Proctor Suite, where she'd always smoke and I'd always pretend it didn't bother me.

The June heat lingered after dark, washed over my bare arms as I sat up on the railing.

Jen took a long drag of her cigarette and watched my bare feet dangle. "Don't fall."

"Don't smoke."

A grin trembled at the corners of her mouth.

"Honestly, Jen, the whole mothering thing doesn't look good on you."

"Honestly, Taylor, I wouldn't want it to." Her gray eyes matched the ash drooping from the end of her cigarette. "Not my style."

Down below in the garden, cicadas sang out.

Jen blew smoke into the night. "Have you told anybody?"

My legs stopped swinging.

"Maybe when I come back this Thanksgiving," she said, "you'll have told your mom."

At the front gate of the inn, I stopped. On the highest landing, the light was on in the Proctor Suite. A tall silhouette shifted. Pulling at the neck of my sweater, I squinted. It didn't look like Jen. I mean, the way she held herself *was* bolder than seventeen-year-old Jodie Foster telling an interviewer she didn't have a steady boyfriend because she didn't "have time," but this silhouette . . . it wasn't rakish the way Jen was. Or slender. It was taller, and beefy. Maybe she was wearing heeled boots, her coat, too.

It had to be Jen. Mom always reserved the Proctor Suite for Jen. She was entitled to it because she'd been our first ever guest. We'd met her six years before, when she'd stayed with us for two whole months, even babysitting me a few times when Mom worked night shifts at Walgreens while she struggled to get the inn on its feet. Since then, the mid-thirties doctor of fine arts would stay with us twice a year—in the summer and over the holidays. After Jen managed whatever exhibition the Peabody Essex Museum assigned her here in Salem, she'd head back to New York City.

Instead of getting out my keys, I rang the bell.

With Jen upstairs, I expected Mom to open the door.

But she didn't.

"Well, well . . ." Jen pressed her side against the open door. "Taylor Parker has *finally* arrived."

My heartbeat fired against my chest. I'd forgotten that we'd been the same height for two years, that our eye lines *matched*.

Her fair hair had grown a few inches since the summer.

It curled around her ears softly, *prettily*, as though it had always done just that. And her gray eyes? They glowed. I say *glowed* because, even though she was wearing a thick sweater, I could make out the swell of her pregnant belly.

I nodded at her middle. "When were you diagnosed with that?"

TWO

$\mathcal{M}$om had made dinner reservations for the three of us at Jerry's Boathouse—Jen loved their pistachio-crusted salmon, Mom loved that she had an excuse to wear the pearl earrings Dad had given her after Affair Number One, and I loved that I didn't have to eat Mom's cooking. When we arrived at the hostess station outside, Mom had to change our reservation to accommodate the Impregnator.

Widowed Wanda had waited tables at Jerry's Boathouse longer than Nathaniel Hawthorne had been linked to the House of the Seven Gables. As Wanda ran her leathery finger down the reservation list, her expression twisted. "You want to change your reservation to three? It already says three, honey."

Wanda didn't see me lingering behind the three of them, trying not to pass out on the dock from the fumes of the Impregnator's aftershave.

Mom ran a hand through her long blond hair. "No, my daughter, too." As she turned to usher me closer, her six-inch heel slipped into a crevice between the pier planks. Tearing her hands from the pockets of her oversized coat, Jen grasped Mom by the arm. *Oh god, Mommy dearest.*

Mom continued. "We have a reservation for three. We just need to add another—"

The Salem Fast Ferry's horn blasted across the harbor,

swallowing up the Boathouse. Wanda stretched her stooped frame across her lectern. "You say you're waiting on another person?"

The Impregnator reached for Jen's hand like a panicked toddler. I bit back a grin. *Well, this is wicked fun.*

The restaurant was full of lingering tourists eager to Instagram Salem's rotting jack-o'-lanterns, so Wanda switched us from our regular window table. "Seriously?" I murmured to Mom as we followed Wanda to a booth in the corner. "The whole point of going to the Boathouse is the view. We may as well have ventured over to the Olive Garden in Danvers with its view of I-95."

"Taylor, don't be a whiny little b—oh, there's Claire Wilson!" Mom grinned so wide, her underbite disappeared. "Go ahead and sit with Jen and Ryan, and I'll be right there—"

"No, Mom, please don't leave me with—"

Too late.

Wanda seated us at Table 13—I should have known the night would only go downhill from there. Jen and Ryan sat on one side of the booth; I sat on the other. Wanda was halfway through the specials menu when she mentioned the pistachio-crusted salmon and Jen pressed two trembling fingertips to her lips. "I'm sorry," she said, and slipped out of the booth.

"Almost five months pregnant," Ryan explained to Wanda. "She's got the tactical vomit down."

Wanda's faded blue eyes flickered between Ryan and me. This wasn't her first rodeo—it wasn't worth relaying the rest of the menu to a teenage girl and a boy-man with a hemp bracelet thicker than his topknot. Wanda was well aware that neither of us would be leaving the tip in ninety minutes.

Please don't leave me alone with him, Wanda. "What's the soup of the d—"

"Clam chowda," Wanda said bluntly. "I'll be back when the rest of your table joins you."

I sank back into the booth. *God, Brooke is not going to believe this.*

Ryan looked around like he'd been led to the table blind-folded and his too-close-together eyes had only just been granted sight. "If you twist around and stretch up a bit, you can still see the harbor." Turning back to the table, he looked me in the eye. "Hey, it's great that you got into the writing program at Emerson. Jen told me all about it. You know, I'm actually a novelist."

"I *know* you are." Did he have early-onset dementia? Enduring the tale of his writing career when I got home had really put a damper on my post–Charlotte Grey euphoria.

"I said to Jen, your application must have been pretty out-standing to get early admission."

"I'm pretty sure I only got in because I used to write to a soldier deployed in Afghanistan who sent a character reference."

"You don't write to him anymore?"

"*Her.* Not really. She's home now, back with her family."

"Well, you must have written something clever for Emerson that spoke for itself. You have to send a sample piece, right?"

"I wrote a mock-humor column."

"On?"

"On people in Salem who lie about their connection to the witch trials."

"People lie about that?"

"Oh yeah. Big moneymaker. Our know-it-all neighbor Linda sells 'I Got Stoned in Salem' T-shirts at this kiosk on Essex Street Pedestrian Mall—'stoned,' by the way, is a totally historically incorrect pun because literally nobody was stoned to death during the witch trials—and she tells customers she's a direct descendant of Giles Corey."

"Giles who?"

"The old guy pressed to death during the witch trials."

"Well, maybe she is—"

"She isn't. She pronounces 'Giles' with a hard *G*—it's 'Jiles.'"

"What did you call the column?"

"'Gallows Humor.'"

"See, I knew it. Emerson's something to look forward to, right? Moving to Boston?"

"I'm not moving to Boston." Mom couldn't afford housing *and* tuition. "I'm commuting from Salem every day." I wiped my water-stained knife against my cloth napkin. I was sick of talking about Emerson, about a future all planned out that I didn't really want. I'd only ever applied to Emerson because Brooke and I had made a pact to go to college together. And then she'd gone and changed her mind. "Where did you meet Jen?"

He rested his elbows on the table. "At a bar."

"But like . . . not *that* kind of bar, right?"

"*What* kind of bar?"

I waggled my eyebrows. "I mean, your profile is startling similar to Ellen DeGeneres's, but I'm having trouble picturing you in a dyke bar. Not that I know *for sure* that Jen frequents dyke bars. But I imagine she would have spent at least some time in them. You know, back when she had a vacant uterus."

As the smile dropped from his face, his Adam's apple bobbed.

"Sorry. I was only kidding."

Bun-head reached for the wicker basket and broke the bread like Jesus Christ. "You know what they say: there's a grain of truth in every joke." He studied me. "It was an airport bar. JFK. My flight home had been delayed, and Jen was there early for her flight out—Chicago, I think. You know how she is about time management. Not my speed. But I love that about her."

I reached for the table water. "You're not from New York?"

"No—the Wolverine State."

"Huh?"

"Michigan. The Wolverine State." He watched in amusement as I struggled to get the flip-top lid back onto the bottle. "You've never heard anybody call Michigan 'the Wolverine—' Oh shit!"

Water spilled across my thighs, immediately soaking through my jeans. My thermal tights were *saturated*.

Ryan leaned across the table to survey the damage. My face burned hotly. I mopped at my lap. My starched napkin was sodden. "I think you'll need another napkin, Taylor. I can flag a waiter over—"

"It's fine."

"That's a *lot* of water."

I laid my coat across my drenched lap and struggled to remember what he had last said. *Michigan!* "Actually, my dad was born in Michigan."

"So you and I both have a bit of *bloodthirstiness* running through our veins." He felt the need to clarify. "The Wolverine thing."

"I wasn't born in Michigan." I shifted in my damp denim hell. "I was born in Tennessee."

"The Volunteer State," he jumped in, like he was on a game show and nobody had told him that he was the only contestant. "So, there's a bit of *generosity* inside you."

Can you give yourself an eye disease from straining to keep your eyeballs from rolling back into your head? If he kept it up, Wanda was going to have a serious opponent in the Salem Cataract Competition.

I looked to the restroom hallway for Jen, then across the room at Mom, who was *still* talking to Claire Wilson. "Did your parents make you memorize every state name or something?"

"My dad lectured in American politics at Michigan State."

"If my dad was a professor, he'd lecture in adultery and parental neglect."

"You don't see him much?"

"I have to see him next weekend. He's touring—he's a comedian, a Christian one—and he'll be in Boston for a couple of shows and Mom's making me go into the city to . . ." *Why the fuck are you telling hipster Jesus the depressing tale of your broken home?* "He has a twenty-seven-year-old girlfriend, and they live on the Cape. So, no I don't see him much."

"You don't like his girlfriend?"

I worked the hem of the tablecloth between my legs. "She's all right. Just a little oblivious. Like, she didn't know who Gilda Radner was until I told her. She had no idea that Gilda was one of the original *Saturday Night Live* cast members in the seventies."

"Right . . ." He edged across the vinyl seat. "I'm going to see what's taking Jen so long. Will you keep an eye on her purse for me?"

That was one of the grossest things, maybe worse than the baby, worse than the Mansplaining Impregnator: Jen carried a purse now. It was the feminine kind of purse that fit everything you needed: your phone, your keys, your wallet, your makeup, the vape pen your boyfriend sucked on like a binky.

One moment, I was playing with the little leather toggle on the side. The next, I was unzipping it, tugging out the black leather wallet Jen always brought to dinner.

I don't know why I pried the wallet open. I don't know why I glanced at Jen's dead mother in the picture frame before I curled my finger behind the little window and pinched my photo out from behind.

Jen had been carrying my wallet-sized photo around for years—I'd watched her put it in there. The photo had been taken the summer before we met Jen, when I was ten, when we'd rented a house on Martha's Vineyard called "Seas the Day." In the master bedroom of "Seas the Day" had been a floor-to-ceiling crab mural. Mom had made me stand up on their king-sized bed and strike poses in my bathing suit while she took photos for the family scrapbook she gave Dad each year for Christmas. Ironically, that was the year Dad caught crabs from a scouting agent in a comedy club and proceeded to give them to Mom for Christmas.

I flipped the photo over and read my twelve-year-old handwriting: *Merry Christmas, Jen! Here is my autograph!* My block-lettered scrawl—*T. PARKER.*

A few seconds after I'd stuck the photo in my coat pocket and zipped the purse back up, Mr. and Mrs. Heterosexuality returned to the table. "I'm getting better," Jen told me, "but sometimes an odd smell will hit me and I just . . ." She slid in next to him.

I slipped the sharp curve of my straw through the fine gap between my front teeth until the ache felt good. If she was expecting my sympathy wrapped up with a shiny bow, I had nothing to offer. She'd spread her legs and brought this on herself.

Meanwhile, Wanda was hot on Mom's six-inch heels, all coral-painted smiles as she followed her to our table.

I felt pretty silly when Mom and Ryan ordered wine and I ordered soda. I felt even sillier when Jen ordered an apple juice and winked at me, like we were both the fundamental partnership of some cool alcohol-free club. The humiliation dissipated somewhat when Ryan took a sip of his Merlot and smiled widely, showcasing a full set of burgundy teeth, and then again when he ordered a *burger*. To be precise, he ordered a prime rib sandwich—in a four-star New England seafood restaurant. I think they were holding hands under the table, but then our food arrived and he needed both hands to manage that cholesterol tower of wheat and grease; I gathered from his red-meat-incited moans that the burger was more important than public displays of hetero affection.

Jen spent most of dinner watching Mom dig her two-prong pick into a claw of her half lobster. She couldn't take her eyes off her. She smiled when Mom smiled, frowned when Mom went off on her Debbie Downer tangents. I drizzled olive oil over the lone piece of bread Ryan hadn't pilfered and watched a glint sharpen in Jen's eye as Mom laughed. I swallowed over the lump of dough—Jen was looking at Mom the same way I'd spent the last year looking at Charlotte Grey. I plonked the oil back in the center of the table. Jesus Christ. *Could she be any more obvious?*

While we were all reading over the dessert menu, Jen snuck off to the restroom—the Diagnosis was "trampolining on her bladder."

I followed.

"Why don't you leave your coat at the table, Tay?" Mom called out.

Jen was already in a stall. "Is that you, Taylor?"

Leaning back against the tiled wall, I glanced down to make sure my coat was disguising the dark patch on my jeans. "You pee really loudly."

"I can't help that—"

I swiped my palm under the hand dryer and let the shrill sound of air engulf the restroom.

When she came out, our eyes locked. The hand dryer stopped.

I cleared my throat. "How long are you staying this time?"

Washing her hands, she looked at me in the reflection of the mirror. "As usual—until Christmas."

"Ryan's staying the whole time?"

". . . Yes?"

"He's okay with that?"

"Why wouldn't he be?"

"Because it's obvious."

"What's obvious?"

"That you have a thing for my mom."

The automatic tap cut off. Blanched, Jen shook her hands into the sink. "Taylor . . . I hope you're joking."

"Course." *Except the way you looked at Mom didn't seem like a joke last summer—and every summer before that.*

Yanking a paper towel from the dispenser, she tried to shift the conversation. "What do you think of Ryan? I thought you two might get along, what with your sense of humor, with his writing . . ."

"Ryan's . . . nice."

"I'm sensing a *but* . . ."

"I don't want to say it."

"Go on. I won't tell him."

20

"No."

"Say it."

"No."

"You're transparent," she said, playful. "Fine. Two days and I'll guess anyway—"

"You two don't match."

A stale, uncomfortable tension settled.

"Maybe that's how you see it," she said, tossing her paper towel into the trash. "I *know* that's how everyone sees it. But I love him, and that means that it doesn't matter what anyone else thinks. Labels are a funny thing. You can go your whole life thinking . . ." She trailed off with a sigh. "Sometimes life works out differently than how you think it will when you're seventeen. Everybody has their own truth."

My voice wavered. "I don't know about the whole fluid thing."

Leaning back against the counter, she appraised me like an absurd art piece she didn't know how to place in one of her fancy museums. Then she nodded, as though she had drawn a conclusion: *Place* The Strange Case of Taylor Parker *in the American Politics wing. Close it off to the public until further notice.*

"Don't listen to everything you read, Taylor. Part of figuring all this out is learning to make decisions for yourself, not basing the rest of your life on what a BuzzFeed article dictates. I know you're having a hard time right now. Coming out is a process. You just have to take your time, do it when you're ready. But you're going to be okay. I know that Carrie can say things sometimes that seem pretty homophobic—trust me, I know that. And I know that coming out seems like the most terrifying thing in the world, but—"

She was trying to be helpful, but she was just coming off

like she was quoting those It Gets Better YouTube videos that celebrities make so that gay kids will stop killing themselves. "Sorry, Jen, I really have to pee." Crossing the room, I closed the stall door behind me.

After a moment, the heels of her oxfords tapped their way across the tiles. Just like that, she was gone.

I pulled the photo from my coat pocket. For a long moment, I stared at it—the picture of who I used to be. My stomach rolled. With a flick of my wrist, I dropped it into the bowl and slammed the flusher like T. PARKER's autographed portrait was marked drug money.

My phone was still charging where I'd left it on my nightstand. I hadn't taken it to the Boathouse.

I could only see the first few lines of a private Facebook message—from Charlotte Grey. *Hi, Taylor, I'm sorry if this message comes off as a bit . . . strange. I was wondering if I could ask for your help with something important?*

Riddled with excitement, I fumbled with my phone. *Yes, Charlotte Grey, I'll run away with you to sunny California! While you audition for a pilot season, I'll work two jobs to cover rent for our West Hollywood studio! On Sundays, we can wander hand in hand through the farmers' market, and I'll even get a third job if you only eat organic!*

I'd tell Brooke all about Jen, about Ryan, about the Boathouse. But not this. Not Charlotte's message. Not when Brooke despised her so much.

I opened it.

I'm sure you've heard in AP History that I'm doing my senior project on the history of Salem. Tacky, but as they say, write what you know. I've heard you're doing an internship at the Peabody Essex because you know somebody who works there? You're lucky!

So . . . I'm documenting the impression of the witch trials on the town—the museum where I work, the Witch House, the Old Burying Point. But I need access to Witch City Waxworks after hours—your manager won't let me take any photos. I know you've been working there for a while, and I was wondering . . . do you think you could get me in? Do you have time to meet up for breakfast tomorrow and talk about it? I have a feeling you'll be really cool about this.

I had a feeling, too. I had a feeling I was about to move mountains for Charlotte Grey.

THREE

I'm not sure what I was expecting to happen when I met Charlotte at Red's Sandwich Shop on Sunday morning.

The streets were deserted, the asphalt shaded charcoal by the early-morning storm. In the drizzling rain, council workers were erecting the Christmas tree beside the *Bewitched* statue in Lappin Park. The tree wasn't decorated—wouldn't be until after Thanksgiving—but they'd hung a lone icicle ornament from Elizabeth Montgomery's fingertips like a promise of the cold to come.

When I spotted Red's, I got all clammy beneath the armpits. *If Brooke had the first clue about what you're about to do, she'd never forgive you.* Rain had saturated the clapboard walls of the restaurant dark cognac, and I stood there on the corner of Central and Front, quivering and perspiring, the *Fun Home* cast recording blaring in my ears—Alison Bechdel's musical memoir about discovering she was a lesbian was really helping me feel welcome in the can't-quite-come-out club.

The bell chimed as I held open the door of Red's for a family trying to collapse a stroller. I fumbled with my umbrella, desperate to get out of their way, and my hands shook so ferally that I brought the plastic shaft down the runner too quickly. The tip of my pointer finger squeezed inside that slight gap and the hairs pricked on the back of my neck. Agony tasted iron, like sour milk. *Fuck.* It hurt worse than the time Brooke and I had

24

watched *Practical Magic* at a sleepover and I'd suggested that we slice into the heels of our feet and declare ourselves blood sisters. We'd cut each other so deeply that we'd hobbled for three weeks.

I must have made a real face at the sight of my purpling index finger—one of the waitresses behind the register mouthed *ouch* with a twisted smile.

I jammed my umbrella into the little bucket.

Charlotte Grey: *I got us a booth in the back.*

Swallowed up in what looked like the world's softest cream sweater, Charlotte had plaited her hair in two braids. Her alabaster skin was three shades paler than her sweater. *Do not joke, Taylor Parker. Do not flirt, do not do any impressions.* I dropped my wallet and phone on the table and slid into the booth across from her. "You look like Wednesday Addams's heavenly twin."

Oh. My. God.

Wrapping her slender fingers around her mug of black coffee, she sat up straighter in the booth. "Oh. I . . . Thank you." Her eyes snapped to my phone.

My heart leapt to my throat. Beside the holder of Sweet'N Low, the *Fun Home* icon was bright yellow.

I flipped my phone over.

Her electric-blue eyes darted all over me as I took off my parka, my scarf. It made me feel as stiff as the time Ms. Glazer had made us do the "calming circle" cooldown where we'd all sprawled across the stage and rested our heads on each other's bellies—when Charlotte's hair had rolled like ink across my ribs for six very still minutes and then she hadn't looked me in the eye for the next sixteen days.

"Have you seen *Fun Home*, Taylor?"

Oh, Jesus Christ. "No."

"I saw *Fun Home* with my mom in New York last year."

Of course she had. Of course Charlotte Grey had willingly sat beside her mother and watched Alison Bechdel sing about her coming out experience

She handed me a menu. "Let's order before we get distracted?"

Food was the last thing on my mind—I'd barely been able to stomach water before leaving the house. I ran my finger down the breakfast column. It *ached*.

"You know," Charlotte said, "this used to be a coffeehouse where patriots met. Before the revolution."

Her bottom lip was caught between her perfect teeth as she perused the menu. I wanted to lick it as badly as I wanted to lick the dimple in her cleft chin. "That's cool." I didn't care where in the hell George Washington took his coffee break, but the way Charlotte's face lit up when I called her fun fact "cool" did matter to me. It mattered a whole lot.

No longer was she rows away from me high on a stage in a Puritan bonnet. She was *there*, across the booth, making conversation with the waitress with the confidence of a grown-ass woman. I admired the way she said *please* and *thank you* too many times, *take your time, we're not in a hurry* when the waitress apologized for the wait on her pancakes.

"I don't see you on Messenger often," Charlotte said when we were alone again. "Ever since you dropped out of drama club, I really only see you in theater."

My chat was permanently turned off—I didn't want anyone to think that I didn't have a life. "I was on this morning. I think I liked your post."

She'd shared a *Hollywood Reporter* article praising Kate McKinnon's rendition of "Hallelujah" on *SNL* the night before.

The three-minute cold open of Kate McKinnon as a mourning white-suited Hillary Clinton on piano had gone viral, and Charlotte had captioned the article with the praise-hands emoji, like Kate McKinnon was the Lesbian Savior and Charlotte one of her twelve disciples.

"How great was that?" she said. "I wish I'd stayed up to watch it. Were you watching live?"

Had I been watching *SNL*? Me, Anonymous, Massachusetts, the secret finalist for the *SNL* internship? *Oh, Charlotte. Buckle up. . . .*

1. There was a framed poster of Kristen Wiig as Target Lady hanging above my bed.
2. When I was eleven, I called Dad when it was his weekend to have me stay over and made up a whole story about having chronic diarrhea, but really, I just wanted to stay home to watch *The Women of SNL* special with Mom.
3. The main reason I asked to stop weekend visitations with Dad was because he didn't have NBC in high definition on the Cape.
4. I cried myself to sleep the night of Kristen Wiig's last episode.
5. I was surer about the lyrics to the "Debbie Downer" jingle than I was of the national anthem.
6. I had a pile of journals hidden in a trunk beneath my bed like dirty magazines, filled with silly, embarrassing sketches I'd handwritten before Mom bought me my first laptop.
7. Every Monday, between five and seven, I secretly caught the bus a few neighborhoods over to Prides Crossing Community Hall for improvisation class.

"Oh, yeah. I was watching live."

The cold open had obviously touched Charlotte more deeply than it had touched me, because she didn't let it go even when our food arrived. She sliced into her gigantic pancake. "I know she was singing about the election and he-who-shall-not-be-named, but it was just . . . it was so *queer*." I liked the way *queer* rolled off her tongue, pretty and strong. "Especially at the end. Right?" Was she talking about when Kate McKinnon had finished singing, looked directly into Camera One, and said, *I'm not giving up, and neither should you?* "It was like she was speaking directly to every gay girl in America. Don't you think?"

There was something in her stare, a sparkling concoction of glory and empathy that made my mouth go as dry as a two-pack-a-day smoker's. Was she trying to coax some kind of lesbian confession from me? As her pink tongue poked out to swipe her syrup-glossed lips, I tried not to stare.

Looking back down at her pancakes, she waved her butter knife in the air. "Sorry if I made you uncomfortable. I just thought it had queer undertones or something."

I swallowed a mouthful of too-hot coffee. This girl was so confident in her queerness that you would have thought she was some kind of time-traveling lesbian who had thrown bricks at Stonewall herself. "I think a lot of her sketches have pretty queer undertones."

Charlotte's eyes snapped up.

I yanked off my sweater and threw it down onto the mountain of clothes beside me.

"You're funny, Taylor."

I looked up at her.

"I'm serious. You're great in theater when we do improv games and stuff. You're the quickest in the class."

Nobody had ever called me *quick*. *Funny*, but never *quick*. "I like improv."

"You always do this thing with your face in the middle of a scene and it just kills me, every time. I don't even think you know you're doing it." Her voice softened. "That's the best part."

We gazed at each other, and I felt it in my knees. Suddenly she dropped her eyes back to her plate. "So, about your wax museum."

"Oh, yeah," I said casually, cutting into my two-egg omelet I'd already let go lukewarm. "I can get you in there."

"Are you sure? I don't want you to get into trouble—"

"I won't get into trouble."

As she raised an eyebrow, I swallowed. *Oh god. Could you be any more obvious?*

"I really appreciate that, Taylor. The photos are going to be great. Your museum is so quirky."

"You should go to Salem Willows, too. There's a fortune-telling machine in the arcade, but it's been redressed as a Puritan witch. The eyes light up red and everything."

"Isn't it shut for the cold season?"

"My boss co-owns the arcade. I worked there the summer of sophomore year while they were training me, and she never asked for the key back." My pulse raced. "I have a few afternoon shifts this week, but I could take you there one day next week after school?"

"You'd really do that for me?"

Since I'd opened her message the night before, I'd had this nagging voice at the back of my mind saying that she was just using me to get her photos. But as Red's grew busier and busier, Charlotte stayed.

I asked her about her college applications. As she talked, she pulled at the sleeves of her sweater. She'd only applied to Boston College, Northeastern, and Columbia so far. I was having trouble focusing—I was too busy imagining how she'd react if I reached across the table and felt that oversized cashmere sweater between my unblistered fingers. "NYU has a great history program too," she finished. "I still have more applications to think about."

"History?" The world tilted on its axis. "I thought you wanted to be an actress?"

She forked an overripe blueberry across her plate. "Acting's not really practical, you know, for the future." The light went out of her eyes. "What about you?"

"College?"

"Yeah?" She laughed. "What else would I be talking about?"

I couldn't tell her about the contest without telling her about the whole diversity thing. "I got into Emerson."

"Why Emerson? You could go Ivy League if you wanted to."

Maybe I would have been offended if I had actually *wanted* to go to Emerson. "Emerson has a great writing program."

"You write? Like . . . poetry?"

For the first time in my life, right there in Red's Sandwich Shop, I told another living, breathing human being about the *thing* that had been bubbling inside me for years. "Actually . . ." My face burned hotter than when she'd brought up Kate McKinnon. "I write sketches."

"Wow, Taylor. Is that what you want to do? Be a sketch writer?"

With all my heart. "Oh, no. I just write sketches for fun. I'm going to be a journalist. Hopefully, write humor columns or something."

"You *would* make a good sketch writer, though."

Something inside me clicked into place. *Lock, clack, snap . . .* peace. No matter what happened after we paid the breakfast check and parted ways, even if she never spoke to me again, even if that voice was right and she'd only used me to get what she needed for her senior project, I was going to be okay because Charlotte Grey thought I'd make a good sketch writer.

She looked like she was going to say more, but then she craned her neck and looked out the window. "It wasn't raining when I left home," she murmured. "I don't have an umbrell—"

"I have one. I can walk you home."

Oh god, there they were—those gorgeous fucking dimples. "But you said you have work at the museum after this. You'd be walking all the way across town and then all the way back. Are you sure?"

Honey, I'd piggyback you across Route 66 all the way to Sacramento. "I'm sure."

As we stepped out into the rain, I opened the umbrella, *carefully* this time. We huddled underneath, arms pressed together as we started downtown. As I listened to her tell me all about her horrible driving lesson the day before, I sent a promise up to Sappho that I would happily accept a plague of a thousand blood blisters if it meant I could have Charlotte Grey all to myself once more before death became me.

My tongue was heavy in my mouth as we skipped puddles. I tried to think of something to say, but I was overwhelmed by how good her hair smelled—like apricot and vanilla—and by the way we fell into step with each other so perfectly, bumping shoulders as we went. She joked that I was hogging the umbrella because I was taller than her, which made me so self-conscious about how I was angling it that I ended up with a soaked sleeve by the time we reached Pratt.

"You live in that big pink house, right?" she asked. "The inn at the end of Essex?"

"We didn't choose that color. It was like that when Mom bought it."

When we'd first moved to Salem, I'd begged Mom to repaint the sickening shade of over-chewed bubble gum. Mom had said that our new house wasn't pink at all—it was the color of cherry blossoms. *There's a difference, Taylor,* she'd huffed as I sat in the bay window and watched her crawl around on the living room floor, sweat dripping from her hairline as she tore up the worn-out carpet with her bare hands. A month later, when renovations were completed and we were open for business, Mom renamed the house Blossom Inn. "Ugly paint job, but I suppose it *is* a Queen Anne Revival," Dad had said when he'd picked me up for our first visitation that week. He'd peered low over the steering wheel to see the tip of the tower. "Do you know when it dates back to, darling? It'd have to be worth over half a million . . ." he'd mumbled as I'd buckled my seat belt and the secrets I shared with Mom.

"When I was a little girl," Charlotte said, "I used to think that it was some kind of castle, that princesses lived in there, up in the steeple. I've always wanted to see inside."

"There's not much to see," I said, and then I wanted to saw my own tongue off with my house keys because here was Charlotte Grey, offering me an excuse to invite her over, and I'd shut her down.

"You know," she said, "when I sent you that message last night, I wasn't sure if you'd agree to meet me."

"Why would you think that?"

"You and Brooke are best friends. We all overheard what she said about me in the tech box that day when the mic was left on."

We stopped outside a two-story brick house with a neat little garden out front. "I . . ."

"What?" she said softly.

After the tech box incident, there was no point in pretending there wasn't tension between Brooke and Charlotte. I gripped the umbrella tighter. "Can I ask you something? About what you told Ms. Glazer?"

She gazed up at me.

"When we had to write and perform that ensemble project last year, when you told Ms. Glazer that Garrett's group copied their script from the internet . . . Why *did* you do that? Tell on them?"

Her lips twisted. "I know what Brooke thinks, maybe what you think too. Maybe what everyone still thinks. But I really wasn't trying to sabotage Garrett's group so that my own would get the top grade. It was just plain unfair. They did the wrong thing, and they were more than okay with taking the A that Ms. Glazer gave them—so I spoke up." She paused. "*Do* you think I did it because I wanted the top grade? That I'm ruthless?"

"I . . ."

"I'm not going to apologize for doing the right thing. I can live with people thinking I'm ruthless if it means I respect myself."

Whooooa.

She stood a little taller. "I put a lot of effort into theater. It matters to me. I love it."

"I know you do." I swallowed.

"I'll see you tomorrow?"

I watched her race down the path to her front porch, her twin braids flying around her head as she skipped up the steps. At the door, just before she slipped inside, she called out, "Thanks, Taylor!" and I swear to Sappho, the rain just stopped. Ceased. The skies cleared and so did my skin and world hunger was one step closer to being solved because I was *full*.

FOUR

"*And as usual*, Mom's on everything Jen says like a moth to a fucking flame—"

"Tay, do you have deodorant?"

"Oh, yeah." I reached under the gap between our stalls. Brooke's hand curled around the stick. "All Jen has to do is poke her head out of the Proctor Suite and give her a sliver of attention and suddenly Carrie Parker's hiking a leg over the banister and drinking the Kool-Aid." I worked the buttons closed on the new uniform shirt Lyn had issued when we'd arrived. Our names were embroidered into the fabric—she really trusted us now. "Even you think it's a weird image, right? Jen having a baby?"

"Yeah, I told you I did yesterday when you asked me on Messenger." She sighed.

"She's not even *that* pregnant yet, but she'll still, like, walk into rooms holding her belly as though the thing's going to just slip right out of her at any moment, like she's holding it in, like she's on *I Didn't Know I Was Pregnant* and—"

"Why's Rita still here with Lyn? It's usually just the two of us and Lyn on the Sunday close shift."

Okay, so Brooke was done talking about Jen. I stuffed my sweater into my bag. "Rita better not be working with us. She fucking hates me."

"She hates me, too." The deodorant stick clattered against the tile as she poked it back under the door. "Ever since her husband put that 'Make America Great Again' sign up in the window of his creeper antique store, she only *pretends* to like me."

"Huh?"

"She's terrified I'll tell someone she's a stone-cold bitch to me, that someone'll think she hates Black people."

"She would trade her goth daughter for you and your filthy-bright MIT future any day."

Brooke laughed. "Stop calling my early acceptance filthy just because you're stuck here in Salem with your mom."

"No. MIT *is* filthy. We made a pact to go to Emerson *together*. You broke the promise."

"Please. We both knew we were settling. Not my fault if you're too scared to go after what you really want."

The room went silent.

Brooke had been my best friend since middle school. Her time on *Teen Dream House Rules* really only proved to me what a decent friend she was—she never let her blossoming popularity come between us. Her whole experience on the show only brought us closer—she wanted to share everything about it with me, and I don't think I'd ever been prouder of someone I loved in all my life.

"Sorry," she murmured. "I didn't mean it like that."

"Hard to tell when there's a wall between us."

"I meant that, deep down, we both knew we were going to set our sights on something better, right?"

". . . I'm going to Emerson?"

"Right. And Emerson's writing program is *amazing*. But you know my dad kept drilling me about my potential. My parents aren't laid-back like Carrie—they went to Dartmouth. You were there that night Dad shot down my Emerson theater design idea. I'd really hurt him if I just threw away how gifted I am in math and physics."

"Yes, you're a child prodigy. You're the Mozart of Massachusetts. It's a wonder the schoolboard actually *allows* you to squander your architectural talents at Nathaniel Hawthorne High."

"Don't be sassy. Architecture at MIT is, like, going to really give me so many more opportunities than theater design. Maybe my dad's right—maybe I *was* born to be an architect. I mean, I have vision, Taylor. I was on *Teen Dream House Rules*. My room renovation was runner-up. *I* was runner-up."

I fake gasped. *"You were?"*

"Shut up."

"Do you actually think I've hit my head and forgotten the four weeks that you abandoned me to film a reality show in Los Angeles?"

"Don't be jealous that I was on international TV," she said playfully. "That I have a hundred thousand followers and the world's most aesthetically pleasing Instagram."

"I'm not jealous." I was pissed off. If I'd never made the pact with Brooke, I'd never have even applied to Emerson. Now I was stuck.

"With me at MIT and you at Emerson, we can literally see each other every day. Trust me, MIT is good for *me* and it's good for *our marriage*." She cleared her throat. "And speaking of people who go to Emerson, I saw my cousin this morning."

My cheeks heated. "Really?" I pulled toilet paper from the dispenser. "Did she, uhh . . . did she get it for you?"

"Oh my god, Taylor, you can just ask if she got you one too."

"Well, did she?"

"It's in my bag. Want it now?"

The door creaked. We paused.

"Girls?" Lyn, our manager. "Are you almost dressed?"

"Almost!" Brooke said.

I zipped my jeans and flushed.

When the flush silenced, I thought Lyn was gone. So did Brooke.

"So, you want it now?" Brooke pressed.

I went a little cotton-mouthed. "Uh, maybe not right now, maybe after work—"

The heel of Lyn's orthopedic shoes screeched across the bathroom tile. I stiffened. *That was close.*

"I was looking at Yelp today," Lyn started.

Grinning, I slipped my deodorant back into my bag. Had Brooke left another review? Ever since Lyn's ninety-year-old mother had died in September, we'd been making fake accounts on Yelp, leaving five-star reviews about the museum, about Lyn—to lift her spirits.

"What did they say this time?" Brooke asked.

"I would like to see both of you in my office in two minutes." The door swung shut.

"Did you leave her another review?" Brooke whispered.

"No. I thought you did—"

"She's pissed off—I could see her face through the gap. Do you think she knows it was us?"

"Why would she be pissed about the reviews? We were only nice about her. She'd just laugh, right?"

"I guess. Maybe."

"*I'd* laugh."

"Yeah, but, Taylor, you laugh at a lot of fucked-up shit."

I tipped the lid down, sat, opened Yelp, scrolled down to the latest review. My groan echoed off the tile. "Oh god, Brooke . . ."

When Lyn closed the door and told us to take a seat at her desk, she already had the Yelp page open on her ancient desktop computer.

She sank into her office chair and pulled her short, stout body closer to cross her arms upon the edge of the desk. She'd always kind of reminded me of Danny DeVito's twin sister, mostly because she'd been balding for years. Her office was dimly lit, and the glow of the screen accented the deep smoking lines around her mouth. She fixed her gaze on both of us. "So . . . which one of you got on the mic?"

My throat constricted. She was talking about the microphone attached to the front desk that was supposed to be used for announcements and evacuations.

Brooke was silent.

"It was me," I said. "Brooke took the group into the presentation and I was at the front desk. Brooke had nothing to do with it. I just did it to cheer her up about the election."

Turning to the computer, Lyn pushed her rimless glasses up her nose until the lenses bogged in the bags beneath her eyes. "Shall we read the review?"

Brooke made an uncomfortable little noise. "We, uh, we just did—"

"'I was thoroughly disappointed by my trip to this museum,'" Lyn started reading. "'I was on the four thirty tour on Wednesday the ninth of November. To give this complaint context, this museum tour involves a prerecorded presentation of the witch trials in a room of life-sized waxworks. The story moves from one diorama to the next, focusing on each event of the hysteria. Apparently, one of the employees of this museum considers it appropriate to interrupt the prerecording and insert a monologue from *You've Got Mail* into the presentation. How absolutely disrespectful! The recording was interrupted when, standing on the gallows, a female waxwork was asked if she had any last words. This was when the recording was paused and a young female voice read one of Meg Ryan's emails to Tom Hanks.'"

Lyn looked up at me. Her brow folded tight.

I wet my lips. "Lyn, I'm really sorry—"

Her eyes darted back to the screen. "'Did the employee stop there? No. After the female waxwork was executed, John Proctor was asked if he had any final words. The employee seized the opportunity to read Tom Hanks's reply to Meg Ryan's email. Appalling! Just appalling.'" Lyn minimized the Yelp page and sat forward in her chair. "*You've Got Mail*, Taylor? Really?"

Brooke laughed. Lyn shot her a look. She fixed her eyes on me. "Why would you do something like this?"

Because an audience loves it when you fuck with their expectations, and because I know how comedy works and it feels good to make it work, and because comedy's tragedy plus time and it's been over three hundred years. "I don't know."

"You've done this before, haven't you?"

There was no point in lying. I nodded.

"What else have you said?" she demanded.

"I read Sandra Bullock's monologue from *The Blind Side*

once." I sat up straighter. "I'm sorry. It was unprofessional. And disrespectful. Definitely disrespectful."

For a long moment, she stared. "Is that all?"

"I can give you a written apology if you need—"

"I'm asking if that is the only other time you've done this."

Brooke shifted on the chair. Lyn caught it. Her eyes snapped from Brooke to me. *Thanks a lot, Brooke.*

I winced. "I may have also read one from *The Notebook*, like, six months ago." I cleared my throat. "Also, *Pretty Woman*."

"*Pretty Woman?*"

"That one wasn't long, I promise."

She skimmed her tongue along the front of her yellowed teeth. "What did you say?"

Christ on a cracker. Bridget Bishop had been asked what her last words were. That was when I'd turned on the mic. "I said, 'Big mistake. Huge.'"

It began with a twitch at the corner of her mouth, a quiver like a fiddle string, the hollowing of cheeks as she tried to suppress it. Slowly, the smile scratched its way to the surface, devilish in full bloom.

She covered her mouth with her hand as though she were as shocked to find herself grinning as we were to see her doing it. Her eyes glistened.

"I'm sorry, Lyn."

She sat back in her chair. "You fancy yourself a comedian? It's open mic night at O'Malley's on Saturday. Take it there, Taylor." The corners of her mouth ticked up again. "Got it?"

I swallowed. "Got it."

Nobody knew Brooke like I did. I knew everything that made her who she was—her allergy to citrus fruit, the way her grandma's house smelled like spices and summer, that tiny scar from when she'd let Levi Pritchard kiss her boobs in the back seat of her car behind a Panera and he'd accidentally bitten her nipple so hard, he'd broken the skin. But just because I knew all that, it didn't make me any less embarrassed that she'd had to ask her older cousin to smuggle me my first vibrator.

We were in her car after our shift, still parked behind the museum, when she pulled it from the base of her bag. "Looks just like lipstick, right?"

I twisted the base. My skin burned. "It's loud."

"Who cares if it's loud? It gets the job done."

My heart thrummed. "I think this makes it even more suspicious. My mom would never expect me to buy lipstick."

"What are you going to call it?"

"Huh?"

"I named mine Dwayne Johnson."

"Because it *rocks* your world?"

She threw her head back against the headrest and cackled. "No. Because he's hot as hell."

I held it tight in my fist. Suffocated in my flesh, it was quieter. "I think I'll name it Oliver."

"Oliver?"

"Because you *twist* it."

She groaned. "That's so lame."

My pun wasn't over. "And because after you're done the first time, it says 'Please, sir, I want some more.'"

"Oh my god, Taylor, stop. You see, this is why you don't have a boyfriend."

"I don't have a boyfriend because I named my vibrator Oliver Twist?"

"You don't have a boyfriend because every time something comes up about sex, you have to make a joke out of it because you get so embarrassed—"

The rapping on the back window was so loud, so sudden, that Oliver Twist leapt from my hand.

"Oh *fuck*," Brooke whispered. "It's Lyn! Quick, turn it off!"

"I can't! I dropped it!"

"Shit, where is it? Quick, Taylor, it's loud as fuck!"

"I don't know where it is—I can't see in the dark!"

"Feel for it!"

"I'm trying! I can't get my hand between the seat and the console!"

At the side of the car, Lyn was gesturing for me to roll the window down.

"Sit back, sit back," I whispered, and pressed the button down.

"Glad I caught you," Lyn said, breath clear in the cold. She poked her head through my window. "When you both open on Saturday morning, because it's been so busy lately, I'm going to have the float waiting in the till so that . . ." She trailed off. "What's that noise?"

I stiffened.

"I think it's just something rattling inside the engine," Brooke said. "From the cold."

Lyn's brow furrowed. "You should get that looked at." She poked her head farther into the car. "Doesn't sound good at all."

"Honestly," Brooke said, "it happens all the time."

Lyn tilted her head. "Promise me you'll get it looked at? A rattle like that could drive a person right off the road."

"You're right," Brooke said. "It definitely could."

When I got in, Mom was in the kitchen with old Nancy from Georgia. I'd met Nancy that morning at breakfast, got her life story while I tried not to fall asleep in my bowl of oatmeal. Nancy was finally fulfilling her husband's dying wish to scatter his ashes in his home state of Massachusetts. Not in one place. Nope. Nancy was scattering her husband's ashes *all over* the goddamn state. A handful of arm in Worcester, a trickle of lung in Cambridge, a few bits of bone drizzled on the state line. I'm pretty sure what Nancy was up to was completely illegal, but when she told us all about it at breakfast, I never said anything, and neither did Mom or Jen.

I stopped in the kitchen doorway, said hello, told them I was going to take a nap before dinner.

"You're a very pretty girl," Nancy said. "Look at that long blond hair, and those blue eyes . . ." She shook her head in disbelief, as though she hadn't seen me at breakfast, as though she'd just stumbled upon America's Next Top Model. "My sons were born with beautiful blue eyes," she told Mom. "But they turned a fairly ordinary hazel a few months later."

"Damn," I said. "You should have asked the obstetrician for a refund."

Nancy choked on her coffee. Mom's eyes widened the way they did whenever I took a joke too far. Her eyes flickered from

Nancy to me. She glared, tilted her head toward the stairs.

"I'm going to take that nap."

Upstairs, I locked my door, piled the blankets on thick to disguise the growl of Oliver Twist, and got under the covers.

Somehow I got to thinking about Ruth and Idgie in *Fried Green Tomatoes*. I'd streamed it the week before after finding it on one of those "21 Movies That Made You Gayer as a Kid" BuzzFeed lists. I'd never seen *Fried Green Tomatoes*, so it hadn't made me gayer as a *kid*, but at seventeen, legs spread-eagle and Oliver Twist humming beneath the covers of my floral bedspread, it sure as hell was about to push me up to Kinsey 6.

You see, in the novel, Ruth and Idgie are in love. They're lesbians. In the movie, however, they're just two Southern gal pals, the kind who raise a child together and tuck stray hairs behind each other's ears—you know, real straight girl stuff like that. I wasn't thinking about the hair tucking though. What I was thinking about was this one scene in the movie that's supposed to be a metaphor for the love scene. Alone in the Whistle Stop Café in the middle of summer, Ruth and Idgie have a food fight. Just two good friends, pouring ice water down each other's backs and dusting flour over each other's skin, slicking handfuls of blackberries across each other's lips, shrieking, grunting, *gasping*. Just two good friends, dragging each other to the floorboards, pulling each other close and pushing each other away, laughing, clinging, clutching, making love the only way they could on-screen in 1991. And that's when an intense feeling cracked between my ribs and lit a fire low in my belly. Suddenly, without warning, my toes were curling and my spine was arching and I was coming, harder than ever before.

I'd never felt anything so intense. As soon as my ears stopped ringing, self-loathing took me by the throat. I felt so fucking ashamed. Ashamed for asking Brooke to get me the vibrator, ashamed that my hand was trembling from holding it so tight, ashamed of this thing inside me that loved romance the way it did. Why couldn't I just think about plain old sex the way everyone else did? It made me sick to my stomach knowing that *Fried Green* fucking *Tomatoes* had taken me to the last stop on the O train.

I wanted too much, all the fucking time. I was a liar, just like Abigail Williams, destroying everything around me because I wanted what I wasn't supposed to want. And I was self-destructive, too. I'd outed myself. *Don't you submit the finalist sketch. You don't deserve it and it isn't worth it.* If I won, NBC's three million Facebook followers would see the announcement. Mom would find out. Dad would find out. It would be the first thing that came up when you googled my name. And there was the other thing: If NBC named me the winner, I wouldn't just be a comedian. Before I even propped open the Laugh Factory door with my funny bone, I'd be a *lesbian* comedian.

I buried Oliver Twist under the loose floorboard next to my dresser, sat back against the wall, and tried to calm down. I'd touched myself a thousand times and never felt anything like this. Had Oliver Twist broken something in me? Had Oliver Twist popped a fallopian tube out of place? A voice hissed in my ear: *It's because you were thinking about two girls in love . . .*

Deep down, I knew exactly where the tacky feeling came from: it came from my tenth summer, when we rented *Seas the Day* during the height of my Kate Winslet phase. My tenth summer, when Bethany Wilcox and I took our watermelon mocktails up to my room. My tenth summer, when I paused *Titanic* on Rose, lounging on the chaise wearing nothing but the Heart of the Ocean, and asked Bethany if it gave her butterflies too. My tenth summer, when Bethany asked if I wanted to re-create that scene from *Titanic*—and not the scene at the bow of the ship. The *sketching* scene.

Mom's soft hands had been rough with grains of sand as she'd slathered my back in sunscreen. *Baby*, she'd said, *we don't ask our friends to take their clothes off in front of us. Our friends only undress in front of us if they're changing or going swimming. You just can't ask them to do that.*

The hot Massachusetts sun had beamed down, searing my scalp. I'd looked out at the Nantucket Sound and wished I were back at home in Virginia, in my own house, in my own room, watching *Titanic* or *The Holiday* or *Finding Neverland*. I hadn't asked Bethany to take off her clothes, I'd assured her. Mrs. Wilcox had it wrong. It was all Bethany's idea.

Nobody should be coming up with those sorts of ideas, she'd said. *It's okay to be curious about your body, but you don't do that sort of thing with other girls*, she'd said. *Don't do it again*, she'd said.

Okay, I'd agreed.

And something about that stuck.

FIVE

I was sixteen the first time I met Gilda Curphey.

It was the middle of October and I was coming out of the Prides Crossing Community Hall restroom after a serious panic spew when I caught her red-handed stealing a slice of apple pie from the Alcoholics Anonymous table outside Meeting Room One. I stopped in the hall. Pie server in hand, she paused. Above, the light flickered. She hadn't been there a few minutes before when I'd been at the opposite end of the hall, too terrified to push open the door to the PFLAG meeting. I *definitely* would have noticed her.

With a wild violet perm and dressed in an emerald velvet suit, Gilda was RuPaul's octogenarian nightmare. She looked like a pint-sized *Rocky Horror Picture Show* extra ready to lip-synch for her life. Lowering the pie server, Gilda pointed to my "Poehler/Fey 2016: Bitches Get Stuff Done" T-shirt. She murmured something, but her Irish accent was so thick that I could barely understand her. "Excuse me?" I said.

There was something about her that reminded me of Supreme Court Justice Ruth Bader Ginsburg—if RBG had visited Manhattan in her early twenties, asked Andy Warhol for directions, and somehow ended up in the basement of Studio 54. Frustrated that she had to repeat herself, Gilda shifted her weight. "I *said* that you must be looking for Stand-Up Therapy."

She nodded toward the room at the end of the hall. Laughter poured from the gap in the door.

Swallowing, I stared down the hall. *Stand-Up Therapy?*

"Improvisation?" she clarified. "We're taking a five-minute break. Well, we're *supposed* to be, but Robert won't wrap his sketch up and sit his ass down." She held up the plate of pie. "Fetch another fork and share this with me before we head back in."

In a daze, I dropped my schoolbag beside the vending machine and took a seat. I was far from hungry, but the apple pie did a great job of excising the rancid taste from my mouth. I forced myself to swallow a second bite. "Improv is therapy?"

"You betcha." Her hand trembled as she attempted to dig the fork in—she had a resting tremor.

As I held the paper plate firmer, her gaze caught mine. Her heavy turquoise eye shadow colored her brown eyes bold. "The first rule of Stand-Up Therapy," she murmured, "is that you don't ask people what brings them to class." Under her fork, the crust crumbled. "Let's introduce you to Frances."

I stared at the Celtic cross hanging over the neck of her blouse. "Who's Frances?"

Frances, the coordinator, was on the steps outside Meeting Room Two. With her wrinkled lips puckered around her cigarette, she said: "You're young . . . the youngest we ever had in the class. Was our program recommended by your guidance counselor?"

The school guidance counselor wouldn't have been able to pick me out of a lineup, let alone help me get my shit together à la Michelle Pfeiffer in *Dangerous Minds*. But according to Tina Fey, the cardinal rule of improvisation is to always say yes . . .

Me: "Yes."

I felt kind of bad about it at first, especially when I walked in and locked eyes on one woman so riddled with nerves that she couldn't raise her gaze from the hardwood floor. I'd come to Prides Crossing to join a PFLAG group, and ended up in an improv class for people who were in *actual* therapy. But after the first half an hour of warm-up games, the guilt just went away. There was no harm in a little white lie. I wasn't hurting anyone. Honestly, they kind of needed me there to get the ball rolling anyway.

People came, people went. All kinds of people. There were never more than ten of us each week, and even less than that who participated. No matter how much Frances encouraged them, a few of the regulars never left their chairs to improvise.

My favorite person in the class was Robert because I got the most laughs out of him and he always picked me as his improv partner. Robert was a thirty-year-old man with Down syndrome and we clicked straightaway. His bus arrived just before mine, so we always set up the chair circle together. "I don't have anxiety," he told me one week while we were unstacking the chairs. Frances was outside puffing away. "I just didn't have a lot of friends before I started coming here." He said it as simply as telling me he didn't like peanut butter.

Robert was a breath of fresh air in the stuffy community hall. He hardly ever broke character and had an imagination wild enough to give Roald Dahl a run for his money. But while Robert was genuinely hilarious, from day one it was Gilda who challenged me most.

Gilda made it hard to follow Tina's improv rules, to constantly say yes. She was a senior-citizen fireball, quick as a fox. I never asked Gilda why she came to Stand-Up Therapy, but I guessed it had something to do with her resting tremor. I never brought it up—I was worried that if I pried, she'd pry right back. She lost her tremor when she was up improvising and moving around, so I tried my hardest to make sure that our scenes were as energetic as possible so that she wouldn't feel self-conscious. I always vetoed Frances's inconsiderate suggestions that we were seated at a bus bench or sharing a cab. I'd suggest building a fire, rock climbing, anything that meant Gilda's hands were busy and calm.

Gilda and I had great comedic chemistry. We were like Lucy and Viv, Maya and Kristen, Tina and Amy. Together, we came up with a whole stock of recurring characters. "Do the train attendants again!" Robert would call out, and Frances would sigh, "No, Robert," because our sassy train attendants did her head in. "But, *Frances*," Robert would say, exasperated, "laughter is the best medicine!" and Frances would excuse herself and step outside to tar her lungs while we followed Robert's orders.

After that first lesson, I was on the steps outside the hall pulling on my fall jacket when Gilda asked how I planned to get home. Bus, I told her. She shook her head. "Come with me."

I followed her out to the parking lot. "Whoa. You have a *Great Gatsby* car." I'd never seen a car like that in real life. I'd *definitely* never taken a ride in one.

"It was my husband's. He passed seven years ago."

I reached for the front handle. "I'm sorry—"

"Uh-uh! In the back!"

She wanted me to ride in the back? "Why?"

"Because I said so—watch your goddarn mouth, kid. And take that heap of a schoolbag off my upholstered seats. This is a Rolls-Royce Phantom, not a public school bus!"

The inside of the Phantom smelled like mothballs and

51

cinnamon. As I scooted across the back bench seat and clicked in my belt, Gilda held up an old homemade cassette tape. The cover was faded, just a small cutout from an old magazine, and it was difficult to make out what I was staring at in the darkness, but there was no mistaking Lucille Ball's bold red lip. "Tell me, Taylor," Gilda said, "do you love Lucy?"

Tonight, Lucy and Viv had pissed off a plumber and, left to their own devices, were attempting to finish installing Lucy's new shower. But they'd locked themselves in the stall, and the water was rising around them faster than they could think to save themselves. As Gilda hyena-laughed over the wheel, it was easy to imagine Lucy's frog dive, to imagine the water rising higher and higher. But tonight I was a little distracted. As we crossed Essex Bridge, I watched the moonlight bounce across the North Atlantic. I imagined Misery Islands to my left, Salem Willows to my right, and wondered what Charlotte was doing at that very moment. Did she ever think about me?

Gilda pulled me from my reverie. "Did you eat before improv?"

"What? Oh, no. Not yet."

"You need to eat—you're losing weight."

"I'll eat when I get home."

"And what *will* you eat?"

"Well, when Mom's stuck at Walgreens on Monday nights, I usually get my Julia Child on with a grilled cheese. I've discovered that you can do a lot with a hair straightener and baking paper."

"*Taylor.*"

"What? I'm good at all kinds of improvising. Hey, speaking

of chefs, when are your daughters coming home from Dublin for Thanksgiving?"

"They aren't." She fingered her crucifix. "Honestly, Thanksgiving isn't a big deal for us. Well, I suppose it is for my girls, having grown up in the States. But not so much for me. I emigrated pretty late in life."

"But I thought you said—"

"Their jobs are highly demanding. Anna's just made sous-chef at a *very* fancy restaurant in—"

"Yeah, I know, you told me last week." Sympathy lodged like a fist in my throat. "But what about you? I'd feel awful leaving my mom on Thanksgiving. Going so far away."

"You may say that now, but one day . . . one day you will."

"But I'll never go *that* far away."

"It doesn't matter how far they go," she murmured so low, I don't think she meant for it to reach the back seat. "The point is, they go."

Dangling from the rearview mirror, the Virgin Mary locked eyes with me. *Go on*, Mary encouraged. *Invite Gilda to Thanksgiving. Don't you know how happy that would make her—* I tore my eyes from Mary to stare out the window. "I'd totally invite you over for Thanksgiving, but my mom's a horrible cook. I wouldn't wish her turkey on my worst enemy."

The quiet was deeply uncomfortable.

"Oh, don't you worry about me, Taylor," she finally said. "I'm serving Thanksgiving dinner with the ministry at a women's shelter up in Ipswich. Tell me—will you see your father for Thanksgiving?"

Lucy: *We've gotta get some help!*

Viv: *Where?*

Lucy: *Well, maybe somebody'll come by the house and save us!*

"Mom's making me go into Boston to see him this weekend." I'd told her that Dad lived on the Cape, but I'd decided against telling her exactly who he was. "But my mom's friend Jen and her"—*oh god*—"her boyfriend are staying with us until Christmas. Jen's sort of like family."

"Your house must be crammed with the extra guests."

"Not really," I said, and then, before thinking: "They're staying in the Proctor Suite."

In the rearview mirror, Gilda arched an eyebrow at me. "A *suite?*"

I swallowed. For the entire year that Gilda had been driving me home, I'd always made her drop me off two houses past our neighbor Linda's house, like eighty-five-year-old Gilda was my drug dealer. The week before, when she'd taken too long to pull the Phantom back onto Essex in the wet, I'd even pushed open the gate to the Grangers' house. "Go on inside," she'd encouraged, "I want to see you get out of this rain!" I'd smiled weakly and made it as far as the Grangers' porch before she'd finally driven off.

She cleared her throat. "You live in the pink inn, don't you?"

Viv: *Did you pay this month's water bill?*

Lucy: *Sure I did!*

Viv: *That was a dumb thing to do!*

A tingling swept across my face. "Yeah. I do. I'm sorry that I didn't tell you. I just . . ."

Her eyes met mine in the rearview mirror. "Your mother doesn't know that you participate in the program, does she?"

"It's . . . complicated."

As we hit a stoplight on Pleasant Street, the laughter of the live studio audience rang loud through the speakers, louder than Lucy, louder than Viv. Gilda turned in her seat. "I found a competition that you're going to enter next summer."

"Gilda, I know you'd love to show off that new bikini in Hawaii, but twenty-five-words-or-less isn't really my forte."

She turned back to the front. "It's a sketch-writing competition, smarty-pants." Green light—Gilda hit the gas. "To win a *Saturday Night Live* internship."

Anxiety hit me like a freight train.

"It's for young people," she said. "I found it on the Facebook. They've already selected the finalists for this year, but the contest opens next year in June for the 2018 intake. You should get to work on writing a sketch. June isn't so far away."

Neither was December—by which I had to be out. How the fuck had Gilda missed the small, minor stipulation that the contest was only open to *diverse* entrants? Thank god I'd asked NBC to keep my name off the finalist announcement. If Gilda had seen my name there and *really* looked into it, she would have found out about me. That I was gay. Panic bubbled inside me. "No point entering next year. I'll be at Emerson by then. And I don't write sketches. I just improvise for fun."

"If you can improvise the way you do, you can darn well write a sketch!"

Can I, though? Every time I'd tried to write my finalist submission, I'd just ended up sweating through my T-shirt. My indecision was as recurring as my mother's UTI. Was trying to reach the finish line really worth what it was going to cost? What if I failed, just like Mom? "I . . . I wouldn't have anything to submit."

"What about that character you do? The school photographer who insults the children. Robert laughs so hard, he almost cries."

I'd used that very sketch for my first submission. *Phillipa the*

Photographer had secured my nomination. "I guess."

"Stop guessing, Taylor. Life is short."

I'd heard the same sentiment from all kinds of people—Mom, Jen, Dad's cliché-young girlfriend when I'd asked her why she sunbathed without sunscreen. But nothing ink-stamped that declaration to your heart like hearing it from the lips of an eighty-five-year-old with a resting tremor.

Gilda pulled up in front of the inn. "So," she said softly, "this is home?"

"This is home." Leaning over the front seat, I kissed the hollow of her cheek. "Thanks for the ride, Gilda Radner."

She grabbed my wrist, her bony fingers curling around my pillowy black parka. "Why are you so reluctant to enter that competition?"

I hesitated. I couldn't tell her the actual truth—that I'd already entered, that I was one of five finalists up for the internship—so I told her the partial truth. "I guess . . . Well, my dad is a comedian. A sort of famous one. My mom was too, but she gave it up to raise me, to let him do it. So . . . I don't think being a comedian is for me. My mom wants me to go to college—"

"You're ridiculous if you don't have a look at that competition. You have a real chance, Taylor."

Oh, Gilda, you have no idea.

"Tell me you'll at least think about it?"

I declawed her grip from my wrist. "I'll think about it."

After locking Mom's bedroom door behind me, I slipped the key deep into the pocket of my sweatshirt.

Moonlight spilled through the gap between her curtains. "Taylor?" she said, groggy. "What's wrong? It's two a.m. . . ."

As I pulled back the covers and slipped in beside her, I told the lie I always told when I felt lonely: "Can't sleep—someone's turned the TV up too loud in the Sarah Good Suite."

She rolled onto her side again. "Night, baby."

I lay quiet, curling the ends of her long hair around my finger, so gentle she didn't even know it, and as rain drizzled against the window, I listened to her breathing even out. And I thought about her tapes.

There were only four cassettes in total—each bursting with forty minutes of material, each labeled *Stand-up* in Mom's perfect cursive. I'd found them in the attic a few winters ago when she'd asked me to haul down the old Christmas decorations we planned to sell at a flea market in Danvers. Mom had no idea I had the tapes, and she sure as hell had no idea that, more than once, I'd fallen asleep listening to them. Now, I know there are podcasts out there for insomniacs, and I also know that a seventeen-year-old dozing off to their mother's prerecorded voice is very Norman Bates-behind-the-shower-curtain. But listening to those tapes helped me to feel closer to her—or, I guess, closer to the person she'd been before me.

In the wind, a leafless branch of the weeping willow brushed against the window. I tugged the thick wad of blankets up to my nose. Deeply, I breathed in the scent of our detergent, our shampoo. I had enough self-awareness to know that I only ever pulled out the tapes when I was seeing Dad soon, when I wanted to get angry, when I needed to remember why I *wanted* to get angry. The tapes were like a laxative—they worked instantly. They made me think about what he'd taken from Mom, about how she'd sacrificed her comedy career for his, about how, when I came along, he'd silenced her voice so his own could be louder.

So, each time I pressed play on the Walkman I'd grabbed for five quarters at Ol Salem Town Antiques . . . Each time the tape started to flutter and I concentrated on the hollowness of her voice buried beneath the ambient hiss of the old cassette . . . Each time I riled myself up over the fact that Mom had more humor in her pinkie finger than Dad had in his entire body . . . it made it a hell of a lot fucking easier to blame it all on him. It also made it a hell of a lot easier to forget exactly where I'd found her tapes—buried in a trunk of *my* childhood toys. And that? That was something I thought about a lot.

I turned my head on the pillow and stared at the back of her head. "Mom?"

"Mmm?" she groaned.

"I . . . I don't want to go to the Marble Room with Dad."

She sighed. "I know—"

"It's so fancy, and I don't even like dessert—"

"—but it's Thanksgiving."

"Thanksgiving? This is about Thanksgiving? You told me he asked you to talk me into this because he wanted to congratulate me on Emerson."

"Maybe it's both." She dragged the pillow deeper into the curve of her neck. "Come on. You haven't seen him in months—Christ, Taylor, your feet are freezing."

"We're not going to have anything to talk about. It's going to be awkward as fuck."

"He's your dad."

On the other side of Mom's door, the landing creaked. Voices murmured. I shifted closer to Mom, slung an arm over her waist.

Instantly, she grasped my hand. "If this is really stressing you out," she whispered, "then you could ask your dad if he wouldn't mind if you invited Brooke along too."

I buried my face between her shoulder blades. "No." I talked too much smack about him to Brooke—he'd be able to read it all over her face. Besides, I couldn't stomach the idea of pandering to him in front of Brooke.

"Mom?"

"Yes?"

". . . Can you come with me?"

She stiffened. "Taylor—"

"Please?"

SIX

Sometimes I looked at our theater teacher, Ms. Glazer, and wondered why I'd never fallen for her.

Ms. Glazer was thirty-five, max. And she was pretty—*really pretty*—with wild blond hair and jingly bracelets and perfect teeth. She'd recently moved from Alabama, but while she had a rich Southern accent, she was no Southern belle. She rode a Harley-Davidson and cursed like a sailor (which was actually hot as hell). But as stunning as she was, Ms. Glazer was also next-level intense.

When the four of us walked into the theater room on Friday night at seven to find Charlotte and Ms. Glazer waiting, Ms. Glazer gripped her sternum as though Brooke hadn't told her I'd agreed to help out with lighting. "It's Taylor Parker," she cried. "My drama club dropout!"

She always called me that, regardless of the fact that I still took theater as a subject and saw her almost daily in class. I'd dropped out of Monday afternoon drama club the year before to go to Stand-Up Therapy instead, and Ms. Glazer was always telling me how much she missed me in drama club, that I needed to be "more involved in the arts" because "performance soothed the type of soul the universe had gifted me." I think she liked me so much because, sometimes, when I was passing through Essex Street Pedestrian Mall on my way to work, I bought her coffee at her weekend job at Wicked Good Books. She'd once told me that she'd taken the job to afford costumes for the drama club—coffee was the least I could do.

While Madison handed out everybody's burgers and fries, I locked eyes with Charlotte across the room. *Please god do not let her mention Red's in front of Brooke. . . .*

What I was helping the drama club out with didn't involve the whole club, just a select few of the best. They were rehearsing for the annual Massachusetts Educational Theater Guild drama festival. Ms. Glazer had written a ten-minute script called "The Boston Tea Party"—three Massachusetts writers at a tea party in Heaven, arguing over the 2016 election result. Charlotte was playing Emily Dickinson, Brooke was Louisa May Alcott, and Garrett was Ralph Waldo Emerson. Madison was understudying all of their roles because she had the most impressive memory in the entire school. State champion of debate, she'd already accepted an offer from Brown.

While they all sat around talking about the amendments Ms. Glazer had made to the script, I took my takeout up into the grandstand. They didn't need me in the tech box yet. I wrote down the lighting cues when Ms. Glazer gave them to me, and listened as they talked costume ideas. Everyone was pretty relaxed. Madison was wearing an oversized Disney World sweatshirt, Brooke was in clothes I'd seen her wear as pajamas, and Garrett was wiping his burger-greased hands on his sweatpants. Everyone looked ready to climb into bed—except Charlotte. Charlotte was wearing boots with a small heel, dark denim jeans, and the sweater she'd worn to Red's on the weekend. She was *such* a professional, a five-foot-three powerhouse of breathtaking ambition. All of that on top of the fact that she was so pretty, it was hard to look directly at her. She was the reason there was a lump in my throat. She was the reason I couldn't finish my burger.

Brooke and Madison were finishing their fries, ready to delve into a discussion about the Enchanted Forest theme for the Snow Ball when Charlotte turned to them. "Can we start rehearsing? I have work early tomorrow."

Even Ms. Glazer's focus sharpened after that.

Watching Charlotte in her natural habitat was really hot. Creativity burned in her, like a light switch she couldn't turn off even if she tried. We were like kindred spirits, like those creepy Greek masks hanging above the theater room curtains—I was comedy and she was tragedy. But unlike me, she did not fuck around with her dreams—it was what had drawn me to her the first time I'd seen her play Abigail. She didn't forget her lines like Garrett, or her props like Brooke. I never got to see her so assertive in theater because we mostly did solo performances, and when we did ensemble stuff, it was just warm-ups. But witnessing Charlotte like this . . . Well, I was beginning to understand why Brooke always left drama club on Monday nights so pissed off. While Charlotte seemed to thrive on receiving criticism from Ms. Glazer, that didn't mean that everyone else wanted to hear what *Charlotte* had to say about *their* performances. Especially not Brooke.

Garrett sat out first while Madison understudied his part. When they swapped, Madison sat in the row in front of me. "Taylor, can you braid my hair like you used to in drama club?"

It took me a while to get the hang of it again. A long time ago, Jen had taught me all the different types of braids on Mom's hair. I'd just finished plaiting Madison's thick dark hair into a staircase braid when it was Charlotte's turn to swap roles with her.

Charlotte stopped three rows in front of me. "Want to braid my hair while I'm waiting?"

My throat grew tight. She was asking me to touch her. Charlotte Grey was asking me to put my hands on her. I tried not to self-combust. "W-what do you want?"

She drew the elastic from her hair. "Whatever you decide."

I felt like I'd been handed the Holy Grail.

As I separated strands of her hair, the air between my joints crackled like electricity. Her hair wasn't as thick as Madison's, but it was so smooth, it fell like a black river over my hands.

I chose a waterfall braid—it was the most difficult and I wanted to impress her. The closer I moved to the back of her chair, the harder the scent of her fruity shampoo hit me. There was so much to take in—the heat of her body at the back of my hands, the slight blush on the curve of her ears, the way her sweater gaped at the back and exposed the tiny hairs sprinkled at the top of her spine. My knuckles grazed the pale slope of her neck and my heart skipped a beat. In April, back when we were juniors, there'd been a rumor that, the day after Charlotte had been to the pop-up drive-in at Winter Island with Savannah Hunter, she'd come to school with a hickey on her throat. I'd never seen the hickey, but the part about her being out with Savannah that night was *definitely* true. Brooke had seen it with her own eyes—Charlotte in a car with Savannah, a senior, a *lesbian*, the captain of the cheerleading squad.

I was so wrapped up in feeling sick to my stomach at the thought of another girl's lips on Charlotte that I guess I missed the moment when, down onstage, Brooke screwed up a few lines.

Ms. Glazer sighed loudly. "Come on, Brooke. If Charlotte can remember her lines, so can you."

Halfway through rehearsal, Ms. Glazer's phone pinged and she disappeared outside to "make sense" of an email. We all assumed she was in desperate need of a cigarette.

Brooke spread herself across the carpeted stage. "This script is boring as fuck."

I bit a cold fry. "You know what would have been really lit?"

Across the grandstand, Charlotte looked up from marking beats in her script.

They were all looking at me. I licked salt from my lips. "A script about their staff party."

Right after summer break, someone had hacked Ms. Glazer's iCloud after finding her password on a Post-it in the tech box. They'd discovered photos from the Christmas in July party. The photos had circulated, and by September, everyone in school had seen the evidence of the night our role models had hired a charter boat and gotten absolutely wrecked. There was a photo of Ms. Ehle sitting on Mr. Peel's lap, one of Mrs. Linklater deepthroating a wine bottle, and one of Mr. Jones and Mr. Guzman pretending to kiss.

Garrett leaned farther over the back of his chair. *"Do it."*

I looked to the door. "She'll be back any minute."

"At least do *her*."

The photo of Ms. Glazer was the highlight of the collection. It had been taken in the parking lot after they'd disembarked the charter, and in it, Ms. Glazer was straddling her fiancé on her Harley. We all knew the fiancé—his name was Johnny and he worked at a drugstore in town. We all called him Johnny

No-Cash because he was constantly short-changing us due to being permanently stoned. In the photo, Ms. Glazer was leaning back against the handlebars of the bike, her eyes rolled back so far, it looked like she was having a seizure. There was a blunt in her hand that *could* have just been tobacco, but the general consensus was that she'd been higher than the Chrysler Building.

"Come on, Taylor," Brooke said. "If you didn't want to, you wouldn't have brought it up."

"That's so not true."

Charlotte tucked her pencil into the tight hold of her braid. "You *have* to."

Well, *now* I had to.

I dragged two chairs to the middle of the stage, faced them together. I patted one of the chairs. "Brooke?" Hell would have to freeze over before I straddled Garrett.

"She's doing it," Garrett told the room. "She's legit doing it."

"*She* can hear you," I said.

Madison laughed.

I tore at Brooke's takeout napkin and rolled it into a blunt, then spared a quick glance to the door as I climbed onto my best friend's lap.

I mimed lighting my blunt, took a drag, tried on my best Southern accent. "Out on the prairie, Mama never said it was right to be goin' round with boys who rode motorcycles and smoked mari-juana, but Mama didn't always know what was best for her daw-ter!"

If Madison *loved* it, Garrett was more into it than a gay man at a Bette Midler concert. I took a long drag of my pseudo-blunt and squinted against the harsh spotlight. Elbows on her knees, Charlotte stared down to the stage. Her eyebrows were perched curiously, like she was wondering if I could keep it up.

I held the nape of Brooke's neck in my hands. "When I took this mighty sweet young man back to Alabama so he could ask Daddy for my hand in marriage, Mama was madder than a wet hen!" Beneath me, Brooke shook with laughter. "'Bless that boy's heart,' Mama said, 'but that Johnny was hit with the ugly stick.'" I tilted my head over the back of the chair the way Ms. Glazer had leaned over the handlebars of her Harley. "And I said, 'Mama, you think I don't know that? You're preachin' to the choir! But I love him!'"

Garrett clapped his hands like a frenetic fangirl. I took another drag, tapped the "ash." "Why, when Johnny asked Mama and Daddy for my hand, I was sweatin' like a sinner in church! But you see, what Mama and me didn't know was that Daddy liked Johnny a whole lot. Why'd Daddy like him so much, Lou Ann? Well, Johnny promised Daddy he could get him some of those *real* special cigars with that medical mari-juana card of his. Like water off a duck's back, Daddy handed over my dowry!" Brooke squeezed her eyes shut, cackled as I blew "smoke" over her cheeks. "'Why, I do declare,' Daddy said, 'there's no reason why these two young'uns should not be joined in *hol-ley mat-tree-mo-nee*.'" Stroking a tear from Brooke's cheek, I gathered her head against my chest and looked to the blinding hot lights. "Lord willing and the creek don't rise, we're gonna have a summa weddin'—"

Brooke stiffened beneath me. Her eyes locked over my shoulder and her fingertips sank hard into my hips.

My heart stopped. I turned.

Ms. Glazer stood at the end of the first row.

From the grandstand, the attention of the others volleyed between us. Charlotte's hand swept up to grasp her throat.

My thighs locked tight around Brooke's. "I . . . I—"

"Taylor, I'd like to see you outside for a moment."

I swung a leg over Brooke and stood.

The night was blisteringly cold. In the shadows under the theater room window, Ms. Glazer's eyes glossed over with that familiar intensity she reserved for watching Charlotte perform.

Licking my chapped lips, I gripped myself to fight off the chill. "I should apologize. I was only trying to make them laugh. I wasn't making fun of you."

She was wide-eyed. "I haven't called you out here to . . . Taylor, it's not about that."

"Is it about the window?" A few months before, she'd put on "Respect" for our warm-up, and when Aretha belted the chorus, I'd accidentally kicked a starburst crack into the windowpane. "I said I'd pay for it if I had to."

"It's not about the window, either."

"It isn't?"

"Taylor, I've just received an email. From NBC."

Earlier that night, Brooke had picked all of us up for rehearsal. All of us, except Charlotte. It was inconsiderate, I'd thought, when the four of us had arrived to find Charlotte waiting with Ms. Glazer. But toward the end of rehearsal, inconsiderate changed to just plain rude when Charlotte casually mentioned that her parents were in Maryland for the weekend for a funeral. That was when I realized she must have walked over to school—in the dark.

It was just after ten and we were wrapping up when I caught Brooke searching behind the stage curtain for a Post-it that had slipped from her script. "What about Charlotte?"

"What about her?"

"We can't let her walk home. She has to pass the woods."

"So?"

"*So*, anything could happen to her. And it's, like, thirty degrees out. You should offer her a ride."

"She can ask Ms. Glazer for a ride."

A flash of buttercup yellow caught my eye. I pulled the Post-it from the felt of the curtain and held it out to her. "Don't be bitchy. There's room for her."

She snatched the Post-it from my fingers. "She does her own thing, Taylor."

Brooke didn't offer Charlotte a ride. Nobody did.

Everybody was gathering their stuff, their notes, their backpacks, and I was trying to figure out how to help Charlotte, how to make sure she'd be safe, but I was humming at a frequency so rough, I could barely focus. Somebody at NBC had emailed Principal Moreton to confirm I was a student—that was what Ms. Glazer had said outside.

As Ms. Glazer flicked off the lights and locked the theater room doors, I checked that the others were first out the door before I snuck up behind her. "You know it's a diversity competition, right?"

Her eyes softened. "Yes, sweetheart. I . . . I know."

"So you get why, when we were outside just now and I said that telling people about this needs to be on my terms, it *really* needs to be on my terms. Because my mom doesn't know. Nobody knows."

"I understand, Taylor."

"And you . . . you understand why you *really, really* need

to make sure that Principal Moreton doesn't tell anyone else about this? Like . . . *anyone?* Nobody else but you and Principal Moreton can know."

"Taylor . . . what are you going to do?"

"I'll . . ." *I wish I knew.* "Night, Ms. Glazer."

I followed Madison, Garrett, and Brooke to Brooke's car. I didn't hear a thing they were saying. I looked over my shoulder, watched Charlotte talk to Ms. Glazer, point toward the street. Ms. Glazer nodded, and my blood ran cold as I realized Charlotte was assuring Ms. Glazer that somebody was outside the school, waiting for her.

Brooke turned the ignition and Garrett and Madison argued over who should take the aux cord. As I watched Charlotte turn away from Ms. Glazer and start down the driveway at the side of the gym, my pulse pounded. Charlotte's petite figure was floodlit in Brooke's headlights, and as we came nearer and nearer to driving past her, panic hit me. What if something happened to her? What if somebody grabbed her by the hood of her parka and dragged her into a car? Or worse, the woods.

"Brooke. *Stop.*"

With a groan, Brooke slowed, but she didn't brake. She leaned out her window. "Do you want a ride?"

The cold burned my cheeks as I pressed down the back window. As she turned, Charlotte's eyes locked with mine. She bit her lip, quickening her pace to keep up. "Oh, I can walk," she said.

Brooke turned her entire body in the driver's seat to shoot me that *I told you so* look.

I opened the back door. "Get in. Fucking brake, Brooke."

I slid over to the middle seat until I was right up against Madison, and then Charlotte was right up against *me.*

Brooke's eyes met mine in the rearview mirror. I snapped my gaze away. She'd pissed me off. Like, *really* turned me fucking sour.

Charlotte's thigh was warm against mine, settling the roar between my ribs. *Ms. Glazer knows about me. Somebody knows.*

Charlotte didn't say anything for most of the ride. I think she knew I'd been the one to make Brooke stop the car, and I sensed that it made her feel like a burden, that she hated that. Garrett was arguing with the others over some Chainsmokers song when Charlotte leaned closer to me. "Hey, about Salem Willows . . ." she whispered.

Her lips were full, still trembling from the cold. I wondered what it would feel like to slide my hand around the nape of her neck and warm her mouth with mine. "I can go on Tuesday if you can."

The way she smiled told me that she was grateful for more than just Salem Willows.

After we dropped off Charlotte and Madison, Brooke went out of her way to drop me next. I didn't say anything about it being quicker to drop Garrett first. I knew she didn't want to be alone with me. Well, I didn't want to be alone with her, either. I didn't know what I'd be compelled to say, but I knew it would be something I'd regret. Something I'd really, *truly* regret.

SEVEN

On the train into Boston, Mom and I had decided that the only way we could possibly get through a dessert date at the Marble Room with Trent Parker and his beefy entourage, Midlife Crisis and Self-Absorption, was if we played a drinking game—for every two minutes Dad drawled on about his comedy tour, we'd take a sip.

Dad was talking at me a mile a minute when the waitress passed our booth and Mom leaned over my lap. "Excuse me," Mom whispered.

The waitress halted.

Mom tucked a wave of her hair behind her ear. "I know we just got here, but my daughter and I are going to need another latte and hot chocolate to come out with our crème brûlée."

"Anyway, sweetheart," Dad said, "long story short, she just wasn't strong enough to open for me, not yet. Actually, she reminded me of you, Carrie, when you first started, before you found your feet. But this one, she was hardly old enough to be *in* the bar. And I tell you, the fact that she looked like Aileen Wuornos wasn't doing her any favors. Now, I don't want to sound like some sexist pig, because you both know I'm not, but—oh, here's our dessert!"

As the waitress placed three crème brûlée dishes and our beverages in front of us, her eyes flickered to the woman at the next table who was rudely flagging her down. "Can I get you anything else, sir?" she asked, frazzled.

Slicking a hand over his balding head, Dad swirled the whisky in his tumbler. "My daughter here was offered early admission to Emerson. Isn't that impressive?"

Her eyes snapped to me. "Congrats. Sir, is that all for now?"

Dad rested his chin in his palm and grinned at her. "Hold on, hold on, don't run off. When you seated me, you mentioned that you go to Boston College. Do you have any tips on city life for Taylor here—"

Mom stabbed the crust of her crème brûlée with her spoon. "Trent, if Taylor needs tips on city living, she can consult Lonely Planet." Mom nodded at the waitress. "We're fine. Go, honey, go."

When we were alone, Mom groaned. "God, my crème brûlée is hard as a fucking rock." She tapped the caramelized crust. "Looks like it was torched in '63." Gripping my knee beneath the table, she looked up at Dad. "I wouldn't be surprised if that Masonic grandfather of yours hadn't crawled from his crypt and was back there in the kitchen torching them himself."

I choked on hard caramel.

Dad rubbed at his five-o'clock shadow. "Carrie, for the hundredth time, the Freemasons had *nothing* to do with the"— he lowered his voice—"the KKK."

Mom shrugged. "Same song, different chorus."

As Dad's jaw tensed, I bit back a grin. We'd only been there twenty minutes and already Mom's banter was good enough to bottle and sell on Craigslist.

My phone vibrated. Pulling it half out of my coat pocket, I spied down at it.

Charlotte Grey: I'm really looking forward to Salem Willows

*on Tuesday. Sort of wish we were there tonight, even though it's
storming. . . .*

Dad tapped the rim of my ramekin with his spoon. "How's
yours, darling? As delicious as mine?"

Had he sandpapered his taste buds on the sidewalk before
coming in? It tasted like a house fire. "It's really good." Looking
back down at my phone, I quickly typed out a reply. *I wish. I'm
trapped in a fancy dessert bar in the city with my folks.*

Dad carried on. "Even the *Globe* gave this place an
excellent— Taylor?"

I looked up.

He tilted his head. "Who are you texting?"

"Just checking the time."

"You have somewhere to be?"

"I . . . Kristen Wiig's hosting *SNL* tonight." It *was* true. I *did*
want to be back in Salem in time for the cold open. "Mom and
I have to be at North Station by ten thirty."

"I'd appreciate it if you focused on what's happening right
here." He gestured between us with the tumbler, his charcoal
eyes dancing the Whisky Tango Foxtrot. "We don't get much
time together and—"

Mom's fork dinged against her ramekin. "That isn't Taylor's
fault—"

"—I'm sure whoever he is you're texting can live without
you for a few hours."

Oh, Daddy dearest. "I—I'm not texting anyone. . . ." I trailed
off as, winking at me, he reached across his booth seat for his suit
jacket, fumbled in the pocket . . .

Smirking, he dropped a set of keys on the table. "Congratulations on getting into Emerson."

I stiffened. He'd bought me a car. "I . . . I don't have my permit."

He chuckled. "They're apartment keys."

I blinked.

Mom sat forward. "*Apartment* keys?"

"She needs somewhere to live while she's at Emerson."

Holy fuck balls. At the intensity of his gaze, I looked down at my hot chocolate. "Mom and I decided that I'd just commute from Salem and live with her until I graduated college—"

He shook his head. "Too far to commute to and from every day. This place I got my hands on for you—it's Uncle Danny's, you remember him, don't you? He stayed with us all those years ago when he was touring Virginia? You loved Uncle Danny— it's in Back Bay, so all you'll have to do is take a short stroll up Boylston each morning to get to class. Now, don't get excited, it's only a studio, but . . . what do you say? Your mom's already told me that she's hell-bent on covering tuition without my help—so I'm covering the rent."

And *there* it was, the third member of his all-male entourage: Pride.

Out of the corner of my eye, I watched as Mom pulled the chain of her necklace around the band of her turtleneck, her fingers curling around the locket that held my first ringlet inside. Her thoughts screamed to me: *Don't be proud—take it.*

An ache built at the back of my throat. "That . . . that'd be great," I said. Then I had to say two empty words to the man who'd broken my mom's heart: "Thanks, Dad."

He spread both arms across the back of the booth. "No need to thank me. You've earned this. *However*, you won't be able to take it until next year. There's someone else moving in just before Christmas and they'll be there until June. After that, it's all yours. Danny says you're welcome to check it out anytime before December fifteenth, see if you like it. But it would be a roof over your head and you wouldn't have to share with anyone. And like I said, I'd cover the rent until you graduate."

I had to say it again: "Thank you."

"Your mom wouldn't have to worry about contributing to the cost of rent—not at all."

And again: "Thank—"

Mom shoved her crème brûlée away from her. "*Her mom* is mortgaging her inn to cover the cost of tuition, so you can turn the generosity dial down a notch, Princess Diana. Don't use me to guilt-trip your daughter."

His gaze didn't pull from mine. "There'd just be one rule," he said seriously. "No boys allowed."

Christ on a fucking cracker. "Consider me the Virgin Mary."

He grinned. "I'll write down the address? For you to go and take a look?"

"Thanks, Dad."

He flipped his wallet open and tugged out one of those little religious cards. Hail Mary Full of Grace—he turned over the Virgin Mary and, like God doling out his business card, took a pen from his pocket and *scribbled* on the back of it.

My gaze dropped to his wallet, splayed open beside his half-eaten crème brûlée—in the picture pocket was a tiny sonogram print. A jolt beat through my body. Dad cared enough about me to keep my seventeen-year-old sonogram in his wallet?

I pulled the wallet closer. "Dad?"

He scribbled circles behind the Virgin Mary's back in an attempt to get the ink to run. "Yeah, hon?"

"You still have this?"

As he looked down at the sonogram, his lips parted. "Oh . . . that's . . ." He rubbed at the back of his neck.

Mom gripped my thigh. "Taylor. That's . . . that's not you." She bit her lip, stared hard into me, and suddenly the breath bottled in my chest.

Sitting forward, Mom's eyes fixed on Dad. "Golly gosh," she said, pulling Dad's attention from me. "What a coincidence. Just when we were on the topic of teenage pregnancy."

He pulled a hand over his face. "Carrie . . . You know Brittney's in her *late* twenties."

Her blue eyes flashed with satisfaction. She tossed her sleek blond hair over her shoulder. "*You* aren't married."

He stared out at the cars waiting for the go on Tremont. "Don't start, Carrie."

"Oh, I'm not starting anything. I'm *very* liberal. I'm just curious to know how you convinced your conservative Southern fan base of the immaculate conception?"

Dad turned to me. "I was going to tell you tonight, but . . . I thought we'd be alone." He beamed. "It's a girl."

Oh brother.

"A *sister* for you."

Praise Jesus, Christmas has come early.

He tilted his head. "Taylor?"

He wasn't trying to hurt me. He was just being inconsiderate. It was just like when I was little and we'd go on long drives through the night and he'd wind his window down without thinking about the fact that, behind the driver's seat, I was copping the brunt of the frigid wind.

I stared at the tea light burning in the middle of our table, watched the flame sway to and fro in the pool of wax.

Eyes trained on me, Dad downed his whisky. "Well, then . . . I think I'll go find our waitress and order another coffee, visit the men's."

When he was gone, Mom turned to me. "Are you all right?"

"I get an apartment. And Brittney's daughter gets a dad."

Sighing, Mom linked our hands together. "Trust me, the fetus is the one copping the raw end of the deal." As she ran her fingernail around the rim of her latte glass, I could make out the hurt floating in her eyes. Was she thinking about the miscarriage she'd had all those years ago? Or was she thinking about our old life back in Virginia? About what the three of us had had before it all turned to shit?

Our waitress stopped at the end of the booth. "Here's your husband's soy latte," she told Mom. "Double shot, extra hot." After placing it next to his empty tumbler, she disappeared.

I looked to the restroom doors. *Ticktock, motherfucker.* I reached for his latte—it was time for the triple shot.

Mom tilted her head. "What are you— *Taylor!*" she hissed. *"Don't you dare!"*

I'd been sniffly all day from the thistly wind, and thanks to the creaminess of the custard, it wasn't so hard to vibrate my throat, snort a little through the left, a little through the right, and hock up a phlegmy gem.

Mom's eyes widened as the wad of my spit slinked into the foam of Dad's latte. "I'm not going to let him drink that!"

"Yeah, you are."

"I absolutely will *not.*"

"Yeah—you will. He's going to come back to the table, and he's going to reach for the glass, and you're going to sit here and watch him drink it, and you're going to grab my knee under the table pretending to be disgusted, but really, you're going to love it." I set the scalding glass between us. "Okay—your turn to do the honors."

"I'd *never*."

"Relax your forehead wrinkles, Mom; it's a wad of his offspring's saliva. His immune system has endured *way* worse."

"Way wor— What do you mean?"

"Well, you didn't kick him out after the first affair, did you? I had a good eight months to get creative with my retributive justice." I twisted his latte glass until the handle pointed toward her. "Quick, he'll be back in a minute. Come on, Carrie Ann, you no-good Texan temptress—you can do it."

"No. Absolutely not. Honestly, I can't believe you right now."

"I think you can, Carrie Ann."

"You know very well my middle name is Ruth."

"Come on, Carrie Ann. Look, the foam's even parting for you, like a little Suez Canal, so cute. . . ." I inched the glass toward her with my middle finger. "Ten minutes ago he commented on the fact that you're a grown woman with your own business who can't drive."

"Taylor, he can think and say and do what he likes. I'm done caring. Trust me, I have been for a very, very, very long time."

"Mom, let's be real for a hot minute—he gave you *crabs*."

Her eyes held mine. She swallowed visibly. Then, shooting a quick glance at the restroom doors, she curled her fingers around the handle and lifted it to her lips.

The train ride home was quiet—we weren't so deep in our Thai takeout as we were deep in thought.

I watched Mom's reflection in the darkened windows. As she heaped an overly ambitious forkful of noodles to her mouth, she hocked a choking sound. My chest tightened. If I ended up taking the Back Bay apartment, how was I going to leave her? How were we going to *survive* without each other? And what would happen to us if I entered my finalist sketch and . . . actually won? Moved all the way to NYC? Mom tried to feed the mountain between her lips again, choked again. My eyes welled. What we had was sweeter than a Brandi Carlile ballad. Not only had it been her arms that had first held me, but she was the one who'd taught twelve-year-old me to smother my tampons in K-Y Jelly so they'd slip in faster than you could say Jack Robinson. I loved Brooke, and I was going to miss Brooke, but when it came to Mom . . . Well, there wasn't anyone in the world I was closer to. Seventeen years ago, Carrie Parker had decided to save my placenta and plant it with a peach pit in Virginia soil—like a curse, we'd been bound together ever since.

She nudged my shoulder. "Hey, I bet you the last spring roll I can pick the five people you'd invite to your dream dinner party."

"How will you know I'm telling the truth?"

"I guess I'll just have to take you for your word and you'll have to take me for mine."

"What if we both lose?"

"I'm not going to lose."

"It's actually gross how competitive you are with me. Any other mother would just give her child the last spring roll."

"It's a spring roll, Taylor, not a fucking life jacket. Stop stalling and guess mine."

The train rolled into Lynn. I watched out the window as a handful of passengers climbed off. "Gilda Radner, obviously. Whoopi Goldberg. Robin Williams . . ." Okay, this wasn't so hard. "John Candy." She'd always *loved* John Candy. I paused. ". . . Loretta Lynn?"

Her eyes gleamed with pride. "Very, very close. Such a shame you lost, though."

My eyes fell to the long blond strands caught on her black coat—it was molting season. "What did I get wrong?"

Her underbite was prominent as she chewed her pad see ew. "I'd swap Loretta for Joan of Arc."

"Joan of Arc?" I dropped my fork into the container. "Mom, what the fuck would you talk about at a dinner party with Joan of Arc? You'd have nothing in common."

"Well, I'd ask her questions."

"How? The only French you know is French toast."

"I bought a coffee table book about her last week. Anyway, my turn. So, Krist—"

"Hold on, there's green between your front teeth."

She picked at the Chinese broccoli with her pinkie nail. "Okay, so . . . Kristen Wiig. Tina Fey. Amy Poehler." She flashed her smile like a Colgate model. "Broccoli gone?"

I nodded.

"Molly Shannon—no, actually, Wanda Sykes." She rested her head back against the window and grinned. "And Gilda Radner—*obviously*."

I ground down on an undercooked carrot. "Enjoy your spring roll," I grumbled.

"*See*," she said cockily, "I know you better than you know yourself. It isn't hard to pick what you like, especially when I knew yours would all be funny girls." And then she said the words that made my face ache with heat: "No men at Taylor Parker's table—no, sirree."

My heart fell to my stomach. "What can I say, I'm a mad feminist."

"Feminist, huh? If I didn't know you any better, I'd think you were of Jen's *persuasion*."

My heart rate skyrocketed.

"After all," she added, "you do idolize her."

I swallowed a doughy noodle whole. "I don't idolize Jen."

"Pfft."

I needed to change the subject—and fast. "Were you shocked? When she showed up pregnant?"

". . . Not entirely."

"What's that supposed to mean?"

"I knew."

I spun on the seat to face her. "You *knew*? You knew and you didn't tell me?"

"I don't have to tell you everything. She called me months ago to tell me that she'd gone and gotten herself knocked up. I didn't think for one second that she was actually going to keep it."

Wait. "So you knew she was . . ."

"No longer a dyke?" She dipped the last spring roll into the sweet and sour and offered it to me.

I shook my head—I'd lost my appetite.

Shrugging, she bit into the spring roll. "Well, it just goes to show you, doesn't it?"

"Show what?"

"People sure can surprise you."

By the time we got home, all of the guests—including Jen and Ryan—had gone to bed, so it was just Mom and me in the common room. Fine by me. Kristen Wiig hosting was a special event that only came around once a biennial. I couldn't have anyone mumbling complaints about Salem museum admission prices in the middle of her monologue.

One of the last sketches was a recurring sketch, "Whiskers R We," the lesbian cat shelter commercial. I was glad I'd spread myself across the good rug in front of the fire and Mom couldn't see my face burning hot.

I'd guessed it was coming. They always paired female hosts with Kate McKinnon to be her creepy cat lady girlfriend of the week. Charlize Theron, Reese Witherspoon, Melissa McCarthy—they'd all done it. The girlfriends were never there for the cats, only Kate McKinnon's sixty-year-old shelter volunteer persona, Barbara DeDrew.

"I love this one." Mom sighed tiredly from the couch. "And I don't even like cats."

For a few seconds I watched Mom in my peripheral vision. The way her wet, blond tresses clung to her cheeks like honey, the way the blues and pinks of the television danced across her face. All of a sudden, it struck me—she was starting to look old, the way other moms looked.

I thought about interrupting Barbara DeDrew and coming out to her then and there.

Do it. On the count of three.

One.

Two.

Three.

. . .

. . .

. . .

I should have done it. It would have made everything that happened from that point on *so much easier.*

EIGHT

Salem Willows was a ghost town. The bustling summer strip was so devoid of visitors that our bus driver bypassed the designated stop completely, just pulled in across the narrowly painted parking spaces.

Across the street in the park, the willow trees drooped. The sparse amber vines swayed in the vicious wind beating off the Danvers River and sweeping straight through the park like a specter. Charlotte pulled her wool hat over her ears and buttoned her parka tight against her clavicle.

We followed the fifties-style Salem Willows sign, its light-globed neon arrow pointing down into the arcade. Halfway up the strip, directly outside the shuttered seafood stall, Charlotte turned off the sidewalk. "Want to know a secret?"

All of them, please.

Like a gymnast on her balance beam, she followed a concrete boulder that extended onto the road to divide parking spaces. She pointed at an enormous black scorch mark atop the seagull-pooped divider. "Would you believe me if I told you that I did that last month?"

I grinned. "Seriously?"

"My mom teaches me how to park out here because there's never anybody around. I came at it on a bit of an angle and next thing I knew, the wheel went over and I just sort of . . . scraped it."

"*Scraped* it? It looks like you tried to grill hamburgers on it."

"Funny." She drew the point of her shoe along the burn. "You should have seen the sparks."

"Maybe when you get the hang of parallel parking, your mom could move on to teaching you the difference between the brake and the accelerator."

Her grin was wide. "I have poor judgment, okay?"

"I take it you're an excellent driver."

"Well . . . *I* wouldn't get in the car with me."

"At least you *have* your learner's permit."

"You don't?"

"Not yet. My mom can't drive. I don't really have anybody to teach me."

The roller doors were down over the front of the arcade, so I led her into the tiny alley. I turned the key in the side door and pushed it open. "After you," I whispered over the creak of the hinges.

For a moment, before she climbed the step up, our eyes locked. Her cheeks were rosy—from more than just the cold. She was nervous—about getting caught, or being alone with me, I wasn't so sure. I slipped the key into my pocket and closed the door behind us.

The arcade was dark, the trees behind the giant shed filtering the last of the daylight spilling through the high windows.

Charlotte doubled her scarf around her neck. "It's icy in here."

I felt along the wall for the light. Flick . . . Flick . . . Nothing . . .

I bit my lip. "Light's busted." I flipped on the flashlight on my phone. The light caught on the screen of the *Pac-Man* machine, reflected off the silver cage of the basketball game, off the blackened squares of *Dance Dance Revolution*.

"I'm getting real *American Horror Story* vibes right now," she joked.

"Wait here for a second?"

"Sure."

I navigated my way past the table hockey, around the carousel to the operator box. I dropped my backpack onto the operator's chair and shone the light on the panel. I had no idea how to actually work the carousel—I'd been too young to be trained the summer I'd started working for the Kincaids—but I *had* turned the lights on when I'd worked morning shifts. I flicked the switch at the top right of the panel. A soft glow filled the frosty arcade. The globes that adorned the roof of the carousel lit up like a Broadway marquee, glittering in the mirrored column of the carousel. I flicked the music switch. The classic carousel tune began.

Smirking, Charlotte lifted her schoolbag onto the hockey table and pulled out an expensive-looking camera, one of those professional ones with the long lens. With her camera in hand, she looked from the Laughing Clowns to the Lucky Duck pond, to the stuffed prizes on the wall above, thickly tarped to keep them dust-free. Finally, her eyes landed on the eight-foot-tall Florence the Fortune Teller box at the back of the arcade.

I followed her over. It was way before I'd started working there that the back of the box had been taken out and the bust of the fortune-teller mannequin redressed as a Puritan witch. The Kincaids had even gifted Florence a deviated septum and an unsightly black mole. I crouched at the back wall, reached behind Florence's glass prison, and plugged her in. At the sudden charge of energy, Florence's mouth dropped open like a ventriloquist doll's.

While Charlotte took a few photos, I found the switch to the Hall of Mirrors and flicked it on so that the colored lights inside the mirrored corridor could stream into the arcade and give her better lighting. When I turned back, Charlotte was watching me, hesitant. "Can I put a quarter in Florence?"

"Go for it."

I pulled myself up onto one of the carousel horses, leaned back against the icy, coiled pole, and watched.

The drop of the quarter was loud as it charged into the machine.

I strained to hear Florence over the carousel music reaching a crescendo, echoing off the tin roof: *"Oh, there you are, child. I am Florence, gentle and knowing, here to impart wisdom, if, and only if, you are ready. . . ."*

Charlotte turned to me. "This is actually creepy as hell." She pressed the glowing red button next to the coin slot. A metal arm extended from the side of the box. The coin traveled along the ramp of the arm and shot into Florence's mouth. The mannequin was tight-lipped.

Charlotte pivoted. "Is it broken?"

"Just give it a min—"

Florence spoke up, and Charlotte almost jumped out of her skin. *"Something significant is headed your way in the form of a letter, my dear, that will change more than simply your day."*

"That's accurate," Charlotte mumbled.

Printed on a sheet of cardboard no bigger than a business card, her prophecy popped into the chute. As she bent to retrieve it, the purple and red lights from the machine danced over her glossy hair.

She turned to me, a quarter outstretched in her palm. "You try."

"Do it for me?"

She inserted the quarter. Florence parted her lips, eager to expel more bullshit. *"Look around, look around. Happiness is yours, unexpected where it is found,"* it told her. Another card popped out. Charlotte waved it at me.

"Profound."

Grinning, she crossed the arcade and handed me the happiness card. I looked down at it. "I don't want that one."

"You can't just choose your fortune."

"Sure I can. I'll trade you happiness for the life-changing letter?"

Her nose crinkled. "I don't know. I'm waiting on college acceptance letters."

I slipped my feet into the stirrups. "You don't really believe that a fortune-telling machine is going to determine whether or not you get into one of the Ivy Leagues? You'll do that all by yourself."

She blushed.

I nodded at our fate in her hands. "Gimme the letter. Have my happiness instead."

Our fingers brushed. My heart skittered.

As she pulled herself up onto the mauve-maned horse next to mine, the ends of her cherry-red parka fell over her thighs like Little Red Riding Hood's cape. I caught a wave of her soft perfume, and it made me feel dizzy-good, like my horse was galloping on its golden pole.

I cleared my throat. "Did you ever go through that three-month horse phase that all the girls did in middle school?"

"No. I went through a three-month Rachel Maddow phase."

The wind whip-cracked the roof.

"I watched MSNBC religiously. I haven't been so smart since I was thirteen. But my opinion on politics wasn't exactly the only thing Rachel Maddow helped me understand about myself."

The carousel tune cranked over to "Greensleeves" and something fractured inside me. "Did you ever come here in the summer?" I asked. "Before you moved to Maine?"

She nodded. "My grandparents used to bring me here. My parents were always working."

"Why *did* you move back here?"

"My nonno was dying. He had cancer."

"Oh. I'm sor—"

Instantly, she changed the subject: "Did you ever come here in the summer?"

I shook my head. "I was way too old for this place when we moved to Salem."

"You were in middle school when you moved here?"

"I moved here just in time to start middle school." We'd passed each other like ships in the night. I'd just missed attending—hand to god, no joke—Witchcraft Heights Elementary.

She tilted her head. "Eleven isn't really too old, though."

"I guess this sort of thing wasn't really my mom's scene. I never really had a kiddie sort of upbringing."

"Why not?"

"My mom's always been more like my cool older friend who just happened to potty-train me. Steve Carell and Tina Fey did the hard work when it came to raising me."

"You mean your mom didn't do the whole bedtime story thing?"

"Does Gilda Radner's autobiography count as a bedtime story? She read me that."

Leaning forward, she rested her chin atop her horse's mane. "What about your dad?"

"He's not around." He was around. He was everywhere, just not where it mattered. He was on Facebook, IMDb, YouTube. Would she find it funny to know that my twelve-year-old self had the Frank Abagnale Jr. of YouTube accounts, just so I could give Dad's stand-up videos the thumbs-down? Would she be amused by the fact that KansasGrl87 and ComedyChick's shared password was "DadsAdick2011"? That, when a thumbs-down had not satisfied the daddy issues raging inside me, I'd progressed to leaving profoundly destructive comments like "lame as fuq!" and "you suck, loser"? "My dad lives between New York and the Cape. He's a comedian."

"That explains where you get it from."

A sick feeling tightened in my stomach. "Actually, my mom was a comedian too. That was how they met. But then she got knocked up, so she quit the stand-up circuit and let him do it instead."

She could sense that I was uncomfortable talking about it. She pointed to the back of the room, at the changing rainbow lights that seeped through the plastic-strip curtain. "The Hall of Mirrors is back there?"

I nodded.

"Can I go in there?"

"You don't have to ask for my permission."

She hiked a leg back over the horse. She was halfway to the curtain when she pivoted. "I'm not going to be murdered in there, am I?"

I bit the sides of my cheeks to suppress a grin. "Well, there *was* a clown who mysteriously disappeared from payroll one summer . . . but you're *probably* safe."

She pried apart the strips and twirled like a showgirl in the doorway. "You should know," she started, "the whole circus-slash-carnival-slash-county-fair thing is my worst fear."

"You don't like clowns?"

"Who does?" She bit her lip. "Are you coming in with me?"

With her? Alone? In a confined space? Something bubbled in my chest and made me afraid of what could come out of my filter-less mouth if I followed her in there. "I think I'm good here."

She tilted her head. "You don't like clowns?"

"Clowns are okay. My greatest fear is being confronted by my own reflection."

"Suit yourself," she singsonged as she disappeared into the Hall of Mirrors. There was a dare in her voice, so sugary and melodic, that it reached across the room, took me by the hand, and pulled me from the carousel.

I had to follow her. I *had* to.

When the plastic strips ruffled at my touch, she whirled at the end of the hall. She was bathed in violet, then indigo as it washed to blue. My heart just *dropped*.

All of the fun house versions of ourselves—tall, short, distorted—watched on as we tinted poison ivy, coward yellow, blood orange.

I stepped inside, deeper, deeper. . . .

The wind howled. My pulse went wild as we were dyed warning red beneath the lights. I stopped, five feet between us.

Her lips parted.

Something clicked. That ache I'd had for months felt more acute, more intense than ever before. There was no doubt in my mind that she didn't feel it too.

As we stared at each other, it was *electric.*

I needed to know what it would feel like to be a little bit brave. I moved forward.

Her voice sliced through the tension like a cleaver. "I think maybe we should go."

The breath caught in my throat.

Her eyes pitched to the floor.

I stuffed my trembling hands into my pockets. "Okay. Totally." Had I misread her signals? Had I misread her signals this whole time? "We can go. Whatever you want. Of course."

Heat radiated off her body like a furnace as I held the strips back and she brushed past me.

We grabbed our bags. I locked up.

It was way too cold to walk back, especially around the exposed cove, but there was no other way to get downtown. Charlotte wrapped her scarf up around her face. A quarter of a mile down Memorial Drive, she finally spoke up, and when she did, I could barely hear her in the ferocious wind. "I got a rejection letter from Columbia yesterday."

I licked my wind-chapped lips. "Oh. I'm sorry."

"I haven't told anyone," she said, her words muffled through the knitted wool. "It was the school I really wanted for history."

"I'm really sorry, Charlotte."

"I'm thinking now, maybe that was the life-changing letter. Columbia's rejected me and the rest could too, so now I'm going to miss out on everything I ever wanted to do and instead I'll have to settle down and live vicariously through my children."

"A card doesn't determine your future. You do."

"You don't know that."

"Actually, I do, because I know for a fact that Florence has a range of exactly seven prophecies."

She stopped walking and looked up at me. "I changed my mind." She pulled the happiness card from her pocket. "Have this. And give me mine back. It'll curse you."

"No."

"Seriously," she said. "I want it back."

"Nope."

She stepped in front of me and slipped her hand into my pocket, her fist tapping against my abdomen in her haste to retrieve the card. Instantly, I stiffened, and she must have felt me tense at the touch, because her sweet laugh ceased. But just when she thought she'd won, I wrapped my bare hand around the outside of my pocket and trapped her hand inside.

The bones of her hand were slight, delicate through the goose down and nylon between our fingers. I stared at her, squeezed gently, once, twice. Her cheeks flushed. My grip loosened.

She pulled her hand free and grinned up at me, smug.

Before she could stop me, I snatched both cards from her, tore them into little pieces with my rigor-locked fingers.

"Taylor!"

The tiny paper particles chased the wind like rose petals. "There you go," I said. "The curse is broken."

We watched the cardboard sail toward Danvers River, heading for Prides Crossing. She shook her head. "I think you just sparked it."

NINE

It was the day after Salem Willows and the day before Thanksgiving when I found myself in AP History, only half listening to Mrs. Linklater drone on about Crane and *The Red Badge of Courage*, and decided that, screw it, this was war. I was going to get myself my own red badge of courage. I was going to do everything in my power to win the internship.

The deadline for my finalist submission package was midnight. I only had nine hours to decide between submitting an old sketch or coming up with brand-new material. The word limit was six hundred, which usually took me no time when I was just writing for me. But writing for other people? People who would read it? And *judge* it? A panel of living, breathing, talented writers? I wasn't sure if nine hours would be enough, but I owed it to Gilda my friend, Gilda Radner, and my *Saturday Night Live: The Best Of* DVD collection to give it a shot.

On my way home from school, I went into Front Street Coffeehouse and ordered a hot chocolate. There was something about sitting in the corner window and pulling out my notebook that made me feel like the Little Comic That Could.

But the thing was, I *couldn't*. I had no idea where to begin. Number 45 had just happened, so political sketches were hot real estate, but I didn't know much about politics other than what I inhaled from *SNL*, and that wasn't enough. I sat there, erratically flicking through my most recent notebook and attempting to calm myself down with the hot chocolate. Everything that had seemed funny at the time was pure and utter crap. I wasn't comical. I was barely *funny*. How the hell had I gotten this far in the contest?

I was staring at my reflection in the window, feeling sorry for the girl looking back at me, when I managed to look past my own misery for a hot minute. A crowd was gathering outside. Then I heard the first scream a mile away. Another shriek. The projection of a deep male voice, closer this time. "Goodwife Bishop! Goodwife Bishop! I have a warrant for your arrest!"

Enraptured, tourists scattered to either side of the street to make way for the hourly performance of *Cry Innocent*. Unfazed, a local crossed through, overfilled grocery bags in her arms, not even flinching as "Bridget" squealed and struggled a few feet behind the "town crier." I glanced at my phone. It was already four thirty.

As Bridget Bishop charged past the window, two men dressed as Puritans hot on her heels, I put my headphones on and went into a trance. I started writing a sketch about the real Bridget Bishop watching *Cry Innocent*, pointing out inconsistencies to the crowd, but then I gave up about a hundred words in because in what world was that funny?

The door to the coffeehouse opened. A woman in a long, velvet, gothic dress headed to the counter. I pushed back my headphones. The mauve hem of her skirt was soaked darker, like she'd waded through a shallow stream. My gaze shot to the window. I'd been so engrossed, my music so loud, I hadn't even heard it raining.

As she ordered, Cruella ran a hand through her stark gray regrowth. Her voice was so husky that, if I closed my eyes, I could pretend it was Cher at the counter complaining about Salem drivers skipping the stoplight at Washington and Essex.

The bell above the door rang as it closed behind her. I watched from my booth as she crossed the street to the terrace house with the "Psychic" sign out front.

Bin-freaking-go. Was there any other kind of comedy gold that could even come close to rivaling your classic Salem setup? I jabbed the stud of my notebook shut, took my empty mug to the counter, and chased inspiration across the street.

Cruella's name was Lucinda. "Weren't you just in the coffeehouse?" she asked as I stood in her doorway, swatting raindrops from my brow. The crow's feet at the corners of her eyes set deeply as she focused on me. In the coffeehouse, she'd looked and sounded about sixty, but up close, she was obviously much older. Trying not to choke on the profusion of incense, I fished a ten-dollar bill from my wallet.

"I won't reveal anything about your death, the death of any of your family members, or any specific dates related to harm or devastation," she monologued.

"Wicked."

She led me to a back room and plonked her cardboard coffee cup on a small table between two chairs.

She asked for a piece of my jewelry.

"Oh, I don't wear jewelry."

"Do you have a key ring?"

I felt down the side pocket of my schoolbag for my house keys. She took them from me, ran her finger over the *Little Women* key chain I'd gotten from Louisa May Alcott's Orchard House on an English class field trip sophomore year. "This will work. But take it off the ring. The keys will interfere with my reading and I may read another of your family members who lives with you."

She started a timer on her phone. 9:59. 9:58. 9:57 . . .

Silence. She rubbed her thumb along the spine of the miniature pewter book, raked her too-long nail over the engraved "Alcott." The pad of her thumb slid along the front cover so slowly, so deliberately, I wondered if I was going to get a reading along the lines of "Your father's been injured in the Civil War" or "Your sweetest sister is about to be struck with scarlet fever." Instead her lips parted. "You have a great sadness looming over you." Her eyes narrowed. She rolled the pewter book between her fingertips. "I'm trying to see past the sadness, but I'm having trouble. Give me a moment. . . ."

7:32.

7:31.

7:30.

"You're in love."

All of me heated.

"This boy is older than you."

Jesus H. Christ. I wanted to give her the benefit of the doubt, really I did. Was she getting hetero vibes from my *Little Women* key ring? Maybe. But then again, I always thought Jo March was pretty dykey, and Alcott claimed to have fallen in love with more pretty girls than men, so I put the boy thing down to less of the *Little Women* vibe, and more of Lucinda the psychic trying to scam me for my hard-earned cash.

"Yeah," I agreed, because I was darned if I wasn't going to get sketch gold out of this. "He *is* older."

She fixed me with a hard look—she didn't want me to validate what she was saying.

5:47.

5:46.

"He is not good for you," she said. "It's going to take you a while to see this, but you will." She took a sip of her coffee, left a hot coral lipstick ring around the plastic lid.

I sat forward. "Can you tell me more about my romance?"

She chuckled, like I was *typical*. "You want to hear more about boys?"

For the first time in my life, Lucinda.

4:21.

4:20.

She tossed *Little Women* onto the table. "You need to be . . . cautious when it comes to sex," she said frankly. "I can see you becoming very reckless in the very near future, and it's going to cost you."

Perfect. "Pregnancy?"

"I'm not sure. You just need to be careful." She paused dramatically. "You need to protect yourself."

3:12.

3:11.

"I see the letter *L*. In gold."

"*L* for *love*?"

"No. The letter, it isn't supposed to be there. It's out of place. Floating."

She was quiet then, for a whole dollar's worth of time. I could see my phone lighting up through the thin zipper of my bag. Mom was probably wondering where I was. "You're not supposed to be here anymore," Lucinda suddenly said.

"Here?"

"In Salem. Or Massachusetts—" The "spell" ringtone

charmed from her phone, loud and obnoxious. "Do you want more time?"

I was curious to know where it was she thought I was supposed to be, but she'd pretty much spent the whole session pairing me with boys, so I brushed it aside. "No, thank you. I think I have enough. Had. *Had* enough." I was itching to haul my sketchbook from my bag. I already had a title picked out: "Sylvie the Salem Psychic Meets a Sapphic." NBC was going to froth at the corners of its peacock beak.

Lucinda followed me to the door—she was closing up for the night. In her tiny reception area, a TV sat on a low table. She groaned at CNN. "Gods, am I sick of watching Trump play the victim when it comes to this Russia scandal. Mark my words, he'll be calling it a witch hunt in no time."

"Witch hunt?"

"He'll have John Proctor rolling in his unmarked grave."

When I got home, Mom, Ryan, and peroxide Rachel Maddow were at the kitchen table, eating from Chinese takeout boxes like we lived in a frat house for mature students. I told Mom I had to work on an assignment. "But it's Thanksgiving Eve," Ryan said. "What's twenty minutes to eat with us?"

I faked a laugh. "The difference between a B and a C." I grabbed the container Mom had ordered for me and went up to my room. Between bites of honey chicken, I typed 563 words and titled it, "Witch Hunt: The Nightmare Before Christmas."

I sat back, staring at the NBC address in the recipient bar. This was it. Once I submitted this final sketch, there was no forfeiting my place in the game. There was no backing out. I'd have to come out within the next month. From this moment on, I'd have to really get my shit together and figure out how to be honest—with Mom, with Brooke, with myself.

The way I saw it, I had two options: not send the final sketch, stay safe in the closet, and give up my dream. Or, send the final sketch, come out in the next month, and give myself a shot at the very best thing that could ever happen to me.

I was scared silly, but there was no question.

I clicked Send.

When I stopped in the doorway of the kitchen later that night, Jen turned suddenly in her chair. I'd interrupted. They'd been whispering about the miscarriage Mom had had years ago—the one she had when Jen was visiting. The one they thought I knew nothing about.

Mom looked up from scrubbing the stove top. "Hi, honey," she said, swatting at the blond strands that had come loose from her ponytail. Her face was flushed. "How's your assignment coming along?"

"I'm working on it. What are you talking about?"

"Do you remember when I stayed here for the *Grey Gardens* documentary exhibition at the Peabody?"

"Of course I remember." After that visit, I'd wondered if Jen would ever come back. I'd wondered if we'd been too much for her, too broken for her. I'd wondered if the next Thanksgiving would be just Mom and me, a whole turkey just for two.

It had been one of the first exhibitions that had brought Jen to Salem. *Grey Gardens* was a documentary from the seventies about a reclusive mother and daughter, former socialites from Long Island. When "Big Edie" and "Little Edie" let their East Hampton estate, *Grey Gardens*, go to absolute ruin, the health department threatened to evict them. Stray cats birthed litters in their attic, raccoons peed behind their demounted portraits, and the women lived on a diet of liver pâté and undercooked corn. Eventually, *Grey Gardens* became so flea-infested that the Edies' cousin, former first lady Jackie O, had to make it rain just so they could keep their home.

"I remember teaching you the Little Edie Long Island accent right here at this table," Jen said. "You called Carrie 'muther darhling' all morning."

I reached into the cupboard for a glass. "I still do. And every time Mom and I argue about something, she says—"

"'You can't get any freedom when you're being supported!'" Mom mimicked Big Edie.

As I filled my glass with water, I stared out the kitchen window into Linda's yard, pretending I was gazing at the North Atlantic barely three hundred yards from Little Edie's back door. "*Honestly*," I improvised, "*I'm positively trapped!*"

Jen grinned. "Okay," Mom said. "We get it, you can still do the accent. We don't need a performance of the entire script—"

"It's not scripted, Mom. It's a documentary."

Mom rolled her eyes. "Save it for theater class, Little Edie."

"So what about *Grey Gardens*?" I asked Jen.

"I've been having weird pregnancy dreams about it, that's all."

"It means she's having a girl," Mom asserted. "A *staunch* little girl."

I placed my glass in the sink. It came out before I could stop myself: "Or it could mean that you feel trapped."

Jen's smile dropped. An uneasy tension filled the kitchen.

Fuck. My neck had to be red. It definitely had to be red.

Jen smiled softly, but I knew her well enough to know I'd truly upset her. "I'm going to head to bed."

When she was gone, Mom stopped scrubbing the burner cap and glared at me. "*Trapped?* Why the fuck would you say that?"

I groaned. "I'm sorry. It just came out."

"Well, think before you speak!" She scrubbed vigorously. "I didn't raise you to talk like that. I raised you to have good manners."

"You *raised me* on a complex diet of Chelsea Handler and Sarah Silverman."

"Don't be a smart-ass."

"I'm sorry, okay? I can't help it that I got half of your husband's asshole genetics."

"Don't speak about your father like that."

"As if you care. You spit in his latte too, Carrie Ann."

Her eyes widened. *"Go to bed."*

I pressed a kiss to her dimple. "Good night, Goody Proctor."

She swatted me with the dish towel.

TEN

"*What about you,* Taylor?" Ryan asked. "What are you thankful for?"

I looked around the Thanksgiving table at the faces of all those people I didn't know. When you think about it, it's a pretty fucked-up way to spend your adolescence—living with strangers in your home, having your mom install a chain lock on your bedroom door when you're eleven years old because she's worried some dirty old man will sneak into your room at night and grab you by the pussy. My gaze drifted from Jen and Ryan, to the Italians from the Bridget Bishop Suite, to the British sisters from the Sarah Good Suite. I looked to Mom at the head of the table, drizzling cranberry sauce over her overcooked turkey. My heart shifted in my chest. "I'm thankful for my mom."

Mom's eyes snapped up. She slipped the spoon into the cranberry sauce and then set the dish down. She pressed a hand to her chest. "Taylor . . ." Her eyes got that sappy glow.

Jen's gaze caught mine. Instantly, she reached for the green beans. Embarrassment locked in my chest like indigestion. *She thinks I'm a coward for not coming out.*

My phone buzzed in my pocket. A message from Charlotte.

I excused myself to the guest bathroom, sat on the toilet lid, and opened the message.

I heard you're coming to drama club tomorrow to help us again for dress rehearsal.

For a long moment I stared at it. We hadn't spoken since Salem Willows—not even online. That was two days ago, and I was still thinking about that moment in the Hall of Mirrors.

Yeah, I typed. *I told Brooke I'd come by. Also, I heard there was free pizza involved, so . . .*

I watched the ellipsis bubble. *You're wasting your Black Friday with us just for free pizza?* The ellipsis bubbled again.

I waited.

When the *Mean Girls* "Why are you so obsessed with me?" GIF popped up, I almost bit off the tip of my tongue. Did she really think I was obsessed with her? Was she flirting with me? Was I supposed to flirt back?

She was waiting. I had to do *something*.

I started typing. Then I stopped. Then she started. Then she stopped. Then she started again. *That was a joke*, she wrote. *I don't actually think you're obsessed with me haha.*

I replied with a GIF of Kate McKinnon winking, hoped that maybe some of that swagger would mask my total and complete inexperience, that she wouldn't see right through me.

I'm not sure what she saw, but whatever it was, she didn't reply.

The thing about working the tech box is that it's a one-person operation. High in the back corner and sectioned off from the rest of the grandstand by timber panels, the compartment is so small, so narrow, that in junior year I almost took off a tit slinking in sideways. There are two grandstand seats in there, side by side, but it really isn't a place for more than one person. There simply isn't enough space to breathe.

So, on Black Friday morning, when Charlotte started up the stairs to the tech box, I panicked. There wasn't room for both of us. Well, there *was*—she was tiny, and it wasn't like I had the physical build of a World Wrestling champion—but nobody had ever tried it. Nobody wanted to. It wasn't *comfortable*.

I smiled at Charlotte as she came closer and closer, pretended I was totally oblivious to what she was planning to do. *Oh god.* I pulled my eyes back to the stage, to Garrett and Madison and Brooke at the dining table, the three of them waiting for Ms. Glazer to finish rewriting one of Emerson's lines because Garrett's lateral lisp was making it impossible for him to say "seventeenth-century Salem, Massachusetts." Brooke's gaze darted from Charlotte to me in the tech box. Our eyes caught, held. She looked down at the teacup prop in front of her, sat forward, started saying something to Madison. Things really hadn't been the same between us since last Friday night when she'd been a stone-cold bitch. I hadn't even told her about the Back Bay apartment—or that, this time next year, I'd be somebody's sister.

Halfway up the grandstand, Charlotte hitched up the long black skirt of her nineteenth-century dress. She'd arrived just like that, completely made up as Emily Dickinson. Everyone else had taken their sweet-ass time putting their costumes on at school, but Charlotte had shown up at nine a.m. in full Dickinson garb beneath her parka, her ink-black hair already parted perfectly and gathered in a low ponytail at the base of her neck.

Excitement feathered in my belly as she strolled across the top row of seating toward me.

Squeezing in, she pulled the door locked behind her. Dainty hands tucked behind her back, she leaned against it. "Hey," she whispered.

My throat grew tight. "Hi."

"It's Madison's turn to understudy my part." She tilted her head. "Can I sit with you while I wait to go back on?"

I nodded, maybe too enthusiastically. "Yeah. Definitely. Here . . ."

Our knees brushed as she dragged her skirt around to one side and settled into the decorative pillows Ms. Glazer had shoved up there when she'd "updated the energy of the room." I shifted closer to the brick wall to give her more space, but it didn't change much—the side of her body was still pressed tight against mine, closer even than the week before in the back seat of Brooke's car.

Downstage, Ms. Glazer was chiding Brooke for not having a pencil on her. A good actor had a pencil on them at all times, she said. At the dining table, Garrett was trying to pinch out the candle flame, and Madison was arguing with him, telling him to cut it out. It was all so chaotic. In the tech box, we were silent.

I drew a breath so deep, I knew she'd heard it. "You're a really good Emily Dickinson."

"Thanks," she said softly. She didn't brush off the compliment or make some self-deprecating joke the way I would have. She just accepted it. It made me want her even more.

I brought my knees together tighter. I wasn't listening to anything that was happening onstage, and I'm pretty sure she wasn't either. What *was* she thinking? Was she thinking about how I'd spooked her in the Hall of Mirrors? About that flirty GIF I'd sent the night before? Maybe she was confused. Not about her sexuality . . . but about whether she actually wanted *me*. She'd run away in the Hall of Mirrors, and she hadn't replied to my GIF. What if she thought she'd judged me wrong?

I rolled my fists along my thighs to still my bouncing knee.

Ms. Glazer looked up at the tech box. She stared, curious. "Taylor and Charlotte, can we turn down the houselights and get a spotlight with a tinge of blue?"

I bent my upper half over the switchboard and added the blue light until the theater room drew dark.

"That's way too bright," Charlotte whispered, and then she reached forward across the switchboard and *completely covered my hand with her own*.

Goose bumps stung my jaw.

Her hand moved mine, sliding it lower, lower, lower until the blue was dimmed. Her fingers were warm, her hand much smaller than my own. "There," she whispered. "I think that's good." Turning her hand over in mine, she did the thing that set an ache in my throat: she linked our fingers together.

A muscle in my thigh twitched. Suddenly I felt so shy, so unbelievably shy in a way I didn't even think I could.

She lifted our joined hands and rested them on the pillows. Settling back against the wall, she looked down at the stage.

We could have said anything to each other and nobody would have heard. But we didn't. Maybe, just like me, she wasn't so confident about all this romantic stuff. The thing is, just because a person knows what they want, it doesn't necessarily mean they know how to go after it.

It was so hot in the tech box that I wouldn't have been surprised if the Perspex screen steamed up just like in *Titanic* when Jack and Rose make love in the back seat of the car down in the cargo hold, just before they hit the iceberg. I'd never held hands with anybody for that long. I felt as though, for the first time in a really long time, a switch had been flicked on inside me and, finally, I was really fucking *on*, brave in a way I hadn't been in years. I'd been soaking in shame and self-hatred for so long that my heart had turned prune-y. You know how your skin shrivels in the bath? How it's a survival mechanism so your grip improves underwater? Hating myself for who I was and who I loved was the only way I knew how to adapt to this change happening inside me. Shaming myself was the only way I could grip the seawalls without floating away. I'd been so angry for so long, so bitter and twisted. But as Charlotte's thumb traced the webbed skin between my thumb and finger, it was like something settled inside me. I *calmed*. I *liked* myself a little bit more.

Her voice was a whisper: "Can I ask you something?"

My nerves fluttered. "Sure—"

"Were you going to kiss me in the Hall of Mirrors?"

She said it quickly, like she was worried about losing her nerve. The thought of her being as on edge about all this as I was made the pressure in my chest swell. I ran my tongue along the roof of my mouth, desperate to get some saliva to flow. "I think so."

I could hear her breathing beside me, wondered if she could hear her own heartbeat like I could hear mine. "So . . . you like girls?" she whispered.

Yes. Yes. "Yes."

"We'll stop there," Ms. Glazer said. She turned and looked up at us in the tech box. "Charlotte, are you ready to take your turn?"

It was just before dinner on Black Friday and I was still day-dreaming about Charlotte and what had happened between us in the tech box when I got the call.

"Mom!" I shouted up the stairs. "I'm heading out!"

She poked her head out of the Abigail Williams Suite. "You just got back from theater! Where are you going now?"

I told her that the movie theater had called, that they'd finally taken my poster down.

"Hon, it's getting dark out. If you wait until after I check in the guests arriving at six, I can walk you over?"

I didn't have time to wait. I was like a kid in a goddamn candy store. It was raining out, and there was water in my boots by the time I got to Cinema Salem. "My boss says it's a bit damaged," the guy behind the counter said as he handed over the cylinder, thumb crumpling the edge where Taylor Parker was written on the back of the poster. "We caught a few kids graffitiing the ones in the frames outside last month, but I think they left this one alone."

"That's fine." I'd been waiting five months and sixteen days for them to finally take it down. Mom had even ordered a frame for it. I didn't care about a few crinkles or buckled edges.

The rain was still heavy when I left the movie theater, so I waited it out under the canopy between Harrison's Comics and Hex Old World Witchery. Even though I'd slipped the poster into the protective wrapping I'd saved from my Target Lady poster, I held the roll tight inside my coat. I watched nerd boys come out of the comic store, tourists pour out the doors of Hex, and I judged them all. You heard that right: Anonymous, Massachusetts, clutching her *Ghostbusters* poster against her body like her firstborn, *she* judged *them*.

When I got back, Mom was busy checking in the guests, so I toed off my boots in the coat closet, went up to my room, and unrolled my poster.

My stomach curled. Beneath the *Answer the Call* subtitle, someone had written *Dykebusters!* in Holtzmann's proton stream.

A nasty feeling flushed through my veins like poison.

I fisted the edges in my hands, and I tore those women apart. Those funny, clever women who I'd placed on pedestals. Those sharp-witted women who'd given me more than I'd ever be able to thank them for. I tore them apart.

I thought about tossing the pieces in the trash outside, but I worried Mom would find them and wonder why I'd destroyed the poster, why I cared about a tiny little bit of graffiti when I could have easily Wite-Outed the black Sharpie. I balled up the shreds and buried half of them under the floorboard with Oliver Twist. Not all of them fit, so I stashed the rest behind the wood in the fireplace.

I sat in the shower and watched the hot steam fog the glass until I couldn't see my reflection. No matter how long I'd waited for the poster, it wasn't worth crying over . . . right? The next thing I knew, I was reaching out and tracing *I'm gay* into the clouded glass door. And *then* I was drawing a line right through *gay* and writing *a lesbian* beside it.

For a split second, I panicked that those three little words would hold longer than my ten-minute shower and Mom would see. I rolled my head against the wall, leaned forward, and kissed the letters from the glass. And I'm not talking about a peck. No. I'm talking about completely going to town on my shower door, tongue and teeth and turbulence. At first, I thought maybe the salt on my tongue was mildew, but then a sob tore its way from my throat and I choked against the glass.

It was almost comical. But at the same time, it wasn't funny at all. Because the thing about being closeted is that you're constantly tearing at the seams. And the world doesn't do you any favors. When someone makes a homophobic joke or jab or judgment, Abby Wambach doesn't show up on your doorstep and offer you a two-week retreat to the Hudson Valley to stitch yourself back up. If you're lucky, you get a few miserable, desolate moments to pull yourself back together. And then you pick yourself up and get back out there and you *hope*. You hope that the seam won't split further. You hope everybody will buy what you're selling—that you're totally *fine*.

After I managed to extract myself from the sexual allure of my shower screen, I pulled myself back together, stitched myself back up. I hadn't even had a chance to dress when Mom knocked at my door. "Show me," she said, looking past me into my room.

I clutched my towel to my chest. "They mixed it up with the *La La Land* poster. They accidentally threw it in the trash."

Her expression crumpled. "I already ordered the frame."

I sagged against the doorjamb. "It's not *my* fault."

"I never said it was your fault. . . . Have you been crying?"

"No."

"You look like you've been crying."

"I'm just tired."

She didn't pry or press or tell me that I could talk to her about anything. "Are you hungry?"

I shook my head.

"I've noticed that you haven't been eating much lately. Are you stressed about something? You stop eating so much when you're stressed about something."

"I'm eating the normal amount."

She stared at me with this hopeless kind of look that said *Don't you need me anymore? Not as a mother? Not even as a friend?*

The hairs stood on the back of my neck. The distance between us had been growing for a while. For the past few months, I'd thought I was the only one who could see it.

Panic rolled rampant in my stomach. If I told her I was gay, it would drive a wedge between us. She'd think I'd been lying to her, that we weren't part of each other anymore. But I wasn't part of anybody anymore. I wasn't whole anywhere, with anyone. Pieces of me were scattered all over Salem—sketch me, gay me, the *me* I wore every day that was maybe just a mask. I didn't even know anymore. I was Taylor Parker, Imposter Extraordinaire. I belonged to so many families and yet, at the same time, I belonged to not a single one of them—especially not the one searching my gaze with the same blue eyes that stared back at me each time I looked in the mirror.

"All right then," Mom whispered. "Suit yourself."

ELEVEN

On Sunday afternoon, I was raking a blanket of gray fluff from the lint trap when the landline rang. I looked up the basement stairs. Was Mom going to get it?

As I lifted the damp sheets from the basket and shoved them into the dryer, it kept ringing. On the sixth ring, I lunged for the wall.

Mom beat me to it—upstairs, she'd already answered. I came to the conversation a few words too late: "—theater teacher, and I'd like to talk to you about Taylor's future."

Ms. Glazer? My stomach plummeted. Had she called to tell Mom about the competition? Was she calling to out me?

"Is this a good time to talk, Ms. Parker? I could call back at another time if—"

"No." Mom paused. "Now is fine."

"Fabulous! Well, I'll get straight to the point: I think Taylor needs to consider a performance program for college."

I gripped the edge of the washtub.

"Oh," Mom said. "Y-you haven't heard that Taylor's received early admission to Emerson? She wants to be a journalist."

"I . . . I have. And I'm not surprised—she certainly has a way with words."

"She's very excited about it."

"That's . . . that's wonderful."

"Yes. It is."

Silence.

Ms. Glazer cleared her throat. "I don't want to rock the boat, Ms. Parker. I'm sure Emerson would be wonderful for Taylor. But it's still early on, and I think that, for someone with the range of talent Taylor has, a performance program is worth considering too."

Mom was quiet.

"I don't make these suggestions to all my students," Ms. Glazer added. "Actually, I haven't made the suggestion to a student in years. But this year, I have Taylor and one other student who shows remarkable potential, so I'm making it my mission to see that they both at least *consider* auditioning. These girls, they're *magnetic*."

My cheeks warmed.

"But how would she be qualified?" Mom said.

"Sorry?" Ms. Glazer asked.

"If Taylor enrolled in some sort of performance program? What would she be qualified to do?"

"Well, she'd learn how to hone her craft."

"Her *craft*? Look, Lou Ann—can I call you Lou Ann?"

"Of cour—"

"I wanted to be a comedian. I *was* a comedian. And twenty years later? As we speak, I'm Windexing splattered foundation from a bathroom mirror in one of my guest suites—and my shift at Walgreens starts in an hour. Now, you teach theater? I'm sure that wasn't *your* teenage dream."

MOTHERRRRRR . . .

"Thing is, Lou Ann, it's great to encourage kids, and I really respect that you have Taylor's best interest at heart, calling me and all, but I think you and I both know how important it is to be realistic."

Now Ms. Glazer was quiet.

"Besides how hard it is to break into that world, besides what a discouraging, unpredictable life it is, all that negativity aside . . . Taylor just isn't tough enough to handle a life of rejection. She's too sensitive. She'd take it too personally."

What the fuck.

"She'd get hurt—and then she'd get bitter. As it is, she already has the resting bitch face of a Victorian schoolmarm."

What the actual fuck.

"You obviously know her best," Ms. Glazer said. "Of course you do—you're her mom. But, from what I've seen, Taylor seems to have quite a thick skin—"

"Trust me," Mom said, "she doesn't. Just before Halloween, we had a guest stay who made a comment about millennials and privilege and Uber Eats, and Taylor took it so much to heart that the next morning she went and ordered every one of our guests coffee through Uber Eats—except him. Honestly, I could have killed her."

In the dryer window, I watched myself smirk. That *had* been pretty funny. Evidently, Ms. Glazer thought so too. She giggled. "I don't know if that's necessarily a sign of not being able to handle rejection—"

"Oh," Mom said. "When it comes to Taylor, it *absolutely* is."

The smile slipped from my face.

The next part came muffled—I imagined Mom covering the receiver, the way she did on a call to Jen: "I'd say it's because she's a child of divorce, but the truth is, even when she was little, she wasn't able to hack it."

I stiffened.

"You know," Mom said, "she'd die if I told you this, but . . ."

I gripped the phone tighter.

"When Taylor was a kid, we rented a house one summer, on Martha's Vineyard . . ."

No . . .

"Gosh, I can't remember the name of it . . ."

No, Mom.

"*Seas the Day!* That was it. She made a little friend there. . . ."

No. No. No. No.

"When we first arrived, she *loathed* this girl. Kid was a spoiled brat, threw prissy little tantrums. But then a few days passed and they became absolutely inseparable. Every day, Taylor was up at the ass crack of dawn and running out to see her. And the thing is, other than at school, Taylor wasn't really around many boys when she was growing up, so, to be perfectly honest, I think she developed a little bit of a crush."

My heart slammed against my ribs. *Don't say it, Mom. Please, god, do not say it.*

"Anyway, they were playing, you know, the way kids do, and, well, long story short, Taylor drew a picture of the girl in her birthday suit. The mother found the drawing in the pocket of the kid's swimming trunks."

I bit into the palm of my hand to stifle a scream.

Clearly, Ms. Glazer didn't know what to say. "Well, that's—"

"It's actually a very sad story. When we got back from vacation, Taylor tried to call her little friend, but each time, the mother would make some excuse why she couldn't come to the phone. Taylor was *devastated.* After that, she quickly convinced herself she hated that girl—but she didn't. She adored her. But you see, my point is, that's what Taylor does—she takes the rejection and the hurt and she Band-Aids it up with anger."

I was going to Lizzie Borden my mother. I was literally going to Lizzie Borden my mother in her *sleep*.

Mom's sigh was soft. "So, I hear what you're saying, Lou Ann—I really do. But Taylor couldn't tough it as a performer. She wouldn't cope. A life like that . . . it'd be the death of her. Because, bless her heart, somewhere along the line, Taylor was hit with the sensitive stick."

Forty minutes later I ran into Benedict Arnold in the kitchen in her Walgreens uniform.

"Hello, my darling daughter," she said, mouth full of turkey. "Are the sheets almost dry?"

"Uh-huh." I poked my head into the fridge.

She tapped me on the back, reached out to me with a triangle of turkey sandwich. "You want half?"

I grabbed a container of strawberry yogurt, tore off the foil, balled it in my fist. I narrowed my eyes at her. "That was left out for too long. You'll get food poisoning."

"Many thanks, Gordon Ramsay, but the turkey's fine."

I pelted the foil into the trash. "Choke on it," I mumbled.

Spinning, she locked eyes on me. "What the fuck did you just say?"

"Nothing."

"Taylor," she called after me.

I took the stairs two at a time. "Hope on it! I said, 'Hope on it'!"

The first time I heard someone say that you truly grow up when you have to parent your own parent, I wholeheartedly believed it. I just really thought that, when our time came, Carrie Parker would be paper-skinned, senile, and stealing custard puddings in some sort of second-rate care facility.

In the corner of the running shower, a sob cracked from Mom's lips. "Go to bed." Rolling her head against the tile, she groaned. "It's so late and you should go to bed."

I wrung the mop out in the bucket of disinfectant. "I can't. I have to make sure you're okay." This had to be the cruelest case of divine intervention. *If you hadn't snuck into her room to call her out on what she said to Ms. Glazer—if you'd just let it the fuck go—you wouldn't have found her like this and you wouldn't be stuck cleaning up her mess at two a.m.*

She sighed, long and hard. "If I didn't have you to look after me . . ." Tugging her knees to her naked chest, she cursed me with an image I *very happily* could have gone the rest of my life without ever, ever seeing. "I don't know why I'm so, so sick."

"Judging from the ocean of turkey chunks I just cleaned up, I'm going to bet my college fund on your sandwich." Crouching at the edge of the shower, I shoved my sleeves up to my elbows. *Eugh.* After the ordeal of getting her into the shower, they were *saturated.* "Mom, you need to crawl closer so I can reach you. I need to wash your hair and I can't come in there in my pajamas."

Clutching her stomach, she groaned. "I can do it myself. I'm not as bad as I was before. Go to bed, baby."

"You can't do it yourself—you're pale as a ghost. Come on,

you smell like something the cat dragged in and the kittens didn't want."

She groaned again. "Don't be a bitch."

I reached under the spray for the shampoo bottle on the ledge. "Come on, you puked in your hair."

She cracked an eye open. "I did?"

"Half an hour ago—about two seconds after I found you in here. And about three minutes before you passed out and split your eyebrow open on the toilet bowl." At least the bleeding had finally stopped.

"I might be concussed."

"I think you're just exhausted." I knew how out of it she got when she was actually concussed—she'd once been sitting upright on a beach lounger when the wind had caught the back of it and she'd been so disoriented that, when Dad insisted we head back to the car to get her home, she'd tried to dry herself off with my Twister mat. I dumped my pajamas on the toilet seat and climbed into the shower in my underwear. I reached to unhook the detachable showerhead and then turned it up full blast.

By the time I swiveled her dead weight to slather her hair in shampoo, my thighs were burning from the squat. Settling onto my knees, I lifted the hose higher. She cried out. "Oh Christ, Taylor, you're getting soap in my eye! My eyebrow!"

Who has a thick skin now, Mother darling?

Ducking her head to meet the spray, she opened her mouth and gulped at the jet like a thirsty fucking bird. "Your father's right," she gurgled. Hands shooting up to my hips to steady herself, she leaned over and rinsed the mouthful down the drain. Eyes dancing, she looked up at me. "I *should* take driving lessons."

I rinsed her hair. "Wonderful—I'll call Beverly Driving

School and book you a lesson for six a.m. tomorrow."

She pressed her forehead against the tile. "Maybe not tomorrow."

"You think?"

"I'm a mess. My life's a fucking mess. My ex-husband cheated on me, my mother's stopped pressuring me to visit, you're leaving me to go live in some fancy Boston apartment, my best friend thinks I'm a monster."

Reaching for the conditioner, I sighed. I had to be at school in five hours. "Why would Jen think you're a monster?"

"Because." Her teeth chattered.

"Because *why?*"

"Because of what I told her all those months ago."

The detachable showerhead thrashed across the tile between us like a snake.

"What did you tell her all those months ago?"

"That maybe she shouldn't have the baby."

It had been months since I'd improvised solo. Frances called last sketch when I grabbed my chance.

Like the storm raging outside, the idea had been brewing since I'd woken that morning. Well, technically, it had been brewing since I'd pulled myself out of bed. I hadn't slept a wink since Mom had looked up at me from the shower floor and told me that she'd encouraged Jen to get an abortion.

During the break, I'd prepared for my solo sketch. I'd snatched napkins from the Alcoholics Anonymous table and fashioned a fifties nurse costume over my sweater—a Peter

Pan collar, a vintage nursing cap—and with a handful of plastic straws, I'd twisted together a coat hanger. But it wasn't just the costume and props that had everyone in hysterics over my fifties TV advertisement, a discreet "service" for hopeful Hollywood starlets. It was what I said. I think, when it came down to it, what mattered most was always what I said.

"Are you sick of the sight of wire hangers? Are you tired of free-falling down your parents' basement stairs?" Lightning burst through the windows.

"Don't let a good night in the back of your boyfriend's station wagon get in the way of your Paramount contract." I Uncle Sam'd them: "Hollywood wants you!

I swooped low for my bow. There it was: that perfect, dizzying feeling. The blush, the *rush*. But as I pulled back up to a spinning room, I locked eyes on the front row.

Gilda wasn't laughing.

Out in the parking lot, as we waited for the car to warm, thunder rolled across the roof of the Phantom, heavy as a bowling ball.

Rain pelted hard against the windshield. In the side mirror, I watched Gilda's expression. She was hypnotized by the windshield wipers, but her face had fallen, as though her pacemaker had conked out the moment I'd taken the joke just that step too far.

On tonight's cassette, Lucy and Viv were attempting to install an antenna on Lucy's roof, struggling to keep their balance on the tiles. All the while, I tried to read Gilda's signals. *If this is how she reacts to a joke—a joke—that offends the Catholic*

Church's sensibilities, how the hell is she going to react if I ever come out to her?

Viv: *Can I hang on to you while I get up?!*

Lucy: *No, you can't hang on to me while you get up! I got all I can do to hang on to myself—*

Reaching out, Gilda flicked off the tape.

My voice came at a whisper: "I . . . I think I've offended you."

"Do you?"

My pulse picked up.

"Would you like to know what I think?" she said.

No. I steeled myself. "Okay—"

"I think that, deep down, you're a very angry girl. It may not be the reason why you started coming to improv, Taylor, but it's *certainly* why you've stayed."

My eyes slammed shut in embarrassment.

As Gilda pulled the Phantom out of the lot, the PFLAG people poured out the doors of the hall. In the yellow beam of Gilda's headlights, they huddled under umbrellas, talking, waving, *laughing* goodbye. As my vision blurred, I wondered how differently things might have turned out if I'd been ready that day, all those months ago when I'd first come to Prides Crossing Community Hall. I wondered how differently things might have turned out if I'd never found Gilda stealing pie from the Alcoholics Anonymous table. If I'd never let her drag me into Stand-Up Therapy.

If I'd had the courage to go right ahead and choose Door Number One in the very beginning.

TWELVE

With the promise of Charlotte at close, Wednesday was a more bearable shift than usual.

I didn't care that I wasn't working with Brooke. It had been two weeks since I'd told her to brake, and things were still tense between us. Whatever. I was happy to work with Lyn. It didn't even bother me when one of the visitors decided that our waxworks were "too outdated," that he was entitled to reimbursement for the "grand disappointment" that was our wax museum compared to the other wax museum in town that he'd read about on Tripadvisor. Lyn usually handled complaints, but she had just gone on her dinner break. I was all alone at the front desk, and I figured it wasn't worth arguing over. Not only was *the customer always right*, but he was a fully developed, fully entitled, fully articulate adult and my limited life experience proved that I cried after 2.5 minutes of confrontation, so I didn't even tell him that tickets were nonrefundable. I just apologized, went out the back to my schoolbag, took a twenty from my wallet, returned to the desk, and handed it over to him.

After close, Lyn hung around longer than I expected. I stalled, counting the quarters from the register and filling out the banking book with the agility of a ninety-year-old. Finally, her husband beeped out front, and after double-checking that I had my key, she left.

A few minutes later one of the heavy rustic doors opened and Charlotte stepped into the foyer. The professional Canon dangled heavy around her neck. She pulled off her black wool hat, her dark hair flitting freely around her face. "Is it okay to come in now?"

We hadn't been alone since the tech box on Friday, and even though we'd sent each other a few messages every day since, neither of us had brought up what I'd confessed in there. As she grinned across the foyer at me—a little nervous, a little thrilled—I wondered how I could continue to go so long without seeing her now that I knew what it was like to have her undivided attention. Glances in the hallways or passing by her locker weren't going to cut it anymore, not when we'd shared breakfast and the arcade and now *this*. "Now is perfect."

At the sight of her in the knee-length, cherry-red parka she'd worn to school almost every day since the beginning of November, something sweet and needy blossomed in my chest. What I was feeling wasn't just love. It was *like*. I really, truly *liked* her.

I locked the front doors and led her inside to the wax figures.

Lyn had turned off all the lights—it was pitch black inside the rotunda. I trailed my fingers across the wall and found the switch. The dioramas high in the walls above lit up, the yellow glow of each box casting a faint, ominous light across the room. But Charlotte didn't seem to notice the dioramas in the dome. She went straight to the courtroom scene in the center of the floor, moved around the silicone figures, snapping photos of the girls in the pews, of Betty Parris alone in the witness box. I leaned back against the wall and watched. The way she moved was strangely polite, as though they were real people and she was trying not to disturb them.

"What exactly is your senior project?" I called out.

"The impact of the witch trials on Salem. The houses, the graves, the museums." Kneeling in front of the witness box, she aimed her camera right up under nine-year-old Betty's chin like she had found Betty's tell. "I'm pairing each photo with a story of, you know, persecution. Like . . . LGBTQ persecution." Her voice kind of faltered when she said "LGBTQ," and I couldn't help but notice that it was so different to how "queer" had rolled off her tongue on our breakfast date. Did labels mean more now that we were alone together in the semidarkness and silence?

"That sounds really clever." Ten times more impressive than my senior project. I'd submitted a proposal to do fifteen hours of work experience with Jen at the Peabody Essex. There was a shoe exhibition—Judy Garland's ruby slippers were touring. I figured that I could drivel something about walking a mile in somebody else's shoes, or walking the world into Technicolor. "Pick a project you have an *interest* in," Mr. Gibson had said. Last month I'd been *interested* in Jen, so I'd forged her signature above the mentor line and planned on telling her about it sometime soon.

"Can I press this?" Charlotte's hand hovered over the button next to Chief Magistrate Stoughton's hand.

I shoved my hands into my pockets. "Sure."

Stoughton's brusque voice burst through the room, condemning Bridget Bishop for her "immoral lifestyle."

Charlotte moved around the main floor, slight and graceful as her delicate fingers twisted the canister of the lens to focus on Bridget's profile. Turning, she smiled at me.

Oh god, was I weak for her.

Her head tilted back as she took in the dioramas up on the circular platform. "I forgot they were up there."

"D-do you want to climb up?"

"You'd do that with me?"

I'd swim the Salem Sound with you in the middle of January.

We climbed the ladder to the first diorama. The waxwork girls were seated around a cauldron in the Parris kitchen, listening as Tituba told stories about her life back in Barbados. The ceiling was low on the platform. I had to crane my neck slightly, but Charlotte was tiny enough that there was still an inch between the crown of her head and the roof.

As I sat against the door at the back that led to the next scene, Charlotte ran her index finger across Tituba's neck, just below the line of Tituba's bright headscarf. She held her finger up for me to see the dust she'd collected. "Somebody's going to lose their job, Miss Parker. . . ." Wiping her finger against the pocket of her jeans, she clicked her tongue.

"You can't see dust from a distance."

As the flash of the Canon fired on Tituba's sharp profile, downstairs, the magistrate finished his spiel. Silence washed over the rotunda.

Charlotte lowered the camera into the cauldron and then moved to stand against the wall opposite. With her hair almost brushing the ceiling, she seemed so much taller.

"You should wear your Abigail costume when you present all of this," I said. "Turn it into a whole performance."

She tucked her hands behind her back and stared down at me. "How do *you* know I play Abigail?"

I could have told her I'd heard about it through school or that I'd seen her face on the flyer. "I've seen you do it."

She smirked, coy and knowing, like she'd had an idea about me and she'd finally proved herself right. Languidly, she pulled her arms out of her parka. She waved her jacket between us like a red flag, spread it across the worn carpet in the narrow space between Tituba and the back wall. She lay down upon the quilted coat as though it were a picnic blanket, put her hands behind her head, and closed her eyes.

I chuckled nervously. "What are you doing?"

Smiling shyly, she bent her ankle like a dancer and pressed the toe of her boot into my thigh.

Oh god, grant me strength.

I pulled my hands over my face. They were clammy, smelled like iron from how tightly I'd gripped the ladder climbing into the diorama after her. "Do you want to go through to the next room?"

She gazed at me across the diorama.

There was an ache low in my stomach. "It makes me nervous when you do that."

"Do what?" she whispered.

"Stare."

She wet her lips.

As our eyes locked, something inside me sharpened. She patted the floor beside her.

I moved to her.

The carpet reeked like mothballs and burnt plastic. I sneezed once, twice. "Bless you," she said, a cuteish kind of lilt in her voice.

"You too." *Oh Christ.*

Pulling my phone from my back pocket and tossing it across the carpet, I lay down. Our forearms touched. Static electricity sparked between us. When I yanked away for a split second, she bit her lip. "It's the goose down in my parka," she whispered.

It's more than that. . . .

I was wearing my long-sleeved work shirt, but she was only

wearing a T-shirt. As we lay there staring at the low ceiling, I could feel the heat of her against me. "I feel like we're doing a theater class cooldown."

I heard her swallow. "Do you remember that day we did that breathing exercise?"

"Wh-which one?"

"I think you know which one."

I'd never been so close to anybody, not like that, and it was a bit weird and I was feeling claustrophobic. I tilted my head to the side and looked at Abigail and Tituba, inches away. Their backs were turned, like they were scorning the line we were about to cross. I looked through the gap between them. On the high platform on the other side of the room, Giles Corey was laid out on a bench in his diorama. Two boards rested atop his chest, stones sandwiched between the timber, his head perfectly tilted our way.

"Taylor," Charlotte whispered, her breath hot above the collar of my shirt. As she pushed up the edge of my sleeve, her fingernails tickled the tendons in my wrist.

Fire singed through my veins. My heart thumped. Giles watched me with animatronic eyes. Finally, his famous last words—*"More weight!"*—made perfect sense. I turned my head and met burning blue.

She rolled onto her side. Inches between our faces, she looked down at me. "Can I kiss you, Taylor?"

I nodded.

She whispered my name, breathed it, sweet and kind against the corner of my mouth. And then her lips touched mine.

I *shuddered*.

Her mouth was soft. Wet. Warm. The gentlest thing I'd ever felt. Her lips parted, slowly. So, so slowly . . . *God*. She tasted like the hard caramels Gilda kept in the Phantom. I thought about all those movies where the gay kid said how they "never once thought" about how they were "two girls" or "two boys" kissing—they were "just two people." *Charlotte* was kissing me, and that was amazing. Spectacular. The most important thing, sure. But I also couldn't stop thinking about the fact that she was a *girl* and I was a *girl* and I *loved* it. I loved it.

As her fingers touched my jaw, featherlight, she made a little noise that sent my brain haywire. She was all over me—literally. Her long hair tickled my neck, my ear, and as she pinched my chin between her thumb and forefinger, she pushed up onto her elbow and bent over me. Blood rushed in my ears. I kissed her again. Again. Again. Hunger unraveled in me like twill tape. Her tongue slipped against mine and we both got too eager too quick. I clutched at her waist. Her knee slipped over my thighs. Her hand clawed at my hip. As she pressed herself closer, a whimper tore from deep in my chest. I rose up to meet her lips again, but quickly, she pulled back.

My eyes shot open. Face glowing pink, lips inches from mine, she stared down at me. Her chest heaved. "I kissed you too hard."

My brain was foggy. "Uh . . . no—"

"I did. You can tell me."

My voice came breathily. "You really didn't—"

"I think I did. I'm sorry. I didn't mean to get pushy. I just . . . I could feel your heart pounding against my chest and I'm really attracted to you, and I've been trying to just keep it to myself for a long time, you know, put a lid on it and stuff because I really didn't know if you liked girls or me or other girls, and I think I just got a little . . ."

Her lips were swollen, her pupils dilated. I swallowed over the tightness in my throat. "Charlotte?"

"Yeah?" she whispered.

"You weren't pushy. I promise."

"I wasn't?" Her fingers reached out. She rested the tips of two fingers in the hollow of my throat, light and delicate.

For a prolonged moment, all she did was stare at her fingers, and all I could do to bear the overwhelming rush of vulnerability was will the pulse against her fingers to slow, try not to swallow. Try not to breathe.

My phone vibrated. We both looked over at it. Brooke's photo glowed on the screen. *Fuck.* Hastily, I declined the call.

Charlotte withdrew her touch. "Should we get out of here?"

No. No. Never. We should spend forever right here. Right now. In this moment. "Yeah," I whispered. "Probably."

My legs were wobbly like jelly as I climbed down the ladder after her. I wasn't the only one with boneless limbs; four rungs from the bottom, Charlotte lost her footing and slipped, gasped, thudded to the wooden floorboards below.

I twisted on the top of the ladder. "Are you okay?"

Rubbing at her elbows, she groaned a laugh. The camera was safe in her lap. "I'm fine. I just landed really hard on my butt."

I tried not to laugh too hard. I whipped my pointer finger out at Giles Corey. "*He* did it!"

Charlotte's gaze shot across the room.

"Why," I said, "I saw his specter drag you from the ladder with my very own eyes!"

She laughed shyly.

I scaled the ladder quickly to help her up. I switched off the lights to the rotunda and she followed me into the storeroom while I locked the safe and turned on the alarm.

Quietly—*bashfully*—we headed around the block, down Essex Street Pedestrian Mall. In front of the Coven's Cottage store, the town clock read eight forty.

There was a special kind of eeriness that swept over Salem after twilight twitched into town. It was soft and subtle, but it was *there*. It was there in the warm glow that poured from the shop windows, in the way the cobblestones gleamed like melted chocolate. As we passed the homeless man who always slept outside Wicked Good Books, Charlotte looked up at me. "I have the day off on Saturday, and I want to go to Boston." She fiddled with securing the lens cap. "Come with me?"

When I came through the door, Mom and Jen were alone in the common room weaving Christmas lights around the Christmas tree that had been delivered that morning.

They didn't ask me to help—they both knew I was allergic to pine. I unzipped my boots and lay belly down on the couch, watching them argue over the symmetry of the lights.

"You need to let it *droop*," Mom told Jen. Reaching up, she brushed a strand of hair from the butterfly bandage keeping her eyebrow together. The firelight colored her purple eye blacker. "See, here! You're pulling too tight. You're too *straight*."

Tell me about it, Mom.

Turning to me, Mom winked. I stiffened. After what she'd said to Ms. Glazer behind my back, she had a whole lot of fucking audacity. I pretended to be focused on the TV mounted above the fireplace, on the live telecast of the Rockefeller Center

Christmas Tree lighting. Kate McKinnon and Alec Baldwin were lighting the tree this year—I'd made it home just in time to watch.

The countdown began.

Now, I don't know how it happened, but I *missed* it. I was so busy thinking about how Charlotte's dainty fingers had felt like velvet across my jaw, about how my lips were still tingling thirty minutes after we'd pulled away from each other, that I totally and completely zoned out. One minute, Kate McKinnon was saying that New York was the greatest city in the world, and the next thing I knew, the tree outside 30 Rock was glittering, lighting up Manhattan.

The camera panned upward, high over the very skyscraper inside which my finalist sketch sat waiting to be read on Jane Lincoln's computer.

As Mom and Jen sang along to "Joy to the World," a log split loudly in the fireplace.

It was November 30. In twenty-five days, I'd be out.

THIRTEEN

On Saturday morning, I got up super early to help Mom make breakfast for the guests before I left to meet Charlotte at Salem Station. The house was still asleep, but Jen was at the kitchen table in her huge gray NYU sweatshirt, sipping a cup of tea. They looked up, surprised, when I stopped in the doorway completely dressed.

"Where's Ryan?" I said.

"He wrote until four a.m.," Jen said. "He's asleep. It's seven thirty. Why aren't you in bed?"

"Going to Boston."

Mom pulled a carton of eggs from the fridge. "With Brooke?"

"No."

"Well, who else?"

I squirted detergent into the sink. "I'm going with my friend Charlotte."

"Charlotte's a dated name," Mom commented.

It wasn't a dated name. It was a regal name. It meant "free man"—I'd googled it.

"What's Charlotte like?"

What was Charlotte like? Red parka, black braids, a bonnet, a navy T-shirt. She was purple in the reflection of a fortune-telling machine, and indigo in a mirrored hall. She wore confidence like armor and her heart on her sleeve. She was calm, still like the Mystic Lakes at twilight, wide-eyed as I tore up her fortune. "Talented," I said. "She's super talented."

I dipped the doughy bowl into the sink and tried to ignore the heat of Jen's eyes on my back.

I got to Salem Station with six minutes to spare before our train—and Charlotte was nowhere in sight.

What if she wasn't coming? I'd thought we were okay. I'd thought we were *great*. On Thursday morning, I'd still been buzzing from kissing her the night before in the diorama when I'd found a note in my locker: *I'm sorry I stare, but you're just so pretty*. But what if, now, she was sick with regret?

As my eyes locked on the elevator, relief washed over me. Eyes on me through the glass, Charlotte did a dorky little jiggle dance. Something in my heart unspooled. Descending like the Good Witch of the North, she was wearing a long black coat and one of those maroon felt hats with a brim so wide, you could only pull it off if your blood type was hipster positive. She looked mystical. Like a spell. Like a Stevie Nicks song. The construction workers behind her in the elevator leered, but Charlotte didn't care that her audience was larger than me. Her wicked confidence had her safe inside a huge Glinda-like bubble of not-giving-a-fuckery. I wanted inside.

As she crossed the platform to meet me, I could see that her cheeks were flushed and I knew that it was the cold that lit them pink, not embarrassment from her little dance.

"You look nice," I blurted.

She beamed so prettily, my pulse jumped into my mouth.

"Are you okay, Taylor?"

"Totally fine."

"Are you sure?" She wouldn't look me in the eye. "If you think the other night was . . . I mean, it doesn't have to mean anything."

"It does have to mean something."

She lifted her head. Our gazes locked.

"That was really smooth," she whispered, and the words were playful but they came out charged. "I didn't know you had it in you, Parker."

The train tracks began to sing. We looked in the direction of Beverly for the approaching train. "Is there anything you want to do in the city?" Charlotte asked. "I have something in mind, but if you want to do something else . . ."

"We can do your thing. What is it?" Honestly, she could have booked us on a guided tour of the Freedom Trail, and I would have been over the moon just to walk beside her, alone in a city crowd.

She grinned. "It's a surprise."

Our car wasn't anywhere near full, and still, Charlotte slid in next to me. She undid the belt of her coat and let the warmth of it spill across my thigh like a blanket. Not once did she take her phone from her bag, but she was quiet, gazing out the window as we sped through Salem Woods. November had cast its witchy curse; the trees were leafless bones, nothing more than stalky siblings of the gloomy Stickwork installation the Peabody Essex had dropped on Essex corner for the season. The woods were so skeletal that you could see the Home Depot a mile away on the other side.

When the train pulled into Swampscott, the first stop, Charlotte pointed down the street aligned with the station. "Do you see that yellow house?"

There was a triple-decker on the corner of the second block.

"My nonna lives there. Mom was born in the house. Actually, Nonna was a few months pregnant with her when they arrived here from Italy."

I ran my eyes over the planes of her face. "Do you like her? Your nonna?"

I think what I said came out the wrong way because she kind of pulled back to study my expression. "Of course I like my nonna." Her breath smelled like spearmint. "She's my *nonna*. Why? You don't like your grandmothers?"

Did I like my grandmothers? My dad's parents were dead, and I didn't really have any feelings about my mom's mom—not enough to say I liked her, not enough to say I didn't. She was kind of racist and lived in Texas, so I never saw her. Occasionally she'd call to talk to Mom and I'd have to say hello. But when Mom was working and I'd see Grandma's number on the caller ID, I'd let it go to voicemail. The last contact I'd had with her was when she sent me a seventeenth-birthday card.

PS As I told each of your cousins on their seventeenth birthdays, this is the last time I'll be sending ten dollars. Next year you will be an adult. Next year it will be just a card. Don't expect money.

Oh, what a crying shame, Grandma! However will I afford Emerson without your annual gift of ten dollars? I'd pinned that last ten dollars to my mirror to remind myself to always lower my expectations.

I told Charlotte that I didn't really know my grandparents. Not a single one of them.

"You make it sound like you have more than four grandparents." She laughed. Then she kind of sobered. "I have more than four. In theory. I guess I have eight if biological grandparents count. Because I'm adopted," she said. Simple as that.

She fell quiet again as we moved on through Lynn. Her shoulder was warm against my arm as our train raced across marshland, over the basin of Revere Beach. "What's your favorite color?" she murmured.

"Blue. Why?"

She shrugged. "It just seems like something basic I should know since we spent half an hour making out on Wednesday night."

I grinned. She was blunter than I thought.

"You're not religious, are you?" she said.

"No. Are you?"

"I used to be. My family's Catholic. I don't know what I believe, but Christmastime always makes me think about it."

"The closest I ever come to religion is when we spring-clean and Mom makes me scour *every* page of *every* nightstand Bible for 'dick and tit pics'—Mom's words, not mine. Three dick scribbles are fine—Mom says that's why god made Wite-Out—but she draws the line at four phalluses. Those Bibles have to be trashed."

"People really do that? Desecrate Bibles?"

"And *The Book of Mormon*. People do weird stuff when you don't provide cable."

We spent the next thirty minutes playing rapid fire, learning hugely unimportant things about each other. She was allergic to salmon, addicted to milk chocolate, and she could tell me who had won the Best Actress Oscar every year since 1963. I told her that my favorite place in the world was probably

Rockefeller Center, even though I'd never been there. I told her that my favorite flower was a sunflower, and that I couldn't tell the difference between cheap ice cream and what other people told me was the good stuff.

"What are you wearing to the Snow Ball?" she asked.

"Something witchy."

She arched a brow. "So . . . black?"

"You'll see."

That made her laugh.

We bought CharlieCards at North Station and took the Green Line C to Coolidge Corner. I knew what we were there for as soon as we stepped off the trolley. I could read it lettered on the old movie theater marquee all the way from the T stop: *1st Anniversary Screening—Carol—Sat., Dec. 3, 10 a.m.*

Forget the gay agenda Mike Pence was trying to warn America about. Taking another girl to see a first-anniversary screening of *Carol* was the *real* gay agenda, and Charlotte Grey was the real MVP.

"Have you seen it?" she asked excitedly.

I'd seen it more times than I could count on both hands. I pulled my gloves out of my bag and put them on. "Yeah, a couple times."

"I've seen it fifty thousand times," she said proudly, and took my hand as we crossed the street.

We were the only ones inside the movie theater—until the trailers started playing and three elderly women wandered in with reusable shopping bags and coffee cups. They picked their seats in the third row.

Charlotte leaned into me. "They have no idea what they're in for," she whispered, loud enough that I could hear her over the Golden Girls' trailer commentary from ten rows away.

"Maybe they're gay," I whispered.

"They don't look gay."

"You shouldn't stereotype."

Charlotte's laugh was hot against my neck. "*I'm* gay," she said. "I'm allowed to stereotype."

I watched her eat popcorn. "Pretty sure that's not how it works." Smiling, I pulled back to look at her. After coming in from the cold, her face was flushed from the theater's heating.

"They're going to press their personal medical alarms when Carol goes down on Therese," she said bluntly, and a field of wildflowers bloomed in my heart as those crass words left her pretty, salt-swollen lips.

"They're probably going to walk out," I added, and we sat there giggling because, when there's safety in numbers, there's something absolutely hilarious—not overwhelmingly devastating—about people disapproving of who you are and who you love.

But those old ladies didn't leave like we'd guessed they would, and after a while, I forgot they were even there. I was distracted—watching Cate Blanchett stare longingly across a crowded department store at Rooney Mara wasn't any less sexy before midday. Halfway through the movie, when Carol and Therese checked in to motel #567 somewhere in Iowa, Charlotte reached across the seat. She took my hand in hers again, like she had out on the street, and she didn't let go until the movie was over.

When we stepped outside, the Boston cold hit hard, curing me of the deliriousness I'd felt wandering out of the movie theater with Charlotte's hand in mine for all the world to see.

The T ride back to the heart of Boston was jam-packed, so we had to press right up against each other, which was *oh so awful.*

Charlotte hummed fifties tunes against my collarbone until the train doors closed, found her balance with her hands on my waist, and as the train twisted between stations, I felt like I was flying.

The Quincy Market food court was thrumming with live musicians. All of the seats were taken because everyone was watching a seventy-year-old man do an Ed Sheeran cover with a tray of water-filled glasses à la Sandra Bullock in *Miss Congeniality*, so we took our trays upstairs into the dome to find a table where we could hear each other.

"What's the story with the woman who stays in your inn?" Charlotte twirled her plastic fork through her fettuccine. "When I'm leaving work, I always see her coming out of the Peabody."

"Oh, that's Jen. She was the first person who ever stayed with us. She's pretty much family. She's like one of those people you can be really honest with and at the end of the day everything will be okay. And she knows it. She has a hell of a lot of audacity with me."

"Audacity?"

"Disciplining me and stuff. When I was younger. So, like, for instance, one time we had to get a plumber because I'd been lazily flushing tampons and Mom got super overwhelmed because the plumber overcharged her, and Jen was livid, lecturing me on what Mom could and couldn't afford."

"So she's your mom's . . . They dated?"

WHAT?! "No. *No.* They're just close friends."

"Oh. I saw them this summer on Essex and Jen had her arm around your mom's shoulders. I guess I got the wrong idea."

Didn't we all. "Jen's dating a guy now. They're having a kid together. I always just assumed she was a lesbian but . . . apparently not. So *that's* been a major plot twist to wrap my head around."

"Why?" she said plainly. "It doesn't really affect you." She speared a tomato.

I dragged my palms down my jeans. She'd stunned me, without knowing it. Without meaning to. And all of a sudden, I felt pretty fucking ignorant—because she was right. It didn't affect me. "Did you really think they were dating? When you saw them? My mom and Jen?"

"I suppose. I got that warm feeling I always get when I see queer couples in real life. You know, that weird mix of bashfulness and *Please look my way, I'm like you, please see me?* I mean, seeing Carol and Therese together is really nice, but when I see two women together in real life, it kind of makes my day."

"My mom made your day?"

"*Taylor.* I didn't exactly come up with a backstory for your mom, okay? I just thought, *Oh wow, there's someone who feels the way I do about girls.*"

I thought about Salem Willows, about what she'd said about Rachel Maddow. About how she'd called herself gay in the movie theater. "The way you feel about girls . . . Do you only feel that way about girls? I mean, I've heard you call yourself gay in drama club, but I don't want to assume that you *only* like girls. . . ."

She rested her chin on her palm. "The way you assumed with Jen?"

"Oh, I . . ." *Yes.*

She leaned across the table, leaned so close that for a split second, I thought she was going to kiss me. "I only like girls."

Her eyes locked on mine. And right there, under the dome of Quincy Market, she sang a few lines from *Fun Home*. . . .

I went still all over. The corners of her mouth turned up and my throat swelled. *Charlotte Grey, there isn't anybody like you on the face of the planet.*

"Now you know two more things about me," she said. "I'm a lesbian *and* I've had vocal training."

"I was already pretty clear about the second one," I managed. "I watched you in our spring production of *Guys and Dolls*." *And for the entire week after, I couldn't think about anyone but you.*

Over her shoulder, I spotted a homeless woman approaching tables. I tried to warn Charlotte that we were next, but there wasn't time—the woman skipped the table in front and came directly to us.

She looked between us. Her eyes dropped to our pastas and salads, our full soda cups, Charlotte's two paper bags with the toffee apples, my little bag with the decadent cookies from the Boston Chipyard. She didn't have to say anything—Charlotte was already fishing in her bag for change.

People stared—not so much at the woman in her 1,200 layers and the bursting pillowcase wound through her fist, but at *us*. An older couple across the dome frowned as Charlotte splayed her wallet open wider than a Venetian fan and handed the woman a crisp five-dollar bill.

The woman moved along. My first, minute-long impulse was to feel embarrassed by Charlotte's naivete. But that impulse died a sudden death. "I hope she stays warm this winter," Charlotte whispered. "It's only December third and it's already so cold. Can you even imagine?" Her straw darkened as she sucked up a mouthful of Sprite.

I swallowed a macaroni noodle whole, felt it slither its way over the lump of shame growing in my throat. No. I couldn't imagine.

When I got home from Boston, Jen was working at the desk in the common room—now was as good a time as any to tell her about my senior project.

"I can't do that." She didn't bother looking up from her laptop. "I'm only a visitor of the Peabody Essex. Insurance won't cover you."

Plot twist: It wasn't as good a time as any. I'd caught her in a bad mood. Apparently, Mr. Hyde was home. Dr. Jekyll must have been out buying baby formula and diapers.

I whined into the doorjamb. "But I already submitted the proposal!"

"You should have asked me first."

"I really can't do *anything* at the Peabody? I could just sit in your office. . . ."

She looked up at me over the rim of the reading glasses she never wore. "You'll have to come up with another idea."

"I can't." I could. I had until Christmas break to submit the final draft.

She fixed me with a *Not my problem* look and turned back to her laptop.

She can't stand you anymore. She can't even stand you enough to pity you. Suddenly she swiveled. "Do you know what your issue is, Taylor? You've developed a bit of a victim complex and it needs to go."

The blood burned in my cheeks.

"I know you're going through a lot right now, but you can't continue to blame everybody else for problems *you* create when—"

Mom stopped in the doorway on the other side of the common room. "What's going on?"

"Nothing." I dropped my gaze to unbutton my coat.

"What are you going through?" Mom said.

My tongue swelled.

"School," Jen said coolly.

"What happened at school?" Mom pressed.

"My senior project," I said. "It's fine. I'll figure it out."

"Do you need help with it?" Mom offered.

Bile rose in my throat.

"I have to go to Walgreens for a few hours, but I can help you with it when I come home at ten?"

I was going to throw up a deep dish of macaroni and four pistachio cookies on the good rug.

"You just need to ask for help, Tay," she said. "Just ask, is all."

I wanted to go straight across the room and wrap her up in my arms, even in front of Jen. I wanted to tell her everything. *Everything.* But I knew that she'd have questions and that she deserved answers to those questions, and I wasn't sure that I had answers to give, so I told her I'd ask for help if I needed it, and jogged up to my room.

I lay on my bed and closed my eyes. I couldn't cry in case Mom came in before she left for Walgreens. Instead, I lay there thinking about that scene in *Carol* when Carol cuts their first date short, dumps Therese at a train station in Jersey after dark, and sends Therese Manhattan-bound after she *promised* to get her home safely. I imagined Therese ugly-crying snot-nosed against the window of the moving train car, wanting, wanting, wanting. Just the thought of Therese weeping all the way back to Manhattan made me feel a whole lot better.

FOURTEEN

At 4:50 p.m. on Sunday, Facebook clocked Charlotte's off-line time to a record of seven hours. I guessed that she had been asked to work all day and hadn't had a chance to look at her phone during her lunch break. I wasn't expecting a reply or anything. I'd refrained from sending her any messages since we'd said goodbye at Salem Station the night before because I was trying this thing where I didn't act like an obsessed fangirl with celebrity worship syndrome. It wasn't really working, though. I just wanted to be with her. And she finished her shift in ten minutes.

Before I could say no to myself, I was flinging my pajama pants across my bed, pulling on my jeans and boots, and reaping my fluffy brown scarf from the back of Mom's en suite door (she was always stealing my shit).

I'd been sitting on the low wall at the back of Charlotte's museum for a grand total of thirty seconds when the stage door opened. I was still trying to catch my breath from running over there, so I was glad it wasn't Charlotte, only the guy who played one of the judges, or Reverend Parris. I couldn't remember. Old men tended to look the same to me.

A few minutes later, the stage door opened again.

Charlotte had changed into her own clothes—that red parka, too—but she was still wearing her Puritan bonnet.

"Hi, Abigail," I joked, and at her confused expression, I pressed a finger to my temple.

Her hand snapped up to her head, like Mom when she's looking for her glasses. Grinning, she drew the bonnet back. "It's been a *long* day."

It hadn't been twenty-four hours since we'd said goodbye, but seeing her *cleansed* me—my mind, my heart, the damage I'd probably done to my lungs back in July when I'd smoked that half pack of cigarettes Jen had accidentally left behind. "Can we go somewhere?" I licked my lips. "It's okay if you're tired of me, though."

She blushed. "I'm not tired of you, Taylor. It's just that I have family dinner at seven. My nonna's coming over. *But*," she said, smiling, "I can absolutely hang out until then."

It was starting to drizzle again, so we wandered around to the front of the museum, where we were undercover. Night was setting in. Cars traveled down Charter in the wet, their headlights stinging our eyes as they headed north to Essex Bridge, over to Beverly. I wondered if anybody from school would see us there under the lights outside the museum, if they'd say that Taylor Parker and Charlotte Grey were together on Sunday afternoon, that they'd looked *close*.

"Should we go to your house?" Charlotte asked.

The wind went right through me. I didn't want to take her home, not when the whole thing kind of felt like a dirty secret. I scuffed my toe against the garden path. "Umm, the inn is kind of really busy at this time of day."

She didn't offer her house, either. "Maybe we could get something small to eat?" she said. "I skipped lunch."

As we crossed over to the pedestrian street, I desperately

wanted to take her hand like she'd taken mine in Boston. But this was *Salem*, and Boston was far, far away. Even if nobody saw us—even if we were the last two left in town—taking her hand in mine would have felt like *more* there in Salem. I wasn't sure I was ready for that. *Well, get ready*, a voice inside me snarled. *You only have twenty days left.*

We went into the diner in Museum Place Mall. "All I Want For Christmas Is You" was playing. "I was starving," Charlotte told me as she spooned a mouthful of chicken noodle soup. Across the booth, she moaned quietly, like the watery chicken broth had nourished her for all of eternity. "I had a feeling I would see you today—" She paused suddenly, her steaming spoon halfway to her lips. Her eyes were set over my shoulder, boring through the glass wall behind our booth. "Don't look now," she said, "but Isi and Hannah just came out of the movie theater and they've seen us. They're going to go straight to Rachel about this in, like, five minutes, I swear to god."

I didn't really know Isi and Hannah. I'd gone to middle school with them, and every so often Hannah would bag a cinnamon roll for me at Dunkin', but they were popular and I didn't run in those circles. Charlotte did. She was on the yearbook committee with both of them. She knew what they were like. We *all* knew what they were like, but the look on Charlotte's face told me she had a much better idea.

Charlotte sighed. "Okay, they're gone. Let's see how long until I get a text from Rachel."

"You haven't told anyone, have you?" I asked. "About us?"

Charlotte shook her head. "No. *No.* Of course I haven't."

"You haven't even told Rachel?" Rachel seemed to be her best friend.

"Never. Rachel can't keep a secret. Besides, even if she could, I wouldn't out you."

I swallowed a tiny bite of my chicken salad sandwich. "Thanks."

"You don't have to thank me." She drew the soup spoon from her mouth. "I care about you."

There was a lot in that. I blinked once, twice, watched her drink soup from the spoon like a delicate bird. "I can't stop thinking about you."

Her eyes shot up to meet mine.

Oh god. I flushed. *Here it comes*: "I've liked you for so long. Like, so long, ever since you came back to Salem."

We stared at each other. Cheeks coloring, she dropped her gaze. "Taylor . . . I've never done anything like this. I've never had a girlfriend. I don't mean that you're my girlfriend, I mean, but . . ." Her expression twisted. She grabbed at her cup of lemonade and wrapped her lips around the straw. "Wow, I put way too much salt in my soup."

I slid my shaking hands between my thighs. *Girlfriend.* I wasn't ready for that. She deserved more than what I was ready to give. She deserved someone out and proud and ready to hold her hand in town. So I was honest. Totally, 100 percent truthful. "I'm not ready," I said. "I want it, I really do, but I'm not ready."

She nodded. "Okay," she said, sounding calmer. "We'll just go slow. For both of us."

I ran a hand through my hair. "How did you come out?"

Her smile grew wide in an instant.

"I'm not coming out *today* or anything," I said. *Just sometime within the next three weeks.*

"That's not why I'm smiling." She scooped carrot from her

broth. "I'm smiling because, the first time I came out, I'd just had my wisdom teeth removed and I didn't react well to the anesthesia. I came out to the nurse in front of my mom."

"Seriously?"

"It's probably the most humiliating thing that's ever happened to me. The nurse kept telling my mom that it was the anesthesia talking. But my mom had already guessed I was gay, so she knew it was the truth when I told the nurse I wanted to marry her. By the time my dad bought the car around to pick us up, I was sobbing, like, *hysterically*, because the nurse *still* didn't believe I was gay. I actually remember being angry, really angry. I fell asleep as soon as I got in the car and didn't wake up until, like, midnight. My dad had to carry me inside like a baby."

"And did you remember when you woke up? That you'd come out?"

She nodded. "Mom came into my room and all she had to say was, 'Do you remember what you said when you woke up?' and it was kind of just . . . done. It was that simple. It was *awkward*, sure, but we all got over it pretty quickly because Mom had to take out the gauze and repack it in my mouth every two hours. She was up in my face, all day, no escaping her." She wiped at her smile with a napkin. "Also, perfect time to come out because the incisions mean you *literally* can't answer their weird questions."

"That would make a *really* good sketch."

"Write it," she said, and it sounded like she was giving me the most precious part of her to make something that was *ours*. She reached across the table. "Can I steal a quarter of your sandwich?"

I was watching her rake excess mayonnaise off with a butter knife when a guy, twenty, maybe twenty-one, swaggered over to our table *way* too confidently for someone who was dressed like his mom had helped him raid the sale rack at Hot Topic. He looked between us. "Hi, ladies." He focused on Charlotte—he'd made his choice, claimed the prettiest prize. "Mind if I join you?"

Charlotte looked up at him pointedly. "Flattered, but, yeah, we do mind."

Whoa. Who knew my not-yet-girlfriend could be saltier than the Dead Sea?

He studied Charlotte. "You're cute as hell. How old are you?" A smirk. "You're either really young or really old."

She held my eye as she took a bite of the sandwich she'd taken from my plate. "I'm turning six on Wednesday. My party's at Chuck E. Cheese—I'd invite you, but Daddy says no boys allowed."

I almost spit out my water.

Charlotte was too much of an effort for him; he turned to me with a grin. "What about you? Can I buy you a drink?"

He *definitely* thought I was older than I was.

I looked across the booth at Charlotte, and then back up at him. "Thanks," I said. "But I have a drink."

"She's here with me," Charlotte told him. "And we're not interested."

He ignored her. "What's wrong?" he asked me. "You have a boyfriend?"

"No boyfriends," Charlotte said. "She's here with me."

Seconds ticked. He looked between us—he *knew* what Charlotte was implying. "Sure," he scoffed, and meandered back to the bar.

As Charlotte tried to catch my eye across the booth, a new kind of tension grew between us that hadn't been there when we'd been comfortable in our own little world. I couldn't help but feel ashamed for being so passive when Charlotte had turned him away so bluntly. Now it was like she was on one level and I was on another. *Charlotte thinks you're a joke.*

"Hey."

I looked up.

Leaning across the table, she folded her arms, puffed out her slender shoulders. "You're too pretty to be a lesbian," she said deeply, and I laughed out loud. Her smile lifted. "Forget about him. Walk me home?"

On the way home, she told me that she was sorry we'd only had an hour together, asked if I felt like hanging out the next day. "Sorry," I said. "I can't. I have a thing on Monday afternoons."

"Oh," she said. "What thing?"

The guilt hit hard. "I—I have to help out at the inn."

When we arrived, Charlotte's parents were in the driveway unpacking groceries. I'd seen her mom around town before, but never her dad. He was tall. Handsome.

"How was work, honey?" her mom asked.

I instantly felt guilty again because I'd been with her for a whole hour and I hadn't asked. "It was good," Charlotte said.

As her parents looked at me curiously, all of me ignited. It was almost like they knew that Charlotte and I weren't just friends.

"Hi." I waved, like a fucking loser.

"Hello there," her dad said, and it surprised me how deep his voice was, like he should have been wearing a mustache and a toupee just for sounding like that.

"This is Taylor," Charlotte said.

"Would you like to stay for dinner, Taylor?" her mom offered.

"We have plenty of lasagna."

Her parents were warm people—I could tell instantly. Lasagna sounded really good too, but it felt like a betrayal. How could I sit at the dinner table with Charlotte's family, with them knowing what we meant to each other, when I couldn't share that same truth with my own family? I made up a story about having family dinner too and said goodbye.

Mom was still at Walgreens when I got home, so I made a grilled cheese and took it up to my room. I had a missed call from Brooke—I ignored it.

I opened the NBC web page and clicked on the *SNL* episode from two weeks before. I rewatched Kristen Wiig's musical monologue about the origin of Thanksgiving four times, and under the too-hot spray of my shower, I performed it for the shampoo and conditioner bottles until I felt faint.

Wiping the fog from the mirror, I stood naked in front of the sink and stared at my reflection. The light lit my wet hair gold. Mom was right—my baby highlights were yet to fade. I'd been growing my hair out since sophomore year, and it was so long that it covered my protruding collarbones, my kind-of-small breasts. I'd lost weight in the last few weeks. I saw it in my reflection each time I got out of the shower, each time I pulled on a pair of jeans and realized they were a little roomier. I had absolutely zero interest in being skinnier. Waking to feel my belly concaved each morning, hip bones jutting into the band of my sweatpants? It made me feel sickly. It was a daily reminder that, while I stewed and stewed over coming out on Christmas Eve, I was wasting away. I was wound so tight that my body had forgotten how to be hungry. All I wanted was to eat a fucking doughnut and be able to swallow it without getting heartburn.

My body was out of my control.

I went back into my room and snatched my laptop from the middle of the bed, placed it on the edge of the en suite counter, and angled the screen so that I had a good look at where I'd paused the monologue.

I slid open the top drawer and I pulled out a pair of scissors.

My reflection on the laptop screen glared back at me as I analyzed Kristen's new pixie cut, the way it combed over from the side, the way the short blond wisps swept across her forehead.

I linked my knuckles around the handles of the scissors.

FIFTEEN

When I stepped into the kitchen the next morning, still in my pajamas, Mom gasped. "What the fuck?" Two slices leapt from the toaster. From where she stood in the corner of the kitchen counter, Jen burst out laughing.

I smirked.

"It looks great," Ryan said, but I could hear the lie in his voice. He didn't like it.

I shifted from foot to foot. "I haven't really styled it yet." I had.

"It looks amazing, honey, it does, it does," Mom assured me. "What did you do with your long hair?"

"I threw it in the trash—"

"You could have donated it!"

"It wasn't *that* long."

"But it *was*."

Jen was biting the insides of her cheeks in an effort not to smile even wider. I knew that look—she was *impressed*.

I couldn't stop running my fingers through it. I felt like a brand-new person. They could all see my face, who I was without that shield of hair, and it felt good to be exposed like that on my own terms.

I didn't grab a wool hat when I left for school—it was so cold that sleet was falling, but I didn't want to mess up the way

I'd styled my new cut. Everything felt fresher, the way the cold licked at my naked ears, the wind whipping at the ultra-short wisps at the back of my neck.

"Nice haircut."—Mr. Gibson when I walked into homeroom.

"Suits you." —Emmy Wilde.

"Wow, your hair was so long before. Even though you never made it look hot like the other girls, like, it was still long and hot." —Jase Ryder.

When Brooke started toward my locker before first-period AP Chemistry, her eyes bugged. I smirked. I *knew* she'd think it was ballsy. "Hey, hottie," I called out.

She didn't smile. "I called you last night. You didn't call me back."

I dropped my bag to the floor and spun the combination lock. "Sorry. I was studying. When I saw the missed call, it was too late to call you back. I didn't want to wake you—"

"I went over to your place yesterday afternoon. To apologize." She leaned against the next locker. "Jen said you weren't home."

Shit. She'd come by when I was out with Charlotte. "I was home," I heard myself say. "I was sleeping. You shouldn't have bothered asking Jen; you should have just come upstairs and knocked on my door like usual. We could have talked."

Her eyes flashed. "I did. I went up to your room and knocked on your door and when you didn't answer, that's when I found Jen in the common room. She said you'd gone out."

Fuck. Fuck. Fuck. Fuck. Fuck.

Her expression hardened. "What's with the face?"

"Face?"

"You always look so angry lately. And what's going on with you and Charlotte?"

Oh god. Had Hannah or Isi told somebody? Somebody who had told Brooke?

Heart charging, I looked her dead in the eye. Right in the eye. Straight down the barrel of the gun. And I lied. "*Nothing's* going on with me and Charlotte."

Her stare was intense. "Do you have some sort of girl crush on her?"

I felt dizzy. "No."

"Well, seems like you're always with her."

"What are you talking about? Jesus. I'm never *with* her." She didn't know about Red's or the arcade or the museum. Or Boston. Nobody did.

"You *are*, though."

"Tell me one time I was with her."

"Black Friday. You were in the tech box with her on Black Friday."

"Sorry, am I not allowed to talk to her just because she mildly offended you *and* the rest of our class a whole year ago? It's not my fault that you couldn't build a bridge—everyone else did."

"Well, maybe I learned the whole not-letting-shit-go thing from you, huh?"

"Probably," I deadpanned. "I am the closest thing you have to a sister."

She pushed off the locker. "Look, I feel like you've been lying to me for months." Her hands shook as she picked at a hangnail. "You used to be really open and stuff and now it's like you're pushing me away because I got into MIT."

"Brooke, I promise, I'm not—"

"Like you have to go and make friends with Charlotte

holier-than-thou Grey because you want to make a show of replacing me—"

"I'm not *replacing* you. I'd never do that. Ever. You're my—"

"I'm just trying to give myself what I want." Her eyes glossed over, which made mine *burn*. She licked her lips, that chapped patch where she always chewed deep. "You have no idea what I've been through since the election."

"What does the election have to do with us?"

"Christ. See—you're so oblivious. Since Trump was elected—no, even before that—I've been getting hate. In the comments. On Instagram. Every new design I post, there's always someone who has something hateful to say. I've gained followers—so many followers. But the comments. You have no idea, Taylor. There's a new kind of nastiness there and I know exactly where it's coming from."

The thought made me sick to my stomach. "Don't listen to them. You're fucking brilliant."

She scoffed.

"Why the hell didn't you tell me?"

"Because you weren't there to listen."

Heat rose to my cheeks.

"I'm not choosing MIT to hurt you, Taylor. But I'm done letting you make me feel guilty for leaving. You think everyone's out to take things from you, but the thing is, you don't do a whole lot of giving either."

Sickness settled in my stomach, thick and heavy like that expired yogurt I'd inadvertently poisoned myself with last summer. She'd never spoken to me like this before. We'd never seriously argued. Not *really*. Not about anything that mattered. "Brooke. I'm so sorry."

"You never have time for me anymore," she said, so soft that I could barely hear her. "I call you and you're all like, 'I'll call you back in an hour,' but then you never do, and the next day, you never apologize for it, and I want to say something every time, call you out for it, but as soon as I get the chance, it's all about the latest thing you're pissed about—your mom, Jen. Like, honestly, I'm so sick of hearing you criticize Jen for getting knocked up—"

"I'm sorry. I really am. You're right. I'll stop bitching about Jen."

"But it's not just the Jen thing. Like today, I was going to say something about how you never returned my call last night, and then I saw your hair and I was like, *Well, shit, now I can't be a bitch because I have to tell her how great her hair looks.*" She drew a deep breath. "It looks great by the way."

"I don't give a shit about my hair right now."

She slid her hands into the pockets of her knit cardigan. "I love you, Taylor, but if everything's going to be all about you until graduation, then I don't know how to be around you every day without feeling sad."

Guilt curled in my throat. Tears sprang to my eyes. She blurred in front of me. "I make you feel *sad*? Brooke. This is coming out of *nowhere*."

She looked down at her snow boots.

"Not for me."

I caught Charlotte in the hallway before second period. She had the door of her locker open. I bumped it against her hip. "Hi."

Her eyes widened. "Oh my god! *Your hair!*"

She reached up to touch my bangs, but the second she realized what she was doing, that there were *people*, that we were in *school*, she dropped her hand and curled her fingers around the edge of her locker door instead. "It looks *really* cute."

Her stare bore into mine. I burned beneath it.

"Are you okay?" she said. "You look upset."

"Brooke's pissed at me. She says she's sitting with her chem friends at lunch."

"Why?"

"I didn't call her back last night. I told her I forgot, but she didn't believe me. I . . . I think I've really upset her."

"She can be judgmental. If you forgot, then you just forgot. She's your best friend—she should know you're super honest. I mean, I do."

As she smiled up at me, my chest ached.

She tilted her head. "Sit with me at lunch?"

"It's okay. I *do* have friends other than just Brooke." I could sit with some of the art kids.

"I want you to sit with *me*."

I bit my lip.

"Please," she said quietly. "It's just me and Chloe and Rach, and sometimes Chloe's boyfriend."

Charlotte had told me in the diner that she hadn't said anything about us to anyone, but when I found her in the cafeteria later that day, I wondered if her friends had guessed. When we first sat down, Rachel glanced between us. I didn't know if Charlotte knew that Rachel knew, but Isi had *definitely* told Rachel what she'd seen the day before.

"Taylor's in theater with me," Charlotte said, like they had no idea who I was, like we hadn't all gone to middle school together.

I fell into the seat next to Chloe. Charlotte sat opposite, next to Rachel. Rachel smiled widely. "Your hair looks great. What made you cut it?"

"My inn has a lice infestation."

Their faces fell.

"She's joking," Charlotte said.

"Am I, though?" I looked between Chloe and Rachel. "I'm itchy. Are you guys itchy?"

"She's still joking."

Chloe scratched at the back of her neck.

The cafeteria was *loud* and Charlotte's best friends were *quiet*.

"What's it like living in an inn?" Rachel was clearly just looking for an icebreaker. "Do you hear stuff through walls?"

I peeled back the bun of my burger to check for a pickle. "Are you asking if I've heard people enjoying an afternoon delight?"

Her mouth slackened. "Oh, no, I just—"

"Well, I was thirteen the first time I heard two people having sex. They only lasted about two minutes so, to be perfectly honest, I wasn't particularly impressed. However, I have to hand it to them, it *was* somewhat educational—I learned that *come* had another meaning entirely." I popped a grape into my mouth.

Mid-bite into her burger, Chloe stilled. Eyes on me, Rachel chewed slowly. I swallowed the grape half whole. *Okay, too far. Safer waters, safer waters* . . . "So, you all went to Witchcraft Heights Elementary together? That's how you met?"

"That's how we *met*," Chloe said, "but we really became friends when we took our First Communion together. Well, some of us *almost* didn't take it." She winked at Charlotte.

Charlotte rolled her eyes. "Can we not go there, please?"

I looked between them. "What does Chloe mean?"

"Chloe *means*," Rachel said, "that Charlotte almost didn't take the Sacrament."

I turned to Charlotte. "The wafer thing?"

"The Body of Christ, yes," Charlotte said shortly.

"What, was the wafer stale or something?"

Chloe giggled. Rachel scoffed a laugh. "Poor Charlotte thought taking Communion meant she was legit marrying God. She freaked out in the church. Her godparent was her cousin in his twenties and he had like *no idea* how to help her. He just patted her head like she was a golden retriever and looked the other way. I held her hand while we walked down the aisle. She silent-cried through the whole thing."

Charlotte folded her napkin on her tray like she was about to have high tea at the Omni Parker House in Boston, not a soggy fruit cup in the cafeteria of Nathaniel Hawthorne High. "Give me a break. I was eight. And you guys may not remember, but those were the exact words the Sacrament teacher used—we were marrying God." She cast a quick, timid glance at me. "Something felt very off about the whole thing and the weight of expectation was overwhelming."

"What did you think you were expected to do?" I was genuinely curious.

A blush lit her cheeks. "I don't know. The white dress and the veil, all that talk of sin, of confessing . . . it was all very confusing. But mostly . . . the veil was just *really itchy*."

We grinned at each other.

Rachel leaned over her tray. "Don't worry, I've got your back, babe. As your self-appointed maid of honor, I've decided that we'll all wear flower crowns—not a veil in sight."

Chloe laughed, and as they started on about the Snow Ball, I thought about how simple and easy and *good* it was that they were so supportive of Charlotte and her future. They wanted to be her bridesmaids one day. Would Brooke ever be that cool about my sexuality? She'd stand beside me, that I knew. But when she said she was proud to be there, would she really, honest-to-god mean it?

A few minutes before the fifth-period bell, Chloe picked up her tray. "You should sit with us again, Taylor." She elbowed Rachel. "You coming?"

When they were gone, I turned to Charlotte. "How did the photos from my museum turn out?"

"They're probably the best set I've taken so far. And I have you to thank for that." She paused. "Actually, I was wondering . . . Do you want to come on another trespassing adventure with me sometime before Christmas? After the Snow Ball? I already have a key this time—"

"Just the girls I'm looking for." Ms. Glazer fell into the seat next to Charlotte. "I have Christmas gifts for both of you," she whispered. "But you can't let the others see—I only have candy canes for the rest of 'em."

Bashful, Charlotte tucked her hair behind her ear. "Gifts? Christmas is still so far away."

"Far away?" Ms. Glazer tilted her head. "I don't think so. It's closer than ever. How many days are there until Christmas, Taylor?"

I ran my tongue along my teeth. *Nice one, Lou Ann.*

"Open them now, girls. They're the same."

The same? I was less careful with the wrapping.

"Oh," Charlotte said, breathy.

It was *Oh, the Places You'll Go!*

Charlotte's eyes were glossy. "This is the nicest thing any teacher has ever done for me. Why us?"

Ms. Glazer wouldn't peel her eyes from mine. "Why you?" she repeated.

I stiffened.

"Taylor and me," Charlotte said, soft.

The corners of Ms. Glazer's lips ticked up. "Oh, I just think it sums up your future paths quite nicely."

A lump set in my throat.

The fifth-period bell rang loud and clear.

That week, the Danvers Men's Shed Association booked our community room for their Christmas party, so Monday night improv was switched to Wednesday.

"Gilda?"

As we turned onto Essex Bridge, our eyes met in the rearview mirror.

I tugged off my scarf and tossed it across the back seat. "Are you okay? You seemed a little . . . off tonight."

She reached for the dial and quieted Lucy. "There's something I've been meaning to tell you. I . . . Well, I won't be able to take you home next week. Or the week after."

I moved as close to the edge of the bench seat as the belt permitted. "If this is about the sketch I did last week, when I upset you—"

"I'm surrendering my license tomorrow."

Sadness sank like a stone in the pit of my stomach. Surrendering her license? Was she unwell? Was her tremor getting worse? Was it somehow related to her vision? Gilda always said that driving was her lifeline. *She must be devastated.* "You're . . . You'll still be able to get to improv, right?"

"Oh, of course," she said, and she tried to make it sound casual, but I heard the skip in her voice. "My daughter had one of those motor things delivered, one of those scooters all the old fuddy-duddies have down at the senior center." In the reflection, I watched her swallow. "But God strike me down if I ever need to be hoisted from the aerobics pool into one of those goddarn things like Mavis Beech. A beached whale, that drama queen thinks she is. Poor darned pool boy's going to need a back reconstruction before his thirtieth birthday. No. I'd rather stay in the water, prune to death."

As I looked out the window, the hairs lifted on the nape of my neck. Was I this obvious when I was masking *my* hurt with humor? "Well, I'm still going to need a ride home, so I'm *totally* happy to double," I joked. "We could even fit your scooter out with one of those rain canopies for when we're flying over Essex Bridge in the snow."

As we rolled into Salem, Gilda didn't turn Lucy up again. In the silence, the sadness settled. Eyes burning, I stared out the window. Why did horrible things have to happen to good people? I bit down on the tip of my tongue. Why were Gilda's daughters so selfish? As a midwife, Gilda had dedicated her entire life to looking after mothers and their babies, and now, when she needed her own babies to look after *her*, they were off downing pints of Guinness in County Couldn't-Give-a-Wee-Fuck.

The click of my seat belt was loud. Gilda half turned in the driver's seat. "Just what do you think you're doing?"

Planting a hand on the roof for balance, I hiked a leg over the front seat. "Riding up front in a Rolls-Royce?"

"Taylor! Watch your boot on the glass—good Lord!"

"Sorry—"

"Mind your goddarn feet! You just booted the Virgin Mary!"

As I dropped onto the bench seat beside her, she shot me a glare. I waggled my eyebrows. Desperate to hide her grin, she molded her lips into a thin line. "Well . . . hurry up and get your belt on then!"

"I am, I am. Hey, you haven't told me if you like my hair. Robert likes it."

"I find long hair more becoming on young ladies."

"Oh, and just when I had my heart set on you taking me to the opening of *Casablanca* and asking me to go steady."

I caught the twitch of her lips. "You were very funny tonight, missy. When you were doing that bit with Robert."

"Which bit?" I'd spent most of improv partnered with Robert.

She slowed at a red light. "The bit about the friends who want to become blood siblings, accidentally nick the arteries in their feet."

"Oh. That one." Pulling a hand through my hair, I thought of Brooke, of how she'd stared down at her snow boots on Monday morning by my locker, of how her eyes had turned glassy and her voice way too soft. We'd been officially not talking for two whole days. Everything was such a fucking *mess*.

"Gilda?"

"Mmm?"

"Could you drop me off at the Hawthorne Hotel?"

She pulled her eyes from the intersection to look at me curiously. "This isn't Gilda's taxi and you're not Miss Daisy. What's at the Hawthorne Hotel?"

"I need to make a reservation."

"For?"

"For Mom and me. For Christmas Eve lunch." It was going to be expensive, but it was worth it. After all, this was going to be my coming out lunch.

"That's nice," Gilda said. "I'm sure she'll be surprised."

I swallowed thickly. "I think so too."

SIXTEEN

$\mathcal{B}$*rooke lived down* the street opposite the House of the Seven Gables, directly behind Ye Olde Pepper Companie, America's oldest candy company. Oprah's cousin once visited Ye Olde Pepper, carted a couple of chocolate turtles back to Los Angeles, and Oprah declared the chocolate the best in all the land. Almost a decade later, the store still boasted Oprah's declaration like they expected her to show up on their doorstep any day and holler, *You get a car, and you get a car! Everybody gets a carrrrr!*

After I popped into Ye Olde Pepper Companie and bought Brooke a box of truffles—if they were good enough for Oprah, they were good enough for my seventeen-year-old best friend who flossed in bed—I wandered down Hardy to the blue-shingled house with the white shutters.

I reached into the Christmas wreath and lifted the brass knocker. Mr. Coleman's voice was muffled through the door, then Brooke's. The wind hit hard. I wrapped my coat tighter around my body, bit my lip, watched the pansies dance in the snow-filled planter boxes. The temperature had dropped overnight—winter had finally arrived.

The door opened. Brooke's eyes widened. "It's early."

"It's almost ten, and I know your Saturday shift usually starts at two, so I figured you'd be home." I handed over the chocolates.

"Are you trying to buy my affection?"

I drew a deep breath. "I'm really sorry. I didn't realize I was being such a shitty friend, that I was taking you for granted." My breath was a cloud. "I'm not mad about MIT. I swear to god, I'm happy for you."

She arched a brow.

"I *am*. But it doesn't mean I'm not worried about what's going to happen to us when you're gone. Can we go for a walk?"

"I don't know. It's snowing."

"Barely."

"I told my dad I'd help him with the Christmas lights."

"An hour? Please? That's all I'm asking."

". . . Let me grab my coat?"

We were both quiet as we wandered down Derby to the waterfront.

"I saw the comments. On your Insta posts. I'm really sorry, Brooke."

"I'm not deleting Instagram."

"Good."

"My parents were really upset about it. So I thought about deleting it."

"I think anyone would think about it."

"But I'm not going to. I was runner-up on *Teen Dream House Rules*. I'm not ever giving up my platform."

"Fuck the trolls—"

"Easy for you to say, Taylor."

"No . . . I . . . I know that."

"Know better. Be better."

"I'm trying to—"

"Thank you for apologizing for not calling me back."

"You don't have to thank me for that. I was all wrapped up in my own shit, and I didn't consider you. That's on me."

"What's going on, Tay?"

My throat ached. "My dad's girlfriend is pregnant. I'm going to have a sister. I'm going to have to *be* a sister."

"Oh."

"He's being really insensitive about it. He downloaded this baby photo-sharing app, and he's been posting updates of the baby's room renovation like"—I put on a posh British accent and pretended to look down my nose at her—"*the royal nursery is now open.*"

Brooke grinned.

"Like, fuck off with your notifications, King Henry. You Anne Boleyn-ed my mother's comedy career."

"You're really bitter about that, huh? Your dad being so successful at comedy when your mom's—"

I stopped dead on the sidewalk. "Let's not go there. Not today. Right now I want to make up for being a crappy friend. I want to buy us tattoos."

She looked up at the storefront—Hysteria Ink. Her eyes grew wide. "Taylor. *No.*"

The Salem Trolley pulled alongside the curb to let tourists disembark at the House of the Seven Gables stop. Brooke started to say something, but I could hardly hear her over the tour guide pontificating about *The Scarlet Letter.* I pulled Brooke closer to the door of Hysteria Ink.

Brooke groaned, but she followed me up the double steps, didn't say *wait* until my fingers curled around the doorknob. "I don't know about this, Tay. I wasn't exactly one hundred percent serious when we were talking about it last month."

"It's just a little bit of ink. We'll just get small ones."

She tried to peer through the slit in the blinded window. "What if we get infections and can't go to the Snow Ball next Friday?"

"Honestly, I can't think of a more badass reason to get out of that fucking nightmare—"

"I'm serious, Taylor."

"So am I." I pushed open the door. "Fingers crossed I'm deathly allergic to tattoo ink."

Brooke went first.

She insisted she couldn't wait—watching it happen to me would traumatize her and she wouldn't be able to go through with her own—so I sat, gripping her hand, watching her eyes squeeze shut as she cursed beneath her breath. But it wasn't watching that put me on edge—it was who was holding the tattoo gun that incited my Hysteria Ink meltdown.

Over the buzz of the tattoo gun, I ran my eyes over Ursula's face. From her neck to her elbow was a colored tattoo of a femme fatale, an emaciated mermaid. It had to be recent—the summer I'd caught her coming out of Jen's room when I was fifteen, her arm had been bare.

She'd aged a lot since being Jen's fuck buddy. Her long blue hair was held back in a high pony, exposing her slight regrowth and the seven piercings in her left ear. She was pierced *all over*—her tragus, her nostril, her *cheekbone*. The bar through her septum was so bulky that I wondered if a tug was all it would take to have her mooing *The Little Mermaid* soundtrack—yank once for "Under the Sea," twice for "Poor Unfortunate Souls." I tried to picture her with Jen in the Proctor Suite, but that made me feel nauseated, so I cut that out before it could get too *Blue Is the Warmest Color.*

Ursula didn't ask many questions, hadn't even when we'd shown our fake IDs and paid up front. Our ages didn't exactly warrant an investigation—it wasn't like we'd asked for full sleeves. The tattoo I'd ordered wasn't much larger than an apricot, and Brooke's was cent-sized—a raindrop. "I Think It's Going to Rain Today" was her grandma Connie's favorite song, Brooke told Ursula. Grandma Connie had been on dialysis for a long time, she said. They didn't expect her to make it to next summer—she wouldn't get to see Brooke graduate. As Brooke looked over at me, I squeezed her hand harder.

She winced in pain. "A-are you still sure about the theater masks?"

I'd decided on the sock and buskin, the ancient symbols for comedy and tragedy.

Not ten minutes later, I was taking off my coat and trading places with Brooke. "You don't have to take your top off," Ursula said as she changed the needles. "Just lift your shirt up to your bra line so I can trace it on."

An ultra-sexual Rihanna song was playing when the Girl with the Mermaid Tattoo moved closer and pressed the tracing paper against my ribs. Her gloved hand was cold against my skin. I stared down at her scalp. Her sky-blue hair was dull, oily. I could *smell* it.

Brooke sat forward. "You want me to hold your hand?"

I shook my head.

The gun whirred.

Those first few seconds were the longest, rawest seconds of my life. Ursula didn't try to talk to me like she had with Brooke. While Brooke rambled on about how we'd be recovering from the Snow Ball this time next weekend, I focused on trying to distract myself from the half dozen needles firing into my dermis at a rate of fifty rounds per second. The vibration against my ribs was so chilling, so fucking agonizing that when it stole the breath from my lungs, my sanity escaped me too—that's the only excuse I have to explain why I was suddenly staring down Ursula's shirt, glaring at her small, creamy breasts, concentrating on the blue vein that crossed her flesh like an electric eel. I wanted to lean down and trace my tongue across it, to zap myself on her bloodstream, to . . .

Ursula stopped, looked up. My stomach bottomed out. Dropping her gaze to her cleavage, she lifted her eyes back to mine. She smirked. And then she returned to torturing me.

Staring up at the ceiling, I smacked my lips together. Thank god Brooke had been checking her phone, that she hadn't seen. *Oh god.* I felt sick, even more perverted than that time I'd assaulted Oliver Twist.

I couldn't breathe. I was drowning in still waters. I rolled my watery eyes over to Brooke, but she was staring at her own tattoo through the bandage.

"Is it almost done?" I rasped.

"We're almost halfway," Ursula murmured.

Brooke pried my hand from the edge of the chair. "It doesn't hurt *that* bad. Tay, are you seriously *crying*?"

The next thing I knew, I was yanking my hand from Brooke's, panting *stop, stop, stop*, trying to slide off the chair between Ursula and the tattoo machine.

"Christ, hold on," Ursula said, "just hold on!" With the gun in one hand, she tried to wipe the blood from my ribs, but I was already up, reaching for my coat . . .

Ursula grabbed my wrist so hard, her nails cut crescents into my skin. "You're not going anywhere until you lift your shirt back up and let me wrap you. *Sit.*"

I couldn't tell if Brooke looked panicked or frightened or confused. As Ursula wrapped my unfinished tattoo, I tried to look anywhere but at my best friend.

Ursula sealed the bandage around my front and pulled my shirt down. Her gaze tracked over my face. "All done."

"Taylor . . ." Brooke tried.

As I hurried down Derby, I could barely see in front of me through my tears. I tried to get my arms into the sleeves of my coat. Behind me, Brooke called out my name.

I crossed the soggy grass of Salem Maritime National Historical Site and made for the bench overlooking the tall ship wharf where, once upon a time, Salem greeted cotton and rum and sugar and slaves.

It had stopped snowing. Sitting in the thick morning fog, I glared at the *Friendship of Salem* docked beside the wharf.

Brooke fell onto the seat beside me. "Are you going to tell me what *the hell* that was about?"

The sails of the *Friendship* lashed against the wind. I couldn't tell her about the internship. What if I told her and then I lost? Deep down, I knew there was another reason, maybe even a truer reason, why I hadn't wanted my name on the finalist announcement. I wasn't just buying time because I wasn't out of the closet. When it came to being a comedian, I had a terminal case of imposter syndrome. I wasn't good enough to win. I was ambitious enough and bold enough, but I wasn't *good* enough. I was like John Proctor at the end of *The Crucible*, crying out with my whole soul, going to the ends of the earth to stop myself from signing away my name—because I couldn't "have another in my life."

"Taylor?"

"I'm a lesbian."

The moment hung, suspended. Shame spiked hot in my bloodstream.

"Oh," Brooke said.

The bitter wind made my ears ache.

Her fingers were warm on my jaw as she thumbed the tracks from my left cheek. "You know this is, like, a nonissue, right? This doesn't change anything."

I drew a sharp breath. My ribs were on *fire*.

"What are you so scared of, Tay?"

"I don't want things to change."

"Nothing's going to change."

I scoffed.

She played with the bandage over her tattoo. "Okay," she reasoned, "so some things might change."

I clutched the edge of the bench. "It's going to be awkward with everyone."

"You're making this bigger than it is. Nobody's gonna care." She paused. "Are you sure?"

"Sure?"

"That you're a . . . that you're gay? Maybe you're bi, or pan."

"I'm not bi or pan."

"You don't really have to know."

"Feels like I do." Not because people would want answers

from me, but because *I* wanted answers from me. *I* wanted to know where I belonged. *I* wanted a label. But what if I labeled myself and then discovered I was wrong? I didn't want people to think I didn't know who I was, that I was some incomplete, half version of myself. And that's every teenager's greatest fear, isn't it? Adults thinking we don't know who we are. Being able to see it as plain as day on their faces.

"Maybe you're just queer, Tay. I mean, you've liked guys, right?"

I shook my head.

"You told me that you've liked guys? You made out with Robbie Haylock behind the middle-school gym. He deep-throated you with his tongue."

"And you wonder why I *don't* like guys."

"Why did you tell me that you did?"

"I don't *know*, Brooke, *Jesus.*" I stared out at the tall ship.

She was quiet then, and so was I. I think she was quickly realizing that this was why I'd been so distant with her, why I'd been pushing her away the same way I'd been pushing *everybody* away.

"Does Jen know?"

I nodded.

"If Jen was anyone else, I'd be offended that you told them before you told me, but . . . I guess she's more like family than a friend. I mean, your mom and Jen are pretty close."

A noise caught in the back of my throat.

"*Really* close."

I looked out at Derby Light. "I think Jen's been in love with my mom since forever."

She sat back against the bench. "Yeah. I've thought about

that too. I mean, that night we stayed up to watch that Wanda Sykes stand-up special, your mom and Jen were pretty much spooning on the couch—"

"Yeah, okay. Thanks. You've thought about it. I get it. Let's leave it there."

"Do you . . . *like* Jen?"

"No. Maybe I had a bit of a thing for her, you know, before, but . . ." My knee bounced. "I, uhh . . . I think I'm . . ." *Jesus Christ.*

"You think you're what?"

"I think I'm in love with Charlotte."

She stared, hard. "You're joking."

"We've . . . we've kissed."

"You've kissed *Charlotte?*"

The wind picked up.

"How many times?" she demanded.

"Once."

"You've kissed Charlotte *once* and now you think you love her? You don't love her." She gave me that Dr. Brooke Coleman, Disappointed Therapist look she'd been freezing me with for years. "This is just you getting obsessive the way you do with everything."

"God, I'm so tired of being told that I want things too much." This was why I just kept my feelings to myself. My feelings were always being judged by a jury of people who knew me best but didn't have the first fucking clue what it felt like to be me. "It's more than just the kiss."

She hugged her knees to her chest. "More?"

"We've had . . . moments. Before we kissed. Romantic moments."

"Moments are just foreplay."

"No." I pulled my coat tighter around my middle. "They're not just foreplay." They were everything.

She sighed loudly. "I'm sorry. I guess I'm just a little shocked that you're into *her*. I can't really see you together. You don't really match."

Digging the toe of my boot into a maple leaf, I let it burrow into the grass. I thought of Jen. I thought about the moment in the Boathouse bathroom when I'd said the same thing to her. And I thought, *Taylor Parker, you're a conceited little c—*

"I guess I shouldn't be surprised about this."

"You guessed I liked girls?"

"No. Not about you. About *her* liking you. I've seen her looking at you. Like, in a gay way."

"Since when?"

"Since she showed up in Salem again."

Charlotte had been looking at me since *last year*? "Why didn't you say something?"

"Why would I?"

I guess that makes sense. I turned to face her. "Is it . . . is it okay that I like her?"

She clicked her tongue playfully. "If you *must* have a thing for her, I suppose I'll find a way to live with it."

"It's not just a *thing*. I really like her."

"You mean *loooooooove*."

It wasn't a joke to me. I felt too much for Charlotte to let Brooke belittle it. When it came to her dramas with Levi, I'd always listened and cared. I deserved the same.

She pulled back the sleeve of her parka. "Dude, I'm frozen to the bone but my wrist is on fucking fire."

"So is my rib." I lifted my T-shirt. The cold wind smacked my skin. Beneath the cling film, my flesh was blotchy red. I'd escaped from Hysteria Ink before Ursula could begin tattooing the second mask. *Jesus Christ.* Why had Ursula decided to start with the tragedy mask? I slumped against the bench. "What a goddamn tragedy."

She laughed. "You did it to yourself."

Oh, Brooke, you have no idea.

"You know, Tay, you don't have to stress over the gay thing." She squeezed my shoulder. "You do you. Take your time. It's not like there's a time bomb ticking down or anything. Right?"

I swallowed. "Right."

SEVENTEEN

After improv on Monday, I was following Gilda out into the hallway when she turned to me. "How are you getting home, missy?"

I tugged on my wool hat. "Bus. How about you—"

Parked against the wall, below the bulletin board, was a red scooter. With a grimace, Gilda looked at the floor—she was embarrassed.

I slung an arm over her shoulders. "I've always wanted to double on one of these."

"Really?"

"Are you kidding?" I tucked her scarf in where it had come loose from the collar of her coat. "Scoot my lazy ass to the bus stop?"

Even through the thickness of her wool coat, Gilda was warm against me as we cruised down Hale. The brim of her cloche swiped my cheek as she turned her head. "Are you going to tell me who Charlotte is?"

"Charlotte?"

She broke hard at the curb to check for traffic. "Every time we've performed lately, you pick the name Charlotte for your character."

I held on to the belt of her coat for dear life. "Doesn't this thing go faster?" Resting my chin on her hunched shoulder,

I breathed in her Chanel No. 5.

In the side mirror, I watched her lips tremble into a smile. Heat radiated through me. In the short amount of time I'd known Gilda, I'd only ever seen her face light up like that once. We'd been listening to Lucille Ball stomp grapes in a vat in Italy. Just before the best part—when an Italian local told Lucy that she wasn't allowed to stop stomping—the cassette had caught. Trapped deep in the Phantom, the tape had squealed. We'd held our breath. Was it about to snap? Seconds later the tape found itself again. "Hallelujah!" Gilda had cried, slapping the wheel with the enthusiasm of a Southern preacher.

I tightened my grip around her middle, and I pretended. For that short moment before we reached the bus stop, I pretended that she was my grandmother. That was something I'd never had—a grandmother who wanted me. As much as Charlotte excited me, as close as I was to Brooke, to Mom, to Jen, when I searched myself, I knew I was happiest when I was with Gilda. I could laugh when I was with Gilda.

I could breathe when I was with Gilda.

I could only hope that, when she found out who I was, she wouldn't break my heart.

On Wednesday night, Mom and I took the train to Boston.

Hands on her hips in the middle of my Back Bay studio, Mom ran her tongue along her teeth. "Smells like a fucking morgue in here."

I threw my coat on top of Mom's on the kitchenette counter and pulled my eyes around the empty space. "How would *you* know what a morgue smells like?"

The heavy tap of her boots as she crossed the room to the bay window told me everything I needed to know—this was ten times harder for her than it was for me.

I climbed up onto one of the two swivel chairs at the counter and tried to spin away the ache that had wound my chest tight the moment we'd unlocked the door. "I can hear you thinking. You think louder than anyone I know."

"So do you." She turned. "What's with the grin, Miss Parker?"

"Nothing." I spun again.

"Tell me."

I threw out a hand to stop myself on the counter. "When I was little, I used to think that you could hear my thoughts. Like, I *genuinely* worried that we had a *What Women Want* situation going on."

"You thought I'd toppled into the tub with a blow-dryer?"

"I thought you loved me so much that we were somehow telepathically connected."

Fingering the scooped neck of her blue sweater, she stared. All of a sudden, she dropped her gaze back to the street.

Oh, Mom.

"You know, Mom, I probably won't even be staying here a whole bunch. Maybe I'll just sleep here on the odd night. When I have a late class."

She perched on the edge of the window seat. "You don't have to do that." She patted the cushion beside her.

With our boots abandoned and our socked feet in each other's laps, we were quiet as we looked down on snowy Boylston. Taking my right foot between her hands, she rubbed it warm.

As she did the same with the left, I rested my temple against the cold glass. "You wanna know something?"

She inspected a hole in the heel of my sock. "Mmm?"

"I found your tapes."

Her hand gripped my ankle. "Tapes?"

"The cassettes." My breath painted the glass cloudy. "Y-your stand-up."

"You . . . You listened to them?"

Warmth tingled out to the very ends of my fingers, my toes. As we stared at each other across the bay window, her eyes filled with tears.

I swatted wetness from my upper lip.

Mom chortled. "Why are we crying?"

"I—I don't know."

"You started it."

"*You* started it."

Her laugh quieted.

As I watched her wipe at her cheeks with the cuff of her sweater, my gaze caught on her locket. "Mom?"

Her thumbs dug into the arch of my foot. "Mmm?"

My voice was little. "Did you really tell Jen she should get an abortion?"

Her hands stilled. "Did Jen tell you that?"

"No. You did. Just after Thanksgiving, when you had food poisoning."

She drew her fists along her thighs. "I didn't tell her that she *should*. I just . . . I told her that, if she kept the baby out of some sense of obligation, with time, she might . . . end up wishing she'd taken a different path."

A different path?

"What's wrong?" she said lowly.

"Is that what happened to you?" My pulse pounded. "Did you end up wishing you'd taken a different path?"

As her eyes widened, my heart quivered like a violin string plucked too hard. Somewhere outside Richmond, Virginia, a peach tree shuddered in the earth.

Reaching out, she ran her fingers through the hair above my ear. "Honey," she said, so soft that my breath hitched, "how could you *think* a thing like that?"

As I focused on the slowly healing split above her left eyebrow, my chin trembled. "Because I get it. Because I'd feel that way. If I were on my way to becoming a . . ." *Don't say it.* "If I were on my way to doing something that I really wanted to, and if *something* stopped me when I was *that* close, I'd resent it—"

She gripped my chin between her thumb and forefinger. Her eyes bore into mine. "What I told Jen, what I suggested . . . that has absolutely nothing to do with you. *With us.*"

I looked down at the street.

"Hey! Look at me." As she tilted my face up, our gazes locked again. "*I had a choice.* And, one day, so will you. You'll always have a choice. God, you'll have more choices than you can possibly imagine." Her grip tightened on my chin. "And if you *ever* find yourself stuck . . . in that situation. If you need to make a decision, I want you to come to me. You hear me?"

Guilt built in my chest like the Berlin Wall.

"I don't ever want secrets between us, Taylor. Okay?"

Billie Jean King was right: pressure really was a privilege. I was scared because I was loved. And I was loved *fiercely.*

Mom's eyes burned. "*Okay?*"

I nodded. *I'm working on it, Mom. Trust me, I'm working on it. . . .*

She tilted her head. "So . . . the Snow Ball is this Friday, huh?"

EIGHTEEN

It is a truth universally acknowledged that any seventeen-year-old who ever walked a mile in their mother's shoes only ever succeeded because they didn't have a mother like Carrie Parker.

I didn't *have* to take her stilettoed boots from her closet. It wasn't like anybody at the Snow Ball would know that the boots were thigh-high—the hem of my gown was so long, it licked the ground. But I needed to be tall. Towering. The look I was going for was formidable with a capital *F*. Formidable, like my mother leaving for a second date after she'd made me paint her nails bloodred and tweeze the darkest hairs from her dirty-blond mustache.

Mom was out on her date with her new Tinder boy toy, and with Jen and Ryan out for dinner, that only left Linda to witness the glory of me stumbling down the garden path to Brooke's honking car, trying not to trip over the long black skirt of my Snow Ball dress. Linda had come out to her porch to see what all the honking was about, and the moment she laid eyes on me, she did a double take.

If Mom had been home, she would have murdered me right there on the front lawn. Mom wasn't exactly an orthodox parent, but proms and dresses and silly school events were important to her. To me? Not so much.

Levi was in the front passenger seat, so I pushed my broom-stick through the back window and climbed in after it.

He turned in his seat, mouth open wide.

"Good evening, Ozians!" I nodded at him. "Nice bowtie, Bill Nye."

Brooke met my eyes in the rearview mirror. Pulling away from the curb, she groaned. "You have got to be fucking kidding me."

Whoever had insisted on green lighting for our Enchanted Forest–themed Snow Ball really hadn't thought it through. While it worked wonders for my painted complexion, everybody else looked like they'd just disembarked the *Mayflower* with a heavy case of the Black Death.

It was warm with all those hormonal bodies inside the gym, the air thick with the anticipation of who would get laid after a *highly* arousing round of Christmas-themed karaoke. It smelled surprisingly good in there, though. Bianca Gomez's dad had parked his popcorn machine over by the table of virgin eggnog, and everyone seemed pretty happy to have him there to fulfill their munchie cravings. It had to be the *least* classy Snow Ball in all of New England, but I wasn't in a position to complain—my outfit didn't exactly help matters.

I couldn't see Charlotte, but I *could* see the snack table. I'd been so busy making the molds and painting my face that I hadn't touched the casserole Mom had left for me in the oven. I'd skipped lunch, too.

My history teacher, Mrs. Linklater, was manning the snack

table. She'd been the one to recommend Emerson to me, and in an ironic twist of fate, without her knowing, I'd accidentally written about her for the mock-humor column I'd submitted to Emerson. Here's the 411: Mrs. Linklater lived directly opposite the Rebecca Nurse Homestead in the next town over, Danvers, the old Salem Village where the witch trials actually took place. One night, Mrs. Linklater looked out her bathroom window and caught old Rebecca Nurse wandering around the red Colonial in the clothes she was hanged in in 1692. My whole AP History class believed it, including Brooke. Not me. Mrs. Linklater had a chronic case of pathological lying going on, which was an *absolutely wonderful* trait to have in an AP History teacher.

As I rested my broomstick against the table, she started. "Taylor?"

I smiled, bit off a mini spring roll. Between the prosthetics, my perfectly green skin, and my long black wig, I was almost unrecognizable.

"The Wicked Witch of the West?" she asked.

I lifted the hem of my black velvet dress to show her the striped stockings I'd pulled on over the skintight leather of Mom's boots. "East. Pre–falling house. But I understand your confusion." I tapped the base of my plastic chin, the tip of my molded nose. "The resemblance to my sister is uncanny."

"It's refreshing to meet an adolescent who doesn't take herself so seriously. A little personality will take you very far at Emerson."

That was me—blessed with a chronic case of personality. I thought of *Saturday Night Live*. Of my entry. What the actual fuck had I gotten myself into?

"Why the costume, Taylor?"

"I figured that if my inner introvert decided to make an appearance, I could just click my heels and *no place like home* it out of here."

"I don't see any ruby slippers?"

I winked. "You mean silver."

"Ruby." She plunged a mozzarella stick into the blob of marinara on her paper plate.

"But in the book they were silver."

"Definitely ruby, hon."

I tried not to look directly at the blob of mozzarella stuck in the wide gap between her front teeth. "In the *movie* they were ruby, but only because MGM wanted to show off with Technicolor. In the book they were silver."

She folded her plate. Marinara squeezed out the point and plopped to the floor beside my boot. "They're at the Peabody right now, Taylor—and they're ruby."

And I live with a Peabody curator, I wanted to call out as she stalked off. *She bought me my first pack of tampons and taught me how to write a bibliography!* Teachers thought they knew *everything*, but this ditz didn't even know the original shoes were silver. I'd taken monumental life advice from somebody who didn't have the first fucking clue. I swiped a punch cup from the table. Why the hell had I taken her Emerson advice in the first place? It was too bad she couldn't tap her ugly-ass Mary Janes three times and . . . Suddenly, the pastry of a vegan spring roll lodged in my windpipe. . . .

Down by the stage, Charlotte was dancing—with Matt Reiner. Rachel and Chloe were close by—technically, they were all kind of dancing in a group, I guess, except Matt was clinging to her like a leech and she was smiling and laughing and he looked *smug*. His giant quarterback body loomed over her like Lurch over Wednesday Addams, his huge hands high on her baby-pink bodice. Jealousy tightened low in my stomach. Knowing Charlotte wasn't interested in guys didn't make knowing *guys were interested in her* any easier to digest. Of course boys wanted her. She was confident and calm and gorgeous, and with her hair pinned up and wearing heels, she looked more grown-up than usual. Unlike every other sleeveless sweetheart-cut conformist in the room, Charlotte wore long sleeves to her elbows, protecting her from the harsh green rays of the UV plague. A quiet green tulle flowed wide from her hips, and under the light, the beaded flowers that linked across the skirt glittered like droplets on a petal. She looked *ethereal*.

Brooke sidled up next to me. "I've consulted my moral compass and I know you think it's corrupt to hack into Glazer's iCloud, but I need to know I've at least got a B on that Brecht essay. Don't judge me. I know you'll judge me but . . . just . . . don't."

"Cool." Whatever she was saying was barely registering; I couldn't take my eyes off Charlotte.

"The future mother of your children has given Matt Reiner a hard-on."

I handed her my cup of punch and turned to pour another. "They're just dancing."

"That's not all *he* thinks they're doing. He's about two seconds from jizzing on her dress."

"Now you're just exaggerating—your back is to the dance floor, just like mine."

"Eyes in the back of my head, baby. Are you going to make sweet, sweet love to her tonight?"

My whole body warmed. "Excuse me, it's *way* too early to be thinking about that."

"Why? You said it yourself—you're wild about her. And who knows? I mean, this costume of yours could be a real turn-on for her. She's so into theatrics that she'd probably ask you to go down on her to the *Rent* soundtrack."

A voice behind us piped up. "I'm more of a *Chicago* kind of girl, actually."

We spun.

"Charlotte." Brooke straightened. "I—"

"It's 'Mister Cellophane' that really gets me going. Do you mind?" She slipped between us to the punch table.

Brooke's brows shot into her hairline.

I jutted my chin at the dance floor. *Go before you put your other foot in your mouth!* "Didn't Levi ask you to dance, Brooke?"

With Brooke gone, Charlotte leaned back against the wall beside me. "When you told me that you came out to Brooke, I didn't realize you meant you'd told her about me, too."

"Is it okay that I did?"

"It's more than okay. It's brave." She pulled her eyes over my costume. "So *this* is what you meant when you said 'witchy.'" As she took a sip from her punch cup, her arm brushed against mine. "Is it un-American of me to admit that I'm attracted to a witch?"

"Only if you're a Republican." I tried desperately to calm my heart. What had she overheard?

". . . Do you really think it's too early for us?"

Oh god. "Have I told you how pretty your dress is?"

She chewed on the lip of her punch cup. "I got it at Macy's. My nonna embroidered it. Don't change the subject."

191

"Your nonna did a great job—"

"I wish you'd ask me to dance, Taylor. But I know that would probably make you feel uncomfortable."

That sick, shameful feeling crawled over my skin. As I pulled my eyes from Charlotte's, my gaze caught across the room—Ms. Glazer was watching us.

Delicately, Charlotte raked back a few strands of hair where they'd come loose from her bun. "*I'd* ask *you* to dance, but I know you'd do anything to make me happy, and you'd say yes, and we'd go out there on the dance floor and people would look and I'd feel like I'd pressured you, and trying to make me happy can't be the reason you come out to our entire grade."

My tongue grew heavy.

Dropping her gaze, she sighed heavily. "I'm sorry. I'm just feeling a bit frustrated tonight, seeing other people, couples, and . . ." She trailed off. "This is hard and lonely—what we're doing—but when I stop and remind myself of the way you looked at me that day in Red's, I know this is more than worth all the hard stuff."

Charlotte, I love you. "Charlotte . . ."

"Yes?"

"I— Elijah Riccardo's coming over here. He's going to ask you to dance."

Eli was a fun guy, a real prankster in a whoopee-cushion, amateur-magician kind of way. Maybe if he took Charlotte out for a spin, she'd come back to me a little less serious—and I'd have time to pull myself together and stop myself from saying anything foolish.

"Hey, TP." He'd been calling me that since middle school. "Wanna dance?"

Me? "No, thanks, Eli. Slow dancing to acoustic covers isn't really my style."

"Come on, TP. I'm not proposing." His breath smelled unnaturally fresh, like he'd chased a pack of mints down with a bottle of Listerine. "I'm just asking you to dance."

Charlotte swiped my cup from my hands. "I'll hold this while you dance with Eli." She made her voice a whisper: "And you *should* dance with Eli."

If I had to claim anyone as a three-minute beard until "Fast Car" was over, I was glad it was Eli. At least I didn't feel so delicate in his arms. He was the only soccer player whose growth spurt had yet to *really* kick in, and with me in Mom's boots, he matched my height. If one dance with Eli kept everyone from whispering about how much time I was spending with Charlotte, well, a closeted lesbian's gotta do what a closeted lesbian's gotta do.

"Why did you wear your Halloween costume?"

The green light caught on his braces. I looked briefly at his chapped lips—the thought of kissing him didn't exactly make me feel like I was coming out of my skin. I glanced over his shoulder at Charlotte. Her expression was unreadable. "How dare you assume it's a Halloween costume. This was my mother's wedding dress. A family heirloom." Across the room, Ms. Glazer's stare flickered between me and Charlotte. Something akin to realization flashed in her eyes before they locked on me. *She knows. She knows that Charlotte is so far from being just my friend that it isn't even funny.*

Eli's hands shifted, his touch firmer, pressing the fabric of my dress into the tattoo. "It's your Halloween costume. I took my little sister to your inn on Halloween and this is exactly what you were wearing when you tripped down your front steps and the bucket of Tootsie Rolls went flying. I helped you pick them up, remember?"

"You want the Medal of Honor?" Ms. Glazer was moving around the snack table—toward Charlotte.

"You always do this. I remember when you dressed up as Jessie from *Toy Story* for our Sadie Hawkins in middle school—"

"Jessie from *Toy Story*? *Dude*, I was Calamity Jane." What was Ms. Glazer planning?

"I don't know why you didn't just wear a dress like the other girls." His hands shifted higher—again. "You make a joke of all the dances, but you're one of the prettiest girls in our grade."

"I'm not." Ms. Glazer and Charlotte were *talking*. My stomach hardened. What if Lou Ann didn't *think* with her *Little House on the Prairie* head and assumed I'd told Charlotte about the internship?

"You *are* pretty." He was trying to hold my eye. "There's something alluring about funny girls."

"*Alluring?* Christ, Riccardo, write one college admissions essay and now you're Hawthorne?"

He twirled us around. "Are you going to the after-party? I have my car. We could go together."

I could barely focus on what he was saying—Ms. Glazer and Charlotte were staring. My knees locked. "Thanks for the dance, Eli."

When she realized I was headed straight for her, whatever Ms. Glazer was saying died mid-sentence.

Linking her arms around herself, Charlotte looked up at me. "Taylor?"

My chin quivered. I couldn't just drag her out of there,

away from Ms. Glazer and her mouth. As an acoustic version of "Waterloo" skipped into the gym, Charlotte looked past me to the dance floor, wistful, and I knew then and there that if I didn't do what my heart was telling me to do, I'd let my sadness steal something from me that I'd regret until the day I was ashes to ashes and dust to dust.

As I took both cups from Charlotte's hands and tossed them into the trash, her eyes widened. I peeled her fingers from where they were buried in her elbow and I led her out into the crowd.

Burning from the inside out, I drew her against me and turned us completely so I didn't have to spend another second looking at Ms. Glazer.

Charlotte stared up at me, stunned and devoted and adoring. Something crumbled inside me. She had it all upside down. I hadn't pulled her onto the dance floor because I was brave. "What was Ms. Glazer talking about?"

Her hand settled gently on my shoulder. "Just . . . the future."

I shifted our clasped hands higher to my collarbone where she couldn't feel my heart trying to spring from my chest. Across the gym, Matt Reiner pulled on Isi's arm to spin her. As they whispered, eyes on us, my other hand trembled against Charlotte's back. "Matt has a crush on you."

Her laugh was breathy against the very spot she'd rested her fingertips weeks ago in my museum. "Well, you'd know, wouldn't you?"

"How would I know?"

"Because *you* have a crush on me."

Fear and want rumbled in my chest. *Snap, crackle, rupture.* "You have a crush on me too."

Her blue eyes were wicked green in the light. "They say

crushes only last three months before they burn out or turn into something more. I've liked you for way longer than three months."

There it was, muffled in the background: the battle cry that bugled *Send in the clowns because I'm so unbelievably proud and I'm so unbelievably done.*

As "Waterloo" drew to an end, Charlotte tilted her chin up. Her breath skated over the shell of my ear. "I need to get something from the theater room. Come with me?"

We'd talked a big game flirting all night, but the moment we were alone, we both turned shy.

"So, what are you looking for?" I asked as I followed Charlotte behind the curtain. We'd turned the houselights on, but behind the stage, deep in the wings, it was difficult to see what wasn't right in front of me.

"We're looking for my corset. The North Shore Children's Theatre is holding auditions soon, and I'll need it for my monologue. I left it here after we did *Guys and Dolls* last spring."

"I remember in vivid detail."

"You remember my corset in vivid detail?"

I blushed. "No. The production. Brooke made me come to see it all three nights."

She cringed. "All three nights? You poor thing. It was really bad, wasn't it?"

"I wouldn't say *bad*. You were great, Brooke was great. . . ."

"It was awful—you don't have to tell me that. I wanted to play Miss Adelaide," she admitted, "but Ms. Glazer said I was better suited to Sister Sarah, that Brooke was better at comedic relief."

Christ, I was glad Brooke had played Miss Adelaide, the showgirl. I think I would have choked on my own tongue at the sight of Charlotte in Miss Adelaide's costume. I mean, Sister Sarah's fifties missionary uniform *alone* had had me sitting up straighter in my seat, and I hadn't even been seriously crushing on Charlotte at that point. "I don't know," I said. I stepped over a beanbag. "I really liked you as Sister Sarah."

Charlotte opened the overfilled costume closet. I leaned against the side of it, took her in. "Hey?"

She was distracted, surfing through the costumes. "Yeah?"

"You look really beautiful tonight."

She pulled back. She looked surprised. "Thank you." She ran her eyes over my face in the semidarkness. "I wish I could say the same about you." She smirked. "But that nose, and that chin . . . Are you going to Hannah's after-party like that?"

"I'm not going to the after-party."

"Me either. I have work tomorrow. Besides, I wouldn't have anyone to go with, really. Chloe and Rachel will be too busy working on 'losing their virginities' at the after-party."

"Seriously?"

"Their words, not mine. There's no such thing as virginity— it's a patriarchal construct. But they think 'losing it' on prom is too cliché, so they decided tonight was best."

"Oh." I felt hot beneath my costume. I reached inside my cape and scratched at my tattoo.

"They're both cliché if you ask me." Sneezing, she pulled the corset from the dusty closet. "I wouldn't have sex for the first time on either night." She closed the closet doors and rubbed at her nose. "*Especially* not in the guest room of Hannah's parents' house."

My tongue turned to lead in my mouth—she'd never had sex either. "Where would you want to have your first time?" I managed.

She moved closer, trapped me in that narrow, shadowed space between the curtain and the back wall. "Where would *you*?"

Oh god. I'm not brave enough for this. "Wh-what makes you think I've never had sex?"

She bit her lip.

I leaned back against the wall, tried to remember how to breathe. "At a zoo after hours. Or on Route 66."

She folded the corset over her arm. "Come on. Be serious for once."

"I don't know. A hotel maybe." I leaned against the side of the wardrobe as she closed it. "What about you?"

She looked me in the eye. "Somewhere memorable."

For a few long, intense seconds, we just watched each other in the dark. My stomach flipped. I was so attracted to her. I was so, so attracted to her, and in that moment, nothing could have drawn my attention away, not even if Charlize Theron turned up in a suit and asked me to be her trophy wife.

Down the hall, a Taylor Swift song purred from the gym. I wanted to kiss Charlotte. It had been a long time since we'd kissed in the wax museum, and so much had happened since then. Boston. The diner. It was different between us now. Deeper. Truer.

"I need to tell you something, Taylor. I need to tell you about what Ms. Glazer and I were talking about back there in the gym."

A bout of nausea washed over me. The contest. They'd been talking about the contest.

"I got into NYU." She wrapped her arms around her middle.

"I got into Tisch and I'm going to accept it."

My heart leapt to my mouth. She was going to New York? "Wait." Tisch was NYU's performance school. "I thought you wanted to study history?"

"Ms. Glazer, she called my parents, and she encouraged it a while back, way before I applied for the history programs and . . . Anyway, I didn't think I'd get in, but I did. Tisch feels right."

I wished that I could have what felt right. I thought of my finalist entry. Had it been read yet? Or was it just waiting in Jane Lincoln's inbox inside 30 Rockefeller Center, my heart and soul unopened?

Realization struck me. "Did you go to New York to audition?"

"I'm sorry I didn't tell you. I just didn't want to tell anyone I'd auditioned and then not get in."

God. We were more alike than I'd thought. "You don't have to be sorry, Charlotte."

Her voice was timid: "Are you happy for me?"

She'd shocked me so much that I'd gone and lost my damn mind, hadn't even congratulated her. "Oh my god!" I said, slapping my forehead like a Disney cartoon. "*Of course* I am." I pushed off the wall, closer to her. "Seriously, Charlotte. Congratulations."

Her lips twitched into an anxious smile. "I'm really nervous about it—"

"You shouldn't be. You deserve this more than anyone I know. I'm *so* happy for you."

We locked the theater room and started down the hallway to the gym.

Her news about Tisch had me so riled up that I'm not sure

what came over me. I was just so happy for her. All I knew was that the world around me was spinning fast, and if I wanted to be part of it, I had to jump on the carousel and join the carnival I dreamed about when I closed my eyes at night.

I reached for her hand and led her down a side hallway.

"Where are we going?" she whispered.

I pinned her against the lockers outside the guidance counselor's office. "Can I just kiss you? *Please?*"

Her eyelids fluttered shut. She nodded.

This wasn't sweet, not like the wax museum. It was *sugary*, because she tasted like lemon punch, but it wasn't sweet. This was long and languid. Our hands were everywhere, on each other's necks, jaws, and then it turned kind of feverish, so feverish that my plastic chin and nose hit the ground with a *thud-thud*. We'd touched a lot, held hands so many times, but this was something else.

As she dropped the corset, it pooled at our feet. Taking her waist in my hands, I pressed my whole body against her, tried not to wobble in Mom's boots as Charlotte's warm hands grazed my jaw, sent my mind fuzzy. Her tongue slipped against mine, and she hummed a little sound at the back of her throat that made my chest ache.

There were voices down the hall leaving the gym, coming closer. I tore away from her.

The voices disappeared in the other direction.

Charlotte's chest heaved. Her neck and cheeks were flushed pink. Green paint was smeared across her chin, her nose. I guess my eyes went sort of wide because, instantly, she brought a hand to her mouth and looked at her fingers. "You got me all green."

Her stare was so intense, I had to look away. I bent low,

picked up my nose, my chin, her corset. I tucked my nose and chin down the front of my dress and slipped her corset under my arm.

Frenetically, she wiped at her face. "Is it gone?"

I could hardly hide my smile. "Nope." I wiped at her face with the pads of my thumbs, the way mothers do with their dirty children. "*Now* it's gone." I wet my lips. "Want to get out of here?"

NINETEEN

The moment we were through the front door, I peeled off my wig. "'Welcome to the Blossom Inn,'" I whispered. The headlights of Brooke's car floodlit the empty common room as she drove off to the after-party with Levi. "I'm sorry if it embarrassed you. What Brooke said in the car. Asking where my nose and chin went."

"I was really tempted to tell her that she was right about what she'd said at the punch table—I really did find your theatrics a turn-on. But I didn't want to say something like that, you know, in front of Levi. Even though we danced together . . ."

The inn was silent. It was after ten and there weren't any guests in the common room. The TV was on mute but the Christmas lights were still flashing on the tree, and the fire danced strong, as though someone had recently thrown a log on to keep it going.

I dumped my broomstick in the coat closet. "My mom isn't home." At the base of the staircase, I unzipped Mom's boots and dusted the point where snow had dampened the leather. Wiggling my toes, I sighed in relief.

Charlotte gripped the end of the banister. "Is she working?"

"No. She's on a Tinder date and she usually doesn't get home until really late. I don't want to think about why."

She giggled.

I led her upstairs. When we passed the Proctor Suite, I couldn't make out light coming from under the door—Jen and Ryan were still out.

On the top landing, Charlotte pointed to the door next to mine. "Does that lead up to the tower?"

I nodded.

"This is *so* cool," she said.

I locked my bedroom door behind us, pressed my shoulder blades against it as I watched her eyes scan my room: the floral bedspread I'd had since I was thirteen; the brass banker's lamp I'd bought for eleven dollars at a yard sale; the string lights above my window, clipped with Polaroids of Brooke and me; the stenciled Tina Fey quote that ran from one wall to the other above my dresser—*Say yes, and you'll figure it out afterwards.* Her gaze landed on the Target Lady poster that hung above my bed, watching over me each night the way the Virgin Mary did for other people. "*This* is quirkier than I expected. I love it."

I didn't want to put on music and make it seem like I was trying to start something, so I just turned on my TV and left it on a Charles Manson *Dateline* special, you know, to really set the mood. I gave her pajamas to change into, a sweater. She set her corset down on top of the trunk at the end of my bed. "Can you help me with my dress?" she asked. "My nonna insisted on adding these little buttons, and my mom had to fasten them for me."

It wasn't like a cliché flirty move—there really were little hooks and buttons over the zipper. I was careful, gentle, so worried about ruining her nonna's hard work. Then something strange happened: my gay ass started thinking about wedding dresses. Unzipping *her* wedding dress. I'd never been one of those little girls who fantasized about her wedding, but there I was, unfastening the clips on Charlotte Grey's Snow Ball dress and *thinking*. I can't explain it, but there was something about the idea of helping my new wife out of her dress at the end of the night that tugged a longing feeling loose in my chest.

She could reach the zip herself, she said. I was relieved. Any longer with my hands against her spine and I would have suggested Central Park's Bow Bridge as a wedding venue.

While she was in the bathroom changing into my clothes, I pulled on a pair of sweatpants and, get this, a *flannel*. I checked my reflection in my dresser mirror. Shit. I'd almost forgotten I was still green.

The bathroom door opened. Charlotte's slight frame was swallowed up in my sweater. She'd rolled my sweatpants to her ankles. I swallowed. The girl I loved was wearing my clothes.

She looked past me to where *Oh, the Places You'll Go!* was propped up against my mirror. "What did she write?"

"Write?"

"Ms. Glazer. She inscribed the books for us."

She had? "Oh. Right. She wished me luck at Emerson." I stared at the Snow Ball gown hung over her arm.

"Does the fireplace work?" she asked.

I nodded. "I have no idea how to light it, though." I grasped the bottom bedpost, swept my fingertips around it while I tried to look anywhere but the pale pink bra hanging over the crook of her elbow.

"I can light it," she said. Paused. "*Can* I light it?"

"Sure."

In the bathroom, I scrubbed the green from my pores. When I was done—there was still green in my hairline and inside my ears, but that was as good as it was going to get—I went back out.

Charlotte was kneeling by the fireplace, my sweater discarded beside her on the rug. She was wearing the "Poehler/ Fey 2016: Bitches Get Stuff Done" T-shirt I'd given her, and as she leaned forward to stab the poker into the burgeoning fire, my eyes locked on the pale strip of skin at her hip, just above the double-folded band of my sweatpants.

I looked to the fire, blinked. "Were you a Brownie?"

She grinned. "No. It's not rocket science. I just used the shredded paper in there as kindling."

My throat tightened. She'd set fire to my *Ghostbusters* poster.

I joined her on the rug and pulled a cleansing wipe from the packet.

"Let me help you?" she offered.

She took the wipe from my hand and moved closer, so close that our knees touched. The warmth of her hand through the wet wipe made my heart race. As her hot fingers curled around the shell of my ear and drew the wipe over my earlobe, my mouth grew so dry that I had to look over her shoulder. There was no way I could look her in the eye when she was touching me like that—like I was something fragile.

She slid the wipe down to my collarbone. As she gently pressed the cloth into the hollow of my throat, my chest threatened to burst. I was so goddamn overwhelmed. Thank god I'd had my quarter-life crisis a week before in Ursula's tattoo parlor—if I hadn't, I know I would have broken down then and there under Charlotte's tender touch.

"'I'm melting,'" I rasped. A joke. To fill the silence.

"Done," she murmured. She tossed the last wipe into the fire, cavalier, as though she hadn't just stripped me of my mask and bared my soul.

We watched the flames rise and catch, catch and rise, listening to the crackle and pop. . . .

"So . . ." she said, "what's the story with your dad?"

I rested back on my palms. "There isn't much of a story. He lives in Cape Cod with his new girlfriend, spends some time in New York. He has another house in the Hudson Valley." I paused. "He's a Christian comedian."

"I know about the Christian part," she confessed.

"How?"

"I googled your name a couple of weeks ago and that *New York Times* profile on him was the first result."

She'd googled me? I felt hot. "There's a *New York Times* profile on him?"

Her expression grew tentative. "It was about his girlfriend being pregnant."

I stiffened. "Oh." *That tiny little detail.*

"The article mentioned you by name. That he had a daughter in high school, too. To be honest, until I read his profile, I didn't even know Christian comedians were a thing."

"He was never really *that* successful, you know, as a regular comedian, until he decided to tack that part on. People can find God pretty quick when there's something in it for them."

"You think it was all a farce?"

I shrugged. "At first it was. He was away a lot touring, mostly the South. After one of his longest trips, he came home and started going to church. That's when it kind of took a turn. I think after a while he really did talk himself into being religious."

"Did you ever go to church with him?"

"No. We had this old lady neighbor in Virginia who had a honeybee farm, so Mom and I used to go to the farmers' market with her on Sunday mornings and help set up the stall. Dad wanted us to go to church with him, I think just to try it at least, but Mom took the honey trade, like, super seriously. She had business cards made and everything."

"How old were you when your parents divorced?"

"Ten. He cheated on her."

"What a good Christian man. Do you see him much?"

"I saw him just before Thanksgiving. He . . . he's not all bad. I mean, he's secured me an apartment in Boston. He's paying my rent while I'm at college."

"Whoa."

"You want to know the one condition he gave me when he handed me the keys?"

She smiled. "What?"

"'No boys allowed.'"

As she giggled, her cheeks turned rosy. My pulse quickened. Charlotte Grey was in *my bedroom*. I was the luckiest lesbian in Essex County.

An old clip of Sharon Tate in *Valley of the Dolls* was playing on TV. Her candied voice filled the silence. "Do you wonder what your dad would think about you liking girls?" Charlotte asked.

"No." I *thought* about it—all the time—but I didn't have to wonder. "I've seen some of his sets on YouTube, and I know what his thoughts are on gay people." I shifted on the floor. "Doesn't matter, though. I don't care what he thinks."

Charlotte moved so close, our elbows were touching. "When did you first know you liked girls?" she said, tender.

A log shifted, fell deeper into the blaze. That time watching *The Crucible* was the most memorable. But lately, I'd been remembering little things I'd felt way before we'd ever come to Salem.

"Maybe when I was, like, ten," I said. "I mean, I didn't know, but I knew, you know? I had a bit of a thing for Kate Winslet."

"Oh?"

"I watched *Titanic* a lot. I used to pause it on that scene where he draws her naked." As soon as the words were out of my mouth, I wanted to shove them right back in. "I mean, not to look at her, you know, her . . ." I waved a shaky hand over my chest. "I just liked looking at the curve of her hip. That's all."

Her sharp blue eyes tracked over my face. "You're blushing."

I wasn't just blushing. I was on fire. I felt like a slingshot stretched too tight.

She nudged my shoulder with hers. "I did stuff like that all the time."

"Like what?"

She winked. "Wouldn't you like to know."

I *did* want to know, but I didn't have the courage to ask. I felt so safe with Charlotte, so understood, but at the same time, I felt like there were worlds between us. She was so far *ahead* of me.

There was chatter out in the hall, the click of a door as someone went into the room opposite mine. Charlotte looked to the door.

"Just guests," I mumbled.

"Right . . ."

The fire crackled loudly. She folded her legs underneath her as she stabbed at the smallest log with the poker.

"You know," she started, "I know how it feels to not be out. The shame, the depression." Her face grew serious as she looked at me. "It doesn't magically go away the first time you come out."

How was it that she knew exactly what I needed to hear? "But you're so confident."

"I just fake it really well."

"I feel like I'm faking everything." I looked at my toes. "I feel like a liar. I feel like I'm lying to everyone."

"There's a difference between lying and protecting yourself." She poked the log again.

Suddenly the strangest feeling hit me: I wanted my mom. I wanted to tell my mom. I wanted to hold my mom.

As Charlotte stared at me, something shifted between us. The air in the room thickened. She looked up at the bed. "Can we sit up there?"

I ran a hand through my hair. "S-sure."

My headboard creaked loudly as we settled back against the pillows. I could feel her eyes on the side of my face. "Rumor has it you and Brooke got matching tattoos."

"We got tattoos together, but they *definitely* aren't matching." She grinned shyly.

I smiled. "What?"

"Are you going to show me?"

"It isn't finished."

"I don't care."

I got to my knees and lifted my T-shirt to the band of my bra. "I have to go back to get the comedy mask finished." As she shifted toward me, I inhaled sharply. "I—I had to leave early. I had a bit of a meltdown."

She was at eye level with my stamp of tragedy. "Because it hurt?"

"No. I just . . . It was a hard week and it all got to be a bit too much and . . ." She didn't need to hear about my quarter-life crisis. "Anyway." I sighed. "I have to go back sometime—"

As she stretched forward and pressed her lips to my

209

tattoo—light, sweet, *soft*—I gasped.

Her lips curled as she looked up at me. "*Now* it's smiling."

She was beautiful. She was so, so beautiful, and she was so, so loved by *so* many people. Everybody talked about how intense it was to fall in love with the dark and the lonely and the unloved—the Heathcliffs, the Mr. Darcys—but they didn't talk about what it was like to fall in love with someone who already had all the love in the world. Charlotte had all the love in the world—from her friends, from her parents, from Tisch. She had all the love in the world, and she still wanted mine.

I cupped her face in my hands and I kissed her—hard.

She pushed me back and climbed on top of me, sighed into my mouth like she'd wanted me as long as I'd wanted her.

Her lips grew eager, her kisses bolder. A bolt of need gripped me. When I made a noise, she pulled back, smiled down at me shyly, and hunger tugged low in my belly. "I've never done anything like this before," she whispered. "With anyone. I've only ever kissed one other girl, and that was when I was nine, so it doesn't really count."

That surprised me. I really thought she'd done *something* with Savannah Hunter at the pop-up drive-in. I kneaded her hip. "I haven't either."

"Really?"

It was impossible to think with the full weight of her sitting on my hips. "Really."

She kissed my jaw, my neck, my throat. Her hand peeled mine from her waist, brought it to touch her breast through the T-shirt. As I held her softness in my hand, something swelled inside me and made me want to sob with the relief of it all, from the sudden, unbelievable rush of certainty. She pressed her lips to the skin just above the neckline of my flannel. "Taylor?"

"Yeah?" I brushed my thumb over her.

She gasped. "I think we should have sex."

I pulled back.

Her eyes widened.

I licked my lips, tried to calm myself.

She traced the swell of my bottom lip. "Do you want that?"

I wanted it so badly, I could barely breathe. "Yes."

"Me too," she said, all breathy.

"Tonight?"

Her fingers fluttered against my belly. "Yeah."

I stared up at her. "Why?"

"Why?"

"Yeah. Why?"

Her eyes closed. "Because I really don't want to stop."

Those words sparked bright in my blood. As her breath fanned my lips, I squeezed my eyes shut. Her fingers were slipping inside the cup of my bra and they were *touching me.* "I think it's you, Taylor. I think you're the one I've been waiting for."

My nipples were harder than Linda's fucking Giles *G.* I brought her hands to the top button of my shirt.

"Are you sure, Taylor?"

I'd never been surer of anything in my life. But before I could tell her that, there was a knock at my door.

Charlotte sat up on my hips, stiffened.

My name came muffled through the door.

"Fuck. It's my mom."

Charlotte was off me like a shot.

I pushed off the bed, slid the chain across and pulled the door open, only halfway.

One look at Mom and I could tell she was wine drunk. It rarely happened, so when it did, it was obvious—to me, anyway. She was still wearing her date outfit—her little black dress, her heels, her caramel trench. Leaning an arm against the doorjamb, she looked me right in the eye. "You think I don't know what you did tonight?"

I gripped the door handle. "What?" I rasped.

The faint creases at the sides of her eyes deepened as she grinned. "Don't play me," she drawled.

My heart slowed.

She pressed more of her weight against the doorjamb. "I saw my boots in the coat closet. And the broomstick. And the wig."

Oh.

"Why're you holding the door closed? What've you got in there? Hillary's emails?"

"No—"

She looked around me. "If you've stretched my boots with your gargantuan feet, I swear to—" Her eyes widened as she spotted Charlotte sitting up against the pillows. Straightening, she glared at me. "Fucking warn a person," she hissed.

Pushing past me, she crossed my room and collapsed on the end of my bed. "I remember you," she said, her eyes tracing Charlotte's features. "You played the uptight one in *Guys and Dolls*."

"Mom, this is Charlotte."

Mom swung her heels up onto the comforter. "Tell me about the Snow Ball. Who did you dance with?"

I felt dizzy. "Um, not many people."

"I mean *guys*." She rolled her eyes at Charlotte as if to say *Get a load of my daughter*. "I'm not interested in hearing about every friend you danced with." She looked between us. Her eyes were unfocused, but I don't think Charlotte could tell that she was drunk. At least, not at first . . . "Tell me, Charlotte, does Taylor have a boyfriend I don't know about?"

Jesus H. Christ.

Mom fixed her gaze on me. "You look flushed from the fire."

I needed something to distract her. "Mom, Charlotte got into Tisch."

Mom's mouth fell open. She grasped Charlotte's big toe. "New York! Congratulations!"

Charlotte smiled bashfully. "Thank you, Ms. Parker." She looked down at Mom's grip on her foot. "I . . . Taylor's told me a lot about you—"

Mom cut her off. "What did *you* wear to the Snow Ball?"

Charlotte pointed to her dress on a hanger on my closet door.

Mom gasped then, as though Charlotte were her own goddamn daughter. "Honey, that's a beautiful dress. I wish I could have seen you." She crossed the room to my closet and ran her fingers over the beads of the dress. "You know, I was married in New York."

"Mom."

She traced her touch over the tulle skirt of Charlotte's dress. "I haven't worn a dress like this in years." She twirled on the spot. "We should celebrate! Why are you both holed up in here? Come downstairs! We can drink champagne!"

"Mom, no."

"Seriously, come on! Jen's just come in; she'll drink with us."

"No, she won't—she's six months pregnant."

"Right. Of course." Shaking her head, she headed for the door. "I'm just going to change out of this"—she *shimmied*—"and then I want you to come downstairs. We can dance." With a heavy click, the door closed behind her.

Falling back against the pillows, I ran a hand through my hair. My heart was still firing from the sudden shock.

Charlotte stretched her legs out on the comforter. "Well, that was close."

"Yeah."

"Your mom's really young. And charming."

Charming? Jesus Christ. "She's a bit wasted, I'm sorry." I brought my knees to my chest. "We don't have to go downstairs."

"We should. I want to."

"No, you don't."

"Yes, I do."

She was being polite.

Mom called my name up the stairs. Christ Almighty. How many guests were going to ask for a compensatory discount after *this*? When she called for me a second time, my name cut off, like someone was down there with her, reprimanding her. *Jen.*

Charlotte grabbed the sweater from the rug. She chuckled. "Come on, let's go downstairs."

As we reached the base of the stairs, Jen was coming from the kitchen in her pajamas. She slowed by the grandfather clock, her tired expression lifting in surprise when she saw that I wasn't alone. "Hello . . . ?"

Charlotte extended her hand over the banister like she was Jackie Kennedy. "I'm Charlotte."

"Jen." As she shook Charlotte's hand, Jen looked pointedly at me. "Carrie's home earlier than usual. I think she had a bad date."

I arched a brow. "Yeah, you *think*?"

She gestured to the common room. "She's in there burning her wedding dress."

Huh? "She can't be. She gave her wedding dress to Goodwill before we even moved here."

"Well, she's burning her wedding *something*."

Just as I was following Charlotte into the common room, Jen gripped my elbow. "Carrie wouldn't let you have a boy in your room, would she?"

I stiffened under her glare.

"Bringing a girl home? Going behind Carrie's back? It's blatantly insolent, Taylor. And you're a better kid than that. So . . . I think we're going to have to have a talk, you and I."

A talk? I pulled from her touch.

With the common room lights out, the amber glow of the fire lit Mom's face where she stood, arm perched on the mantelpiece like a Victorian gentleman contemplating the effects of industrialization. She'd changed into her pajamas, and with her knee-high bed socks eating her pant legs, she looked ready to leave on an Antarctic mission at Bear Grylls's first call. In her hand? She twirled a white lace garter belt too close to the fire, aggravating the flames.

Oh fuck.

I peered around Mom. Over the end of a log, her bridal slip was shriveling. I squinted in the semidarkness. *Is that an underwire bra melting on coals?*

Charlotte moved closer to me. "Um . . . are those your mom's panties on the fire poker?"

I groaned internally.

With a careless toss, into the fire went the bridal garter belt, then the white panties.

Stepping back, Mom noticed the three of us and brushed against the Christmas tree. "Oh, girls!" My "Baby's First

Christmas" ornament jingled. Mom reached across the mantel-piece for the bottle of red and fixed her eyes on Charlotte. "Do you drink red wine, honey?"

I didn't mention the consummatory underwear. The safest thing to do was let the woman burn her bra without asking questions—the last thing I needed was for her to start up about Dad giving her crabs.

Jen hovered in the doorway as Mom poured red wine into champagne flutes—one for me, one for Charlotte. With the stems locked between her fingers, the flutes wobbled, threatened to tumble wine all over the good rug. God, she was more hammered than I thought. "Mom, let me help you."

"I'm fine, Taylor." She handed one to me, then Charlotte. "Here you go, Chelsea."

"*Charlotte*, Mom. Her name is Charlotte."

She pressed two fingers to her lips. "I'm so sorry. *Charlotte.*"

I led Charlotte to the couch. There was only a small gap between us, but after what had just happened upstairs, it felt wider than the Serengeti. My head spun. Ten minutes earlier, she'd been on top of me, telling me that she wanted to go all the way, and now we were sipping sour wine in the common room watching Mom scroll through Spotify as she stood before the fireplace.

The opening notes of "You Don't Own Me" slipped through the speakers. Mom spun to face us so quickly that the flames leapt. As she planted both hands behind her on the mantelpiece and popped a hip from left to right like she was Roxie fucking Hart, her pajama Henley rode up, exposing her C-section scar. I looked to Jen. Standing against the doorjamb with a cup of tea, she had the nerve to be *amused*.

I looked back at the hot mess. *And I thought getting inked was painful.* What was this, an audition to find the fourth member of the First Wives Club? *Christ.* She lifted her arms above her head, shimmied so low that I worried she'd topple over and whack a veneer out on the corner of the coffee table.

A guest halted beside Jen in the doorway with a cup of coffee. I'm pretty sure he was coming in to watch TV on the big screen, but he took one look at Mom dancing before the fire, clearly decided this was some kind of nasty, feminist coven shit, turned away, and went straight upstairs.

Mom extended a hand to Jen, grabbing at the air with her fingers. "Dance with me?"

Jen shook her head.

Mom pouted.

Jen sipped at her tea. "One of the girls will dance with you."

Mom's gaze stuck on Charlotte. Panic fanned in my chest. "No," I said firmly. "Charlotte's not dancing with you." My eyes flashed to Jen. *Help!*

A tickled smile playing on her lips, Jen put her tea on the coffee table and took Mom in her arms.

It was smooth, the way they sort of fell into each other, even with Jen's belly between them. Jen was soft with Mom. Patient. She always had been. Mom calmed with her in a way that she never did with anyone else. Maybe it was because Jen was the only person Mom had ever really asked for help.

The song kicked in again, on repeat. I watched Charlotte out of the corner of my eye. She seemed to be enraptured, in awe. I brought the flute to my lips and took a swig so long, my eyes watered. Was this my punishment for sneaking Charlotte into the inn? For not finding the courage to come out even though I had T minus eight days until Christmas? I dropped my mouth to Charlotte's ear. "I am *so* sorry."

"Are you kidding?" She sipped her red wine. "This is more captivating than the time my aunt Gloria took me to New York to see Cate Blanchett in *A Streetcar Named Desire.*"

I looked to Mom's garter belt at the edge of the fire, all but melted. I thought of Charlotte's dress hanging up on my closet door, about how I'd unbuttoned her.

"Hey," I whispered.

Charlotte looked up at me. Her lips were stained red from the wine. "Yeah?"

"You know how earlier you said . . ."

"Yeah . . ."

"I don't think I can do it when my mom's in the house."

Her gaze softened. "I think maybe that's best." She moved closer. "I don't have to stay over," she whispered. "I can go."

"I don't want you to go."

Jen looked at me, then at the door, inclining her head as though she were saying *Go on.* I reached for the bottle of wine, but her eyes flashed. We both put our glasses down. *Worth a try.*

Upstairs, we climbed into my bed together. We lay there talking, not about anything important, not like we had in front of the fire. Mostly we talked about school, about the drama festival at the end of January. It was *almost* like sleeping beside Brooke, but at the same time, it was different, because lying beside Charlotte, I had a little flame burning in my chest that set me on edge.

We didn't kiss each other, or touch each other. We didn't even hold hands. I think we were both worried that if we started something, we wouldn't be able to stop.

Six thirty the next morning, the inn was still sleeping when I walked Charlotte downstairs, her Snow Ball dress and corset over my shoulder. She couldn't stay for breakfast—she had to go home and put her Abigail costume on before she left for work at eight.

Quietly, I unlocked the front door. It was cold out, but it wasn't snowing. I followed her to the steps of the front porch and kissed her on the cheek.

Flicking both her braids over her shoulders, she beamed. God, she looked so cute in my sweatpants, my sweater, her coat, a pair of old snow boots I'd outgrown in middle school.

"So . . ." she said. "Last night was fun." She tilted her head. "Why are you smiling like that?"

"Because 'last night was fun' kind of sounds like something Sorority Girl Number Two would say in an Owen Wilson movie."

Rolling her eyes, she took her dress and corset from my arms. "Well, it *was* fun. I mean, your mom, especially—"

"I promise my mom isn't an alcoholic."

"I didn't think she was."

I pulled my coat tighter around me. "She's really been trying to keep the bra burning to a minimum, too. BBA just gave her her first chip."

Her brow furrowed. "BBA?"

"Bra Burners Anonymous. Twelve-step program."

Grinning, she hitched her Snow Ball dress over her arm, but as her gaze lowered, she turned a little shy. A little melancholy. "Do you think this is pointless?" she said softly. As she stared up

219

at me, her lips twisted. "We only have until graduation, and then the summer. After summer, I'm going to Tisch. You're going to Emerson. There'll be a whole state between us." Her gaze dropped again.

There was a tingle in my chest as the word ripped from the back of my throat. "No."

She looked up sharply.

Right there on the porch, I reached for her hand. "I think my *whole life* has been building up to this December."

Her eyes sparkled. She squeezed my hand. Leaning forward, she pressed her lips to my cheek. "Well then," she said, her breath warm against the shell of my ear, "we better make sure January is one for the books."

TWENTY

Later that Saturday, Trent Parker's text did not catch me in a good mood.

Sweetheart, Brittney is feeling blue because you haven't acknowledged our happy news. I understand that it came as a shock to you last month at the Marble Room, but Brittney's low mood isn't good for your little sister's health. I have deposited $150 into your savings account—please buy Brittney a Christmas gift that will make her feel appreciated. You're a clever girl—I know you'll think outside the box and come up with something that's personal, just for Brittney, this Christmas. God bless you, Taylor.

Oh boy, did I make fulfilling Daddy Warbucks's Christmas wish a priority. First thing after work, I took the bus to Northshore Mall.

No matter how many times I told the Macy's sales assistant that I was fine—I was just buying perfume, I didn't need help—she refused to leave me the fuck alone, holding the fragrance test strips too close to my nostrils, wanting me to sniff every scent under the sun until I passed out right there between the MAC and Clinique counters.

I picked a bottle of Dior for Charlotte and a bottle of Chanel for Mom. After the bra-burning debacle, I was still avoiding Mom, but I knew that would pass by Christmas Day. Jen, on the other hand? I planned to avoid her until the day she packed her bags and vanished back to New York. I wanted to have that "talk" of hers just about as much as I wanted to give myself a Brazilian sugaring.

"You're making your decisions mighty fast," the saleswoman said, waving the coffee beans under my nose like she was casting a spell.

"I guess I know my mom and my friend pretty well."

"You wouldn't believe how many men come in here and haven't the first clue about their wife's taste. Fruity? Floral? Woody? Not a clue. I may be sixty-eight, but between you and me, sometimes I wish I were a lesbian."

Lord, give me strength.

I'd inhaled so much that I was light-headed by the time she took the bottles to the counter and told me to give her five minutes while she gift wrapped them. I lifted the bulky drugstore bag onto the counter. "Ma'am, I know I didn't buy these here, but could I pay extra if you'd gift wrap these, too?"

As she looked inside the bag at Brittney's gift, her brow furrowed. "You want to gift wrap . . . these? *All* of them?"

"Absolutely." I couldn't wait to stop by the post office next.

While I waited, I went into the lotion aisle, rubbed sample hand creams into my dry nail beds. I peered over the rack. The sales assistant was mumbling to herself as she unrolled ribbon. I reached into the pocket of my coat and pulled out *that other thing* I'd bought in the drugstore. The box of dental dams was thin—it had been the smallest on the shelf. In the drugstore, I'd been so nervous that I'd barely had a chance to read it over. I flushed. *God damn it.* They were mixed-flavor dams. There were four inside—Blueberry Blast, Chocolate Temptation, Mint Tingle, and Strawberry Crush. I bit down on the insides of my cheeks. Could I ever actually use them? What if Charlotte got the wrong impression? What if she thought I'd picked these out especially for us because I knew she liked blueberry pancakes?

At home, I hid the perfume bottles under my bed. I pulled the box from my pocket, went over to the *30 Rock* DVDs on my bookshelf, and opened the first season. I stuffed the colored foils inside, all four of them. Better to be safe than sorry, I thought. And until the moment came when I had to *actually* be safe, Liz Lemon would keep my great gay secret.

I was remaking the bed in the Abigail Williams suite when Mom stopped in the doorway. "I just found the strangest thing." She waved a receipt. "It was on the stairs, must have fallen out of somebody's coat pocket. . . ."

Folding a fitted sheet around the corner of the mattress, I swatted sweat from my upper lip. "Why's it weird?"

"You'll never believe it."

"Try me, Carrie Parker."

She squinted down at the receipt. "Somebody's gone and bought one hundred and fifty dollars' worth of extra-long maternity pads—and they weren't even on sale."

I was changing into my pajamas, ready to head downstairs and watch the *SNL* midseason finale with or without Mom when there was a knock at my bedroom door. It wasn't Mom, and it wasn't Jen.

"Hey, stud." Looking past me to my bed, Brooke lifted her eyebrows. "So *this* is where the magic happened last night."

I rolled my eyes. "I already told you on Messenger that nothing happened."

"Sure."

I scoffed, held the door open for her, but she just stood there in the doorway, unmoving. *Staring.*

"There anything you want to tell me, Tay?"

"I told you . . . the big thing."

"Hmm . . ."

". . . What?"

She poked her tongue into her cheek. *"Live from New York . . . it's Saturday Niiiiight!"*

Her meaning crept across the landing and my skin barbed, bristled, *crawled.* I stiffened. On the wall above the staircase, the drawing of Giles Corey fogged in its frame. *More weight. More weight. More weight more weight more—*

"Congratulations, Anonymous, Massachusetts. I've known since last night."

She'd found out at the Snow Ball? *How?* I was going to retch. "Ms. Glazer told you?"

"Not *exactly.* I found an email from NBC in her iCloud when I was looking for my grade. Your sketch was attached to the email. I read it. Taylor, Taylor . . . my Taylor. You need to *own* it." She pulled me into a hug, hard. "Oh my god." She laughed. "You're shaking."

My eyes burned.

"You have no idea how hard it was keeping a lid on this when I dropped you and Charlotte off."

Horror hit me. What if Brooke tried to sway what happened from here on out? "This has to stay between us. Charlotte can't know."

"Why not?"

Because she's on her way to Tisch. I clutched at her back. "Because nobody can know. When I lose."

"But what if you *win*, Tay?"

I couldn't cry. I wanted to. But I couldn't. *Brooke knows.*

She squeezed my waist. "Get your coat."

"Why?"

"Because we have unfinished business."

This time, when Ursula said she was ready for me, I told Brooke that I wanted to go in by myself. As much as I didn't want to be alone with Ursula after she'd caught me looking for the lost city of Atlantis in the depths of her cleavage, Brooke had asked way too many questions about *SNL* on the walk across town.

As I lay back in the chair and Ursula worked the comedy mask transfer onto my skin for the second time, she didn't say anything about my breakdown. In fact, she didn't say much at all. All she said was that the tragedy mask was healing really well, that I was taking good care of it. *That's me*, I wanted to say, coddling my very own tragedy like a goddamn pro.

"So why the comedy faces?" she said.

"I don't know." I think maybe I was getting it because part of me felt like inking comedy into my skin gave me a reason to have to go after it. If it was a visible itch, nobody could blame me for scratching at it until it bled.

Across the shop, behind a curtain, someone else was getting inked. There was the faint slur of male voices, the unrelenting whir of a tattoo gun. As Ursula pulled the transfer paper from my skin, I wondered if she could feel the thump of my heartbeat against her fingertips. My gaze darted down. Ursula's lashes were the longest I'd ever seen, her eyes as moss green as the Common in August. I looked up at the ceiling. "How was your Thanksgiving?"

"Quiet."

"Oh. Sorry." *Well, fuck you too, then.*

"No, you can talk. I meant my Thanksgiving—my Thanksgiving was quiet."

"Oh. Cool."

She swiveled on the salon stool and rolled toward the machine behind me. I listened as she fiddled with something.

I was clammy beneath the armpits. The fine hairs stood tall on my exposed belly. "I remember you from when I was a kid. You dated the woman who works at the Peabody."

She was silent for so long, I wondered if she'd heard me. She rolled back to me with a tub of ointment in her gloved hand. "We didn't exactly date. She's shacked up with that woman who owns the pink inn now. I've seen them around town together. Haven't for a while, though."

The tips of her fingers worked slow circles between my ribs as she rubbed the ointment over the transfer. My stomach hardened. First Charlotte had assumed, now Ursula . . . "People really think they're a couple?"

"I'm surprised they're a thing," she said, absent, as though she were talking more to herself than gossiping to me. She rolled halfway across the room and placed the ointment tub on the bench, then pushed herself back to the tattoo machine. "I think they'd been together, or tried to, sometime around when I knew Jen. But the woman at the inn said it wasn't working because she wasn't really into women."

My eyes prickled. *Been together?*

"Anyway, I do my best to avoid Jen. We didn't exactly end things on a pleasant note. I made a joke. Some joke about lesbians falling for women who just wanted to dip their feet in the lesbian pond, or spaghetti being straight until it was wet, or something, I don't know. I used to say a lot of crap about switching teams. But Jen didn't think it was funny. She told me she was bi and she couldn't be around someone who was biphobic. Boy, did I learn my lesson that night." She turned the machine on. As she leaned over my torso with the tattoo gun, the shrill buzz scorched the air from my lungs. "Are you ready to finish what you started?"

I drew a deep breath and closed my eyes. "I'm ready."

For the first time in forever, I think I was telling the truth.

TWENTY-ONE

Charlotte chose for our Great Salem Trespass of 2016 to take place on a storming school night—approximately forty hours before I was going to come out to Mom at Christmas Eve lunch. Until that night, I'd never been inside the Jonathan Corwin House—the Witch House. Home to one of the witch trial judges, the gray First Period colonial had always sat conserved at the junction of Essex and North.

Rain trickled down as Charlotte unlocked the back door of the Witch House. Somebody who worked with her at the Museum of Witchcraft had managed to get her access to the keys.

"You're pretty badass," I whispered in her ear, and she grinned shyly as she pressed the door open for us to step inside.

We didn't dare turn on our phone flashlights. From the outside, we could see that the casement windows were ready to betray us if we pushed our luck too far.

The storm had yet to truly set in, but our shoes were covered in snow from the walk across the grass to the back door, so we took them off in the gift shop and padded farther into the house in our socks. Even with the rain hammering down upon the gambrel roof, we could hear the ancient floorboards creak as we moved through to the first room.

My eyes adjusted to the darkness. The rain clouds had spread a gray-green glow across the moon. The light of night leaked through the casement windows, outlining each decorative piece, the hard furniture corners, the worn tapestry mounted on the wall. We were standing in some kind of living room with a bed in the middle, each piece of furniture sectioned by braided hemp ropes.

Charlotte photographed the end of the bed frame, the corner of the kitchen table, the fireplace. I got sweaty-nervous when she went over to the window and shot the cloudy, diamond-shaped panels of glass. By the fireplace, I glanced toward the gift shop. What if somebody driving past saw the flash? I sent a prayer up to Sappho that we would get away with what we were doing. Sappho listened—minutes later, the heavens opened up and a fierce bolt of lightning streaked across the sky in unison with the flash of Charlotte's camera.

There was another room downstairs, to the left of the fireplace. I peeked my head inside. "Charlotte? The kitchen is over here."

A roll of thunder broke sharply in a loud crackle.

"I just need another moment in here," she murmured.

I took a seat at Judge Corwin's kitchen table. As I listened to the living room floorboards groan between the crashes of thunder, I thought about how safe I felt in the darkness knowing that Charlotte was a room away. Since our sleepover, I was beginning to feel as though I could tell her anything. Except that I wasn't talking to Mom. And Jen. And that I'd given Stand-Up a miss on Monday night to make out with Charlotte in the back row of Cinema Salem and I felt guilty about it. But I could tell her *almost* anything else.

A draft sailed through the kitchen fireplace. I pulled my legs up onto the chair and rubbed at my frozen toes. Knowing what I knew about Mom and Jen hadn't softened the thing inside me that ached every time I thought about coming out to Mom. It had only pried apart the break between us. If what Ursula said was true, Mom had tried with Jen—and it hadn't worked out. Why hadn't it worked out? Because Mom was straight, just as I'd always assumed? Or was there more to it? As reluctant as I was to admit it, Mom and Jen *did* have chemistry. In theory, they were compatible in almost every way. Had they been close to something real and requited and Mom's shame had convinced her to call it quits? That was the thought that terrified me most—if Mom felt that way about *herself*, what did that mean for how she'd feel about me?

Charlotte stopped in the doorway. She lifted her camera and shot a picture of me at the table in my parka and wool hat, like she was Diane Arbus and I was her circus freak. *Girl in Witch House Holding Her Heart in Her Hands* . . . I blinked against the bright light. She smiled down at the picture of me on the little screen of her Canon. "You look so much older without all your hair."

Our eyes locked. Held.

I took her gift from my coat pocket and placed it on the table. "Merry Christmas."

Lowering her camera, she stared at the little wrapped box. "Taylor . . . I haven't brought your present tonight."

"I don't care. Open it."

She pulled out the chair next to mine and carefully unwrapped the glittery icicle-print paper.

I got hot.

She turned the box over. "Oh my god. You got me Dior perfume?"

"Do you like it? If you don't, you can exchange it."

"Of course I like it. . . . It's just . . . Well, it's a lot."

"Come on, open it. You're making me nervous just looking at it."

She took the bottle out, sprayed it on her wrists, dabbed it below the point of her jaw.

I swallowed.

She brought her wrist to her nose and closed her eyes.

Her pretty sigh left me light-headed. "Can I tell you something? Something about the way I felt a long time ago?"

Her eyes locked on mine.

The house creaked. "I used to come to your museum. To watch you."

She smiled. "I know. I saw you."

"But . . . but you don't know that I came more than once."

She took my hand in hers. "Yes. I do."

The hairs stood on the back of my neck.

Her expression was gentle. "Is that what you wanted to tell me?"

My heart pounded a hard, steady beat. "The thing is . . . I mean, what I wanted to tell you is that . . . You know at the end of each show, how you ask for audience questions?"

She wet her lips. "Yes?"

My chest ached. "I always wished I were brave enough to just stand up. Stand up in front of all those people and tell you that I thought you were just . . . *the best*." The smell of her new perfume was driving me crazy—I could barely get words to

231

form. "I know it isn't a question, but . . . I just . . . I wanted *so badly* for you to see me."

For a long moment, we were both quiet. Lip between her teeth, she leaned closer in her seat. "Taylor . . . I saw you."

My pulse slowed.

Gently, she placed the lid on the bottle and slid it and the gift wrap into her cross-body bag. "I'm finished down here," she whispered. "Let's go upstairs."

A spell of lightning lit the staircase. It was narrow and steep, and there wasn't any kind of railing to grip. Just a few steps up, Charlotte turned and took my hand in hers. It was hard to see where I was stepping in the dark until we reached the top.

Upstairs was much brighter, and it smelled different from the bottom floor. The house had been closed for the Christmas holiday, and upstairs reeked of that old museum smell. It had a different vibe, too, like those top rooms had been abandoned for hundreds of years and we were the first people to permeate that space since Corwin himself. There was a sense that we weren't alone up there, like the Ghosts of Judges Past were standing in the corners with their arms crossed, anticipating our every move. And trust me, if Judge Corwin's ghost *did* witness what Charlotte and I did next, he wouldn't have approved.

Beside the baby's crib in the corner of the room was a canopy bed. Plain white curtains rimmed the ceiling of the bed, hung low where they gathered around each of the four posts. Like every-thing else, the canopy bed was sectioned off—until Charlotte lifted the hook of the rope and carefully latched it around the pole. The clink of the latch echoed throughout the room.

Just as Charlotte had lowered the Canon into Tituba's

cauldron in my museum, into the padded crib went the camera, her bag. With her back to me, she undid the belt to her black coat and let it drop on the floor next to the spinning wheel. My heart spun.

The mattress was so ancient that it seemed to sink under Charlotte's weight. She sat on the edge, giving me *that* look.

My face grew hot. I didn't know if it was just a replica bed, or if it actually *had* been Judge Corwin's bed, but I couldn't bring myself to care. As the thunder growled furiously, I moved to her.

As I unbuttoned her soft flannel shirt, she pulled off my parka, my wool hat, my scarf. I pressed on her bare shoulders until she lay down on the scratchy blanket. She brought my hands to the front of her jeans and excitement burned in my chest. "Y-you really want me to take them off?" I whispered.

"I *really* want you to take them off."

Her silky hair was damp when I raked my fingers through it and kissed her, soft and deep. As her fingernails trickled up my rib cage, her ragged breathing came hot against my cheek. "Take your clothes off too?"

I shucked my clothes so fast that I didn't allow myself time to be embarrassed that I was naked with her—we were way too into the sensation of skin against skin to stop and take each other in. The frame screeched angrily beneath our weight. "Wait," she whispered. "We won't break the bed, right?" She looked at me like I held all the answers, like I was some lesbian carpenter cliché who would know.

"I don't think so. I mean, probably not, right?"

As I shifted to toe my underwear off, the bed moaned again. She giggled.

My leg slipped between hers like we were meant to *fit*, and as we kissed, I held her against me, moved slowly as she clutched at my back. Goose bumps erupted on my skin as I gripped her tiny waist, felt the point of her rib cage against the pad of my thumb. "Charlotte?"

"Yeah?"

"Am I too heavy?"

"What? No. You're fine." She drew me closer. "You're *great.*"

"Sorry if my legs are hairy. I haven't shaved them since the Snow Ball."

Pressing herself harder against me, she gasped. "Your legs aren't hairy."

"You can probably tell that they are."

"Taylor." Her shoulders arched off the mattress. "I'm not really thinking about whether or not your legs are shaved right now."

"Right. Me neither. Wh-what *are* you thinking about?"

"*You.*" As her fingers traced down over my shoulder to cup me in her palm, her gaze tried to catch mine. "I'm wondering if this feels as good for you as it does for me."

I dropped my eyes to the hollow of her throat. It did feel good—it felt *too* good. The voice in the back of my head slurred that, for as right as Charlotte's body felt against mine in *this* moment, that could change the second it was over.

"Taylor?" Her grip relaxed around my thigh. "Are you okay?" We stilled.

My breath hitched. It felt shameful this way—me above her. "I think we should swap."

"Stop?" she said breathily. "You want to stop?"

"No—*swap*. Maybe you should be on top. I—I think you should."

As her thumb swept over my nipple, my hips jolted against hers. "Why?" she whispered.

My throat grew thick. "I . . ." *Why?* "I don't know." As thunder crashed, I lowered my forehead to her chest and drew a deep breath. "I'm sorry. I don't know what's wrong." I pressed a kiss to the swell of her breast. "I can't think clearly—I'm really turned on right now."

Her fingers traced up and down my back, like she was trying to soothe the explosion happening inside me. "I know," she whispered. "I can feel it."

The need to be honest with her pulled like a slingshot in my chest. I lifted my head to look at her. "Promise you won't make us stop just because of what I'm about to say?"

She was quiet. "I can't promise that," she said. "But I want you to tell me anyway."

My skin tingled as the truth bubbled from my lips: "I'm scared that once we do this—once it's over—I'm going to feel dirty or guilty or ashamed."

She pressed a hand to my cheek. "You feel ashamed?" she asked sadly.

"Not right *now*. And it's not about you, I promise. It's not about *us*. It's just . . . sometimes I feel ashamed after I . . . after . . ."

"After you come?"

Burying my face in her neck, I groaned in embarrassment.

"Taylor?"

I shivered as she skimmed her fingers across my lower back. "Mmm?"

"Are you sure you don't feel ashamed right now? About what we're doing?"

Drawing back, I locked eyes with her. "I don't," I said truth-fully. "I really don't. I *want* this. I mean, if you still do."

She lifted my hand to her lips and kissed my fingers. Slowly, her fingers inched mine between her legs. "I still do," she whispered. "How about I go first? Take one for the team?"

A laugh bubbled from my lips.

She grinned, but as she settled my fingers where she needed them, her eyes closed. She sighed.

A sharp ache hit between my thighs. "Are you sure?"

"Yes," she said, husky and perfect, her knees parting ever so slightly. "Yes. You can."

I did. I did. *I did.* Nobody ever talks about what it's like to feel another girl lose control like that, how they whimper and gasp and make you feel powerful, *wanted.* I touched her for so long that I worried that I was doing it completely wrong, but just when I was on the verge of asking her what she needed, her whole body went still beneath me and her mouth fell open and it happened.

I bent down and pressed my lips to the side of her head, left them there against her clammy temple for a moment. She smelled like the perfume I'd given her. Lifting a hand, she held it over her eyes. "Oh my god." Her lips trembled with a smile.

I wanted to tell her she was beautiful, that watching her had sewn up parts of me that I hadn't known were starting to tear at the seams, but I felt like I was going to cry from the joy and goodness and purity of it all, so I just kept my mouth shut and held myself above her.

"I want to touch you," she murmured.

Yes, god, yes.

"Do you want that?" she asked.

A hot shudder passed through me. "Yes."

As she looked down at her own hand, amazed at how it disappeared between my legs, her long black hair fell like a curtain around her face. Her eyes had turned dark. Sapphire. I heard myself say her name. She lifted her head from the pillow and pressed her lips to mine. "I'll take care of you," she murmured against my jaw. "I'll be here."

It was too much, too intense. I buried my face in the crook of her neck, let my hips roll, let the exhilaration spike, and as Charlotte whispered to me, those little sparks of need began to charge up and down the back of my thighs like bolts of electricity. The feeling washed over me, hammered down on me. I closed my eyes and let it happen, let the familiar white heat take me with her breath warm on my chin, and I *spiraled*.

She ran a hand through my hair. "Are you all right?" she whispered. "With what we just did?"

My body hummed, my heartbeat firing bare and full against hers. "I am so totally *okay*."

We held each other on top of that musty bed in the dark, listening to the storm calm and anger, anger and calm. My hand drew circles between her shoulders. My goose bumps were long gone, and Charlotte was warm and sweaty in my arms. As she traced patterns across my sternum, I thought about how the house had seemed creepy when I was standing around watching her take photos, but now it felt like a safe haven that was ours.

"The rain's getting heavier," she whispered. "Should we go?"

I pressed my face into her neck. "No." I wasn't sated. I wanted to do it again. I was burning to do even more, especially to go down on her. But Charlotte's chest was still heaving and she looked so relaxed, so content, that I didn't want to ask for more. I was dying to tell her that I more than just *liked* her, but I'd read enough fan fiction to know that we weren't there yet.

The storm grew so loud that I could barely hear a thing. With her hands in my hair, I was dazed. "I have this dream in my head. Of us."

She pressed her lips to my cheek. "Tell me."

"It's a couple of years from now and it's close to midnight and I'm waiting for you outside a Broadway stage door. It's winter, wicked cold. You're in a play. Something smart. Ibsen or Chekhov."

". . . Oh?"

"You're still young, still at Tisch, so you only play a side character. But it's a big deal. Obviously. It's *Broadway*."

"Those are great expectations for me to live up to."

"Someone at the stage door asks me if I'm waiting for an autograph. And I gesture to the coffee tray in my hands and I say that I'm waiting for someone in the cast." Her nails slipped across my scalp and I didn't fight the shiver. "I'm waiting for my fiancée."

Her fingers stilled. "Your fiancée?"

My grin splintered, sharp.

Her voice was gravelly. "And what do you do?"

"Well, I wait. For you. And then we take the subway home to our grungy little apartment in our grungy little neighborhood—"

"No, what do you *do*? What do you study? Or do for work? How do you see yourself spending your days?"

What I *saw* was myself riding the NBC elevator twice a day. "I . . . I wish I knew."

She rolled away from me and swung her legs over the side of the bed.

I pushed up onto my elbow. "Charlotte?"

"You can't just follow me to New York for . . . I can't be the only thing you want."

"But you are."

As she turned to look at me, her eyes dropped to my chest, and suddenly she was a picture of pure panic.

"No. I mean, you aren't. I mean—" Hurt blistered in my lungs. Didn't she think it was romantic? Didn't she want my vision of us?

"Where's my coat?" she muttered, desperate. "I'm cold and I want my coat."

I jumped off the edge of the bed and pulled her coat from the feet of the spinning wheel. *What have you done?*

Stock-still on the lip of the bed and shrouded in her heavy coat, her dark hair was wild and messy. "You thought about us being engaged while I'm at Tisch. I'm only there four years. You think we'll do something that huge before we're twenty-one? Taylor, I don't know how to boil pasta without it sticking to the bottom. I can't even parallel park. I can't be someone's *wife*."

"It's okay, pasta gives me heartburn. Mom thinks I *could* have celiac, so probably best to avoid it. And as for parallel parking, we'll be taking the subway—MetroCards mean neither of us will *ever* have to parallel park."

She blinked rapidly.

"I'm joking, Charlotte—"

"I won't give up my dreams." She was hoarse, like her vocal cords had been sandpapered. "I won't be distracted by someone needing me to hold them up."

Standing, she pulled from my touch at her hip, and an ache throbbed at the back of my throat. "I don't need you to hold me up. There are other things I imagine. Things I'm leaving out—"

"I think I'm having a panic attack." Clutching her coat closed with one hand, she raked her fingers through her hair.

Worry set me stiff.

"I'm naked and I'm having a panic attack." She grabbed her jeans and hauled them on.

"Charlotte." The way she fumbled with the buttons of her shirt—desperate, *disturbed*—made me feel like there was a pendulum in my chest, solid and swaying and clocking every breath between us: *shame, mistake, shame, mistake.* "*Please,* Charlotte."

She yanked the belt of her coat tight. "I have to go."

I couldn't get the ankle of my skinny jeans over my heel fast enough—she was already halfway down the stairs, her bra forgotten beside my parka on the bed. I snatched up my parka, my hat, my scarf, her bra, then plucked the Canon and her bag from the crib and, tugging on my sweater, chased after her down the stairs.

In the gift shop, I held on to her elbow as she slipped her boots back on. Her whole body was vibrating, shaking like we'd just murdered somebody and buried the body together. "Let me walk you home," I begged.

She slipped her camera over her neck and then pushed it down her coat, where it would be safe from the rain.

"Please, Charlotte, let me walk you home. You're not okay."

"No, Taylor," she said firmly, and it sounded like she was mad at me, but then she reached up on her tiptoes and pressed her lips chastely to the corner of my mouth. She slipped her hand into the pocket of my parka and retrieved her bra. She pushed it into the pocket of her own coat until the pale blue straps were out of sight. "You can't follow me to New York. You just can't."

What I *could* do was follow her home. She didn't know. I lingered almost a block behind, but close enough to be sure she was safe, close enough to know she made it inside and out of the rainstorm.

Jen was in the kitchen—alone.

"Where's Mom?"

Her eyes shot up from her laptop. She hadn't heard me come in. "She's working until close—" She gasped. "Why the hell are you *completely saturated?*" Her brow furrowed. "I thought you were upstairs this entire time."

Shivering, I pulled out a chair and fell into it. "I've done something really bad."

She lowered the lid of her laptop. "What's happened?"

I told her everything that had happened since I'd left home that night at nine—sneaking into the Witch House, giving Charlotte her gift. Taking the camera up to the second floor. What we'd done up there. How I'd overwhelmed Charlotte by saying what I'd said. "I know it seemed like what I was saying was so much, but I couldn't tell her the rest of it."

"The rest of it?"

My teeth chattered.

She sat forward.

"I've entered a contest, Jen."

"A contest?"

". . . I'm a finalist in a contest to win an internship. At *SNL*." My shrinking stomach twisted itself into a rolling hitch.

"At *SN*— Fuck, Taylor."

"It's a diversity internship. I told them I'm gay. The winner is announced soon. I have to come out by Christmas. And I'm going to—on *my* terms."

Sitting back in her chair, she pulled her hands over her face. *"Taylor,"* she groaned. "Why would you do that? Why would you enter something like that when you aren't even comfortable enough to come out?"

I didn't have an answer for her.

"That's so . . ." She waved her hands around. "Why would you put that kind of pressure on yourself?"

I stood. The feet of my chair screeched across the floor-boards. "I'm sorry."

Her eyes widened. "Hey, hey, don't cry, it's going to be okay. You know that, right? I'm going to be here the whole time. I'm here for you."

But you aren't. I shivered in my soaking wet parka, my drenched wool hat. "I . . . Jen, I *miss* you so much."

"You *miss* me? Taylor," she choked, "I'm *right here.*"

"Not like you used to be."

"I love you like you're my kid."

"But I'm not your kid. Even if I could've been."

". . . Could have?"

I tried to look anywhere but at her hand on her belly. *I always feel safest when you're here.* "You . . . you would've been the best decision my mom ever made."

Her face fell. "What are you talking about?"

She was frightened. I'd frightened her. Which meant it was true. Something had happened between them.

"Taylor . . ."

I raced up the stairs to my room, furious at myself for so many things—for letting myself want Charlotte so desperately, for entering the contest, for confiding in Jen when I knew I'd only disappoint her.

There was an elderly woman on the landing outside my room. I hadn't met her, but I'd heard her complaining to Mom about our lactose-free cream cheese at breakfast that morning. She was rummaging through the owner's closet, clearly labeled off limits, but I didn't give a fuck that Mom must have left it unlocked again. Old Mother Hubbard could pinch every plastic underlay in there, take all of our fitted sheets back to Wyoming or Wisconsin or wherever the hell she was from. I had bigger fish to fry.

"You're the daughter?" Old Mother Hubbard snapped. "Reach me down another pillow. The one in my room isn't good enough when I'm paying two hundred and thirty dollars a night!"

I reached for the bottom pillow on the top shelf. Her stare bore into the side of my face. As I handed her the pillow, she could see that my eyes were swimming with tears—but she didn't care. She fluffed the pillow. "Still too flat. Find me another."

I could barely see through the tears. "One moment," I choked. I went into my room and pulled my pillow from its yellow slip. I went back out and gave it to her.

She appraised it. "Is it clean?"

Taking a pillow slip from the closet, I shoved the pillow inside. "Practically brand-new."

I didn't stick around to hear any more—the last straw was me shoving her against the wall and suffocating her with the pillow.

Old Mother Hubbard was muttering about manners and millennials when I slammed my door and slid the latch across the runner.

I swiped *Oh, the Places You'll Go!* from my dresser and flipped it open:

Taylor Parker, funny girl extraordinaire,

Stay bold—in your impressions, in your laughter, and in your joy.

And for the love of god, never put out your own fire.

Amy Poehler once said that it takes years as a woman to unlearn what you've been taught to be sorry for. Tomorrow was December 23, the last day of school. Tomorrow I'd tell Charlotte all of it. And I'd try my very best to be anything but sorry.

TWENTY-TWO

At the sight of Brooke at Charlotte's locker, my stomach turned.

It was early, the hallway half empty. Over Charlotte's shoulder, Brooke's eyes landed on me. She stilled—like she'd been caught.

As Brooke whispered something and disappeared around the corner, Charlotte spun. A beat rippled up my throat. Why was she staring like that? Had Brooke told her about the internship?

I strode to her locker and turned myself toward her. "What did Brooke just tell you?"

"Nothing."

"It was obviously *something*."

"She was offering to drive to the drama festival together in January. Just the two of us. That's all."

"*What?* Why did she offer that?"

"Because I told her I was planning to get the train to Boston that day, but she said it would be way too cold by then, and with costumes and props, it'd be so much easier if we just drove in."

Easier? I blew air from my cheeks. I'd find out what *that* was about later. "You didn't tell Brooke about last night, did you?"

"O-on what planet, in what universe, would I ever, ever want to do *that*?" Her blue eyes were so wired, they looked ready to slip from the bone. "I already feel pathetic enough. I don't need Miss *Teen Dream House Rules* knowing I panicked."

Something cracked in my chest.

She tore her eyes from mine and began to hunt in her locker.

I leaned in close. "We need to talk about last night. I know I pressured you. But there's more to it. There's something big, something really big you need to know. When you hear what I'm about to tell you, everything I said last night will make total sense."

"Not now." Her voice shook. "I got splashed waiting for the bus, and I feel like I'm standing ankle-deep in a puddle."

"We can't talk about the fact that I'm the reason you had a panic attack last night because . . . your socks are wet?"

"People are *looking*, Taylor. They've been looking and talking ever since the Snow Ball. You should be careful being close to me if you're not ready for that."

At the locker opposite, Emmy whipped her eyes away. A lump crept into my throat. Kicking back a foot, I tugged off my rain boot. As I held it in midair, Charlotte drew back from her locker. "Taylor, what are—"

I dropped the boot. Emmy laughed. *Thump* went the other.

Charlotte clutched her history textbook to her chest. "What the hell are you doing?"

Dropping to my knees, I grasped her ankle and tugged at the zipper of her boot. "Taking away your troubles one sock at a time so that *maybe* you'll find the headspace to listen to me."

She sucked back a breath, hands pressed against the lockers for balance as I stripped off both her boots *and* her damp socks.

"Taylor, people are *watching*. Stop it. Stand up. Put your socks back on."

I gathered my sock to the toe the way Mom would with the pantyhose she'd make me wear to church when I was little. I looked up. Charlotte's eyes were alight. Quickly, she Cinderella'ed into my sock.

I balled up her wet socks and pegged them into her locker. As I pushed to my bare feet, Charlotte's stare was loud with guilt. *I'm ready, Charlotte. Are you?*

I swung my boots over my shoulder, and I shoved a hand through my hair. "Sorry," I whispered, "if I made you think I needed you to hold me up."

Brooke jabbed her fork at my peach pastry. "When are you going to tell Carrie?"

"I'm taking her to lunch tomorrow."

Charlotte was across the cafeteria with Rachel and Chloe. I stared, blatant, until that invisible string between us pulled tight and Charlotte's eyes snapped up from whatever Chloe was saying and locked on mine.

I hated the Corwin House with a nasty intensity, but in that moment, I would have given anything to be back there on that freezing second floor on that rickety bed with her before I'd ruined everything.

Passing with his tray, Jase Ryder gripped my shoulder. "We noticed you've been *swapping socks* with the girl Matt's obsessed with."

A few students at nearby tables turned. So did my stomach.

Brooke cursed beneath her breath. "Matt needs to let it go. Charlotte's *gay*, Jase."

"Hey," he said. "You shouldn't label people, Brooke."

"Label? She's said it herself. Also, her entire locker door is a collage of Sarah Paulson pictures."

Charlotte couldn't hear, but she *was* watching as Jase patted me on the back and took off to his own table.

The phantom touch of his hand pulsated between my shoulder blades. Brooke stared across the cafeteria at Charlotte. "What the hell was the sock thing about this morning? Everyone's talking about it."

"I . . ." *I was trying to prove to her that I didn't care what anyone thought. I was trying to make her see that I'm ready and I went about it all wrong.* "She wouldn't listen to me because her socks were wet."

"See?" She pointed her fork at me. "She's already high-maintenance—"

"Why did you offer to drive Charlotte to the festival?"

She paused. "Because I think you're under a whole lot of pressure right now and I just . . . I wanted to be nice to her. Forgive her. For you. To make things a little easier."

"That's . . . that's actually really nice. Thanks. If today was any other day, it'd totally make things easier. But last night I went and royally fucked up."

"Last night? What did you fuck up last night?"

"I gave Charlotte a panic attack after what we did and I think she's still riding the end of it."

". . . What did you do?"

Our eyes locked.

"*Oh.*" She looked across the room. "Is she okay?"

"*You* asking if Charlotte's okay? That's a first."

"Well, is she?"

"She *was*. Until I got all sappy and romantic and said too much." My eyes welled. "I don't know. Maybe she's starting to see that I'm not good enough for her. I just need to tell her about the contest. I think maybe if I could just rip off the Band-Aid . . ."

"Hey." She reached for my hand. "You're extraordinary. She'll see just how damn extraordinary you are soon enough. *Trust me.*"

Laughter crept behind the curtains of the theater room—a bunch of them had already arrived and were messing with the colored lights in the tech box. In the darkness of the wings, I stopped by the desk at the door and took my stapled script sheet from the pile. Days ago, Ms. Glazer had told us that our last lesson would be pretty chill, just duologue exercises from a few plays. There was a duologue sheet stuck to the window—we had to sign up for a partner. I squinted in the low red light. Charlotte hadn't signed in yet. But Brooke's name sat high in the *Character: Salem Witch* column, partnerless. I filled my name in beside hers, in the *Character: Trump* column.

Trump . . .

My heart went haywire. I think I went deaf for a moment. I looked down at the script in my hands.

Time of death: 2:14 p.m.

Ms. Glazer rounded the curtain. "You're early for once—"

"You've outed me."

"*Excuse me?*"

The tips of my ears burned. I couldn't speak. Humiliation was like a terrified cobra coiled around my throat. *Charlotte.* Charlotte was going to find out. And she wasn't going to hear it from me. I shoved the sheets at Ms. Glazer.

Her eyes scanned my sketch. She choked on a breath. "*No.* I had *nothing* to do with this."

"You're the only one who has a copy of it."

She looked past me to the desk, searching. "I printed duologues from *August: Osage County.*"

My mouth went dry. "This isn't *August: Osage County.*"

The houselights changed. She went blue. We both did.

I followed Ms. Glazer out of the wings.

Kinsey fours, fives, and sixes were scattered all across the stands. In fact, it was mostly the queers who'd made an effort to come into school that day—the homo-to-hetero theater ratio was 2:1. Oliver was queerer than Oscar Wilde, Nathan was out and proud, and it was the general consensus that Garrett was a little bit bi. In my heart, I knew I wasn't sick to my stomach because the header at the top of the page read "Taylor's Entry to the Diversity Competition"—because it confirmed I was queer. I'd danced with Charlotte. I'd stripped off my socks. I'd given myself *that* death by a thousand cuts. But being outed for being a comedian?

In the center of the stage, Ms. Glazer was *frantic.* "Where are my *August: Osage County* scripts?"

From high in the grandstand, Brooke stared, incredulous.

Green light bled over the theater and stuck. "I'm going to ask again," Ms. Glazer said. "*Where* are my *August: Osage County* scripts?"

I held myself up against the Boston Tea Party prop table. "I think you're missing the point, Ms. Glazer."

Brooke pushed to her feet. "The *point* is that my best friend is the most talented person in this room and everyone needs to know it."

Nausea climbed my throat.

Brooke grinned. "Tay, I'm so proud of you. You deserve this. You deserve a *moment*."

On her way in from the wings, Charlotte stopped behind me. "What's 'Witch Hunt: The Nightmare Before Christmas'? I thought we were performing *August: Osage County*? Ms. Glazer, I stopped by Walgreens for Tic Tacs to use as pills?"

I squeezed my eyes shut tight.

Emmy spoke up: "It says at the top of this script that Taylor wrote it. That she's nominated for an internship at *Saturday Night Live*."

Crossing my arms, I held my ribs so they wouldn't combust.

Charlotte's voice was soft as wax: "*Saturday Night Live?*"

I scrolled the script in my fist. I was going to be sick. *You're not good enough for her, and what's worse is that you're actually going to have to stand here and witness the exact moment she figures it out.*

Ms. Glazer didn't reach out to soothe me—I knew she wasn't allowed to touch me, and I was glad for it. Instead she lunged out to sweep the sketches from Emmy, from Garrett, from the others sprawled on the carpet. "*This* belongs to Taylor," she said, furious. "*This* is Taylor's intellectual property, and it was at Taylor's discretion if and when she shared her news."

Charlotte fell into her seat in the front row. Ms. Glazer was saying things, rambling, but I couldn't hear past the storm rolling through me as Charlotte's brow furrowed and she looked up from the sketch, up at me, right at me, right in the eye. She knew.

She knew now what I'd been talking about in the Witch House.

"Wait," Garrett said. "How's Taylor even diverse? She's white?"

I twisted, and I threw up in the prop teapot.

Silence swept the room like a ghost.

Eyes glassy, I lowered the lid to the teapot. My feelings fountained, overspilling in spurts so strong, I couldn't put down the teapot. I needed the weight of it in my hands, heavy with my sick, to hold me down, to keep me from floating away. I cast a glance at Brooke. She looked as mortified as I did. This had not gone the way she'd planned.

"Ms. Glazer," Garrett said. "We have to drink tea out of that pot."

I stared up at Brooke in the grandstand. "I want to know the truth. Why did you really offer to drive Charlotte to the drama festival?"

Her gaze pulled from me to Charlotte. ". . . Because it's kind?"

"*Kind?* We both know you'd rather cheese-grate your nipples than spend time alone with Charlotte." I set the teapot on the props table. "You offered to drive her for one reason—you're trying to control what I have with her. Just like you're trying to control me now."

"Con—I'm trying to do something really nice for you right now. We're *celebrating* you, babe."

"You're humiliating me, *babe.*"

"Oh my god, here we go again. So much for last week's apology, huh? Your drama is like a broken fucking roller coaster that I can't get off. I know it, your mom knows it, Jen knows it—"

"My drama?" My voice shook. "You play all nice taking me to finish my tattoo, but just when I think I can trust you, you go and play this card."

"Card? You've lost your goddamn mind. I'm doing something *nice* so that you'll get out of your own fucking way and take credit for this."

Ms. Glazer stepped in. "Maybe you'd like to discuss this privately."

"You have tattoos?" Garrett said.

Brooke turned to Ms. Glazer. "It's fine. I'm actually done talking about this with Taylor."

"Well, *I'm* not." I looked around at the others. Charlotte was pale. Coils of resentment snaked inside me. "This is just like middle school when we took those karate classes."

Brooke's face turned to stone. "What does a karate class five years ago have to do with me offering to take Charlotte to the drama festival?"

Ms. Glazer tried again, but she was only background noise. Our history of hurting each other was a wildfire in my gut. "When I leveled up to orange belt, you were so jealous that you were stuck on yellow that you suddenly decided you didn't like karate, so we stopped. You knew my mom didn't drive, you knew I couldn't get to Danvers without your parents driving, but you never cared. Even back then, even when we were so little, I knew it was your way of controlling things." I shoved a hand through my hair. "I loved karate and I was good at it and you took it away from me."

"For Christ's sake, Taylor, you didn't love karate—you loved the butch sensei. You talked about her nonstop, fucking *fawned* over her. And let's be real—you weren't that good."

"I was *great* at karate. Sensei said I could have gone to championships one day."

"*Championships?* You couldn't roundhouse the punching bag without flinching when it swung back and hit you in the tits."

Anger whipped through my veins like venom. I was so *angry*. Angry at Jen, angry at Mom. Lashing out at Brooke—who I was always so safe with, who was the closest thing I had to a sister—was the ultimate release, the highest of highs. "I can't have anything good unless you get to control it."

Brooke's gaze raked the room. She scoffed, and it was an embarrassed scoff, a now-we're-getting-too-close-to-really-raw scoff. "*You* can't have anything good? You've been nothing but a sulky bitch about MIT from the moment I got in."

"Yeah, well, maybe I *was* a sulky bitch, but at least when you have something I don't, I don't try to take it away from you." Spittle built in the corners of my mouth. "I can't trust you anymore."

She shot to her feet. "You take one more thing out on me just because you're having a hard time coming out, and I might just walk away. *For good.*"

Her words struck something inside me—something ugly and volatile and acidic. My tongue swelled behind my teeth. "We both know you walked away from me the moment you applied to MIT."

Her cheeks were hollowed—she was sucking them, the way she had all those months ago when she'd told me about her grandma's diagnosis. "God, no wonder your girlfriend had a panic attack."

My eyes snapped across the room.

Charlotte was ashen-faced.

TWENTY-THREE

The door chimed behind Charlotte. Slipping her umbrella into the bucket, she looked around Red's. Our eyes caught. Pain burned at the back of my throat.

She tossed her red parka onto the seat along with her cross-body bag. The string of Abigail's bonnet dangled from the zipper.

I blew air from my cheeks. "I didn't know if you'd come. After what Brooke said this afternoon."

She settled into the booth. "You mean, after you told her something that should have stayed between us?"

"I'm so sorry."

"It hurt."

"I know. I broke your trust. I'll never do it again. I hate that I hurt you."

"It hurt just as much to know you'd kept something so special from me."

"I was trying to tell you. This morning. At your locker."

"I wish you'd told me sooner. Your best friend knew."

"I didn't *tell* Brooke. She hacked into Ms. Glazer's iCloud and found the email NBC sent Ms. Glazer. She did what she did today because she's always had a penchant for organizing other people's lives based on her own vision."

Charlotte's eyes dulled. "Brooke apologized to me. *You* need to apologize to *her*." She looked the way I felt—there were dark circles under her eyes, and she was paler than usual. She took a wrapped gift from her bag and slid it across the table. "Merry Christmas," she said, plaintive.

It was a journal, pale blue . . . and embossed with my initials in the corner of the cover. "You can write sketches in it. You know, when you get your internship. The internship you never told me about."

My chest tightened.

"Taylor, why didn't you tell me about the competition?"

"I didn't tell anyone."

"But why not *me*?"

The last time she'd looked at me so wretchedly, I'd been holding myself above her on that old bed in the Witch House. She'd been waiting for me to tell her I wasn't ashamed. At the memory of her tender hands drawing up and down my naked back, my heart fluttered like one of Mom's cassette tapes. "You didn't want to tell anyone you'd auditioned for Tisch and then not get in. If nobody knows when I lose, I haven't really lost, have I? I haven't disappointed anybody."

"*You'd* still know. *You'd* still be disappointed."

"I already exist in a Disney World of my own disappointment."

She rested her chin on her steepled fingers. "When do you find out?"

"After Christmas."

"What date?"

"Just, *after Christmas*." I offered her a menu.

She smoothed a hand over where her braids began behind her winter-blushed ears. "I already know what I want."

"Blueberry pancakes?"

She forced a smile. "Blueberry pancakes."

After the waitress took our order, Charlotte folded her arms on the table. "I need to apologize for last night. I ruined it. What we did in there was . . . one of the nicest things I've ever done."

"Nice? Salem in fall is *nice*. Being with you was—"

"*Taylor.*"

When she smiled like that, *blushed* like that, it was contagious.

All of a sudden, she sighed deeply. "I didn't know why you imagined what you imagined for us. It felt like the weight of your world was suddenly on my shoulders, like your happiness depended on me. But now I look back on everything that went wrong in the Witch House, and I can see we were having two totally different conversations. You weren't imagining following *me* to New York—you were imagining following your dreams to New York." Her voice came at a whisper: "I know it was really awkward the way Brooke did what she did today—"

"She outed me."

"You half outed *yourself* when you danced with me. People had already guessed. You know that. All Brooke did was tell people about the contest. She thought she was doing a nice thing."

We were quiet.

"Taylor, ever since I found out about the contest . . . I think I've fallen for you even harder. There's nothing more magnetic than someone who knows what they want and goes after it."

I ran a fingernail around the lip of my coffee mug and tried not to throw up again.

"Taylor? Are you okay?"

"Having me for a girlfriend is . . . I'm the human equivalent of a participation ribbon."

". . . Huh?"

"I look pretty good right now—you'll take me home and pin me up—but a little while from now, you'll come to your senses and realize all I represent is—"

"Did you literally just come up with that metaphor now?"

"I stole it from my mom." *I steal everything from my mom.* "She threw it at my dad when she was telling him what a shitty husband he turned out to be." My heartbeat thrashed in my ears. "I'm trying to say that I'm not exactly first prize, and you'll realize it soon enough."

The tendons in her throat tensed. "I really like you. Please don't say things like that—"

The waitress stopped at our booth. "All right, I've got one of the blueberry pancakes, one of the chocolate chip?"

As we ate, dough lodged in my windpipe and brought tears to my eyes. One day she'd look back on all of this and realize it was nothing but a silly mistake. Fifteen years from now she'd pull her Abigail costume from a moving box in her Brooklyn brownstone and laugh with her wife about that time she spent with a funny girl in a First Period colonial.

"Are you going to talk to your mom?"

My breath came quick. "Y-yeah."

A forkful of pancake hovered before her lips. "Tonight?"

"She's at Walgreens. I'm taking her to lunch tomorrow."

I didn't want to talk about Mom with her. I *couldn't* talk

about Mom with her. Not when I couldn't stop thinking about what Ursula had said about Mom and Jen. Not when I couldn't stop wondering why it couldn't have just worked out between them if part of Mom had wanted it.

Sitting back in the booth, Charlotte gripped the juncture of her neck and shoulder like she was working out a knot. She plowed the blade of her butter knife across the plate, parting violet syrup like the Red Sea. Suddenly she dropped the knife to her plate and sat forward. "I know things are hellish right now, but that's going to change. And if we both end up in New York, it'll be *so* different." She threaded her fingers through mine. I couldn't look at her. "It'll be really nice," she said softly. "Everything you imagined."

And if I don't end up in New York? Electricity crackled between us. "Maybe you'll find someone better than me in NYC."

My words fell like *lead*.

She looked at me with wide, nervous eyes. "I don't want anybody else."

"You'll probably change your mind about me."

"I didn't *change my mind* about you last night. If that's what you mean."

"You must have changed your mind a little. You left me—"

"I *left* the Witch House."

"Yeah, and you left *me* in there."

Yanking her hand from mine, she pulled a ten from her wallet and dropped it beside her plate. She slipped her arms into her parka.

My stomach dropped.

"Don't follow me, Taylor."

Hurriedly, I paid the check. Through the windows, the

cherry blur of her parka vanished left—she was taking Charter. I rushed out after her.

Snow battered my cheeks as I watched her struggle with her umbrella by the gates of Old Burying Point. "Charlotte!"

One glance at me and she was gone.

Sighing, I pulled on my gloves. Where in the hell was she going? Her house was in the opposite direction.

When I reached the corner of Charter and Hawthorne, I mumbled under my breath. "A church, Charlotte? Really?"

Evening Mass had just finished at Immaculate Conception. A small crowd of pearl-clutchers lingered just inside the doors. As I jogged up the stone steps, the priest's head turned. "Merry Christmas," he said kindly.

"Merry Christmas."

In all my Salem years, I'd never stepped foot inside Immaculate Conception. Brooke and I'd shared an inch of a joint in the shadows of the church parking lot the summer we were fourteen, but that had been the extent of our spiritual experience. It was nice inside. Warmer than outside. It smelled a little odd, a little churchy, a little like my Texan grandmother's suitcase—mothballs, not pecan pie. But it was . . . nice. There were stained glass windows and people chatting above in the mezzanine and a natural wood organ and an ornate nativity scene. And there was Charlotte, sitting in the third pew from the altar. As she wrenched her eyes from a statue of the Virgin Mary, our gazes caught. Quickly, she spun back to the front. I rolled my shoulders. *Lord, give me strength.*

I stopped at the end of her pew. "This is very Lifetime Christmas Special." I dropped into the padded blue seat. "Ingénue runs from her comedian lover after a misunderstanding, only for the two to be reunited in a church together on Christmas." I set the journal between us. "Honestly, I'm just waiting for Della Reese to show up as the church flower arranger and tell us there's a light at the end of the tunnel—"

"If you've followed me here to flex your funny bone with *Touched by an Angel* references, you should go home." She pulled her gloves off. "Can you see how hurtful it was? What you just said about me changing my mind about you? I thought I was hurt today in theater when I realized you hadn't trusted me enough to tell me about the contest, but this day just keeps getting better and better."

My heart fell. "Charlotte, I'm—"

She twisted back to the altar. "Stop talking. You're not supposed to talk in church."

"But I need to apologize?"

She refused to pull her gaze from the red light that flickered above the tabernacle.

Reaching forward, I took a pocket pencil from the back of the pew. I opened to the first page of the journal she'd gifted me. *I'm sorry I kept the contest from you*, I wrote.

Her eyes flickered down.

And I'm even sorrier for what I said back there in Red's. I hate that I was a jerk. I hate that I upset you.

I turned to a fresh page. *Even if you are very cute when you're angry.*

"*Cute when I'm angry?*" She huffed. "Just because you're a lesbian doesn't make it acceptable for you to sexualize women's emotions. I thought you were more intelligent than that, but I'm quickly realizing that maybe you aren't at all who I thought you were."

After everything we'd been through together, *that* was like a stake to the heart. I bit my tongue against the sting of tears. She didn't mean it. *If she really meant it, she wouldn't still be sitting here beside me.* I wet my lips. *If I could just make her laugh* . . . I put pencil to paper.

What did Adam say to Eve?

Her gaze dropped.

I'll wear the plants in this family.

Blue eyes slipping to black, she twisted on the seat again. "You're uncomfortable so now you're making jokes? Grow up. And stop wasting pages in the journal. I went all the way to Boston to get it embossed with your initials—it's supposed to be special, for your sketches."

I don't think Charlotte's animosity was about how I'd kept the contest a secret, or about all the shitty things I'd said in Red's. Although I'd definitely been a total and complete jerk, I don't think any of that really mattered to her—we were way past trying to be beautiful for each other. I think the real reason she was lashing out was because something had shifted between us in the Corwin House. Something had shifted between us in a really big way.

This time, she didn't even pretend not to see what I was writing.

Charlotte,

After last night, I think being bold with you might be my favorite thing in the world. It scared me, really scared me, and I think maybe it scared you, too. But even though it scared me, I'm going to try to be bold, to stop being so sorry for wanting all the things that I want. You deserve to feel special and safe and wanted and seen and heard, and I want to be the one who makes you feel all those things. Even though you deserve better than

Her fingers curled around my wrist. "Stop saying things like that."

"Things like what?"

Her gaze became a little less cloudy, a little more focused. "You said you thought I was the best. In the Witch House, before we went upstairs, you said that every time you came to my museum, you wanted to stand up and say that you thought I was the best. Can you say the same about yourself?"

"What?" I rasped.

"Tell me something you like about yourself."

Something I liked? "About myself?"

She nodded.

"I . . ." My throat bobbed. Gently, I nudged her shoulder. "Well, I like that *you* like me."

Her tired eyes climbed to meet mine. "That's not something you like about *yourself.*"

As her gaze dropped to my neck, I imagined that she could see the pulse jumping there, beating like a war drum. My mind blanked. *Say something. Say anything.* Tearing my eyes from hers, I looked to the sanctuary light and tried to hear through all that white noise, through the static of my shame that ran deeper than the smuggling tunnels under Salem. *Make something up! Make anything up!*

Charlotte's thumb was warm against my cheek as she brushed away a tear. "Taylor, it's okay." I heard it: the way the syllables of my name broke on the wave of her breath. I knew that sound. I hadn't been able to think of anything else since I'd traced the delicate bones of her chest in the Corwin house.

I let a breath shudder from my lips. "I *do* like myself. I do. I just . . . I . . ."

As her hand covered mine, she flinched—my fingers were frozen. "Here," she said, soft. Lifting my wrist, she slipped one of her gloves onto my right hand, working the fingers of fleece over my knuckles so gently, so carefully, that I felt it in my bones. The night before, I'd been inside Charlotte, and she'd been inside me, but this, *this* . . . This moment, where she was slipping her glove onto my hand and waiting for me to find *one* fucking thing that I liked about myself, was the most intimate moment I'd ever shared.

The heat of her gaze burned into the side of my face. I looked at her.

"If we're going to do this," she whispered, "if we're really going to be together, you need to like yourself." Her brow furrowed as she worked her other glove over my left hand. "I need to know that you like who you are so that you can like who you are when you're with me. Otherwise, we're both going to get hurt."

I swallowed past my cotton mouth. "But I'd *never* hurt you." The lump in my throat had swelled so thick that it was almost impossible to get the words out. "I'm going to come out so that I can be with you."

"Oh, Taylor. You can't come out for me." Her eyes glistened. "You have to do it for yourself." She let go of my hand, curled her bare hands around the edge of the pew, and pulled herself to her feet.

"Charlotte?"

"I have to go now," she said. "I'm sorry, but I have to go now."

TWENTY-FOUR

At two the next day, I found Mom unpacking Christmas groceries in the kitchen in her Walgreens uniform.

"Hi," she said coolly, bandaging plastic Walgreens bags around her knuckles. "Are we on speaking terms yet?"

"You didn't show."

"Huh?"

"The Hawthorne Hotel. We had a reservation. I waited for you outside, just now, for an hour, and you didn't show."

"You . . ." She stared at me, incredulous. "You waited for me? I was working, Taylor. You knew I was working."

My head was spinning. "But all those weeks ago when I told you I'd made the reservation, you said you'd get someone to cover the end of your shift. You said you'd finish in time to meet me there at twelve thirty."

"Honey." She held the fridge wide open. "I assumed you'd canceled it. Taylor, you've barely said two words to me since your friend slept over. I'm sorry," she said bluntly, "but I figured the last thing you'd want to do was have a three-course meal with me."

Nothing was as it was supposed to be. "I *did*. Want to."

265

Her eyebrows gathered. "We could make another reservation for after the New Year?"

It was too late for that.

She gestured to the groceries. "Help me unpack?"

My feet took me over to the counter, to tomorrow's eggs and flour and wine bottles. As she pried eggs from the carton and placed them in the container, she asked questions about the last day of school, about my senior project. My heart hammered in my empty stomach. The afternoon sun was breaking through the clouds, shining through the kitchen window and catching the glossy black of her name tag. *Carrie.* She wasn't just my mom. Just like me, she was other people, too.

I wasn't ready, but it was time. Time for me to go away and move on and be better and be more and be who I was. Time to stop feeling so alone, so angry, so tired, so guilty. It was time to make a decision, to choose whether or not I wanted to make sense to people. Because living like this . . . I'd grown paper-thin. I was done with crumpling at the edges, tearing at the creases.

"Mom?"

"Yeah, hon—"

"I like girls. Only girls."

Her eyes whipped up. Her long fingers curled around an egg. "What?"

My insides ignited like dry tinder to an indigo flame.

"Really?" she breathed.

Don't cry. Do not cry.

Gently, she lowered the egg back into the carton. "Well, that's . . ."

I'd known in my heart there would only be a whole lot of love. I'd expected her to be awkward, but I hadn't expected her to be so

266

thrown by it, especially when I knew that *something* had happened between her and Jen. Her vacant look made me terrified of the winding yellow brick road my confession paved out for us.

She fell into a kitchen chair. "Have you . . . I mean, do you have a girlfriend?"

What she was really asking was if I'd ever been with another girl—I wasn't going to answer that. "No," I choked. Charlotte wasn't *officially* my girlfriend. "There's a girl, but . . . Charlotte."

"Pretty Charlotte?" She stared. Then it happened. A delirious smile broke on her lips. She pressed her hand to her cheek like she was Katharine fucking Hepburn. She shook her head, grinning.

I held myself around the throat. God, my neck was on fire. "Are you okay, Mom?"

She raised her eyebrows. "Am *I* okay? Oh, Taylor," she said. "How long have you known?"

"About a year. Maybe a bit longer than that."

The light went out of her eyes.

A surge of guilt slithered through me, sparking sneaky little synapses. "I'm sorry. I wanted to wait to tell you until I was sure." I left out the part where I had yet to reach a point of complete certainty.

"You have nothing to apologize for." She reached for my hands. "You're so fierce," she said, and frowned, like she was quickly realizing I'd spent the last year soaring through rings of fire just to meet her there at our kitchen table. "When did you get so fierce?"

"I—"

"This makes sense when I think about it." She rubbed at my wrists. "It makes sense. It does. Christ Almighty, here I was thinking that you binged *Orange Is the New Black* three times because you appreciated the female gaze. But it turns out you just appreciate the female gays."

"Mom . . ."

"And you've never had a boyfriend. I mean, you're seventeen, that's—"

"Mom?"

She looked up at me with wide, wet eyes.

"Everybody at school found out. Brooke showed them. She thought she was doing a good thing and she showed them all."

"Showed them what?" As her thumbs stilled on my wrists, her nails marked tiny half-moons against the ridges of my veins. "What did she show—"

"I'm a finalist in a contest."

"What kind of contest?"

". . . A sketch-writing contest."

Groaning, she shook my hands. "Oh no. No, Taylor. Oh Jesus, I suspected something like this might happen one day. There were so many signs. But I thought you'd have enough sense to choose an easier life for yourself. Don't make the same mistake I did."

"This is *different*. You barely even got started before you gave up."

"I *need* you to go to college. I have worked my whole life so that you can go wherever you want to go—"

"It's an internship, Mom. At *Saturday Night Live*."

She choked a sound. "*Sat—Saturday Night Live?*"

Heart thumping, I wet my lips. "It's called the Emerging Writers' Diversity Award."

Her head jerked back. "Diverse . . . Oh."

I rubbed at the back of my neck. "I was planning on telling

you today . . . you know, about the diversity part. The gay part. In case I won. That's why I reserved a table at the Hawthorne. To tell you. I wanted you to be the first person I told but . . ."

"Taylor. Taylor. What on earth did you write to get this far?"

I went and got my laptop. I sat opposite her and pulled my legs up onto the chair, opened my sketch, and turned the screen around.

We sat in silence. "Taylor." Her eyes were trained on my laptop screen. "Stop shaking your knee—it's distracting."

"Sorry."

She read. She didn't laugh.

"You get it, right? Mom? Trump's woken up in the middle of the night and he thinks what's happening to him, being called out on the Russia stuff, he thinks it's sort of like a witch hunt. So the victims of the Salem Witch Trials, like Rebecca Nurse and the Proctors and all those people, they've appeared in his bedroom, at the White House, to tell him that he has no clue what a witch hunt really is. Y-you kind of have to see it performed to get it. It's not really funny just reading it—"

"It's very funny. I get it." Her expression was blank. As she studied the screen, her head tilted so far to the left that her ear almost brushed her shoulder. "Taylor, you've written here that John Proctor calls the forty-fifth president of the United States a 'whiny little—'"

Jen stopped in the doorway. She saw that Mom was red-eyed. Her gaze flickered between us. "What happened?"

Mom gestured to my laptop. "Taylor wrote a sketch and now she's a finalist for a very important competition. For an award." She cleared her throat. "A *diversity* award."

I glared at Jen. *Mom knows!*

Mom looked from me to Jen. "Did you know?"

Jen lifted a hand to her belly. ". . . Know?"

"That I'm gay."

Jen lowered her briefcase to the table. "Yeah." She pulled out a seat. "I knew."

We were all quiet. I looked over at Mom, trying to make her look at me, but she was in a trance, watching Jen's hand smooth over the life growing inside her. Mom's gaze lifted, and their eyes met across the table. Locked. Held.

Something happened then. It was in the way Jen's eyes went cool, careful. The way Mom's turned silver hot. I can't explain it. All I know is that this *energy* kindled right there at the table, and it was *weird*, really fucking weird, like I shouldn't have been in the room with them. They were in their own little world, where me and my problems didn't belong—where *nobody* else belonged.

Jen broke the spell. She pulled my laptop to her. "Let's take a look at this award-worthy sketch."

We watched Jen read, listening as my down key crushed a sesame seed from lunch last week. Mom's eyes raked over Jen's face, gauging her reaction. Her lips quirked when Jen chuckled, her eyes narrowed when Jen's tongue skirted along her teeth. But it was when Jen *cackled* that Mom was shocked out of her stupor and stood, humming a low sound as she moved across the kitchen to fill a wineglass.

My mouth grew dry. Mom was freaking out. Her fight-or-flight response was kicking in. If they handed out Pulitzers to people for removing themselves from situations that made them uncomfortable, Mom's would have taken pride of place on her bookshelf, propping up *Under the Tuscan Sun* and *Eat Pray Love*.

She had running away down to a fine art. I'd seen her do it with guests who made complaints, with men who asked too much. She'd done it with Dad, she'd done it with Jen, and now she was doing it with me.

"Mom?"

As she turned from the counter, wine sloshed up the sides of the glass. "Taylor . . . are you sure you want to do it this way? As a *gay* comedian?"

Jen looked up.

"*What?*" I said softly.

Mom took a long sip. "I just . . . I'm sure there are other opportunities available—other contests you could no doubt *win*—that don't require playing the diversity card."

My stomach dropped. The room spun, and my eyes grew hot.

Mom drew a hand across her cheek, pulling her skin so low, so tight that her eye looked ready to bounce from the bone. "I'm sure *Saturday Night Live* has some sort of diversity quota to fill, no?"

The blood drained from my face.

"Carrie." Jen stopped her. "Their intentions are good. It's becoming increasingly important, I think, for studios to welcome a diverse group of writers, for different perspectives to enrich—"

Mom held up a hand. "Jen, all I'm saying is that I know how the comedy world works. Trust me." She fanned her fingers against her breastbone. "If anyone knows, it's me. The moment I included one joke about female sexuality was the very moment they started introducing me to the stage as a 'comedienne.' From that moment on, always, it was *comedienne*."

I looked past Mom out the kitchen window. I could feel Jen's worried stare trained on me.

"I just wanted to be a *comedian*," Mom continued, waving

her wineglass through the air. "That's what I was—a goddamn comedian." She reached for the wine bottle and refilled her glass. "But I never demanded to be called that, did I? For two years, I showed up to every goddamn 'comedienne' hour in the basement of that dingy fucking sports bar, and every Thursday night I accepted that one a.m. stand-up slot without hesitation. *Sure, I'll go on after the boys.*" As she spoke, she focused on Jen. "I never stood up for myself. I thought, 'Hey, one day this comedienne thing might actually make me stand out in the sea of men with their dick jokes and sex shtick and disgusting little bits about women who dare to say no.' I thought, 'I'll just work twice as hard and maybe someday somebody important will show up to scout.' But nobody ever came to scout. Not once. Not to '*comedienne* hour.' Because comedy is a boys' club, and if you aren't a man, then you might as well just forget—"

"Carrie," Jen tried. "I can understand why you wanted to be called a comedian—of course I can. For you, your gender as a comedian was beside the point, and 'comedienne' was a dated and sexist label. But this award is *embracing* Taylor's diversity, welcoming what she can bring to the table in *recognition* of exactly who she is. It's *celebrating* her perspective as a female comedian, as a woman who is attracted to other women."

My face heated.

"Carrie," Jen finished, "this is *very* different from your experience."

Wide-eyed, Mom spluttered. "It's no different at all. I never let the fact that I was a woman define my comedy, and Taylor shouldn't let her sexuality define her comedy either—"

"But it *can*, Carrie," Jen said firmly. "And *that* is a *wonderful* thing."

After everything I'd put her through this winter, hearing Jen defend me was like having acid poured into an open wound. At some point in the last year, everybody else in my life had let me push them away—Mom, Brooke, Charlotte, Gilda. But not Jen. I'd pushed her the hardest, and here she was, calling me *wonderful*.

Mom rubbed at her cheeks. "Don't get me wrong, Taylor, I'm very happy for you. God, it's *Saturday Night Live*." She groaned. "But I don't know if I want it for you this way."

I palmed the sweat from my upper lip. "Maybe you don't want it for me at all," I whispered. "Maybe you want it for *yourself*."

The air was sucked out of the room.

Mom paled.

Shame curdled in my belly. Deep down, I knew it wasn't true—Mom wasn't jealous of me. She didn't want what I had. She was only reacting this way because she was in shock. She was trying to protect me. But I was trying to protect me too.

"Okay," Jen murmured. "Okay. Let's just take a minute and take a breath, some space, before anybody says anything they're going to regret—"

I stood from the table.

Mom pinched the skin at her throat. "Where do you think you're going?"

"To give you space."

Her eyes flashed—she was terrified. "You're not going *anywhere* alone when I don't know that you're all right—"

"I'm fine." I wasn't fine. "And I won't be alone." The lie came easy: "I'll be at Brooke's."

TWENTY-FIVE

Gilda owned a beautiful home in Prides Crossing. I'd only been there once, to change her bathroom lightbulb one night after improv, but it wasn't hard to remember which mansion was Gilda's. At the very end of Paine Avenue and backing onto the water, Gilda's ivy-cloaked home was so elaborate that it had a name—*Sláine*—tattooed to the cement above the door. Meaning "health" in Gaelic, *Sláine* was woven into the cast-iron gates of the driveway, too.

Half a minute after I rang the bell, Gilda pulled open the door. "Missy! You're shaking like a leaf!" She reached for my gloved hand and pulled me toward her. "Get out of the snow this instant."

In the hallway, I drew my wool hat back. "I'm sorry—I know it's almost eight and I know you go to bed at nine and I should have called ahead but I lost service in Beverly, just before my bus got to Prides—"

"The tower was hit by the storm earlier tonight. I've been trying to get on the Facebook for hours but—"

"There was a storm?" After hiding in Cinema Salem watching a movie about Jackie Kennedy, I'd come out into the pedestrian street at seven o'clock to find the cobblestones shining, but I hadn't heard thunder. Guilt kicked my heartbeat into second gear—here, Mom wouldn't be able to reach me.

"Why weren't you at improv on Monday?" Gilda demanded.

I tugged at the fingers of my gloves. "I . . . I've been really busy."

"Busy?"

My teeth chattered. "Yeah."

She tightened the belt of her robe. "Is everything all right, sweetheart?"

I'd never seen her like this—comfortable, not made up with heavy eyeshadow, not dressed in a brilliant, bright pantsuit. I dropped my gaze to my boots. "Can . . . Do you think I could stay here? Just for tonight?"

Gilda reached for the zipper of my parka. "Of course you can stay."

After I changed into a pair of Gilda's rose-printed winter pajamas, I padded up the hall and found her in the guest room turning down my bed.

She smiled sympathetically. "Feel warmer after your bath?"

"Thanks for heating my towel for me. You didn't have to do that. Or make up a bed for me. I could have slept on the couch."

"I didn't make it up for you. My eldest daughter is arriving tomorrow. She'll be here in time for Christmas dinner."

God, was I happy for her. "That's . . . that's really nice."

She spread a spare blanket over the end of the bed like a scarf. "Ready for bed?"

She insisted on tucking me in—literally. The mattress was ancient; as she folded the tightest hospital corner possible, a spring dug into my shoulder blade. "Hey, Florence Nightingale, with all due respect, I think you're cutting off my circulation."

"The tighter the tuck, the better the sleep. Now, there's your glass of water next to the tissue box, and when you're ready, tap the base of the lamp twice to turn it off. What else did I have to tell you? Oh! The electric blanket will kick in soon, but don't you dare sleep with it on—I don't want you burning in your bed. Promise me you won't fall asleep without turning it off."

"I promise."

As she turned to leave, I struggled against the hospital tuck and pushed up onto my elbows. "Gilda?"

"Yes?"

"Can I ask you a hypothetical question?"

"Of course."

"Can . . . can you come and sit here for a minute?"

As the edge of the mattress dipped beneath her weight, the moment stretched. I fell back onto the pillow, shifted against the spring probing the edge of my spine, tried to work the too-short pant leg of Gilda's pajamas down with the arch of my foot.

"Taylor?"

"Yeah?"

"Are you going to ask your question?"

"Uh-huh. I just . . . need a minute."

Over the scratchy blanket, I took her hand. "Say there was this girl," I started, "who entered a writing contest. Say it was called the NBC Emerging Writers' Diversity Award. . . ."

Her fingers tightened around mine. "Do we know this girl?"

"No."

"All right . . ."

"Say this girl entered the contest before her friend even recommended it. Say this girl was named a finalist, to win an internship at *Saturday Night Live*—"

She gasped. *"Oh, Taylor—"*

"But she decided not to tell anyone that she was a finalist."

"Why on earth not?"

"Because there was a catch, a catch I don't think her friend realized when she told the girl to enter. The contest was only open to diverse applicants—writers of color, writers with disabilities." My mouth grew dry. "Writers who're . . . gay."

"Mmm?"

I squeezed her hand like a reflex. "And this girl, she hadn't told anyone she was gay. And because she hadn't told anyone she was gay, she couldn't tell anyone about the contest. But when she did tell someone—that she was gay, that she was a finalist, all of it—this person, this really important person said that they thought the girl was playing the minority card."

"And who was this important person?"

"Her mother."

Gilda hesitated.

I lowered my voice to a whisper. "What . . . what would you think about that? About what the girl's mother said?"

Her thumb slipped across the back of my hand. "I'd think that if this mystery girl were named a finalist in a contest of such magnitude, it would be the most wonderful thing in the world."

I squeezed my eyes shut tight against the sting of tears.

"And, Taylor," she whispered, "if I knew this girl—if I were lucky enough to call her my friend—I'd be very, very proud."

Her voice, choked with tears, set a ringing in my ears. "I thought that you'd be upset with me. Because . . . because you're Catholic."

"What in the world would make you think that?"

"The way you reacted when I did that really cringey abortion sketch."

"Oh, Taylor, I wasn't upset that night because I'm Catholic. I was hurt because, when I was fourteen, my eldest sister was sent to live in a Magdalene Laundry."

A Magdalene Laundry? "What's a Magdalene Laundry?"

"They were asylums, in Ireland, run by the Catholic Church. *Fallen* women, unmarried girls, were sent there—to carry their children. To give birth. *In secrecy.*"

My stomach turned. "Was . . . was your sister okay—"

"No." Expelling a shuddery breath, she lowered her chin to her chest. "She was never the same. Not after that."

Reaching out, I took the point of her crucifix pendant from where it rested against the collar of her fluffy robe. I rubbed it between my thumb and forefinger. "How can you still believe in God?"

She curled my fingers around her crucifix. "Institutions like those . . . they're not God, honey." In the lamplight, her eyes were so brown, I could see myself in them. "If I know anything," she said, squeezing my hand around her pendant, "it's that nobody deserves to live with a secret."

My throat constricted.

She rested our hands between us on the edge of the mattress. "Taylor . . . That very first day you came to the community hall . . . I saw you outside that meeting room. The one where the gays have their talks. I saw you, trying to push open that door."

What?! She'd known this *whole time* that I was gay? My breathing came rushed. It felt like my chest was caving in. She knew. *She knew?!*

"I knew the NBC competition was for people like you. And while I knew that you weren't quite ready to push through the door at the end of the hall, I knew there was another door that you were more than ready to open. That's the thing, sweetheart—there's always another door." Shifting closer on the mattress, she thumbed the tears from my cheeks. "Don't let anybody tell you that you aren't worthy. You make sure people treat you as good as you treat them. You hear me?"

I nodded tightly.

"All right then," she said, solemn as the chime of the grandfather clock in the hall. "As long as you know."

On her way out, she stopped in the doorway. "I'm going to leave the door ajar," she decided, "to keep the warmth flowing through."

Early the next morning, while Gilda was still asleep down the hall, I quietly stripped the bed for Gilda's daughter and made it up again with a spare set of sheets I found in the hall closet. I folded the extra blanket and placed it on the seat below the window that overlooked Salem Sound. As pearly flakes fell against the glass, I tore a page from my sketchbook and left a note on my pillow: *Merry Christmas, Gilda Radner.*

As my train rolled through pink-skied Beverly and horned hello as we passed another, I drew my name in the frosted window and watched the lavender and yellow-banded cars chug by.

Gilda once told me about a horrible crash at Prides Crossing in the eighties. A commuter train heading for Boston had collided with a freight train. As the commuter train soared into the air on impact, the freight train's engine was so heavy that it stayed on the tracks, burrowing beneath.

Before the trains struck, Gilda heard two whistles—both of a different pitch—all the way from *Sláine*. With her husband, she'd charged up to the scene to pull passengers from the commuter train onto neighborhood lawns. Four people died that day, all because two dispatchers hadn't communicated properly.

You make sure people treat you as good as you treat them, Gilda had said last night, but in the last six months, I hadn't treated my family very well at all. I'd been dishonest and dismissive and I couldn't keep barreling toward them.

My phone vibrated in my pocket—finally I had service.

Eight missed calls from Mom. Twelve missed calls from Jen. And an email.

To: Taylor Parker (debbie.downer04@gmail.com)
From: Jane Lincoln (jane.lincoln@nbcunicareers.com)
Subject: Winner Announcement for Emerging Writers' Diversity Award
Received: December 24, 2016, 8:38 p.m.

Dear Ms. Parker,

With great delight, I'm writing (earlier than you surely anticipated!) to inform you that your entry has won the Emerging Writers' Diversity Award for 2017. Congratulations!

We would greatly enjoy your presence at the industry awards on January 8 in New York City. Additionally, we would like to schedule a meeting for January 9 to discuss further details of your internship.

While we intended to make the announcement on social media on the 26th, the NBC team has now decided that the announcement will be made public at the industry awards on January 8. Until the ceremony, we ask that you refrain from posting this news on social media.

Congratulations, Ms. Parker. We look forward to meeting you at the ceremony and awarding your tremendous talent.

Happy holidays.

Jane Lincoln
NBCUniversal Careers

The sound that escaped me was guttural—I'd never made a sound like that in my *life*. My eyes welled so fast, the bright screen blurred, and a spiky sort of heat blazed up from where my heart hammered in my chest, higher, higher, sparking my skin just like in *Pleasantville* when Joan Allen's face catches color for the very first time in her monochrome existence.

There was *a time for everything*, my dad always liked to say. There was *a time to be born and a time to die. A time to weep and a time to laugh. A time to be silent and a time to speak.* He's wrong about most things, but that quote always made sense. I knew a whole lot about time. How could I not? I was a comedian. My entire future relied on my ability to play with rhythm and tempo, to carry a pause until it found its feet. Now my pause had two feet on the ground, and I was done stalling. It was time for the punch line.

The train attendant poked his head into the car. "Salem, next stop!"

TWENTY-SIX

Because October's nor'easter had torn most of the vines from the lattice against the east wall of the Colemans' house, climbing the lattice to Brooke's bedroom window was as easy as it had been when I was thirteen.

I peered through her window. Cross-legged on her bed, Brooke was sitting up against her diamond-tufted headboard, pajama shirt rolled to her elbow, uncapping the same tube of antibacterial ointment Ursula had given me. When I danced my fingers against the glass, she dropped the small tube into her lap, her eyes shooting up in alarm. I smiled.

Grimacing, she took her sweet-ass time finding her slippers. After an eternity, she lifted the window and bent at the waist. "The fuck are you doing?"

"Making a grand gesture." After receiving the email, I was feral with adrenaline—and determination.

"I don't have time for this, Taylor. It's Christmas morning. I'm about to go downstairs."

"Just hold open the window so I don't get my torso Black Dahlia-d?"

Headfirst, I heaved myself through. With a grunt, I rolled

off the window seat onto her rug.

A small smile tugged at the corner of her mouth. "You look like you peed your pants."

I looked down at my jeans. She was right. The window ledge snow had gifted me a lovely little wet patch. "Climbing through someone's window is a whole lot less romantic than rom-coms make it out to be."

"Romantic? I thought you already *had* a girlfriend. Close the window, please."

I pulled the stick from the frame and looked around her newly renovated bedroom.

Brooke had saved all year for the overhaul, which had seemed like a totally pointless endeavor at the time, considering that she wasn't planning on U-Hauling the furniture to college. But she'd been hell-bent on the "Old Hollywood Glamour" theme since *Guys and Dolls* rehearsals had begun, and I think she was buzzing with creative energy that she didn't know what to do with—this was just after *Teen Dream House Rules* had finished filming. Of course, I'd shown up every day to help. And we'd had fun. A *lot* of fun. We'd repainted her baseboards Tiffany Blue at three in the morning while we'd silent discoed to Florence and the Machine, and we'd hung wallpaper with an art deco print so dizzying, it was difficult to follow the YouTube tutorial. When we'd finished, her new bedroom had made mine look like a Goodwill delivery shed.

She'd gone a little overboard, though, with the matching chairs. The afternoon that UPS had delivered them, the ostentation meter had hit an all-time high. "You love them, right?" she'd encouraged, and as I'd stared down at the Audrey Hepburn print, it had taken every ounce of willpower to stifle a laugh.

"Brooke . . . you've never even *seen* an Audrey Hepburn movie."

"You made me watch *The Philadelphia Story* last year."

"Babe, that was *Katharine* Hepburn—not Audrey."

"So? I like her mom, too."

"Brooke. Brooke, Brooke, Brooke. My sweet Brooke—Katharine and Audrey were not related."

"I know *Breakfast at Tiffany's*," she'd bragged.

As we'd carried the chairs up to her room, I'd asked her the premise of *Breakfast at Tiffany's*. She'd relayed the plot of *Waitress*.

Now I watched Brooke closely as she struggled to worm the ointment from the near-empty tube. I moved around the Hepburn chairs and sat down on the edge of her bed. "Here. Let me."

She handed it over. I worked the ointment from the bottom and swiped a quarter of an inch from the top.

"That's not enough," she grumbled.

"Trust me—it's plenty."

I rubbed the clear ointment into her wrist. "Does it hurt?" Mine was still sensitive.

She shook her head. "Not really."

I spread the ointment in circles until the stickiness soaked into her soft skin. Until her hand relaxed in mine. Silence settled, solemn and strong. I drew moons around her raindrop, and as I hummed the melody her grandma loved, I felt the warmth of her curious stare. "Your mom's been calling my phone, Tay. I haven't answered." The pulse in her wrist jumped beneath my thumb. "Did you come out to her?"

I traced my finger to the fold in her wrist. "Yeah."

Her fingers clawed at my tickle, but I flattened my palm over hers and wove our fingers together.

The moment swelled with intensity. As I stared at our joint hands, emotion burned inside me.

"Taylor," she said, soft, shaky. "I'm so sorry if I told people something you didn't want them to know. Okay, *two* things you didn't want them to know. I was just trying to make you take credit for what you've pulled off. I was just trying to make you happy because I know you've had a really hard time lately and I know you've felt so insecure—"

There was just so much hope and relief and frustration swirling around in the pit of my empty stomach and I was sure of only one thing—I wanted to be genuine for Brooke. For my very best friend, I wanted to be as real as I could be.

I lifted our fingers and pressed my lips to the back of her hand. Gently, chastely, I kissed the spot where the tendons webbed, the way men do in Old Hollywood films before they draw their leading ladies beneath lampposts to say things like *Last night we said a great many things* or *We'll always have Paris* or *That twinkle in your eye—wrap it up for me, will you?*

Bottom lip caught between her teeth, Brooke smiled. "What was that for?"

"No reason. I just love you is all."

Her features softened. "Yeah?" she whispered.

Throat burning, I nodded. "Sure do, Miss Adelaide." I squeezed her hand once, twice: *I'm sorry, Brooke. I'm so, so sorry.*

"Taylor, why didn't you tell me about *Saturday Night Live*? Before I found out?"

I only had to look at her for her to know the answer.

"But you shouldn't be scared. You're so funny and so smart and I'm so proud of you. Even if you don't win. Just getting this far is—"

As I pulled her into my arms, she buried a laugh in the gap between my neck and my parka. "I know the attention embarrasses you." She sighed. "But you have to get over it. I mean, dude, it's *Saturday Night Live*. You could legit *win*."

We sat like that for a while, me twirling one of her braids around my finger, the both of us listening to the murmurs of her parents down the hall. With the tip of her finger, Brooke traced patterns on my back, just as she had when we were little, lying on a pallet of sleeping bags in Grandma Connie's den playing Who Am I? after lights-out. But this morning, she wasn't tracing answers for me to guess. Just stars and symbols and swirls. The guessing game was over. There wasn't anything left to say that we didn't already know.

When I got in, there was a colony of gold balloons floating in the middle of the common room. Fifteen helium-buoyed letters swayed around the Christmas tree, twisting with the grace of a peacock. *Congratulations*, they read. Well, *Congratulalions* . . .

I spied movement. I turned. At the end of the hall outside the kitchen, Mom was wringing a dishcloth through her hands. She looked to the balloons. "Sorry about the *L*," she said. "Target only had one *T* left."

She didn't say exactly what the balloons were for—for coming out, or for being a finalist. I didn't ask.

"Merry Christmas, Taylor."

I won, Mom. Against the sting of tears, I bit the tip of my tongue. *Mom, I won.* "Merry Christmas."

"Why haven't you or Brooke been answering my calls?"

Oh god. "Because I wasn't at Brooke's."

Her breath hitched. "Well, where the *hell* were you?"

"In Prides Crossing. I stayed with my friend Gilda."

Her expression hardened. "*Gilda?* Is that a joke?"

"It's not a joke. I really do have a friend named Gilda. I met her at Prides Crossing Community Hall."

Her eyes widened. "You stayed with a stranger you met at *a community hall?*"

"She isn't a stranger—"

"Do you know the kinds of people that frequent that community hall? Alcoholics! Addicts! Christ, Taylor, she could be a drug addict for all you know! Or a *dealer!*"

"Mom, she's not a drug dealer. She's eighty-five and she's so nice to me—"

"What in god's name are you doing hanging around Prides Crossing Community Hall?"

"I do improv there on Monday nights."

Her irritation morphed. She flinched—actually *flinched.* "Improv? You do improv?"

I nodded.

"That's . . . Well . . ."

Oh, Mom. I pushed back my wool hat. "I'm so sorry about what I said. About you being jealous. You're not jealous. I know that."

We stood there at opposite ends of the hallway, gazing at each other, cowboys in a Western standoff. The only thing that could possibly go *bang* was one of those balloons because Mom had weighted them far too close to the fireplace. Perhaps that was more dangerous. If I lost any part of her *congratulations*, if any smidgen of her support suddenly burst under pressure, I'd lose her forever. If she wasn't totally on board with who I was, eventually what we had would die. There would be nothing I could do to save us.

But in that moment, I could see that she was only trying to decide if I was any different in the light of day, if she still recognized the girl who had broken free of the glass closet. I wanted to tell her I'd won the internship. I wanted so badly to tell her that I'd won. But the moment was delicate, fragile. And so were we.

"These past few days, I was really scared about coming out to you. Because I couldn't stop thinking about something."

She smiled warmly. *Confused.*

"I couldn't stop thinking about the fact that you gave Jen a chance."

The smile slipped from her face.

"Jen didn't tell me." *Why didn't you tell me?* "I just picked up on things over the years."

Her gaze dropped to the floorboards.

Hurt bundled in my chest. *Were you ashamed, Mom? Is that why it's still just you and me?* "Why didn't it work out?"

She stared at me, stricken, and my heart climbed to my throat. *If it had worked out between you, you would have someone to love when I move away. You would have someone to love you right back.*

Ryan's voice was coming from the kitchen. There it was: Jen's laugh.

"You probably could have made it work," I whispered, and I could hear it: how hopelessly optimistic I sounded. A child's wants coming from the mouth of a grown-up. "She treats you really well. Maybe if you really gave it time, you could have fallen in love with her."

I could see it in her face—she thought there was still so much for me to learn about seeing the world for what it was. "I don't think time could have changed the fact that Jen deserved more than what I could give her."

"I know she's from New York and all, but you're not out of her league—"

"Oh, I'm not out of anybody's league."

A laugh pulled from me. She bit back a grin.

I looked up at her. Her face was flushed, her underbite obvious. "Jen deserved more," she said simply.

"More *what*?"

"More than what I feel for her, Taylor."

My throat grew thick with the relief of it all. She hadn't been ashamed of what she felt for Jen. She just hadn't been all in, heart and soul.

"Come and eat, honey."

Jen and Ryan were in the kitchen with a couple of guests. They all looked up. The Australian who'd checked in a couple of days ago patted me on the back as he carried his mug to the sink. "Merry Christmas, kid. Congratulations on being a finalist in your competition! Just goes to show, you've got to be in it to win it!"

"You sure have." His wife beamed.

Oh, I'm in it. I sat at the head of the table, next to Jen.

"What do you want, baby?" Mom asked. "Eggs and toast?"

I could get them myself, I told her. "No," she said. "I'll get them."

It was snowing outside, but the light of the clouded sun was pouring through the kitchen window, and even though Mom was smiling and talking, I could see the dark rings under her swollen eyes.

Jen leaned close enough that Mom couldn't hear her over Crocodile Dundee's compliments on the breakfast frittata. "So, about the balloons. Carrie called me from Target last night and asked if it was a good idea to get *congratulations* in rainbow or gold. Let the record show that *I* was the one who prevented you from waking up to Pride in the common room this morning, okay? Merry Christmas—you owe me one."

The moment stretched like gum. Lucinda the psychic had seen the letter *L*. In gold. And she'd called it out of place.

Mom had plans to cook all day for Christmas dinner. I offered to help, but I think she just wanted to be by herself. It was horrible, I know, but I didn't really want to be around her anyway. I didn't know how.

After we cleaned up the breakfast mess, I kissed her on the cheek and told her I was going to take a walk. Before I could tell her I'd won the internship, I needed to clear my head.

Salem was slimy, wet stillness. The stores were closed up for Christmas, the cobblestoned pedestrian street puddled with morning snow. I walked two blocks through sleet, thought about just sucking it up and heading back home, but I was shaky with worry. What if, before I could tell Mom about the internship, she started asking me stuff? Stuff I wouldn't want to answer? What if we just spiraled all over again, like we had the day before? And then there was the thing that terrified me most: What if I told her that I'd won the internship and she was disappointed?

I was crossing to the Dunkin' on Washington when Jen

and Ryan pulled up to the stoplight. Jen stuck her head out the driver's-side window of their rental. "Want to come with us for a drive?"

I asked her where they were going.

The lights were about to change.

"Just get in, Taylor."

As I buckled my seat belt and Jen made a left onto Hawthorne Boulevard, they told me that Ryan was doing research for his new crime novel. Location scouting, he called it, said it with such conviction that you would have thought he had a bestseller list to rival Stephen King's.

"Where are you location scouting?" I asked. Danvers? Beverly? Manchester-by-the-Sea?

Ryan shrugged. "New Hampshire. Maine. Who knows."

My eyes widened. "We're going *out of state*?"

I caught Jen's gaze in the rearview mirror. "I can pull over and you can go home if you'd like. I'm sure Carrie would love to spend the day with you."

"I . . . No, that's okay. K-keep driving."

We spent Christmas Day driving up and down the New England coast. Seven beaches, three states, five gas station stops for Jen to pee. I spent most of the drive thinking about how funny people are always the saddest.

I was funny now. Legitimately, award-winningly funny. Did my funniness validate my sadness? Or was it the other way around? I'd been really sad for a long time. I was still sad, but at the same time there was this *thing* flowering inside me that made me think that maybe one day soon I could understand what they all meant about the weight being taken off your chest, about it getting a whole lot better, about that light at the end of the tunnel.

Coming out wasn't quite as sugary sweet. It tasted like lemon icing when you'd been expecting vanilla. It felt like racing toward a crossing and skidding to a stop at the exact moment the walk signal turned red—you had no choice but to pause and watch the traffic move around you. But there was the promise of that green light to come, and that just had to be enough.

"What are we scouting for exactly?" I asked when we started our trek over the half-mile grand allée at Crane Estate. Crane Estate was also known as Castle Hill—a mansion sat at the top, overlooking the decadent promenade that rolled to meet the Atlantic like a giant carnival slide. The allée had given its grand green pride to winter—the grass had died, leaving behind a tea-tainted path. There were only patches of snow, but any day now, the grand allée would be completely white.

"We're looking for somewhere a body would wash up," Ryan said. "Somewhere popular, but somewhere it would still take a while for people to notice."

Jen fell behind, stopping to admire the effigies lining the allée.

The grounds were completely empty—it felt like we were the only people in the world. The closer we came to Crane Beach at the end of the allée, the further we escaped the watchful eyes of Mr. Crane's fabulously grotesque gargoyles. The more the castle on the hill shrank away.

It had been hours since we'd left Salem and neither of them had brought up the night before, but I guessed that Jen had filled Ryan in because he asked me how I came up with my sketch idea.

I watched him zip up his windbreaker. "I couldn't think of anything to write, so I went to this psychic." I knew the wind was carrying my words to where Jen stood on the lip of the cliff. "I thought I could get a sketch out of it if she just took me for a ride. And I did get a sketch out of it. I had this whole sketch planned out in my head. But then right before I left her store, I . . ."

He was distracted—Jen was moving closer to the edge. The drop wasn't high—you probably could have jumped to the sand without spraining your ankle. But there was something about the fall—about Jen standing there on the grassy, slippery edge, pregnant as she was, that made it seem more dangerous. "Jen," he murmured.

She scoffed, but she moved back.

He refocused on me. "I'd love to read it."

"Sure."

A heavy downpour began just as we reached Maine, so Jen took the exit at the New Hampshire–Maine border and circled back onto the turnpike to Massachusetts.

At our last stop, Jen and I waited in the car. Hampton Beach looked really pretty, but it had started to snow and my ears were aching, and Jen couldn't afford to catch a cold.

She caught my gaze in the rearview mirror. "I think it was a good decision—you coming with us today. To give Carrie some time. To process."

"To process the fact that I'm a lesbian?"

"No. To process the fact that you're reaching a turning point, and, for the first time ever, she has to let you turn the corner alone."

". . . Oh."

"Did you tell Carrie you're with us?"

Shit. "No. I totally forgot—"

"Didn't think you would," Jen said. "I texted her for you."

I clicked my tongue. "Why did you ask me if *I* had if you'd already done—"

"Because I wanted to give you the benefit of the doubt. You need to start making your mom more of a priority. Carrie only has you."

I looked out at the whitecaps of the crashing waves, at the vast emptiness of Hampton Beach. Ryan was standing there on the sand with his hands in his pockets, staring out at the ocean. "Your fiancé looks like a poster child for clinical depression."

"Don't deflect. You're all grown-up now. It's time to start making Carrie number one like she's made you number one all of these years." She met my stare in the rearview mirror. "Okay?"

I nodded.

We watched as Ryan disappeared behind a grassy sand dune. "Is he a good writer?"

"Yes. He's very good."

"Did you . . . did you tell him about me?"

"He guessed. A while ago. When we first arrived."

I rested the side of my head against the window. "Oh."

"He's bi, you know. Like me."

Oh.

"Don't look so surprised, Taylor." I could tell she was smiling from the way the corners of her eyes creased as she looked at my reflection.

"I'm not *surprised*," I said too quickly.

"Yes, you are. You assumed he was straight. Just like you assumed I was a lesbian."

We sat, quiet, awkward.

"You know," she finally said, "I realize you thought I betrayed you by falling in love with a man. And that's your biphobia to work through—you're old enough, worldly enough, and it's not my job to help you with that."

My skin heated. "I know. I'm sorry."

"But I will tell you that there isn't a single person on the face of the planet who's one hundred percent sure how their life is going to turn out. Life changes. And the thing is, Taylor, I don't think anyone is ever really happy until they step out of their own way. Until they stop fighting themselves and let life just . . . happen."

But I did, Jen! I wanted to scream. *I did step out of my own way!* Need bubbled inside me. *I won and I'm going to New York!*

"Jen?"

"Yeah?"

"I . . ."

Something stopped me.

As she looked out the windshield at Ryan, she stretched her arm into the back seat, dancing her fingers in a silent request the way she used to when I was little and we'd reach a busy intersection.

The moment I took her hand, her grip squeezed tight around mine.

"Taylor?"

"Yeah?"

"I'm having a girl."

I went a little weak. "Really?"

"You can't tell Ryan, okay?"

"I don't know why Mom insists on buying these tacky-as-hell decorations every Christmas," I grumbled to Jen later that night as I pinched American-flagged toothpicks from the leftover Christmas pastries.

Chuckling, Jen continued scrubbing at the baking tray Mom had charcoaled. "Let her have her little Christmas traditions."

"I can hear you better than you think I can, Taylor Parker," Mom called from the dining room, where she was Saran Wrapping cranberry sauce and biscuits and mashed potatoes. "I know you're talking about my toothpicks."

When we heard Mom go down into the basement, I turned to Jen. "I think it has less to do with tradition and more to do with leftover half-off Thanksgiving decorations at Walgreens."

Plucking one of the toothpicks from the collection, Jen waved it in my face. "Where's your patriotism?"

I pushed down on the foot pedal and dumped a handful of flags into the trash. After picking the last flag from Jen's soap-sudded fingertips, I waved it around, did a square dance on the spot like Little Edie. Then, in a pretty damn great Long Island accent, I drawled, "'It's very difficult to keep the line between the past and the present.'"

Never in my six years of knowing Jen had I ever heard her laugh like *that*. Not when Ryan made a joke, not when she'd read my sketch. Not even in those early years when I'd lie at the top of the stairs, desperate to decipher her common-room whispers as she got wine-drunk with Mom. "God, Taylor . . ." She lifted the baking tray onto the drying rack, "I don't know how we're going to get through the next few days waiting to hear about this internship."

I buried my face in the fridge and pretended to make a space for the burnt turkey leftovers, but really, I was just trying to conceal my flaming cheeks, a mark of my own disgusting, filthy pride.

When Mom came back into the kitchen, in her arms was

a huge wrapped package—I knew instantly that it had to be a frame. "Go on," she said as she laid it down on the table.

It was my *Ghostbusters* poster.

She squeezed my shoulder. "I figured, what's the point in having the frame if there's nothing to put in it?" She nudged her hip against mine. "So this email *has* to come sometime before New Year's, right?"

I nodded. I'd keep the news to myself, I decided. Just for a little longer. There was still one thing left to take care of.

TWENTY-SEVEN

Somewhere high behind where I was seated at the back of the auditorium, the final notes of Chopin's funeral march drowned. In the ray of morning light that slipped across the stage, the dolls dropped from the papier-mâché Proctor's Ledge, and with them, my heart plummeted. It was time.

It was the first performance of the day and the auditorium of Charlotte's museum was half empty. Hiding in the pew behind a large Amish family, I swayed in my seat. *Is this what a heart attack feels like?* I couldn't do small audiences . . . could I? Small audiences were a million times more threatening. When an audience was small, you could read their faces, their judgment, their pity. Small audiences were made up of people, *real people*, and those people had lives and jobs and parents and children and *their own thoughts*. Small audiences let you bomb faster, fall harder from a greater height. . . .

Charlotte reached for Elizabeth Proctor's hand, clasped Ann Putnam's in her other. They dipped for their bow. They beamed. As my knee bounced uncontrollably, I squeezed my eyes shut tight. I couldn't think about the size of the audience. Not now. Not when I was a heartbeat away from saying what I'd crossed

Salem to say. I had to focus on one person, and one person only. *Don't pass out. Whatever happens, don't pass out. . . .*

Center stage, Charlotte stepped forward. Her gaze scanned the room. "Any questions?"

Now! Do it now!

The world slipped away.

Blood rushed to my head. I pushed to my feet. "I like myself!"

The entire auditorium spun in their seats. All those faces. All those people. All those pulses.

Silence. Too close for comfort, the Amish looked up at me. Onstage, Mary Warren murmured something to Goody Osbourne. And then, there was Charlotte. As she took me in from the height of the stage, her eyes were wide.

My toes curled in my boots. *You're embarrassing her. You're making a monumental mistake.*

Charlotte moved out of line. "Taylor?" She held her throat. "What are you . . ." Her voice was shallow . . . shuddery. Staring down at me, she bit her lip. "Taylor?"

One thing was for sure—no matter how loud the voices were in my head, there was no turning back now. I pulled a miniature Blossom Inn notepad from the pocket of my coat.

In the palm of my shaky hand, the list danced. I tried to focus, to find the first name . . . *Gilda.* Sucking in a breath, I looked up. "I like myself," I blurted. "I like myself every Monday between five and seven."

The most unnerving part, the thing that left my arms heavy and sent my heartbeat into overdrive, that had my nerves splintering like glass beneath my skin, was that Charlotte's expression was totally and completely *unreadable.*

I don't think I could have run if I'd tried. I was stuck. My voice came strained, shaky: "Monday is when I go to Prides Crossing Community Hall to do improv with a bunch of really fun people. I-it's where I met Gilda. Gilda's eighty-five and she has hair like cotton candy and she drives a Rolls-Royce Phantom—well, she used to—and she's the funniest person I've ever met." I fisted the pad. "Th-there's so much I want to tell you about her. I think you'd really like her."

Charlotte drew back her bonnet. Feeling tingled through my body. Maybe she wasn't embarrassed. Maybe, *maybe*, she was touched.

Heart beating in my fingertips, I looked at the next name on the list. *Brooke.* "I liked myself a couple of months ago in AP History, too. I don't know if you remember that day when that sub made each of us read a paragraph from the textbook aloud. . . ."

Charlotte arched a brow.

"When I mispronounced *hymn* as *hymen* and you could hear a pin drop?"

Behind Charlotte, Elizabeth Proctor laughed. Loudly. Finally, a full-bodied *cackle.* The corners of Charlotte's mouth ticked upward.

"It wasn't an accident. I did it on purpose. To make Brooke laugh. She'd just gotten some bad news about her grandma. After I did it, she spent the whole class, like, in tears—happy tears—so I let her think it really was an accident because it totally distracted her from thinking about—"

A door behind me slammed. I spun. At the end of the aisle, Charlotte's boss was watching. *Fuck.* I turned back to Charlotte, searching for her *Taylor, stop.* She stared back at me.

I found the next person on my list. "This past summer, I asked Jen when she knew she was gay." I kept going. "She told me that when she was a kid, her foster mom took her to the movies to see *Sister Act.*" And *going.* "Jen said that from the moment she saw the mousy novice take her solo in 'Hail Holy Queen,' she made a real *habit* of noticing the redheads in middle school."

Charlotte *laughed.* I bit back a grin. "I know that one has nothing to do with me, but hearing Jen say it made me feel really good about myself because . . ." I trailed off. It was impossible—absolutely *impossible*—to come up with a single coherent thought when she was looking at me like that. Suddenly I felt it, the way I always did when I was with her—the want, low in my gut, dripping like syrup.

Boots clacked heavily down the far aisle. By the side door that opened to the exorcism exhibit, Charlotte's boss halted. "Charlotte." Her voice was clipped. "Time to wrap this up, please. Right now."

Charlotte stepped closer to the edge of the stage. She had eyes for me—and only me. "Do you have more, Taylor?"

I burned beneath a score of stares. Whipping off my scarf, I tried to focus on the notepad. *Mom.* I searched myself for all the boldness I'd ever buried. "I liked myself last year, too, when I wrote and sold sassy yearbook quotes to self-conscious seniors so that I could afford to take Brooke to see the Boston Pops for her birthday. Mom and I sat up till three in the morning writing them. Mom and I wrote them together, and it was probably one of the best nights of my whole—"

Charlotte's boss clapped her hands. "If Tour Group A would like to stand and make their way to the—"

"Wait!" Startling herself by the volume of her own voice, Charlotte's eyes grew large. Her stare whipped across the room to land on her boss. "Taylor isn't finished," she said, softer this time. "Can we just let her finish?"

As I looked across the room, I gathered my courage. "Ma'am, can I just have one more minute?" I begged. "I really need to say this next one."

"Let her finish," a woman called out. "This is better than the actual show."

Lips pinched, Charlotte's boss jabbed a finger at the clock above the stage. *"Thirty seconds."*

My gaze dropped to the last name on the list. Pulse pounding, I drew a deep breath and looked up at Charlotte. "There've been too many moments with you to pick just one."

Her face flamed.

A lump grew quick and thick in my throat—I'd never seen her so . . . undone. "Charlotte," I said, breathless, "I really liked myself when I followed you into the Hall of Mirrors. And I really liked myself at the Snow Ball, when you realized I was dressed as the Wicked Witch. I mean, the way you smiled that night was . . ." As her face softened, my throat constricted. "And then there was later that night, after the Snow Ball, when we were sleeping in my room . . ." My chin quivered. "When you got out of bed in the middle of the night to find a makeup wipe, to clean some of the paint I'd missed?" I swiped a fingertip over my brow. "I know you thought I was asleep. But I wasn't."

Her eyes pitched toward the floor. Everything I'd ever felt for her flared up. "I know you asked to hear things I like about myself, and I know these"—I waved the paper—"are just a bunch of silly moments. But if I'm being totally honest, this is the best I can come up with right now." I pushed the pad deep into the pocket of my coat. "You were right. About what you said in the church. I do need to find things that I like about myself. And I need to get to

a point where I like myself most of the time, not just some of it."
I bit my tongue against the sting of tears. "But you make me want
to get to that point really, *really* fast. Because, sometimes—most
of the time—you make me too nervous to breathe. And because
I . . ." *Say it! Say it!* "Because I think you're the *best*."

A smile split across her face.

Happiness broke free inside me. As she blurred in my
gaze, my world narrowed to her. I felt *whole*. Not because I'd
finally come out, or because I'd gotten the girl, but because
I'd done the one thing Jen had told me would make me
happy—I'd found the courage to step out of my own way.

I was charging through the backstage maze of the museum,
searching each and every dimly lit hallway for Charlotte, when
Elizabeth Proctor appeared out of nowhere. "You're Carrie
Parker's kid. Haven't seen you since you were *this* big. You look
just like her. And, god, what you did back there—that was *such* a
Carrie thing to do! *Very* funny. *Very* endearing."

"Oh. Thank you." The rush of adrenaline had me breathless.
"Can you tell me where I can find Char—"

She pulled the tie of her shift loose and then touched my
forearm, the way mothers do to keep your attention. "Worked
with Carrie at the store a few years back, and I tell you what,
your mom made that job more interesting than it should have
been. Every damn time she needed assistance at the registers,
she'd do a wicked impression. Wish I could remember who—"
Her eyes widened. "Gilda Radner!" she said, gripping my arm
tighter. "That's who she'd do! Gilda Radner!"

A sudden feeling gripped me. "Really?" I'd never—*ever*—seen Mom do an impression of Gilda.

"You're too young, probably don't know who Gilda Radner is. But your mom would do this one character Gilda would do . . . God, what was her name? I can see her. Big hair. Rosie-something, Roslyn . . . Rose . . ."

"Roseanne Roseannadanna—"

Her eyes caught over my shoulder. "Oh, there's Cynthia with my paycheck! Say hello to Carrie for me, sweetheart."

I stared after her down the hall. There was chatter, movement. *Charlotte.* I exhaled, hard. I could see Charlotte in a moment. Tell her everything in a moment. But there was somebody else who deserved to know first.

I slipped out the emergency exit. The air was so frigid, it hurt to breathe. I squinted against the onslaught of light. The sky was pink—snow was falling, gentle, easy. By the dumpster, I plucked off my gloves and took out my phone.

She answered immediately. "Taylor?" A sharp intake of breath bled through the phone. She knew. She *knew.*

I sucked my bottom lip between my teeth. "I know you're at work, but are you free to talk?"

Her breath came short, excited. "I'm stocking the cold storage room, but if I don't lose my fingers to frostbite in the next few minutes, I can definitely talk."

The picture of her in the cold storage room froze a lump of guilt in my throat—Mom hated working the cold storage room.

"Taylor? You've heard from them, haven't you? You got the email?"

"I know you want to know," I breathed, "but first, I need to ask you something."

"What, baby?"

I drew a deep breath. "When I was born, did you feel like you stopped being you?"

A moment.

Her voice rose, the way it always did when she feigned innocence. "Being me?"

"When I was born, did you feel like I took something from you? A different life that meant a lot to you?" Sleet settled on the point of my nose. "Because I know what you said in the Back Bay apartment that night about choices, but I also know what you gave up for me. I know how huge it was for you to give up comedy, and I know it probably wasn't an easy sacrifice to make—"

"We've been over this," she said firmly. "Why are you asking me this again?"

"Because this internship . . . an opportunity like this could have found you as easily as it's found me." My voice shook. "You worked so hard at this sort of thing for years before you got pregnant, and then you had to let it all go—because of me. You're so funny, and you worked so hard, and I haven't worked hard for this, Mom, not really. Not the way you did. And I'm scared I don't deserve it, that you're right—that I *am* playing the diversity card. I'm scared that I don't deserve this as much as you do. I'm scared that I'm taking something I already took from you a long time ago. I'm scared that I'm taking it all over again."

She breathed my name so soothingly, my chest burned. "Okay," she murmured. "Okay. I'll tell you something. . . ."

I licked my chapped lips.

"When you were born," she started, "I felt like an imposter. I loved you more than I could stand, but for a long time, I felt

306

as though I were walking a tightrope with someone else's kid in my arms. I didn't think I could ever be the kind of mother my own was. And when I felt like that, it was easy—it was so easy, Taylor—to think that I could have taken a more . . . suited path. I had no idea how to care for a newborn, and that made me feel things I was ashamed to feel." She sighed softly. "But then you . . . you finally latched and the tightrope slowly became a plank, and then the plank became a boardwalk, and, after a while . . . we fit. We just fit, Taylor." Her voice sank to a whisper: "And I think I got the hang of it."

I swatted at my cheeks.

"Did I?" she whispered.

"Did you what?"

". . . Get the hang of it?"

My heart splintered in my chest. She'd asked it like she didn't know—like she really, truly, didn't have the first clue that she had built a home for us safer than a cloistered convent. The words pulled from the back of my throat. "Yeah, Mom. You got the hang of it."

Silence.

She exhaled slowly. "Taylor?"

"Yeah?"

"This award . . . whatever happens . . . I think it's amazing. I think *you're* amazing. I'm proud, Taylor. I'm so *unbelievably* proud. And, my god, honey—it's going to be lonely when you leave."

My tongue grew thick, heavy as a paperweight. "I won, Mom," I breathed. "I won, and I wanted to tell you first."

EPILOGUE

January 7, **the** night before I left for New York to collect my award, was Salem's annual bonfire night on Dead Horse Beach.

Bonfire night was a tradition. If Halloween was an outing of witches and warlocks, bonfire night was a purging of society's ills. After Salem stripped their Christmas trees of cringey crafts and carted their Fraser firs down to Dead Horse Beach, the town gathered to croak "Auld Lang Syne" as the local fire department ignited the blaze. It had always been a real community sort of thing, but the hype was dying a slow death—this year, the twenty-foot tower seemed a whole lot less impressive. Or, who knows, maybe the flaming lump was just as tall as ever. Maybe it was me. Maybe my perspective was changing. Maybe the things that had seemed monumental when I was a kid weren't so daunting anymore.

Even at the back of the crowd, the heat of the blazing evergreens pinched my cheeks. Sipping at the hot chocolate we'd bought across the street at the Salem Willows Christmas market, Charlotte looked up at me. "What do you want your life to be like in five years?" Her smile was bright in the firelight.

Pine crackled and popped as the fire department cast another tree into the flames. I took a deep breath—tonight Salem smelled fresh, citrusy, like the duvet in Gilda's daughter's room. "I'm not sure. I think I'm just going to see where this internship takes me."

As the fireman tossed a wreath onto the burning heap, Charlotte hummed a sound. "Who knows," she said, "maybe somebody really important will have read your sketch. Maybe they'll come up to you tomorrow and say"—she put on a gruff male voice—"Ms. Parker, forget the internship. I've read your piece and I'd love to offer you the position of head writer at *Saturday Night Live*."

Ruby red embers lifted from the pile of pine, heading for the waxing moon. I chuckled. "I don't know that anything like *that* could ever happen."

"Okay, maybe it won't happen anytime *soon*." Grinning, she slipped her gloved hand into mine. "But one day. Imagine that."

There's a part in Amy Poehler's *Yes Please* that always stuck with me. She says that, although she's not trying to sound cocky, she always knew she was going to be on *SNL*. She wasn't sure she had "the talent" or the "drive," but she did have a "tiny little voice whispering" inside her. Closing my eyes, I focused on Charlotte's thumb as she stroked the back of my hand. And for the first time ever, I let myself hear that whisper too.

ACKNOWLEDGMENTS

When I sailed into Salem on a fast ferry seven years ago, I could never have imagined that the experience I was about to have would blossom into a book I'd one day hold in the palms of my hands. Ever since, my luck has been enormous, and I owe every stroke of that good fortune to so many kind and clever people.

Endless thanks to my agent, Bridget Smith at JABberwocky Literary, who has had time and love for this story right from the very beginning. Bridget, I'm beyond thankful for all of the doors you've opened for this story—and for me—ever since. You had faith that Taylor would find her feet when this tale was a comedy of many errors, and your unbelievable insight has taught me more than you know.

I'm so grateful to everyone at Page Street Publishing. To my wonderful editor, Tamara Grasty, whose vision and enthusiasm brought so many parts of Taylor's story together to look like they'd always fit. To my thoughtful and patient copy editor, Kaitlin Severini. My talented cover and book designer, Kylie Alexander, and cover illustrator, Agustina Gastaldi. And a big thank you to the very gifted authors who were so generous to read and share kind words about this story.

To my nearest and dearest: your encouragement and kindness means the world. And to each of my girls: as a kid, I thought I'd learned all there was to know about sisterhood from wearing out my *Practical Magic* VHS—and then I met you.

To my brother, Jack, who was not only born with an extra wisdom tooth but an extra funny bone, too: if kissing the Blarney Stone when we were little gave *me* the gift of the gab, then pulling that living-statue stunt at Madame Tussauds when you were seven set your very charming—and very cheeky—personality in stone. I was lucky enough to be your first friend. I'll always be your proudest.

To my dad, Garry, who is the epitome of the improvisation rule "yes, and…". A few years ago, I danced around the idea of entering *Saturday Night Live's* "Biggest Fan" ticket competition—if I was lucky enough to win, I'd have a week to fly ten thousand miles to make it in time for the taping. To that, you said, "so go home, and write something funny, and then see what happens," and I went home, and I wrote something funny, and then *something happened.* This story wouldn't be what it is if you hadn't said "yes, and…". Your love, support, and spirit have given me all the gifts I'll ever need.

My staunch mum, Donna, who is my very best friend. You put paperbacks in my hands and dressed up for our school storytelling days, and for that, and so, *so* much more, I am forever grateful. Thank you for breakfasts at Red's and sunsets at Crane Estate and Thanksgiving on the first floor of a little pink hatter's house. There's nobody I'd rather ride a 30 Rock elevator with, Edie.

This book is written in memory of my nanna, Lola, who had shelves bursting with books. I might be my mother's daughter, but I'm my grandmother's too, and for every story I'd love to be able to tell her, there are twice as many that I'd love for her to be able to tell me. With each year that passes, my questions about her storied life stack up like the programs in her musical theatre collection, but when there's a coveted seat miraculously empty beside mine in a sold-out theatre, it gives me hope that one day, somehow, she'll find a way to show me the answers.

Finally, thank you to each and every reader. The importance of queer stories is indescribable, and by reading, you help make them visible. In the end, Taylor won—in so many ways. As long as inclusive, proud, and *true* stories keep being told, the more we all win, too.

ABOUT THE AUTHOR

Hayli Thomson lives in Sydney, Australia, and writes novels about candid characters for anybody who ever watched Jo March leap a fence and longed to be her best friend. Bizarrely, during her teen years, Hayli was afflicted with a "headache" every third Monday in September, when she was left with no option but to stay home from school and watch her favorite female comedians collect Emmys live on the other side of the world. *The Comedienne's Guide to Pride* is her debut YA novel. You can visit her online at www.haylithomson.com.

*If Only
I Were
A Better
Mother*

If Only
I Were
A Better
Mother

Melissa Gayle West

STILLPOINT

STILLPOINT PUBLISHING
Building a society that honors The Earth,
Humanity, and The Sacred in all Life.
For a free catalog or ordering information, write
Stillpoint Publishing, Box 640, Walpole, NH 03608, USA
or call
1-800-847-4014 TOLL-FREE (Continental US, except NH)
1-603-756-9281 (Foreign and NH)

This book is manufactured in the United States of America.
Text design by Karen Savary

Published by Stillpoint Publishing, Box 640,
Meetinghouse Road, Walpole, NH 03608

Library of Congress Catalog Card Number: 92-80779

West, Melissa Gayle
If Only I Were a Better Mother

ISBN 0-913299-87-1
5 7 9 8 6 4

To my mother, Tibby,
to my daughter, Eloise,
and to the Mystery that births us all

Contents

PART IV: The Return: *Hearts Open Wide*

Foreword

*H*undreds of manuscripts cross my desk every year. From these only a few are selected for publication. We publishers all have our own criteria for the choosing of books that we hope will be meaningful to our readers and thus successful. My interest in a book is based on the degree to which I am moved by its message and the power and skill with which the author delivers her thoughts.

I read Melissa West's book while on vacation. I was so compelled by her message that I called her from a pay phone to tell her we wanted to publish her book. *If Only I Were a Better Mother* has had an astonishing effect on me, considering that my children are now teenagers and older. The inner question marks one collects while raising children don't just evaporate, they sit there in our minds and hearts until answers are forthcoming. For many mothers, those answers never come, and so we never have the satisfaction of knowing that what we felt and did on our "bad days" was as justified as what we did on the "good days," when we thought we were the perfect mother.

I wanted to be a mother long before I actually was one. Like many young married women, I planned my family, anticipating only the rosy glow of motherhood. Being a mother can certainly produce an inner and outer glow, although the fire burns most intensely when our children's immediate needs compete with our longing to direct our attention elsewhere. This fire within us can glow with the warmth and companionship that we've imagined, but it can also consume us.

Melissa West has written a book that deeply touches all parts of our inner fire as women, as mothers, as daughters, and as contributing members of this miraculous planet Earth. Melissa carefully, sensitively guides us through the conflicting mother-feelings that can—and often have—consumed us, to the warm, accepting, and truly nurturing mother-feeling that is the basis for spiritual growth in ourselves and in our children.

Spirituality and mothering are intimately, crucially related, one to the other, if we as women are to allow our unique ability of offering life to the world to carry meaning for ourselves as well. We've taken motherhood for granted, accepting it as part of our heritage; it is what we do to ensure that we'll have a next generation. Yet the total completion and fulfillment that comes from understanding and validating our experience of mothering has often been lost through the misleading ideal of the "good mother." Melissa addresses this problem with such insight.

Women today want more from their lives than a splintered, frantic existence of running from job to family and back again, always feeling guilty and never good enough or available enough. The challenges of trying to have a career and be a mother are overwhelming in the best of times, let alone when the baby is sick and the office calls to tell you that your most important client is waiting at your desk. Mothering is the most demanding profession because it requires the primary nurturing of children who will carry in their hearts messages influenced heavily by their mothers. Of this responsibility we as mothers are perfectly aware. Yet the spiritual journey offers the mother a great deal that suggests she is not alone responsible for this child. She is part of an evolutionary process, and all that has gone before her contributes to this new generation. The idea that motherhood is a spiritual journey is the truest aspect of life itself and forms the basis upon which women can take up the necessary courage to see that the paths they walk are essential—in fact, critical—to their own development as women.

If Only I Were a Better Mother is written with love and humor. But more than that, it is written with wisdom and insight. The memories of times when we responded to our children in ways that seemed unloving, selfish, or not as "good mothers" will haunt us for the rest of our lives unless we discover the nature of wholeness in mothering and permission to put these memories to rest. We do this by honoring our own spiritual journey and the miraculous experience of giving birth and raising, along with others, the children of tomorrow's world.

Melissa's book will make you laugh and cry. Most important, it will make you feel what you've been unable to feel before: a belief in yourself and your own ability to nurture your children successfully. You have in fact chosen this experience of mothering, and the joy and beauty you find together with your children will forever mark your adventure on this Earth.

Meredith L. Young-Sowers
Publisher, Stillpoint Publishing
Author of *Agartha: A Journey to the Stars*
and *Language of the Soul*
February 1992

Acknowledgements

So many people I wish to acknowledge: the Sunday night writing group, all its past and present members, and especially Barbara Turner-Vesselago and Debra Jarvis, for support, love, constructive criticism, and plenty of sillies. For reading the manuscript, and offering helpful feedback, Carla Berkedal, Melissa Smith, Eric Beck, Barbara Fischer, Laura Peterson. Thanks to all the mothers who have shared their stories and lives with me. I am deeply grateful to the community of all sentient beings: people, creatures, ocean, rocks, rain, sky, and forest, at Point No Point, where so much of this book was conceived and labored over. Many, many, many thanks to Eloise's caregivers, Sharlyn and Scott Hubbard, and Melissa Smith, without whose loving care this book could not have been written. Deepest gratitude to my editor, Meredith Young-Sowers, and all the people at Stillpoint, both for their help and support of me, and for their vision of a healed planet.

And, finally, to Rodg, partner in this Great Adventure.

Author's Preface

"*If* only I were a better mother. . . ." How many times has each one of us said that, out loud to friend or partner, or silently in our own heart of hearts?

The journey of ten thousand miles begins with one step, goes the old Chinese saying. The first step for many mothers on this journey to find a fuller, richer, more loving way of being a mother is the acknowledgment that something feels missing. They have a sense deep in their bones that there is more to mothering than the daily round of carpooling, diapering, and picking up.

The gnawing sense of something missing leads many women out of their homes and their daily routines and into classes I offer for "Mothering As A Spiritual Path." The "first step" on this journey of discovery for these mothers is showing up for the first night of class—a step into the unknown. For you, the reader of this book, the first step might be picking up this book and deciding to read it. If that is so for you, welcome to the journey.

In Part 1 of *If Only I Were A Better Mother* you will have

an opportunity to meet some fellow travelers and get a map of the journey of transformation through mothering. The next three parts correspond to the three stages of the journey itself.

Part 2, "Naming the Journey: Getting Past the Lions," concerns the first stage, that of naming what is really happening for mothers, both internally and at a cultural level.

Part 3, "Descent: Dancing with Kali," describes the second stage of acknowledging denied feelings and letting go of destructive cultural expectations of motherhood.

Part 4, "The Return: Hearts Open Wide," describes the third and final stage, that of a new way of mothering—with an open heart and clear mind. This fully-embodied, fully-alive way of mothering is born from the pain and personal discoveries of the previous stage.

The Resources described at the end of the book give you, the reader, exercises for journaling, body awareness, imagery work, food for thought, and practical tips. Blank Journal Pages, in which you can write your thoughts, feelings, and experiences, are included at the end of the Resource section. Finally, you will find a list of suggested reading for many subjects touched upon in the book.

Welcome on the journey. Let's get started.

I

Preparation:
Call to the Journey

*In the middle of the journey of our life, I came
to myself within a dark wood where the straight
way was lost.*

—DANTE

CHAPTER
1

A Map of the Territory

A COMMUNITY OF MOTHERS

Sixteen mothers sit in soft chairs and sofas around me. It is the first night of my "Mothering as a Spiritual Path" class. Each mother has come tonight in response to a brochure mailed to her weeks before. In the class description I defined "spiritual" as "contact with the Sacred; living deeply whatever life brings; being present with a fully open heart to oneself and others." I invited mothers of all ages and persuasions to come explore the ways mothering was a spiritual path for them and the way they might deepen and broaden their experience of that path.

The youngest woman in the living room tonight is twenty-four, slightly frazzled, with a three-month-old baby at home. The oldest is a well-dressed sixty-two-year-old mother of three and grandmother of four. There are women of all ages in between. They have identified themselves as Christian, New Age, Buddhist, unaffiliated.

I open the class by asking each mother to speak about the reasons she has come tonight. There is silence until a thirtyish mother in jeans and a hot pink sweatshirt speaks up. "I think I've always known, since Seth was born six years ago, that mothering is some sort of spiritual path for me. I've done lots of exploring, lots of it, and mothering is both the hardest and the most rewarding one I've ever been on. It's different from any other type of spiritual path I've tried because there's no way to get off—the practice is always there for me in the form of my son. Before him, practicing a spiritual path always seemed optional, something I didn't have to do if I wasn't really in the mood; now I'm doing it all the time, every day, whether I feel like it or not."

"I know what you mean." A woman in her late forties leans forward in excitement. "All those spiritual teachings I've tried to follow all my life, it seems as if I was in kindergarten with them until I had my kids. . . . But you know, I never hear about mothering in that vein; it's as if spiritual practice is somewhere else, and then you come home to your family. I don't believe that; it seems like being with my family really is my spiritual practice, but I never hear anyone talking like that. It's always as if spirituality is someplace else."

"That's right, and I'm so tired of it too," interjects a redheaded woman in her twenties. "I always thought I was the only one who saw things that way, too. I've always kept it to myself: the way being with my daughter makes me feel more spiritual than most things I've ever experienced."

Amid vigorous nodding, another mother, a slightly greying forty-year-old with two teens at home, hesitantly speaks up. She talks of reaching lower "lows" in the course of mothering, as she struggles with her adolescents around dating, school, clothing, than at any other time in her life.

The mood in the room visibly changes. The young mother of the infant begins to cry quietly. Other mothers then open up: they talk of feeling guilty about the anger, fear, grief, despair that they have all felt at times as mothers. Almost all articulate that these "dark times" have blocked their capacity to experience mothering as being spiritual. They say that when they feel these difficult feelings, they lose contact with their own hearts, with their own children, with their sense of the sacredness of life.

A hush falls over the group, a hush that follows the telling of a long-held secret. . . . Rustles break the silence as several women shift in their chairs, adjust their clothing. The grandmother coughs into her hand.

I take a deep breath and look at each mother sitting around me.

"What if," I propose, "your experience of the sacred and the dark with your children are simply opposite sides of the same coin? What if it is possible that, by accepting the darkness and opening into it rather than fighting it, you could emerge with an even deeper sense of mothering as a spiritual path than you ever had before? What if, indeed, the darkness that you all have experienced as mothers could be a gate into an even deeper relationship with your own children, with yourselves, with the Sacred? What if this could be so? What if . . . ?"

I look once more at the sixteen faces around me. Some of the mothers are crying. All of their faces show incredulity, and surprise, and hope.

STAGES OF THE JOURNEY

As the weeks progress the mothers move, at their own individual paces, through what I have articulated as the three stages of this journey. As they move through these stages I tell them that going through these once is just the beginning of a cycle of many cycles, of the deepening of this path. When their children enter a new developmental stage, such as adolescence, this work in all probability will need to be done again, at an even deeper level. Likewise, as they, the mothers, go through their own developmental stages such as entering midlife, or through unexpected turns of life like the death of a partner or divorce, they will in all likelihood go through the process again.

On that first night in a typical class I give an overview of the journey, the way to this new land of a deeper way of mothering. I am delighted to pass on the map as I understand it, an amalgamation of my own experience and all of the other mother-travelers with whom I have been graced to work. Not surprisingly, the stages of this transformational journey correspond roughly to the three stages marked out in other archetypal rites of passage.[1]

The first stage involves naming the old, the status quo,

and then leaving the old and the known behind, relinquishing it at both an outer and an inner level. The next stage, the transition or liminal (*limen* being Greek for "threshold" or "margin"[2]) stage is an interim period of "not knowing," vulnerability, loss, and total surrender to the process, a true "dark night of the soul" (Victor Turner describes this "betwixt-and-between" period as "fruitful darkness"[3]). The final stage is that of initiation: rebirth, the return of spring and new inner and outer life, the stage of incorporating into one's own daily life a new way of being in the world.

The way these stages look and feel in this particular discipline of mothering as a spiritual path are as follows.

NAMING THE JOURNEY

As women and mothers, we have often been denied the power and possibility of naming our experience. We have been denied the opportunity to talk about what it is truly like to be a mother, for better and for worse; we have not been able to talk about the cultural binds and boxes we are stuffed into as mothers. Just to articulate the possibility of mothering as a spiritual and transformative journey is a powerful act. Just to say, "Sometimes mothering is the most difficult thing I've ever undertaken; sometimes, just sometimes, I would rather not be a mother at all," is the first important step toward breaking the chains that our culture has bound us with as mothers.

This cognitive work, this act of naming, leads to the release of feelings long buried in us as mothers, and also, quite often, to fear: the fear engendered by breaking taboos, by telling those truths that our culture has not allowed us to even acknowledge internally, much less say out loud. Someone (I can't remember who) once wisely said, "The truth will set you free, but first it may make you hurt like hell."

Community, whether in a group of mothers, with another friend and mother, or even alone with this book, is very important in facilitating the growth and change that happens when women heal old wounds. In this first stage a mother in the class may articulate feelings that seem very dark, forbidden at a deep level by our culture to say, words like "Sometimes I don't even like my child; sometimes I just want to run away and be all by myself." I see this mother's fear over naming something heretofore unnameable, and the courage she musters to express it. Then I see her surprise at what invariably follows: a chorus of "me too!"'s and "I'm so glad to know I'm not alone!"'s. What starts out as a hesitant solo expression of feelings always seems to lead to a powerful chorus. There is tremendous power in naming.

THE DESCENT

The naming stage soon gives way to a deeper, more turbulent stage. This is the dark time, the time of acknowledging and feeling whatever feelings have been repressed generally for mothers: anger, fear, longing, despair, sorrow; and for acknowledging and feeling whatever feelings I, in particular, have repressed as mother. This is a time of housecleaning for the soul, for flushing out all those things that have held us back from being fully alive and embodied. This is a time of unknowing, of meeting that deepest, unknown place inside ourselves, of being stripped of everything that had once been known, and secure, and comfortable.

This second stage is like the "dark night of the soul" described so often in spiritual literature, a time of purification as well as a deepening and maturing of the spiritual life. Paul Brunton writes, "It is a grave misconception to regard the spiritual progress as passing mostly through ecstasies and raptures. . . . It passes just as much through broken hearts and bruised emotions."[4] This is a time of despair, of inner darkness, a time of helplessness and of being undone in order to prepare for something greater.

In the literature of various cultures and spiritualities, this stage is often portrayed as a descent. Many heroines and goddesses had to descend in order to find healing and salvation. Jungian analysts claim that mythic descent represents going below our normal consciousness to reclaim those parts of ourselves that have been lost. In the Greek myth, Demeter descends in order to reclaim her daughter-self, Persephone. The Sumerian Innana and the Babylonian Ishtar descend to reclaim their lost sons and lovers. Innana is a perfect example. Sylvia Brinton Perera, in *Descent to the Goddess* (see Recommended Reading), uses the Innana myth beautifully as a metaphor for the journey women must make in order to reclaim their wholeness. Christ and Mohammed both descend in their journeys. Dante, in the quintessential Christian mystical journey, must travel down through the Inferno before he reaches the Paradisio. These descents may be seen as metaphors for the often painful self-confrontation and stripping away that is necessary before transformation and new life.

For myself, and for many other women, there is as well another meaning for "descent." In this time and culture, we are encouraged to live much of our lives in our heads, up and away from the truth of our bodies. Likewise, much of our spirituality involves going "up" and "out": God, we learn, is someplace else, and the further we can rise out of our bodies the more likely we are to find God, our Higher Power, the Source of Life. (Please feel free, if you have difficulty with the word "God," to substitute whatever term you wish for the Source of Life whenever the word occurs.) Part of our healing as mothers and as women is to make the journey back into our bodies, descend into our bodily homes and hearts, and reclaim the truth, the power, and the sacredness that resides within.

In order to receive this new life, within and without, we must first be emptied of the old. I tell a Zen story to illustrate this stage. A student comes to study with a famous Master. This student is very eager to learn, but he is filled with knowledge, filled with his own ideas of how things are and how things should be. The Master invites him into his simple hut for tea. The student chafes at this, wanting to get directly on to learning about Life and Spirituality, but reluctantly assents. The Master hands him a full teacup and then proceeds to pour tea into it, and pour, and pour, until the cup in the flabbergasted student's hand is overflowing onto the bare, clean floor. "Stop!" cries the student, "what are you doing? My cup is overflowing!"

"Ah yes," replies the Master, putting the teapot down, "How difficult it is to put anything into a cup that is already filled to the brim!"

And so it is with us, and with mothering. This second

stage, this dark night, is a time of emptying, of letting go of the known, so that we may in the next stage be filled with far more life and love than we ever dreamed possible. This is often a time when one is even emptied of spiritual solace, experiencing a sense of loss of whatever spirituality one has been practicing, when it seems as if one has even been abandoned by God Her/Himself.

What I hear most often in this stage from mothers is "I can't survive this much pain; how can I keep on doing this?" This stage is most like transition in laboring to give birth to a child. Just as in labor, we need a partner or coach or community at this time, for support and encouragement, and to remind us, when we have lost the ability to remind ourselves, that this pain is in the service of something greater, of bringing new life into the world. This coach, this friend, this community, can hold us in a bigger and more loving space than we can possibly create for ourselves when we are in so much pain. They remind us both that this pain has a purpose, and that the pain will have an end.

At some mysterious time in the process, there is a turning, the beginning of release from pain and the sense of something new being born within. A moment comes, perhaps an hour or even a morning, when the first glimmer of a new life, a new way of being so much more filled with life and light and aliveness than we had ever dared hoped for, emerges. The possibilities of an entirely new way of being a mother open up. The baby, so to speak, is coming down the birth canal. There may be some hard work still ahead, but the time of dilating and stretching far more than we thought it was possible to stretch is mostly behind.

THE RETURN

Words can only approximate in a pale fashion what this last stage, ineffable, is truly like. Many mystics call it "living the Unitive life," and that is indeed how it feels. We have learned that we can stay open to *whatever mothering brings us*, no matter what, that we can stay open and responsive to our children, no matter what, and this learning is generalized to the rest of our lives.

Staying open, connected, unified with ourselves, our children, and the greater web of life into which we are all woven is the way of this last stage. We learn that, no matter what occurs between ourselves and our children, we can keep our hearts open and soft. We learn that, as we stay open in this way, life brings us more and more moments of grace as mothers, both a feeling of grace within and grace between ourselves and our children.

I call this way of being with our children and the world "dancing on the razor's edge," the razor's edge in Eastern spiritual literature referring to that place of spiritual transformation within and around us that is always available for the asking. Since it is a razor's edge, though, we may fall off from time to time, forget how to dance in that special place, begin to contract again and lose that soft and powerful openness to life and to our children. After going through this process, however, we will always carry in our bodies and souls the memory of the way mothering, and living, can be if we breathe, open, and soften our hearts and say "Yes" to the present moment. And so each time that we fall we can get up and brush ourselves off. We can then acknowledge that we have fallen off, and climb on once again to resume the Dance with our children, and with life.

In this final stage our bodies feel more alive, more flexible, safer and livelier places to be, since many of the dark and taboo corners have been cleaned out. We feel a new sense of power as mothers. Before making this journey, our sense of power came from "power over"—trying to force things to happen in mothering. Now we feel "power within"—our own potency and liveliness in our own bodies, the power to be fully present, the power to feel what we feel and know what we know, the power to do whatever it is that we need to do, moment by moment.

Our greater sense of spirituality has been transformed as well. We feel a stronger presence in our own lives of the holiness and grace embedded within the ordinary, the transcendent shining through our everyday lives with our children. This newfound sense of the sacred within the daily does not depend upon our children being "good," upon our being "good." We can sense the sacred even when we are at our worst; life comes through us no matter how we behave. We have a stronger sense of the community of all life, of all sentient beings, in which we are all deeply embedded, and we find that we can practice honoring this community of all life as we mother our children.

Finally, in this "homecoming" stage, we can see what great gifts we have given our children by passing through darkness and out the other side. First, the gift of fully alive and embodied mothers. Second, the gift of giving our children, as well, permission to be fully alive and present in the world. And, finally, the greatest gift of all, the gift of acknowledging all life as holy, of all acts, great and small, as carriers of grace, of celebrating within even the most daily motions with our children the great and gracious web of life within which we all live.

SETTING OUT

The journey we are about to share in this book is Everymother's journey. This book is also a chronicle of my own journey as a mother, the journey into motherdarkness and out into a changed life. *If Only I Were a Better Mother* is the story of my first passage through these three stages of change that I've described briefly. I have included some journal entries I've written during that journey so that you may feel safe in "naming" your own struggles and triumphs. My experiences are often intense, as I am an intense woman. Other women on this journey have experienced a wide range of feelings, ranging from quite subtle to very intense.

Please know that no matter how upsetting, fearful, or seemingly off-base your own feelings during your own journey may be, they are within the range of what others have felt. Some feelings you may be able to integrate well on your own and with the help of friends; other feelings as they surface might require the additional support of professional help. Ask for, and open to, whatever sort of help and support feels best for you.

This book is an affirmation of what both I and increasingly many other mothers have found: that, amazingly, our own tender and spacious hearts lie in the depths of that inner darkness. That after making this journey, and continuing to make it over and over (for it is an ongoing process), I find myself in a larger, more sacred space with myself and with my child than I have ever imagined. The boon, the incredible gift, of this journey is the discovery that all of mothering, *all of it*, is inherently sacred.

Come now and make that journey with me.

Naming the Journey:
Getting Past the Lions

*One does not become enlightened by imaging fig-
ures of light, but by making the darkness
conscious.*

—CARL JUNG

2

Where Did I Go Wrong?

We begin to be mothers from the time we are born. We form our first impressions of mothering from the time that we are cradled in our own mothers' arms. Our experiences of growing up and being mothered by our own mothers, grandmothers, and aunts shape our sense of ourselves and ideally give us the tools and resources necessary to successfully mother our own children. Some women are thrilled when they get pregnant, some are terrified, and some are ambivalent. Whatever the state of a woman's mind, pregnancy opens doorways to new emotions and spiritual opportunities.

We are complex beings, with rich, multi-level experiences that make profound impressions on our emotional and spiritual senses. When we begin the journey into motherhood, we awaken the inner messages that have been developing since our birth. The ways we were nurtured or abandoned, loved or ignored; the television shows we watched growing up; the nursery rhymes and stories we were read and the songs we sang; all critically shaped our inner selves and our expectations of the way to be a mother.

Our own struggles to be acknowledged, nurtured, and valued may have gone unnoticed until the time comes to mother another. Then the unheard messages leap to the front of our awareness, demanding attention when we have the least amount of time, energy, and patience and when we are supposed to be attending exclusively to our own child's needs.

How do we heal our own inner wounds when we aren't aware they exist before we have children of our own? How can we understand and make room for our needs at the same time we handle our children's needs? How can we be fully alive human beings and mothers at the same time?

When my daughter Eloise was born I did not know the answers to these questions; in fact, I was unaware of the questions themselves. Like most mothers, I wasn't prepared for many of my feelings, or for my child's responses.

PREGNANT AT LAST!

After waiting so long to have children, after doing all the things I wanted to do before settling down, my feet finally slowing down after years of restless travel, I was ready to stay put, be domestic, pull back on my career. I was ready to be a mother.

I had motherhood all figured out: I knew what I wanted, and I was going to create it. I was going to be a Good Mother: calm, patient, unconditionally loving to my child no matter what he or she did. I was going to give endlessly to this child inside me, this child I wanted so much and already loved so much. I was going to love this child from a bottomless source of love inside me.

Oh yes, I sometimes acknowledged: of course there would be bad moments—after all, that's a part of mothering too, isn't it? But those moments would pass quickly. Mostly, mothering was going to be about me giving to my child and loving my child from a pure and spiritual place inside me. I was going to give this child all the love I felt I missed in childhood. I was going to mother better than I had been mothered; I was never going to raise my voice against my child, terrify my child with my anger, hit my child. I would be there for him or her, always, gladly. I was going to be a Good Mother, a perfect mother.

That summer of waiting for my child to be born was a hot one. I lay on my sofa after working, bare feet propped up on pillows, hair pulled back in a ponytail. I rubbed my beautiful burgeoning belly with swollen hands, singing songs to and loving the growing child inside of me. I couldn't wait. . . .

REALITY SETS IN

The period of waiting and dreaming that pregnancy brings reinforces all our previous programming that tells us motherhood is going to be wonderful and whatever difficulties arise can be worked out easily. We are rarely

prepared to face the struggle of dealing with our own
unmet needs and at the same time give so much concentrated attention to our children, especially in the first
few years of their lives.

I remember, as perhaps many of you reading this book
may also recall, the first time I crossed some invisible
line and reacted to my child in a way that not only scared
me but brought into conscious awareness all the old programming inside of my head that I had been so unconscious of.

My daughter, Eloise, was two years old when the enor-
mity of my mixed feelings about mothering finally sur-
faced. For the first few years after Eloise was born, I'd
been relatively successful in ignoring or pushing un-
wanted feelings into the background. But suddenly
something had gone wrong, and Eloise and I had come
to an impasse where I could no longer ignore my internal
maelstrom of conflicting feelings.

I remember the incident as clearly as if it had been
yesterday. It was nine o'clock in the morning, and Eloise
was still in her nightgown, playing with Gumby and
Pokey at her table in the living room. I felt tired, de-
feated, and housebound. I knew I didn't have the energy
to get Eloise dressed. The timer rang. "Eloise," I said,
"it's time to get dressed now."

"LA-ter." She flung one look at me, a "back-off-
Mama-if-you-know-what's-good-for-you" look, and went
back to giving Gumby his twentieth pretend bath of the
morning.

"Not later, Eloise, it's time to get dressed *now*."

Silence. I reminded myself to take a deep breath. That didn't help. I took another.

"Eloise. Eloise, do you hear me?" (Oh God, was that my mother speaking across the years?)

No response. I took another deep breath, calm on the outside, the real drama unfolding silently inside my head: (ELOISE! ELOISE, DO YOU *HEAR* ME? ARE YOU DEAF? I LEAN OVER AND SHAKE HER, HARD, UNTIL WHATEVER INFERNAL THING THAT SELECTIVELY BLOCKS OUT ONLY HER MOTH-ER'S VOICE IS JARRED LOOSE AND FALLS OUT.)

Outwardly, after yet another deep, slow breath, I reminded myself that, after all, she was only two and this was the way two-year-olds were supposed to act; it was good for them to learn independence (YES, BUT WHAT ABOUT *ME*?), and so I tried again: "Eloise, it is time for you to get dressed; I need to go to the bank, and remember I said we'll go to the playground after that" (ANYTHING, I'LL PROMISE ANYTHING, JUST THIS ONCE GET DRESSED WITHOUT A SCENE).

"NO, Mama, LA-ter," she said condescendingly, as if tired of trying to explain to me that what she was doing was far more important.

I squatted down eye level to her as she sat at her little table. "Eloise, listen. I don't want a scene, and I know you don't want one either. We can cooperate. Do you remember that word, 'co-op-er-ate'?" I said this in my best modulated, Mr. Rogers, gentle-but-firm) voice. (What I really wanted to shout is: DAMMIT, ELOISE, JUST PUT ON YOUR CLOTHES *RIGHT NOW*. IT'S

NINE O'CLOCK IN THE MORNING AND YOU
GOT ME UP AT FIVE O'CLOCK IN THE MORN-
ING IN THE MIDDLE OF A NICE DREAM AND
I COULDN'T SAY, "LA-TER, ELOISE, LA-TER,"
OR PRETEND I DIDN'T HEAR YOU AND I'M SO
TIRED OF BEING THE ONE TO DO ALL THE
GIVING, ALL THE WAITING, AND WHEN IS IT
MY TURN?)

"Mama, LA-ter."

"OK, Eloise, I hate to do this but I have to get to the
bank so my weekend checks don't bounce," and I picked
her up, "NNNOOOOOOOO" right in my ear as I carried
her, wriggling and kicking and wailing, to the lazyboy.
Calf roping, I thought grimly, would be a breeze, as I
tried to pull a tee shirt over her blond head while she
thrashed her arms and legs.

"NNNNNNOOOOOOOOOOOOOOOO."

I wondered how many of my neighbors were convinced
that I beat and tortured my child.

"NNNNNNNNNOOOOOOOOOOOOOOOOOOOO-
OOO."

Shirt on now, I went for the pants. When I got them
up to her knees she managed a kick hard enough to send
the pants flying.

"NNNNNNNNNNNOOOOOOOOOOOOOOOOOO-
OOOOOOOOOOOO."

"Eloise. ELOISE. Stop it, STOP IT, I hate this too."
For a brief moment the struggle ceased, we locked eyes,
both panting. Maybe, I prayed, just maybe I could get
her pants on without more struggle, maybe she was worn
out as I was. "C'mon, Eloise, let's just get your pants
on and move to something that's more fun for both of
us. Please, Eloise, let's get going."

"NNNNNNNNNNNNNOOOOOOOOOOOOOO-
OOOOOOOOOOOOOOOOOOOOOO."

The struggle began anew, and with renewed determination I reached for the pants, pinned her down, and
wrestled them on. Gone was any gentleness or tenderness in my handling of her. What I was stripped to
was rage barely checked and a willingness to match her
obduracy, whatever that took. Part of me simply
wanted to throttle her. Anything. Anything that would
restore to me peace, and stillness, and quiet, all long
fled from the hubbub that now was my life.

I lifted Eloise up, still thrashing, and yanked the
pants on. My jaw was clamped shut so hard my teeth
hurt. "OK, Eloise, all done, I know how angry you feel
but this is something that needs to be done. I'm sorry
I have to do it this way."

Breathing hard, she stopped crying, gave me a hating
look, and rolled off my lap by pushing me roughly
away. She landed on her back, lower lip jutted out de-
fiantly, still pushing me away with her eyes.

I drew a breath. A shaky one was all I could manage.
At that moment, listening to both of us breathe, I hated
my child.

I hated myself for my feelings, but I wished her gone.
I stood up, legs shaking, and walked to the kitchen.

This was the place of recognition where I began the
process of naming, where I began my inner journey.
Many mothers say their journey began in a similar man-
ner, with a flash of understanding that the old ways of
mothering couldn't work. This is the time of beginning
to name and sort out our feelings: those that are angry,
those that are hateful, those that are loving and caring,

and the so-strange ways these feelings get all convo-
luted together inside.

THE   VOICE   OF   THE   "GOOD   MOTHER"

Perhaps the worst part of becoming conscious of difficult
feelings about our children is the concomitant discovery
of the voice of the "Good Mother" inside our own heads.
This voice speaks the messages of our culture and families about how to be a good mother. The messages may
be found in many parenting books, on television, in novels and poetry. For this voice, and our culture, the only
way to be a Good Mother is to be a Perfect Mother,
always loving, cheerful, and giving. When we start to
feel those feelings about mothering our children that we
have repressed, this voice begins to speak up, to get us
back on track in our struggle towards perfection.

This voice tells us how to be a good mother, but what
she really speaks of is our false self, a false mother-self
we need to construct in order to try and squeeze ourselves
into the life-denying mold of motherhood we are given
by our culture. Throughout the rest of this book I will
refer to this voice as the Good Mother, not because she
represents good mothering, but because this is the guise
in which she presents herself.

I became aware that when I said I loved my child after
this episode with Eloise, this Good Mother voice inside
my head would whisper to me, "You lie."

"You lie," she whispered, "look how angry you are at
your child. See how you want her to be gone . . . . You
lie. No Good Mother ever feels that way about her children. No Good Mother ever does."

I was confused. I never knew, before having my child, that I could love someone with such passionate intensity and delight. Loving her was always the easy part. What was difficult for me was the rest—harboring such strong feelings: anger; despair; sadness; the difficulty of truly letting go; the resentments, all engendered by the day-to-day realities of caring for a child. I was not prepared for these feelings, or for their intensity. How could I be a good mother and wish my child wasn't there? What did it mean about me if I was so angry at her sometimes that all I wanted to do was shove her against the wall? ("IT MEANS YOU'RE A BAD MOTHER, THAT'S WHAT IT MEANS," said the Good Mother within me.) It was hard, as it is for most of us when we hear her voice inside us, not to believe her.

I turned to books to find answers. I haunted bookstores and scoured libraries to find reassurance that something wasn't wrong with me, that I wasn't a bad mother for sometimes feeling these feelings. I found little help. The most that was given to me in the parenting books I found was an occasional acknowledgement that in the course of mothering there sometimes were bad days.

I looked to the major spiritual traditions. Again, I read anything I could find, talked to those steeped in their traditions. The most I could find was an idealization of motherhood, totally selfless and giving women: the Virgin Mary, Kuan Yin, Earth Mother. Nothing about raging mothers, grieving mothers, mothers who wanted, at least for split seconds, to "kill" their children. All this searching only made me feel worse. What was wrong with me? Why couldn't I be a Good Mother and be calm, serene, in control? Was I the only mother who ever experienced these terrible feelings?

SEARCHING FOR ANSWERS

Journal Entry
December 15, 1989

I spent this morning at the University library. Going through the Reader's Guide to Periodicals, *going through* Books in Print, *going through* Psychological Abstracts, *page after page after page of reference. And what did I find about motherhood and darkness, motherhood and grief, motherhood and despair? Nothing.*

Plenty of books and articles to tell me what a joy mothering is ("The Delights of Motherhood," "Celebrating Our Kids"), but none to tell me as well how truly difficult mothering can be. No one writing about being awake in the middle of the night, in between visits to a sick child's room, no sleep for days, crying from weariness and frustration and helplessness. Nothing. Silence. It can't be that I'm the only mother to have felt as if "me" was disappearing, suffocating under the giant midden of daily tasks. I can't be the only one. Why is nothing written? Why?

My throat tightens as I write this question; I want to shout I KNOW WHY. Because I'm never supposed to feel these feelings, ask these questions (the Good Mother inside my head clears her throat, gently reminding me that this is what she has been telling me all along). Because my image of motherhood, my culture's image of motherhood, is that of the serene Madonna, smiling down at the child on her lap.

Being a mother means having radical surgery. It means having that part of me that cries and despairs irrevocably cut away. It means having a lobotomy so that I don't think about what it's really like to change two thousand diapers, or pick up every day only to have the same chaos descend upon the room five minutes after picking up. It means having my heart cut out so that it doesn't break when my daughter says she hates me. It means getting de-barked, like a dog, so that I will never raise my voice to my child in frustration or rage. So much of me to cut out, get rid of, in order to be a Good Mother. A mutilated Melissa, but a good mommy.

Actually, I was incorrect when I wrote that I found nothing this morning in the library: I did, in my time there, find evidence of despairing mothers, dark mothers, depressed mothers. I found these mothers in Psychological Abstracts. *What, or who, I found there were Abnormal Mothers: mothers who hated their children; mothers who were severely depressed; mothers who sometimes didn't want to be mothers. Articles describing in cold, clinical terms how I sometimes felt: Abnormal. These articles, for the most part, were written by men, authorities on mothering: psychologists, physicians, psychiatrists. Men who have never been mothers.*[5]

I read none of these articles. I have had enough authorities, inner and outer, telling me the same thing: how deviant I am to feel these feelings and ask these questions. I want no more of that. I want to find, I hunger for, affirmations that these feelings are, at least in this culture and at least at times, a normal part of mothering. I want affirmation that there might be good reasons for these feelings. I want affirmation that these feelings have some meaning.

I feel the anger slowly subsiding now. I was so angry back there in that library full of quiet concentrating students. So easy, too easy now to go back to being a good mother, a nice mother. Behave myself. Choke back my angry words and feelings. Join the ranks of the voiceless mothers, mute. Say nothing. Write nothing. Just be good. A Good Mother.

LOOKING INSIDE

I began to understand the futility, at this point in my journey, of looking outside for answers. There were none outside. Fortunately, I had the support of a group of women with whom I met weekly. Many of them were mothers, they understood my feelings, and they supported my questioning.

Outside support is so important in this process. It is difficult for us as individuals to question the status quo, the cultural norms we are given. The journey is eased greatly when we can find others who are asking the same questions, feeling the same feelings. Others can't give us the answers; the answers will emerge, eventually, from within our own hearts, bodies, and souls. Others *can* encourage us, as Rilke once wrote to a struggling poet, to live into the questions.

I began to pay more attention to my dreams, hoping for some guidance at a level deeper than my conscious mind could provide. One night, during those months of questioning and searching, I had a dream, a dream that I awoke from in a sweat:

Journal Entry
Jan. 2, 1990

Someone—I can't see who, she is cloaked in darkness—
tells me that I have a brain tumor. She tells me that it
is an especially virulent one that will soon kill me. I
am terrified. I don't want to go through all that pain
and suffering. I don't want to die. I grieve also for
Eloise, that she is to lose her mother so early in life.

I didn't understand the dream, but I understood in-
tuitively that it had something to do with my search to
be a better mother. Then, soon after that, I had another
dream, not once, but several times:

Journal Entry
Feb. 8, 1990

I've had almost exactly the same dream for three nights
running now. It's slightly different each time, but the
dream basically goes like this:
  I am shot in the head. I cannot see who shoots me;
they are in the dark, as I am. I feel excruciating pain,
my life draining away in the blood flowing from the
wound. I am terrified. Then, somehow, I am carried
beyond my own death. After all the pain, I feel alive,
so very alive.

  I'm confused by the dreams, and afraid of them.
What are they trying to tell me, what do these wounds
and illnesses mean, and what do they have to do with
my search for some bigger picture of mothering?

DYING TO BE BORN

After these dreams I was again reminded of the importance of community. Friends with whom I shared dreams
reminded me that dreams of death and dying often augur
transformation. These frightening dreams that often precede an inner transformation remind us that in order for
something new to come into existence—for instance, a
better way of mothering—something else must die first,
to create room for the new.

This journey, this searching, is neither a quick nor an
easy one. There are no simple answers, no one-minute
ways to manage it. It is, as I have found in my own and
other mothers' lives, a life-long process of discovery, a
cycle that will be repeated, in various degrees of intensity
and increasing depth, whenever our children enter a new
developmental phase or when we ourselves go through
expected or unexpected life crises and changes.

Often this journey starts at an emotional, practical level
("Help! I want to be a better mother, but I don't know
how!"). We search parenting books for answers to questions that we often aren't even aware of at a conscious
level, questions such as, "Isn't there something more to
mothering than what I'm doing?" We look for permission
to be whole persons as well as mothers. We look, perhaps
unconsciously, for ways to be mothers that will enhance
and transform our lives emotionally and spiritually.

If a mother sticks with this process, it often deepens
into a spiritual journey, a journey in which one asks who
one really is, where one is really going as a mother, what
mothering really means. Father Thomas Keating defines
the spiritual life as one of letting go of the false self and
looking progressively deeper to find out who one really

is. Mothering can be a way of awakening this search, of learning to let go of this Good Mother/False Self so that one may find the treasure buried deep within, the jewel of one's own real self. One dies to the old ways so that new life, a way of mothering that keeps one connected to one's own deepest self, may be born.

CHAPTER
3

The Dark Mother

*D*eath. What does that have to do with with mothering? And darkness? Why darkness? What are these dreams trying to tell me? I asked myself these questions over and over, at night in my bed, while driving on the freeway, while playing with Eloise.

This culture we live in is death- and darkness-phobic. We whisper about "passing away" or "expiring"; we perfume and cosmeticize corpses. We push away darkness with lights. We have lost our connection to the larger rhythms of life: plants die back in winter in order to be reborn in spring; we die to being childless in order to become mothers; our babies die to intrauterine life in order to be born into the world. We have forgotten the rhythms of light and darkness: night fading to day and darkening once more to night; the moon waning, and waxing, and growing darker and thinner once more. As Marion Woodman says, we have forgotten that night is as important as day.

In my search to become a better mother I was focused on light because I was a product of my culture and times. I wanted to smile more, to laugh more, to let more love shine through me. I thought somehow I could do this simply by willing more light into existence. I wanted to be a mother full of Light. I would ultimately reach this point, but first I had to learn about darkness, about the place of the Dark Mother inside of me. . . .

UNDERSTANDING DARKNESS

Later that spring my husband Rodger, my child, and I went to Hawaii to warm up and remember what sunshine looked and felt like. I was looking forward to the trip, for R & R with my family, for a break from my work as a therapist in private practice, and for a break from my inner mothering search, which seemed to be taking me nowhere. I had continued to be haunted by those dreams of the preceding winter and was anticipating being able to forget about them while we vacationed on the Big Island.

Because I had always been fascinated by volcanoes, I relished watching the current Kilauea volcanic eruption up close. I was moved by the awesome power of the destruction and surprised by the little time it took for trees and scrub to begin growing on the cooled lava. The deep connection between destruction and creation amazed me; I saw that even as Kilauea destroyed trees, plants, and homes, the lava was creating new land where it poured into the ocean. I learned that the lava's chemical constituents were exactly right for encouraging new plant growth once it had cooled.

As I watched the eruption, it felt somehow comparable to the process that was taking place in me: that what seemed frightening, and dark, and bore images of death was often a mysterious carrier of new birth and life. I began to see, a little, that what was so frightening about death and darkness was not knowing that light, and life, would come thick on its heels.

On a hike around the old caldera of the volcano, Rodger and Eloise and I happened upon an offering place for Pele, the powerful goddess of the volcano: oranges and bits of change and some colored paper, now faded, had been placed upon the folds of the old lava. Both Rodger and I felt the power of Pele's presence, and after some silence we each added some change, the only offerings we could think of, to the small pile.

We stayed in Volcano House at the top of the volcano, in a room overlooking the old caldera.

Journal Entry
May 18, 1990

Something amazing just happened. I'm still shaking a little bit—I hope I can read this later. I've got to get it down so I can remember it. It was like a prophetic daydream that was very real, a vision that foretold a greater truth.

Rodg was out taking a hike. As Eloise napped I was enjoying curling up in the black vinyl armchair by the large window and looking out over the miles of still-

smoking lava. I gazed into the distance. . . . Suddenly,
someone was talking to me. My heart skipped several
beats; I thought I was alone in the room. I turned my
head back toward the room, but no one was there.
Whose voice was this? Words and images tumbled into
my awake dream state. I didn't know what I was expe-
riencing but decided to listen anyway to see what the
voice had to say to me:

MELISSA, MELISSA YOU FOCUS TOO MUCH
ON LIFE, YOU LEAN TOO HARD UPON BIRTH
AND LIGHT AND LIFE. THERE IS NO BIRTH
WITHOUT DEATH; THERE IS NO LIGHT
WITHOUT DARKNESS. HEED MY WORDS. YOU
FOCUS TOO MUCH UPON LIGHT AND LIFE.
HEED ME. HEED ME WELL, FOR THIS IS
THE POWER AND TERRIBLENESS AND AWE-
FULL BEAUTY FROM WHICH YOU RUN.

From some inner place I knew then that the voice
represented Pele, goddess of the volcano. The voice
shook me, it was like lava, the molten lava pouring
down from the volcano, destroying everything in its
path, trees surrendering their lives in a blaze of wild
flames. The voice was the roaring wind spawned by the
unfathomable heat of the volcano's power. The voice
shook me, ripped my composure to shreds, stripped me
bare of certainty the way Pele's great winds stripped
limbs off trees.

Then there was silence. Powerful silence. Not sure
where I was, or even who I was, I looked down in
mild surprise to see my hands folded quietly on my lap.
Such silence. I heard faint noises carried up to me on
the ever-present wind from the overlook three floors
below. I unclasped my hands and ran them along the

broad armrests of the chair; the cool, dry surface felt
reassuring and brought me back to the room. I turned
to the window and looked out over the smoking lava
landscape poured out to the ends of the world.

FIRST   ANSWERS

This inner vision unnerved me for the rest of the trip.
The words I attributed to Pele were obviously directed
specifically to me. Light, nurturing, tenderness were all
important to me as a professional therapist and a mother;
yet here was this voice telling me something new, chal-
lenging my assumptions about what was important in my
life. What did Pele mean? What connections did her
words have with my questions about mothering?

When we begin to ask questions without demanding
to know immediate answers, synchronicities begin to
happen. If we can stay present and alert to these seeming
"coincidences," answers will begin to appear, although
quite often in a form different from what we were expecting. In a bookstore, a book that normally might not
intrigue us almost jumps off the shelf toward us, begging
to be read. A friend we haven't talked to for quite some
time calls, the conversation takes an unexpected twist,
and we hear from her what seems like an answer to our
predicament. We take a walk in the woods, and something that catches our eye and our heart, perhaps the
falling of a solitary leaf, illuminates a shadowed corner
of our questions. An old saying spoken by a partner in
casual conversation suddenly takes on new meaning.

This is what, at least in part, happened to me in Hawaii. My dreams had frightened me. I didn't understand

what death and darkness had to do with becoming a better mother. When I saw the volcano's destructiveness and learned at the same time how fertile the cooled lava was, how easily plants could soon grow in its rich and life-giving medium, I understood at a deep level the connection between death and birth, between darkness and light. My encounter with Pele, that powerful presence that epitomized this union for me, illuminated an important aspect of my own inner struggle to find meaning in mothering.

RE-MEMBERING THE GREAT MOTHER

Back home I recalled a quote from a book that I had bought and read right before the trip to Hawaii. I went out to my studio and pulled *The Mother Archetype in Fairy Tales* off an upper shelf of the bookcase and turned to a dog-eared page. There it was, underlined: "A woman destined for individuation must come to terms with the Dark Mother figure."[6] The author explained that if a woman becomes conscious of the darker side of mothering, the unspoken, secret aspects, she will then be transformed. The writer asserted that she considered this process, the personal encounter with one's secret self, to be the prerequisite of all spiritual renewal.

This is what, or who, had been released in me when I birthed my child: the Dark Mother, the complement to the Light. Powerful forces and feelings that I didn't understand before now had a name: they were the Dark Mother coming through—my own darkness, my own shadow, all for the purpose of emotional and spiritual transformation. Not only did this all now have a name, but there was meaning as well, a path that pointed me toward reclaiming a part of my own femaleness, a part that I had sacrificed long ago in order to be Good.

Excited now, I remembered another book I had read recently. I searched my shelves once more until I found it. I curled up on my flowered sofa with *In Her Image: the Unhealed Daughter's Search for Her Mother* and thumbed through the pages until I found the passage I was looking for. It told me that

> The woman who is infinitely supportive, nurturing, unselfish, and caring, who can feed others without needing to feed herself—is an archetypal image. . . .The mistake that we make as a culture is to expect one woman to *be* the archetype, and further, to be only that aspect of the mother archetype we want, that we see as positive. The cultural stereotype of the "Good Mother" is but one part of a much larger entity; the archetype is more complicated and bi-valent than we would choose.[7]

This image of the Great Mother, which appears in so many cultures and times around the world, represents both birth and death, both destruction and creation. These cultures acknowledge that life is a process that incorporates both light and darkness. The people of these cultures understand at a deep level that the darkness of gestation, of the womb, often precedes the light of creation.

In our culture we have split this image, labeling the darker side, that which precedes birth, as "bad" and relegating it to our unconscious, where it remains no less powerful for the banishment. What we, as a culture, are left with is only the Good Mother.

Even if she were to try very hard, a woman can't simply *make* herself into this Good Mother. In fact, the task is impossible, and the woman who tries this is doomed to perpetual failure. One of the main tasks for modern women to accomplish, in order to become whole, is to differentiate themselves from the powerful cultural expectations to be this Good Mother and learn to re-incorporate their darker side.

As we find affirmation and insight from others, as I did in my studio that afternoon, we know we are not alone and that our questions do have answers.

I understood the bind I was in: by trying to be the Good Mother that my culture expected me to be, I had moved further and further away from my true self. For too long I had felt like a perpetual failure as a mother because I'd tried to do the impossible: be someone I never could be no matter how hard I tried.

As we deepen on this journey we uncover in ourselves a wounded region, a place which must be healed so that we ourselves may be healed and whole. The realm of the Dark Mother, where darkness is as important as light, where darkness and light dance with each other in the great rounds of birth and death: this is the place of emotional and spiritual transformation, the womb of unconditional love and life.

This dark place is where our small mother-selves die, these small mother-selves who have been so constricted and crippled by the demands of the Good Mother. This dark place is to be both womb and tomb: tomb of that smaller self and womb of a larger, fuller mother-life.

CHAPTER

4

Crossing Over

As we become aware of the possibilities for healing that opening to our inner darkness holds for us, we begin to be even more aware of the Good Mother voice within. This voice has been directing many of us since our children were born, but we remain unaware of her existence until we begin this healing journey. The Good Mother's voice is the one we have listened to about how to be a mother, how to feel as a mother, how to behave as a mother. Her demands are the ones to which we yield. She is always Right. We are always Wrong.

As I became more aware of the way out of the binds I was in as a mother, about opening up to my darker side, exploring and accepting my pain and anger and grief and despair, the Good Mother voice inside my head stepped up her attacks on me. I had hoped that, once I had named the problem, had discovered what was causing so much of my unhappiness, that I would immediately feel better, but the opposite happened: I felt worse instead.

There were days when every action I took as a mother, every feeling I felt, was judged and attacked by this Good Mother/False Self. As I began to question how this voice, this cultural programming, had put me in chains, she was fighting back, protecting herself and what she stood for. There were days when I felt devastated by her and her demands upon me, but I was determined to find a way to be whole and healed as a mother.

I began to ask myself questions, even though at that point I had only a nascent idea of what the answers were. Who was this Good Mother inside my head? How did she get there? What were the costs for listening to her? Whom did she represent? How was I to get beyond her to find this dark and healing place inside me? And I realized that behind these "smaller" questions, these questions about my life specifically as a mother, loomed much bigger questions: Did I want to be less at war inside myself, less numbed, more alive? Was I willing to say "Yes" to the direction life was taking me to be healed?

ENCOUNTER WITH THE GOOD MOTHER

Journal Entry
July 14, 1990

It has been a sleepless night. I'm sitting here writing in bed. Rodg is out of town, Eloise has an earache, and

I've been up every couple of hours in response to her crying. It's dawn, finally, and I'm tired. I want to go check into a motel somewhere by myself and sleep for six weeks. Soggy grey light washes my bedroom as the day begins.

Through the monitor I hear Eloise starting to stir again. Something in me, already frayed, snaps. I don't think I can do this anymore. I can't get out of bed another time. Here we go. . . .

I'm back with a cup of coffee. I've given up on sleep for tonight. Maybe I'm not meant to be a mother. . . .

GOOD MOTHER: *Maybe you're not. This is what mothering is about, after all. What did you think it was going to be, a tea party? Why, I never even had a babysitter in all my years of being a mother. And I* loved it, loved it, *every minute of it.*

ME: *Why don't I feel that way all the time? Why can't I love being a mother all the time, no matter what? What is wrong with me?*

GOOD MOTHER: *You just must not be a good mother. Good mothers love to take care of their little ones. I so looked forward to the chance to stay up at night with my sick children to show them how much I really cared.* They *knew I cared about them.* They *knew I loved them unconditionally.*

ME: *(I'm starting to cry): But I'm so tired.*

GOOD MOTHER: *Good mothers never get tired. The love carries you through. If only you loved your child enough . . . .*

ME: *But I do love her, she's my treasure, it's just that I'm so tired, so very very tired—*

GOOD MOTHER: *No excuse, my dear, no excuse. If you loved your child enough, if you just tried hard*

enough, there would be no problem, no problem at
all. . . .

TRYING HARDER

After this sleepless night with a sick child another piece
of the mothering puzzle fit into place. I began to see that
the advice of this Good Mother inside my head was always to try harder: that if I just tried a little harder I
could be perfect, always nurturing, never ruffled. Her
voice had a siren quality: she promised me that if I became the perfect mother I would be loved, I would be
happy, and my child would be spared all the pain that I
had suffered as a child.

I had wanted to believe the Good Mother. I wanted
my daughter to have a happier childhood than I had had.
I wanted to be a happy mother. I wanted to be loved. I
had wanted to believe the voice, and I had tried harder.

The Good Mother promises us wonderful gifts if we
only successfully carry out her demands. She promises
us perfect happiness. She promises us the happiness of
our children. She promises us the admiration and love
of our children and partners when they see what wonderful mothers we are.

What she doesn't tell us, though, is that there is a
hidden price-tag attached to these gifts, a hefty price-
tag. We must be perfect mothers, cheerful, loving, self-
sacrificing. All of the time. In all circumstances. And if
we fail to measure up to these excruciatingly exact stan-
dards, it is always our fault. And if we slip up, we are fit
to be called only one thing: Bad Mothers. Failures. And
the Good Mother within will never let us forget this.

NUMBING THE PAIN

As hard as I tried at this point, though, the grief and anger and pain still arose at times. What to do?

When we listen to the Good Mother, we do our best to forget about these feelings. We hope, sometimes desperately, that if we disregard the pain it will retreat magically, slinking off like a rejected child. We try to push the pain down and away, but some part of us knows that we pay a great price for doing this. We expend a great deal of energy trying not to feel what we do feel sometimes as mothers, trying to lie to ourselves and others about our own experience. As a result we become numb: physically, emotionally, and spiritually.

What was it like, for me, to be a numbed mother? It was like this:

I got bored around Eloise. At times everything I did with her seemed grey, stupid, lifeless. I found myself counting the minutes until her next nap, until Rodg got home, until it was time to take her to day care.

I felt drowsy, stuporous around her. I couldn't stop yawning. All I wanted to do was curl up on the couch and sleep for a long time. I couldn't attribute this completely to lack of sleep, for I sometimes felt this way even after a good night's rest.

I felt resentful of her, but not *too* resentful: Good Mothers don't resent their children.

I left her by daydreaming in her presence. My imagination took me to exciting adult jobs, beautiful tropical beaches. I designed gorgeous quilts in my head, dreamed of having a svelte body. I would be far away, until Eloise yelled "Mama!" or pulled at my sleeve.

I spun my wheels, trying hard to do "something useful" when I was with her, so at least I would have "something" to show for my time.

I got restless, itchy; I wanted to get away. I had a hard
time sitting still.

I took Eloise to the mall, took her to the drugstore,
the grocery store, took her shopping to distract myself
from my own pain and from my child.

I ate too much, and too much of the wrong things.
Too often, the oatmeal cookies I made with Eloise were
for myself and not for her.

I tried to avoid her, tried to erect an invisible wall
between myself and my child. I was a master at being
present physically and absent in every other way.

THE COST OF NUMBING

Going numb in these ways, and in many others, means
closing our hearts to our children, to ourselves, to Life,
and hanging a "Keep Out" sign on it. We want to shutter
our hearts when we are in pain, even if it means shutting
everything and everyone else out as well. Some part of
us, listening to the Good Mother, would rather die, emotionally and spiritually, than feel such pain. Joanna Macy
writes eloquently about emotional pain: "We block it out
because it hurts, because it is frightening, and most of
all because we do not understand it and consider it to be
a dysfunction, an aberration, a sign of personal weakness.
We know she is right."[8]

STAYING AWAKE

Journal Entry
July 22, 1991

*I've been thinking a lot about this whole numbing busi-
ness that I do with Eloise. Does the numbing work?
NO. All of "those feelings" come out anyway, but in
uncontrolled ways, like lightning from a troubled sky. I
get irritated and angry more, in little ways, as if there
were a hair shirt around my heart. I become more critical of those around me. I feel isolated from Eloise,
from my husband, and most of all from myself, from
my own creativity and juices. Life itself seems duller.
Colors are muted, sounds less acute. An edge is gone.
Some part of me recognizes that I am lying to myself
about my own life as a mother. Everything is out of
joint.*

*It's late at night. I can't sleep after another difficult
evening with Eloise, so I've come downstairs. This
time, though, it's different; I've let myself cry, feel the
pain and anger and frustration and helplessness. And
somehow I feel clearer, lighter inside, even though nothing has changed on the outside. C.G. Jung's statement
that "There is no birth of consciousness without pain"
just came to me. I ask the darkness around me: Is
something trying to become conscious in me with the
pain I feel around mothering? Could something new
and alive and powerful be trying to come to birth
within me, and I keep telling it to lie down and die?
What is begging to be born? And why am I so terrified
of this birth?*

Holding back and numbing such powerful feelings as grief, anger, fear, and despair takes an extraordinary amount of energy, rather like trying to hold a huge beach ball under ten feet of water by oneself. When we make the choice to stop repressing our pain, to stay awake, our life begins to shift. More energy, a "higher voltage" begins to pulse through us. This energy is often felt initially as fear, fear of the new and unknown.

This energy, however, does begin to be felt in other ways as well. Even in our fear and our emerging pain, the world comes back: colors are noticed again, the timbre of voices around us, the poignancy of quiet moments of holding our children. It is as if our hearts begin to open, both to our own pain, and to life around us. And as our hearts begin to open, we take our first steps away from the internal tyranny of the Good Mother.

LEAVING THE GOOD MOTHER

Journal Entry
July 25, 1990

Who is this Good Mother inside my head? Who is she? At first she was not separate from me. I carried her not just in my head but upon my back, my back so tired from her great burden of guilt; but this, I thought, this is what mothering is about. To feel so tired. To feel so guilty. To feel so inadequate. Somehow other mothers always seemed to be so collected. I felt isolated in my churning and questioning.

Something, however, is beginning to work itself loose

*in these days and nights of questioning. That something
is a nascent me, a me not immutably joined to the Good
Mother inside me. Bit by bit I understand that this
Good Mother voice inside my head represents everything
I have heard or read about mothering, from parents,
culture, religion. When I heeded her roaring inside me I
could do nothing else, because listening to her dictates
and demands, and trying to obey them, was a more
than full-time job. As long as I listened to her voice I
could not be me, Melissa; all my energy was channeled
into being a Good Mother. Likewise, Eloise did not
have me, Melissa, for a mother; she had some numbed,
whitewashed, sanitized version.*

*I'm beginning to connect my faith in and obeying of
this Good Mother voice to my chronic fatigue and guilt.
Slowly I'm beginning to be able to separate my own experiences and feelings from this Voice. Slowly I'm beginning to feel more awake, more alive. As the numbing
lessens I feel even more the intensity of those feelings,
dark and powerful. I feel as if I am in labor with my
own soul.*

The Good Mother voice, and all the other voices of
our culture, exhort us to be a Good Mothers. These
voices are the many child-rearing manuals we have read
over the years, counseling us to be in control, say the
right things, feel the right feelings. They are June
Cleaver of "Leave It to Beaver" and Donna Reed and
all the other TV mothers of our childhood: smiling, un-
flappable, always rising above all the chaos of a children-
filled house, always moving confidently toward a quick
and happy resolution of any problem with the kids.

These voices are those of our own mothers and fathers,

teaching us as children to always stay in control, be good, take care of others, put ourselves last, not show our feelings. They are the Virgin Mary-as-Mother: blue and gold, with demure smile, meek, mild, serenely loving. They are our own inner Good Mothers, a particularly heady distillation of all these sources.

All together, these voices of experience and culture are like roaring lions barring the entrance to territory forbidden to mothers in this culture. This taboo country is where mothers, and women, can truly be themselves: loving, powerful, imperfect, free. Alive. The borders to that territory gradually become visible to each mother on this spiritual journey, and once this happens each mother is faced with the challenge of going forward in spite of her fear, of finding her own innate courage.

THE CLOSER WE GET TO THE LIONS, THE LOUDER THEY ROAR

Mothers may be afraid of these lions, as I had been for so long, but they soon become less afraid of their own fear, more ready to challenge these ferocious guardians of the taboo land of fully embodied, fully alive and loving mothers. The closer we get to the lions, the louder they roar: YOU WILL DIE! (they may be right). YOU WILL NEVER COME BACK! (it is a risk we must take). YOU WILL NEVER BE THE SAME! (this may be true). YOU WILL DESTROY YOUR CHILD! (this we are afraid of, for we have listened to their voices for too long; but something inside us knows, *knows* that this is a lie).

What the lions fail to tell us is that they, the Guardians of True Motherhood, will also die if we make the crossing into the new and taboo country. They will starve, for their sustenance is our willingness to listen to and believe them. They feed on our insecurities; their ribs will soon show if we stop letting them gnaw at our souls. For when we recover our own power, our own darkness, our own lives and creativity, we will not listen to them again. We will not cower before their roaring. We will not use their measure to gauge our own worth as mothers and as women.

This reclamation of our own true mother-nature means going over and down into the regions of the Dark Mother, down into the darkness of our own souls, to face the darker side of our mothering. This may seem frightening, but the only alternative is death-in-life, to be devoured by the hungry lions barring the entrance to new worlds.

GOING DOWN, GOING WITHIN

When we come to the parting of the ways with the Good Mother we find ourselves ready to continue on to the next stage of the journey. We have named the Good Mother voice inside our heads. We can recognize her judgments and criticisms of us. We understand how she has come to be there. We are able to name the costs, both for ourselves and for our children, of listening to her. We understand, finally, that the suffering engendered by our attempts to cauterize our painful feelings lead to a far deeper sort of suffering, both again for ourselves and for our children.

Waking up in these ways is both empowering and frightening for us as mothers.

Empowering, because the naming gives us choices:

we can choose to see the Good Mother as the internalized voice of our culture and all its mothering practices, rather than believing her an integral, essential part of ourselves; we can choose not to heed her voice any more; we can choose to go beyond her to that deep and dark place within, in which we need to sojourn for our healing as mothers.

Frightening, because we see the power she has had over us and our daily lives with our children. Frightening, because we know if we choose to stop listening to her, and go beyond her, we will be in a new territory, an unknown country.

AUTHOR'S NOTE: For help along the way, see the exercises described in Resources, especially those under Stage 1: Naming.

III

The Descent:
Dancing with Kali

*We can know the dark, and dream it into a
new image.*

—STARHAWK

CHAPTER
5

Meeting the Shadow

CHOOSING LIFE

I knew, at this point in my own journey, that to find a better way of being a mother, to choose darkness over light at this time, was paradoxically to choose life. My mind certainly couldn't make sense of this, but my body and heart could. I chose their wisdom and went on.

We need now, as mothers, to reclaim the Dark Mother and to remember her with Madonna, Dark and Light. To do this we must make the journey down, within, into her regions and meet her face to face. Allow her to be fully embodied, once again, within us.

We must claim her. We must let ourselves be claimed by her as her own. Then, carrying her in our bodies and wombs and hearts, we may journey back to our own lives, graced with her boons: the gift of being fully present in our own lives and bodies and relationships; the gift of the unleashing of the dark and fiery heat of love and creativity; and, finally, the gift of being able to mother our children in a powerful, loving, and embodied way.

At this stage in the journey dark goddesses, goddesses who have appeared in many cultures and spiritualities, dark-skinned goddesses who have wept, raged, and grieved, may be seen as powerful metaphors and guides for the next step. Dark Goddesses who personify the deep connection between destruction and creation, between dark and light: Kali, the Black Madonna of Christianity, Pele, the Black Tara, many others.

These goddess images represent two things for mother-journeyers: first, those feelings that so many of us have firmly repressed as mothers: grief, anger, despair; second, the truth that destruction, the breaking away from the old order, must precede creation, the birth of the new, that these two processes are inextricably linked.

This next stage in the journey is about the destruction of being a mother in the old way, in the cultural models we have been given and have swallowed whole. This destruction, this dying, can be frightening, but by learning about these dark goddesses we can see how important this dying is, no matter how painful, so that a new way of mothering may be born.

WORKING WITH FEARFUL IMAGES

I was personally intrigued by, and a little bit frightened of, Kali, the black Hindu goddess, who, as Fred Gustafson writes, "personifies those terrible stirrings and forces in the psyche that seem like death to an individual, but which in the end turn out to be part of the vital process needed to transform life into something of greater value and meaning."⁹

As I sat down to my typewriter late one night, I had definite ideas about describing the integration of the internal Dark Mother. I sat at my table in the dark and quiet house, rolled a blank sheet into the typewriter, took a sip of tea, and raised my hands to the keyboard. Immediately, a Dark Mother image appeared before me. I sat back and rubbed my tired eyes with my hands. Perhaps I really just needed to go to bed instead of writing. . . . I turned off the lights and called it quits for the evening. The next night, however, and the night after that as well, this same image appeared in front of me whenever I sat down to begin the second part. It was one thing for me to read and speculate about dark goddesses as metaphor for the process but another thing entirely to open to the power and darkness of what these images represented for me.

Finally, I knew I had to respond to this image in front of me as I wrote, even if I was afraid. I sat down with a pen and my journal, said a brief prayer for my own healing, and met this Dark Mother image. I wrote down what I was experiencing as it happened, using a journal technique I sometimes use for Active Imagination. As I wrote, I realized that I was discovering one of the most significant doorways in my journey: the opening into my own darkest fears and feelings. This image of Kali blessed me with her presence as much as her words frightened and confounded me.

MEETING   KALI

Journal Entry
August 3, 1990

*Darkness. . . . Where was I? Quiet. . . . I could no
longer hear the roaring of the lions. I seemed to be
alone. . . .*

*As I write now in my journal I know I have discov-
ered one of the most significant doorways in my journey:
the opening into my own darkest fears and emotions.
This image of Kali has blessed me with her presence as
much as the words scare and confound me.*

This was the experience.

*As my eyes got used to the dark, I saw something—
no, someone—in front of me. A She. I could barely see
her, it was so dark and she was so dark.*

*Who was she? Her skin was night, dark of the moon.
She looked at me with wild, focused eyes. What was she
looking at me that way for? Who was she? Those fierce
and untamed eyes moved back and forth in the darkness; her body had to be moving as well.*

*She must have been dancing, although her movement
didn't look like any dance I'd ever seen: rolling eyes,
dipping head, and arms, many arms, crossing, twin-
ing, untwining. I heard no music, but she must have
heard some, for she danced with a clear and steady
rhythm. She was a beautiful and sensuous dancer if I
could look past her wild appearance and strange, flowing movements.*

Why did she look so intensely at me? What did she

*want from me? Why couldn't she stop for a moment
and talk to me? And who was she?*

*Then I recognized her. She was Kali, "the Black
One."* ¹⁰ *Quick, what do I remember about her? Kali,
Kali, yes, ancient goddess, goddess of destruction and
creation. Wild one and tender mother, Great Mother in
all her contradictions.*¹¹ *Yes, I remember her now.*

*What did she want from me? When I asked myself
this, she acknowledged me for the first time with a tilt of
her head, as if to answer me. I understood. She wanted
sacrifices from me, something I had to let go of, release.
If I was to surrender to her, how would I do it?*

*She nodded at me, almost imperceptibly, a slight
weaving of her head added to the undulations of her
dance. Mouth dry, I took a step toward her. My legs
shook. Her fierce eyes fixed briefly on me once more; her
head nodded me yet closer. I took another hesitant step,
and another. By then we were so close that I could feel
waves of heat emanating from her writhing body.*

*I felt naked, alone, exposed. What was happening?
Her heat and energy penetrated my body. My arms and
legs, feet and hands, felt tingly, electric.*

*She was beckoning me to the dance. I, who had been
so immobilized as a mother by the roaring of the lions,
was being called to surrender to Kali's dance of Death
and Life, inner death and rebirth. I felt embarrassed,
uncertain how to start.*

*Then I heard, faintly, a pulsating rhythm. My feet
responded, tapping out the beat on the raven ground.
My hands made curious motions in the air. What was I
dancing?*

*Immediately, I knew the answer: I was dancing with
Kali, my fear. My grief. My anger. And all of the other*

things that I was forbidden to dance when I obeyed the lions up above.

   ME: *Oh, Kali, so I am to learn your dance of transformation. Where do I begin?*
   KALI: *Begin with endings. What must be destroyed to make room for new life?*
   ME: *What must be destroyed?*
   KALI: *Yes. Destruction births creation. What must die so that you may come alive as mother?*
   ME: *I don't know. . . .*
   KALI: *Yes, you do. Look inside. What must die?*

ACTIVE IMAGINATION

Many people use Active Imagination, the process of working with internally generated images, to heal, to get acquainted with unknown parts of themselves. This is a process by which one closes one's eyes and allows an image to arise. One then responds to the image, holds a dialogue with it, gets to know it. One begins to work with the image in a way similar to the way one works with a dream image, assuming that the image contains seeds of wisdom and self-knowledge that, if opened to and conversed with, may lead to healing. Barbara Hannah, a Jungian analyst and author of *Encounters with the Soul*, tells a story about a wise woman who, on a long tour, had to share a room with another woman unfriendly to her. At first the wise woman felt staying with a person she didn't like would inevitably spoil the tour—until she realized that she would waste one of the most interesting times of her life if she allowed her dislike to spoil it. So, writes Hannah, "She set herself to accept her uncongenial companion. . . . This technique worked marvelously, and she managed to enjoy the tour immensely."[12] Hannah then explains:

> The first figure we usually meet in the confrontation with the unconscious is the personal shadow. Since she . . . mainly consists of what we have rejected in ourselves, she is usually quite as uncongenial to us as the woman's traveling companion was to her. . . . If we are friendly (to the figure)—realizing its right to be as it is—the unconscious will change in a remarkable way.[13]

Kali represented for me all those parts of myself as a mother that I had denied: pain, grief, anger, despair. She also represented the enormous healing potential available if I opened myself up to this cut-off part of myself.

All of us carry somewhere within ourselves symbols or images of those parts of ourselves that we are most uncomfortable with. The more uncomfortable we are with these split-off parts of ourselves, the more frightening the images may appear to be. If, however, we can be with our fear, breathe through it, and befriend these images the way the woman on the tour befriended her uncongenial roommate, new vistas of healing and wholeness heretofore undreamed of may open up before us.

For most mothers, what is contained in the shadow is all that our culture demands that we distance ourselves from in order to be a Good Mother: our griefs, our fears, our angers, all naturally engendered by the day-to-day process of being a mother. In other words, our humanness. If we are to be healed as mothers, it is that very

human-ness that needs to be reclaimed, felt, transformed.

If you are interested in exploring Active Imagination
as part of your own mother-healing, see Resources. For
some women, however, simply feeling the pain, the central task of this part of the journey, is enough; other
women, more kinesthetically oriented, find that getting
some bodywork done is their preferred method for rein-
tegrating their shadows. We are, each of us, unique, and
it is important for our own healing that we find the most
congruent way for ourselves of doing this work. Trust
your own judgment in this.

Since Kali was such an important inner symbol for me
during this stage of the journey, my dialogues and experiences with her will appear from time to time in Part
III. She represented for me those parts of myself that I
had split off from as a mother, at first so alien and frightening: my grief, my despair, my anger; my fear of loss
of control, and my fear of letting go. Since I was so afraid
of those parts of me, I was frightened of her. The more
that we open to these orphaned parts, though, the friend-
lier the inner figures become, and healing of that inner
split happens in a profound way.

DYING TO NEW LIFE

What must die? Kali asks. What must die?

This Good Mother we carry within ourselves. This
Good Mother who has such a stranglehold on our aliveness, our creativity, our love, our heart.

This Good Mother within, who must always be in
control of us and our children. This part of ourselves who

must always be sweet and kind, even if she is howling inside. Who must always be the perfect mother: calm, loving, ever-giving. Who must always have a perfect child: sweet, docile, well-behaved. Who would rather have her children be Good than Alive.

This Good Mother within must die, this Good Mother who forfeits what *is*, in the present, for what *should* be. Who must numb herself in order not to feel the sorrow, anger, despair that comes as part of motherhood. And who, because she is numb, does not feel the joy, silliness, holiness that are part of being mother as well. This Good Mother who sacrifices the living heart of the present on the cold stone of what Must Be.

This Good Mother, who is terrified of death, of darkness, any death, any darkness. This Good Mother who shuns the unspoken truth. This Good Mother, who seeks the Light, who repudiates at any cost the parts that are different.

KALI: Yes. The agony of the Good Mother's death and the labor pains of your own true motherself's birth are the same. I, Kali, am both your undertaker and your midwife. This dying is your own birth. Trust it.

ME: This is too disturbing. I don't like it, I'm afraid of it.

KALI: This disturbance is your salvation. Trust the disturbing: it is the labor pain of your new life, a life as mother where you can be yourself, truly yourself, with your child: free, alive, vital. This disturbance will lead to peace. Trust me. . . . What must die?

ME: This Good Mother, this false self, within me. This false self that, although seeming to think of others first, really has only her own self-interest and preservation at heart. This Good Mother, who seems to be giving, giv-ing, always giving, always putting others' needs before her own. Underneath the giving, the sacrifice, though, is a secret demand: if I do all this for you, you *must* love me, you *must* cherish me, you *must* never leave me. So even though all this looks like giving, it is really about getting, getting love, getting security. Both the false giv-ing and the demands for security and love must go. This tight and clenching false self, this Good Mother, must die.

KALI: Yes. And your true and vital motherself will be born.

As we consider all of this, all of this letting go, all this dying, we may feel tired, discouraged. How can we do this? How can we really let go of so much? This is what we've known. How do we know, really, that something else will take its place? What if all we're left with is loss? What if there *is* nothing beyond this?

The quiet inner response may only be "keep going, keep remembering."

WINTER TO SPRING

I remembered the previous winter. It was such a long one: it started about October, really, and lasted until April. Long, long days of darkness. I, my husband, my child, woke up in darkness. Ate dinner with darkness pressing in at the windows. Lights on in the house the entire day. Even when the sun was up, the light, filtered through low grey clouds and endless drizzle, was watery, subdued. No hint of blue sky or honest-to-god sunshine for weeks, months, eternities, on end.

And outside . . . bare, barren. Leafless lilacs, dead black stalks of summer flowers in the boxes on the deck. The ground dark, and cold, and sodden.

By February, no matter how many layers of clothing I wore, no matter how many lights I turned on in the house, I too felt dark, and cold, and sodden. I wanted to admit defeat, crawl up the stairs to bed in my dark room, pull the blue down quilt over my head, and sleep until light and warmth and life returned to the earth. Part of me despaired that spring would ever return. Perhaps all that was left to me was winter. . . .

Kali, representing for me that quiet inner response, kept after me in my journal to persist, to keep feeling the awakening feelings that had been buried so long.

KALI: Don't stop there, Melissa. Keep going.

ME: I can't. I'm tired. This hurts too much.

KALI: Don't stop. What happened then?

What happened then? Spring. . . Not all at once, little clues at first: thin green spikes of crocuses pushing up through the winter blanket of dead maple leaves; mornings of sunshine, warm, dry, life-giving; waking up to morning light in the bedroom, dinner eaten by twilight. Day by day, more life, more color: pale yellow daffodils pushing up out of the warming soil, red tulips opening, bright splashes of primroses thriving in boxes and borders.

The part of me that had crawled under the quilt in despair peeked out from under the quilt, saw the nascent light even in the bedroom, concluded that life was returning after all. This hibernating me decided to get up, swung herself out of bed, stretched, opened the window to see life leafing and blooming, joined me downstairs in the kitchen. We went out together into the garden. Eloise was swinging on her swingset with Chris and Corinne, next door neighbor children. Their shouts and laughter blessed me, consecrated the new emerging garden. Spring, and life, had returned once more.

KALI: Yes?

ME: Yes. Spring did return. . . and always does.

KALI: Remember the moon, too, Melissa. Remember the moon.

ME: What about the moon?

KALI: Think of the phases, the everlasting cycle: full, three-quarter, half, crescent, dark, crescent, half, three-quarter, full. . . .Dark, light, dark, light; waxing, waning, waxing, waning. Every month the moon surrenders her luminescence, becomes dark. And every month she shines once again. You know this, Melissa, you know this deep within your body. You carry the moon in your womb.

ME: I don't understand. Why are we talking of the turning of the seasons, the cycles of the moon? What do they have to do with my tiredness, my despair?

KALI: You are cradled now in the dark arms of the moon. It is winter in your soul. All this, though, shall pass in its own time. You will be lightened, greened, again. Now is the time for dying, for darkness. Trust the cycle. . . . Write more. . . .write about betrayal . . .

TRUSTING THE CYCLES

Kali, goddess of Death and Life, Destruction and Creation, was to be my guide into the new territory. I had no sense at all of "where" Kali was as she appeared, and to me it didn't matter whether she was "out there" or a creation of my own deep imagination. She knew this territory—indeed, it was her home—and she had offered to be my guide through this painful place. She talked to me of death, the death of the Good Mother within me. She reminded me that we see the dark and the light, death and rebirth, all around us, all the time, in nature.

It is important in this process to remember that we, as humans on this earth, are embedded in larger cycles of birth, death, and rebirth that recur throughout our lives. Any of us who has ever tended some sort of garden knows at an intuitive level of the cycles of nature. We know that the garden beds must lie fallow in winter in order to bring forth new life in spring. Any time that we compost our leaves, our refuse, we are making a statement of faith that out of this "dead" matter will rise nutrients to bring forth new life.

We witness the moon "dying" and being reborn every month. Seeds must be laid in the ground, cracked open, so that the life of the nascent plant may rise up through the dark and fertile soil. The sun dies every night, into darkness, and blazes forth anew each morning.

We can relearn to trust these cycles, allow ourselves as well to become embedded once again within these greater rounds. Then, as we begin to die to the old way of mothering, some part of us will understand that this is necessary, this is good, so that we may be reborn into a new, more lifegiving way of being a mother.

EMBRACING   PARADOX

Kali spoke to me in paradox: she told me that the death throes of the Good Mother/false self and the labor pains of the new self to be born within me were one and the same. She told me that she was both my undertaker and my midwife. She told me that this disturbance was my salvation. My mind balked at the paradoxes, but some deeper part of me understood.

Paradox is employed in many of the world's spiritual traditions as a tool for awakening. Paradoxes stop the thought process and make the student ready for a wider, nonverbal experience of reality. A koan, an example of the use of paradox in the Zen tradition, "grips the student's heart and mind and creates a true mental impasse, a state of sustained tension in which the whole world becomes an enormous mass of doubt and questioning."[14] From this impasse, this dying of the old ways of comprehending and mentally controlling the world, arises a newer, freer way of being.

Paradoxes abound in this stage: dying so that new life can come through; opening to our own anger and fear and grief and despair, our own personal shadows, so that we may be better mothers; making friends with that which we are so afraid of. These paradoxes make no sense to the conscious mind, but that is precisely the point: much of the work of this stage, and most of the healing, is done at a non-rational level, at the level of heart and and body and soul. With paradox there are no easy answers: we are invited, instead, to live into the questions, to allow the answers to come in their own time, rising to sweet awareness within open hearts rather than critical minds.

○   ○   ○

I gratefully accepted Kali's help. I knew that I could not do this on my own, under my own conscious steam. Little did I know then what a difficult taskmistress she was to be in the service of my healing, and what difficult lessons I would have to learn . . . .

CHAPTER

6

Descent

And so, in this stage, we are to open to those very things that have scared us the most, those feelings we have spent so much energy trying to repress and deny. We are to name those feelings, those thoughts that before this have seemed unnameable, taboo, descending into our own inner darkness and pain in order to be healed. In order to be the kind of mothers our hearts have always dreamed of being.

Begin with whatever thoughts, feelings, words, or images rise up in you. Begin wherever you are. For me, the word "betrayal" tightened my heart. I said to myself: Everyone knows that a Good Mother never betrays her child. What a terrible thing, to betray one's child. And yet this was where I began to write.

BETRAYAL

Journal Entry
August 5, 1990

*I found this excerpt, written a couple of months after
Eloise was born, in an old journal this morning:*

> *This morning, after nursing Eloise, I held her and
> rocked her, and she fell asleep in my arms. We were
> alone together in the house, except for the two cats
> curled up on the sofa with us, and I felt cocooned
> together with her in love. I looked down at this beau-
> tiful sleeping baby in my arms: straight red-gold
> lashes, soft pink cheeks, downy gold hair, nursing
> blister puffy on upper lip. As her round tummy rose
> and fell in sleep I matched my breath to hers; nestled
> against my breasts, she and I shared the very stuff of
> life.*
>
> *Oh my child, I breathed to her as she slept: I
> promise you, my sweet warm baby, I am here for
> you, always. I will take care of you. I will protect
> you. I will comfort you. And never, never will I be-
> tray you. Never. Never.*

*But now I think, How many times have I already bro-
ken that vow? How many times have I, busy or angry
or preoccupied, communicated in some way to you,
Eloise, that you are not important? How many times
already have I not been there for you at a time that you
particularly needed me?*

*Something inside me counters, Oh, those minor times
are unimportant, too insignificant to matter, nothing*

really at all. Yes, perhaps minor (to me at least; no one has asked Eloise), but betrayals nonetheless. To date, as honestly as I can see it, no major betrayal has taken place (again, I am acutely aware that this is my perspective, not my child's; she may have an entirely different story to tell someday).

But someday, sometime it is inevitable that a bigger betrayal will happen, even though I try my best to prevent it: I will let her down, disappoint her, fail to protect her in some way that feels vitally important to her. In spite of my vow. In spite of my best intentions. In spite of my love and concern for her. Therein lies the rub, and a certain death of innocence for myself, about myself: that I will inescapably hurt my child, in large ways and small, consciously and unconsciously, despite all efforts I make not to do so. I resist knowing this. I want to struggle and say, No, this is not true, I will never hurt my daughter.

And yet, sadly, I know I will. This is not the kind of mother I would ideally be for my daughter. But this is the kind of mother I am: human, fallible, mortal.

FALSE GUILT AND REAL GUILT

This writing about betrayal touches a sensitive area for mothers, one in need of healing. Our culture, and the internalized voice of our culture in the form of the Good Mother/False Self, tells us that as mothers we should have no needs of our own. We should always be giving, loving, and cheerful. We must *always* be there for our children, no matter what.

This voice, this culture, says to us that if we acknowl-

edge our needs, if we say "No" to our children on oc-
casion so that we may say "Yes" to ourselves, we are bad
mothers and should feel guilty. And we comply. Many
of us are in a no-win situation: either we try to be there
for our children all the time, sacrificing our own selves
totally in the process and feeling drained and resentful
as a result, or we make time and space for ourselves,
setting limits with our children, and end up feeling
guilty.

This is false guilt, the result of a lie we have been told
about how to be a mother. All of us, *all of us*, need at
least occasional time and space away from our children.
We simply cannot be there for them a hundred percent
of the time, and we become ill as mothers when we
swallow the poisonous belief that we must be so. When
we can make boundaries with our children, take time for
ourselves, we ultimately become better mothers. No one
can make withdrawals from an empty bank; when we
take care of and nourish ourselves, we are making generous deposits that we may later withdraw without becoming bankrupt.

Our children, too, need for us to make boundaries in
this way. They need to learn, in developmentally appropriate ways, that we cannot satisfy all their needs. As
they get older, this gives them chances to discover more
and more their own internal creativity and resources. We
are, at the same time, modeling for them healthy self-
care and nurturing. Love has many faces, including, at
the appropriate time, one that says "No, I can't be there
for you right now."

There is, however, a darker side, one that is sometimes
even more painful to acknowledge. This is that, sometimes, we are not there for our children at times important

for them, whether out of anger, resentment, or simply ignorance. Times, that, in the future, our children will remember with pain, grief, anger. Times when they felt betrayed.

Healthy guilt arises from the experience of betrayal. In order to heal, we need to recognize those times we have let our children down in ways that were healthy to none of us. We need to feel the pain of this, open our hearts both to the pain and to ourselves as the feelers of the pain. To make amendments, if appropriate, to those betrayed. And, finally, to forgive ourselves for being human and mistake-makers, to find a merciful place for ourselves within the recesses of our own hearts.

ANGER

Journal Entry
August 10, 1990

Why do I get so mad at Eloise sometimes, anger gone beyond anger? When she is having a temper tantrum, or talking back to me, or giving me the silent treatment, why do I want to shake her until her teeth rattle? What is it? What turns me, normally a reasonably even-tempered person, into a pedicidal maniac?

I know. What turns me into an unreasonable, angry mother is my need to have it my *way. When Eloise was and is out of control, whether as a screaming infant, a kicking toddler, a howling child, I get scared. I've tried so hard all my life to be in control, nice, good, that when she detonates, my foundations shake. If I can't control her, how can I control me? She is breaking all the rules that I have tried so hard to keep, about being good, about putting others first, about not rocking the boat. Eloise, when out of control, doesn't seem to give a damn about anyone else. There is a small child in me terrified about the consequences of someone going out of control in this way. My own internal sweet small child remembers what happened to her, the terrible consequences that happened to her if she went out of control long ago. She also remembers with a shudder how frightening it was when her own mother and father went out of control. This child in me wants to stop Eloise at any cost, get her back in line, under control.*

This child in me wants something else as well. She would relish the chance to be "selfish." She would love, for once, to lie down on the floor and kick and shriek and not have to be frightened of swift and severe retribution. She would like to run wild, leave mayhem in her wake. She never got a chance to do that in a safe environment, and she is jealous now of Eloise. She says it's not fair that Eloise doesn't get spanked, hard, when she screams; it's not fair that Eloise has parents who take her anger and frustration seriously; it's not fair that Eloise has parents who try to understand what's causing the anger, grief, pain.

This jealous child inside me wants Eloise to get what she got, to get walloped as she got walloped, to have rage met with rage. This little girl inside wants justice meted out swiftly and harshly. Get Eloise back under control the way her parents did it to her. It's not fair to do it any other way.

The Good Mother/False Self within also rages when our children misbehave. Hers is a righteous rage. When our children are born, this part of us makes a pact with the infant: "I will sacrifice everything, sacrifice my very Self, to be a Good Mother for you. You must, in turn, be a Good Child for me, sweet, pliable. In order to redeem my sacrifice, such a great sacrifice, you must love me always, make me feel good, do what I say."

When our children act up they are breaking this secret pact that we made with them long ago. No matter that our children had no chance to say, "No, this is not good, I will not agree to this devil's bargain." And so we rage at the betrayal of our sacrifice.

This Good Mother in our heads tells us, as well, that if our children are upset, acting up, out of control, it's our fault: we must have done something wrong for them to behave in that way. Our children's "negative" feelings and behavior become a reproach to us. If we truly are Good Mothers, says this Good Mother within, then our children will always be sweet and sunny and docile. If they become otherwise, it's invariably our fault, and we become Bad Mothers. An out-of-control child means that we are failures.

In order to become Good Mothers once again we must get our children to behave, no matter what that takes. If we need to kill our children's spirits, kill their capacity for life—well, then, that's just the price. A Good Mother must be a Good Mother no matter what the cost. . . .

LETTING GO

How tightly we often hold on to our children, asking or demanding that they act in certain ways for us so that we may feel better about ourselves, so that we may feel as if we're being Good Mothers.

I was shocked to find how many demands I'd made of Eloise, unconsciously, to be a certain kind of child so that I could feel better about myself. I had always prided myself on being a relaxed and non-demanding mother. I was surprised to find, in my shadow, this mother who was rigid and full of expectations for her child.

What would it mean to let go of our children, not to have to control them at such life-denying levels? What would it mean to let them feel what they need to feel, to learn the lessons they need to learn?

It wouldn't mean avoiding saying "No." It wouldn't mean giving up being firm about limits and the consequences for broaching them. Every mother will have different limits, depending upon her temperament, background, values, and philosophy of bringing up a child. All of us, however, do have limits, lines over which we will not let our children pass. Wherever we as mothers draw the line is where the control issue will arise. It doesn't matter where we are on the continuum from lenient to strict; the control issue will always be there at the outer limits of the boundary we have drawn.

Letting go would mean acknowledging that, after a certain point, we have no control over our children. We can't force them physically to bend to our will. Letting go would mean drawing a line between our past pain and our children's present pain, releasing the demand that

they always be happy to redeem us from our own un-
happy childhoods or own feelings of low self-esteem.
Letting go would mean giving up basing our own self-
worth upon the way our children behave.

I can't *make* my daughter stop having a tantrum. I can't
make her behave the way I want her to behave. If and
when I get hooked into trying to control her, the battle
lines are drawn, and both of us invariably lose the war.

The questions then arise, "How do I let go of all this?
How do I let go of demands that she be a certain way,
behave in certain ways, so that I can feel better? How
do I do it?"

There are, unfortunately, no easy and simple answers.
What I can say, though, is that the release comes inevitably when we stay faithful to the process of letting go
of the Good Mother/False Self and open ourselves to all
within us that we have so painfully denied for so long.
Letting go is connected to loss, and loss is where we
shall move to next.

LOSS

Journal Entry
August 25, 1990

Sometimes I want Eloise to vanish, go somewhere far
away so that I'm not responsible for her any more. The
desire doesn't arise like a thought: it's more like a fan-
tasy, a split-second fantasy, of her dying of childhood

leukemia, or being hit by a car, or disappearing. Experiencing the fantasy, I feel punched in my gut: I don't want my child to die.

But yes, part of me would like freedom again. Free to sleep as long as I want to when I want to. Free to stay up all night and write or play the piano or visit friends. Free to stare off into space. Free to take a walk around Green Lake. Free to enjoy unscheduled time with my husband. Free to have an argument with him and not have to worry about how it's affecting Eloise; free not to have to put the argument off until after her bedtime, when we're both so tired that we're likely to have forgotten what the argument is about but are still carrying the hard feelings of the argument itself. Free to eat what I want to, when I want to. Free from carpooling. Free from noise, and mayhem, and chaos.

Oh yes, I know that I would lose much that is precious if she were gone, but sometimes I would give anything, almost anything, to recover some of the old freedoms.

Sometimes I am afraid I will lose my happiness with Eloise. I wonder if I deserve the fresh, unencumbered happiness that she has brought into my life: rolling together on the carpet tickling each other; rediscovering through her eyes the magic of a moon that follows you everywhere; telling silly, impossible stories; drawing pictures together of silly, impossible creatures; splashing each other in the bathtub; rocking her at night in the lazy-boy.

Such gifts. What have I done to deserve such gifts? How have I earned them? Can they possibly be free? If they are truly gifts, will somebody take them back?

Have I been good enough to deserve them? What is
"good enough"? What if I stop being "good enough"?

*I feel afraid when I think such thoughts, afraid that
somehow a mistake has been made, that she really
wasn't intended for me, that such simple happiness
wasn't intended for me. I want to hunker down, not
laugh so loudly with her, not sing quite so clearly to the
moon and stars and trees. Maybe if I modulate my own
happiness, keep it under cover, under wraps, then it
won't be noticed. And won't be taken away. . . .*

*Sometimes I am afraid Eloise will die. When I read
about a child dying of cancer, hear about a child killed
in a traffic accident, see a poster for a missing child, I
feel torn apart. For a split second, sometimes for an
afternoon, I see, and feel, Eloise there instead of that
other child. How could God have created beings as in-
finitesimally fragile as children? Whatever did God
have in mind?*

*My mind chants the litany of what could happen to
her (being in a car crash, coming down with cancer,
drowning, being burned, being kidnapped), and my
heart cries out, No, no, those things can't happen, those
things will not happen to her. And yet they do happen,
to other mothers' children. Mothers who have taken
every possible precaution to keep their children safe, to
create a barrier between their children and death. And
still death comes. Mothers who have said to themselves,
My child is safe, those terrible things happen to other
mothers' children. Mothers who now have holes in their
hearts where once were their children's lives.*

*What separates me from those grieving mothers, lost
children? How can I inoculate my child against death?
When I hold my daughter I can feel her small heart*

beating, bringing blood and nutrients and life to her
body. How can such a miracle be? How can such in-
tense fragility survive in a world of nuclear bombs,
rapists, carcinogens? How can I make my own body a
barrier, an impenetrable barrier, between her and all
that could happen to her? And how many times have
the mothers of those sick and dead and missing children
asked the same questions?

NADIR

Loss represented for me my nadir on this journey, the
lowest point to which I could sink, although I did not
know it at the time. Each of us has a nadir, some core
pain about mothering that will generally be the last pain
to be revealed and felt. It is as if the journey isn't just
"down," it's a peeling away as well, like the peeling of
an onion. Each layer represents a deeper level of pain
and truth, peeled away until the core is revealed, a jewel
of healing encrusted by long-forgotten pain.

This core is the nadir and is experienced as the dark
night written about in Chapter 1. For each mother, the
core issue will be different. For some, like me, it will
be loss; for others, it might be anger, control, guilt. This
is the time that despair usually arises, when one feels as
if the pain will never end. This pain will be felt in varying
degrees of intensity by each different mother and be felt
in different ways.

This experience of deep pain represents, though, the
turning, the mystery, the darkest night before the dawn.
Vivekenanda, a spiritual teacher, writes, "Never are we
nearer the Light than when darkness is deepest." The

transition stage of labor, the "ring of fire," that most radical opening of our cervixes and souls, prepares the way for the baby to make its trip through the canal towards birth. This pain breaks us open, cracks our husks so that new life may arise within.

CHAPTER
7
The Turning

Meister Eckhart writes, "What is this darkness? What is its name? Call it: an aptitude for sensitivity. Call it: your potential for vulnerability. Call it: a rich sensitivity which will make you whole."[15] This is the dark night. We can read such mystics as Meister Eckhart, who assures us that this darkness has as its purpose the healing and regeneration of our psyches and souls, but that assurance is difficult to believe in the middle of the dark night. How could good come out of so much pain and grief and anguish?

This is an important time to recognize both the need for community and the need for solitude. Other mothers, one's own mother, one's partner, a therapist—all can be of help in supporting, listening, simply being with one's pain. People who can listen, support, without trying to fix or solve our pain for us. People who can love us at our most broken. People, also, with whom we may take a break from the pain, which is also needed; people who can be silly with us, laugh, be light.

Solitude is also necessary at this time. Time and space for us to be naked with our pain, befriend it, let it stretch us in ways we have never been stretched before. This pain, if we can simply open up and learn what it has to give us, can be the greatest teacher we have ever encountered, if we can simply open up and learn what it has to give to us.

This may be the time when we need additional time away from our children, and it is important to be as honest and clear as possible with our partners and fellow care-givers about getting this need met with additional care for our children.

We may need at times to remind ourselves that this pain, this healing we are undertaking, is not just for ourselves. It may be the greatest gift we can ever give our children, for we will emerge from it able to love, give to, and receive our children in ways undreamt of before the journey. Not only our children benefit from this. At this end of this passage our partners, our friends, and our families will encounter a transformed person. Our culture, and our planet as well need, at this critical point in our planetary history, such a person as we can become: a woman, open-hearted, clear-visioned, honest and aware, committed to living what life brings to the fullest.

HEARTBREAK

At this point in my own journey I felt the necessity to retreat, to find a place where I could simply enter into my despair without having to function as mother, wife, therapist, friend. I went to a cabin on the west coast of Vancouver Island, a place my family and I had gone before for rest and recreation, a place where I could be blessed and surrounded by strong winds, grey ocean, dark firs, and living creatures.

I wrote in my journal, I slept, I walked along the grainy beaches, I cried. I called upon Kali to help me. I knew I couldn't do it alone.

Journal Entry
August 25, 1990

As I write these words in my journal this morning I know I am allowing my deepest feelings to arise, to come to awareness. I have to remind myself that feeling these painful feelings is part of the process of becoming whole and healed as a mother.

How can I deal with such letting go, such loss? My mind rebels. I want to believe that, yes, I can keep my child from death; that, yes, I can keep death away from myself as well. If I just try hard enough, am careful enough, then no harm will ever befall either myself or my child.

KALI: This is not true.
ME: I want it to be so. I will make it so.
KALI: This is impossible. You are deluding yourself.

*Death is wild, untamable. You cannot domesticate it,
put it on a schedule. It will not be.*

ME: *How can I open, truly open, to the possibility of
my own child's death, without its tearing me apart?
Without its killing me as well?*

KALI: *Trust the darkness. Trust it.*

ME: *What do you mean?*

KALI: *Trust the darkness inside yourself. Trust the
reality of it. It is ground.*

ME: *What does this have to do with the death of my
child? With the fragility of my child?*

KALI: *Everything. Everything. It is the not-knowing
that is destroying you. What if? What if? And when you
question like this you become hard, contracted. These
"what-ifs?" you ask yourself are unanswerable. Yes,
your child may die. Yes, your child is fragile. Yes, you
are fragile. . . . It is the not-knowing, isn't it?*

ME: *Yes. I want to know the future, predict it, control it. I want to be in control of my child's safety and
well-being. I want her to be okay. I'm afraid I could
not survive the death of my child; how could I live
through that much pain? How could I do it?*

KALI: *You died when you birthed your child. You
would also die if your child died. Dancing with the
pain, the darkness, the not-knowing, is what matters.
You cannot control the rest. You are powerless there.*

ME: *I don't know how to dance like that, dance with
not-knowing, dance with pain. How do I learn the
steps? How can I learn the pattern of pain?*

KALI: *You have been learning. Each time that you
have stayed with your uncertainties, your anger, your
grief, you have learned some of the dance. Here, would
you like to learn more?*

ME: *Now?*
KALI: *NOW.*
ME: *(deep breath) Yes. . . . I put my pen down.*

Later—
This is what has just happened. I feel as if I'm still
living it:

I lie on the bare floor in this island cabin where I'm
staying for a few days. The room is a little bit cooler
down here. I hear from outside the muffled boom of
ocean waves breaking on rocks. My heart is beating fast
and hard. (Let go, breathes Kali. Go into the fear.) It's
hard to breathe. (Breathe into the fear, says Kali, not
away from it. The breathing will carry you through.)
What am I doing? I don't know how to do this. (Keep
going, keep going. Trust it.)
Oh my child, oh Eloise, you are so precious to me.
How could I lose you? (You are losing her, says Kali.
You lost her from your body when you birthed her.
Each step of your life is about letting go of her, losing
her, a little bit more. Keep breathing.) Loss. Loss. Loss
of control. Loss of certainty. Loss of my child. Loss of
my baby at one, loss of my toddler at three, loss of my
preschooler at five. I am always losing her. My heart
feels so tight, so small, so scared.
I don't want to lose her. How can I lose her? How
can I survive losing her? I will lose her someday, just
as I have lost my infant, just as I will lose my teen-
ager. I will lose them all. How can I bear such loss?
My heart feels so tight, a clenched fist. A fist pound-
ing no, no, NO against my ribs. No, no, I won't let
go. I can't breathe. I'm going to die of this pain and

grief. (No you aren't, whispers Kali, keep going.) How can I do this? My heart wants out. No pain, it says, no letting go. No loss. Hammering on me to get out. GET ME OUT OF HERE, it's hammering on me. I hate this. I want to get up and forget this. (Stay with it, whispers Kali, fiercely, to me. Stay with it, you're almost there.)

Where? Where the hell is there? . . . The panic of labor returns to me, the knowing that there is no out, only through. Only through. Keep breath-ing. . . . Something's happening to my heart. It's going faster and faster, out of control. Help, something's hap-pening. Help. HELP. . . .

My heart. . . . My heart just exploded. . . . It's bro-ken into a million pieces. I'm lying in the rubble of my own shattered heart. . . .

It's very quiet. . . . I hear the waves breaking again, only now they are breaking through me. Going right through me. No resistance. . . . Just open space, and quiet, inside me, around me. . . . The waves are wash-ing through right where my clenched-tight heart used to be. . . . And the wind, too. Wind blowing through me. No resistance. . . . I finger one of the pieces of my heart lying by my side. Such sharp edges. The piece is hard, smooth, like glass, like china. . . .

What is inside me now that my heart is in shards all around me? What is inside now? Space. . . . The ocean. . . . Grey-green firs bending in the wind. . . . My daughter's countenance in all its weath-ers and seasons. . . . Just what is. No more. No less.

BEGINNING TO OPEN

I returned from the island cabin to my home and family with a heart softer and wider open than I had ever dreamed of.

This turning will be different for different mothers. Some, like me, will have dramatic turnings; others may simply wake up one morning and fell lighter, different, returned to life. For still others, the turning may be so subtle that they can't even articulate what has happened until talking about it with me in a therapy session. For all, though, there is a sense that something important has shifted, that although there still may be some pain, that a corner has been turned, that they feel engaged with life once more, that the baby has crowned.

I think that the turning may have more to do with the transformation of our relationship with whatever is most painful for us rather than with the passing away of the pain itself. At some point, through grace, timing, whatever, we learn to breathe into our pain, soften into it, let ourselves into our own hearts as feelers of great pain, and we ultimately allow our hearts to be broken. A broken-open heart, says Joanna Macy, has room to contain the whole world.

The ultimate letting go is letting go of the demand of life, of God, that we be pain-free. Once we let go of this demand we can stop contracting around pain and grief and fear and anger, and we can instead soften around them, be merciful and compassionate toward ourselves even in the midst of trauma.

At first this learning, this softness and openness, may feel fragile and tentative, like the beautiful tentacles of an anenome ready to suddenly pull in at the slightest hint of danger. But, as Steven Levine says, the wider open our hearts have become, the greater the distance it takes them to close. Contraction soon becomes too painful a state in itself to support for very long.

And such gifts begin to present themselves when we make the first small steps toward living with an open heart.

EMBRACING THE CYCLES OF LIFE

Journal Entry
September 6, 1990

Something has changed inside of me. Today, while drawing with Eloise, I knew this, in a moment, and had to go sit by the window and look out over the late summer garden to take it all in.

I'm not me, any more than I'm Eloise, or Eloise is herself, or either of us is my own mother. Rather, Life is dawning itself with Eloise, nooning itself with me, twilighting itself with my mother.

We are all moving round in a Great Circle as Life pours itself, herself, through us, moves in the Sacred Circle through us. Such a deep, visceral sense of the fleetness and insubstantiality of our individual lives, like waves washing endlessly up on a long, grey shore. Somehow we are no more than spokes on a great, sacred, everturning wheel, and who or what the spokes are is not important; what matters is the turning. The

*Sacred Turning. Coming round, and round, and
round.*

*Somehow, before having a child, it was possible for
me to convince myself that everyone else but me aged
and died. Particularly this last week, with Eloise sick
and me so sleep-deprived, I have looked at myself in the
mirror and seen, shocked, an old woman looking back
at me. That future time no longer seems so far away. I
cannot dream of Eloise's future, something I do mostly
with pleasure, without seeing also in that picture my
own face and body, grown also that much older.*

*My beautiful young daughter, moving into the morn-
ing of her life as the prow of a graceful ship plows deep
waters, just moving into her life as I reach high noon,
and what? What beyond that?*

*Such a short short time ago it was, really, that my
own mother sat pondering the same imponderables with
me, her firstborn, on her lap, and here she is, so soon,
so soon, a grandmother, growing always more intimate
with death as friends, relatives, age and die. And so
soon, so soon may Eloise, grown old, be staring out at
trees newly leafing with heart open wide, and marveling
and grieving over the same wonders. My mother has sat
thus, and my grandmother, and her mother, and her
mother before her. And they are all dead now, they are
all who knows where, Oh mothers do you hear me?*

*Pondering, ageing, dying; pondering, ageing, dying;
and here am I, pondering, and ageing, and dying a little bit every day.*

Such sweet relief, to be able to let go into Life, to open
our arms and embrace whatever Life will bring us. Such

sweetness, to let go into our own mortality through our children, through the lineage of mothers that we are all descended from. Such grace, to make friends with our inner darkness.

DESCENT INTO DARKNESS: DESCENT INTO LIFE

We come from darkness, our mothers' dark and life-bearing wombs. We bring forth our own children from the moist, dark, interior regions of our own bodies. At death our bodies return to darkness, the earth, womb and tomb of all life.

At night, in sleep, we dip, are dipped, into our own dark wells of dreams, returning both full and empty to face daylight once more.

The earth herself descends into darkness every winter, turning from the sun, before turning round once more to warmth, light, life.

All around us and within us are places of darkness, places of destruction and renewal, places where life and death meet and are one.

So we too must return to darkness, not once, but many times. What if the earth decided, "No night"? What if she decided, "No winter"? "No darkness"? How could we die, and live?

So, too, how can we live, truly live, without dwelling in our own darkness and finding there the deepest center of our own life, of Life itself?

GIFTS

Journal Entry
September 10, 1990

Kali, explains The Book of the Goddess, *offers an ultimately liberating knowledge: "that the bright and dark sides of the sacred are but the human bifurcation of one holy reality."*[16]

Kali, Kali. She is standing before me once again. She is different now, though—transformed. (Or is it I who is different, transformed?) Rather than looking terrifying, she looks beautiful. Her eyes have softened. Her grin is more like a smile. Her gestures, as she dances, are less vigorous, more graceful.

As I adjust to the changes in her she gives me a gentle nod of welcome. Why didn't I see her sensual and raven beauty at first? All I could see at our first encounter was death, destruction, terror. Now I am encountering, she is showing me, another side of herself. Now, though still sometimes slightly menacing, she dances peacefully and gracefully. Her hands bestow gifts and peace upon me.

What is this peace that she now grants me? Peace not born from avoidance of pain, a willed peace, but the peace that I experienced after my heart shattered. The peace of the darkness. The peace of a heart broken wide open. The peace of going through to the other side, the peace following birth. Yes. Kali looks at me, nods "Yes." A dynamic peace. An alive, thriving peace.

I look at her once again. She is lifting her hands, gift-giving ones, for me to consider. (Do I even detect a

*glint of amusement in her eyes?) Gifts: gifts of aliveness,
of juices flowing freely, of being fully present in my own
body, in my own feelings; a gift of finding my own dark
and fertile center; a gift of learning to dance with what
is, no matter what it is; a gift of being broken open, of
discovering wide-open spaces inside me, filled with emptiness and love.*

*Kali nods at me once again: don't forget, don't forget
the rest. Yes, her wildness is still there, black hair
flying, eyes flashing. I feel stretched once more, saying
"Yes" to the stretching that allows me to behold her in
her totality, allows me to contain all of me as well. I
have learned, finally, to dance with Kali.*

DANCING WITH OUR INNER IMAGES

When we begin to open to ourselves, all of who we are,
when we begin to learn how to be in life with an open
heart, our relationship with inner images that may for-
merly have been threatening shifts. When we began this
descent, our waking images and our dreams may have
been filled with frightening figures. These figures
seemed wholly foreign to us.

As we keep opening to our pain, to our shadow selves,
the figures change, slowly but surely, into friendly figures, still a little wild and untamed, perhaps, but there
to offer us guidance, help, support. As we begin to integrate these figures, they begin to transform. Quite
often, those figures that have frightened us the most, if
we can stay with them, converse with them, befriend
them, have the greatest gifts to give us.

SEEING IN A NEW WAY

Along with the shift in our relationship to inner images goes a new way of seeing both our inner and our outer worlds. Many Eastern religions speak of a "third eye," an eye of wisdom that opens at a certain point in one's spiritual development. This is a potent image, one that speaks of the shift in seeing that we experience at this point in the journey of mothering.

With this new eye, this new seeing, we can see/feel that place within us where stillness and dancing meet and join, the still point of the turning world. We behold the interconnectedness of all life, sense the sacred matrix from which we, our children, and all of life have emerged, the dark and holy Love pulsating at the very center of Life itself.

We see that it is our love for our children, their love for us, and Love itself that have brought us through all the pain and fear and grief and anger to this soft, dark center, this matrix of all life. We feel gratitude. We see, with this new vision, that we have been graced by our children: to have this opportunity for healing, for integration, for being rewoven into the web of life that surrounds and upholds us all.

Mechtild of Magdeburg writes: "From suffering I have learned this: that whoever is sore wounded by love will never be made whole unless she embraces the very same love which wounded her." We see now, with our "single eye," that the pain, grief, and despair seemingly brought on by bearing and raising our children have been some of the greatest opportunities we have ever been given for opening to love and healing beyond our wildest dreams.

AUTHOR'S NOTE: For help along the way, see the exercises described in the Resources section of this book, especially those listed under Stage 2: The Descent.

PART

IV

The Return:
Hearts Open Wide

*The higher goal of spiritual living is not to
amass a wealth of information, but to face
spiritual moments.*
—RABBI ABRAHAM HESCHEL

CHAPTER
8
Does This Really Work?

*A*fter the turning, we are ready to be with our children in a new way: with a welcoming heart, ready to stay open to them and to ourselves, no matter what comes up between us. Ready to use any circumstance as an opportunity to keep breathing, a chance to practice keeping our bodies and our hearts open and soft. Ready to say "Yes" to life and whatever life brings in the course of mothering.

A part of us may still hold back, though, asking: Can I really put all of this into practice? I asked myself that question often in the first weeks after my shift into a different way of being. All that I had learned sounded wonderful when I was alone, but was it really translatable on a practical, day-to-day level with Eloise? When I felt up against some wall with her, could I really stay soft and open?

For many mothers there may be concerns as well about boundaries between themselves and their children. Can we say "Yes" to life and an open heart and at the same time say "No," set limits with them? If we let our children, and life, into our hearts more, will we also know when to draw the line?

PRACTICING

Journal Entry
October 3, 1990

I had an opportunity tonight to practice what I have so recently learned, to see that even when I forget it, all I have to do is take a breath, return to center, return to that sacred space . . . .

Eleven P.M.: Eloise had been in bed, restless, since eight-thirty. I had seen a lot of clients today and was tired and still a little sick myself and all I wanted to do was crawl into my bed, pull the down comforter over me, and get lost in the Agatha Christie mystery I was reading. Eloise started coughing. Hack, hack, hack. Quiet. Hack, hack, hack. Poor sick one, bronchitis still in her lungs. Hack, hack, hack. I went in, murmured to her, gave her more cough medicine, stroked her forehead damp from coughing. Hack, hack, hack. She closed her eyes, room quiet again except for the soft hissing of the humidifier. I kissed her warm head and returned to my room, weary.

I eased myself beneath my comforter and breathed,

*tired. Hack, hack . . . gasp, hack hack. I grabbed one
of my pillows and returned to her room.*

*"Here, sit up, sweetie." I propped both her pillow
and mine against her headboard. "Here, now, lie down
against these, this will help." Her small body was limp
with fatigue. I settled her into the pillows. She coughed
more; I stroked her forehead. The coughing ceased. I
kissed her once again and walked softly back to my
room, not wanting to ruffle the quiet.*

*I leaned over my bed; hack, hack, gasp, hack fol-
lowed me through the monitor. I was all ready to be
angry, put out, resentful, but none of that came. I hurried back to her room, calling to her as I went. She
turned her head toward me as I crossed her threshold.
Her room was dark except for the meager light in one
corner from her nightlight, but I could see the dark circles under her eyes, the shadows in her face, the damp
hair plastered against her cheeks. My heart felt as big as
the room and as soft as the darkness enfolding us both.*

*"Sit up once more, Eloise," I whispered, and I
crawled onto her bed. I squeezed between her and the
headboard, put both pillows behind my back, slid my
legs around her, encircling her. "Now lean back, lean
into me. That's right. Just close your eyes now." I felt
her slightness against me, so little weight for me to
carry, such intense sweetness to sit there, in the dark,
Eloise leaning against me, feeling her breathing, her
back against my chest, such sweetness.*

*She coughed and I stroked her forehead, she quieted,
she coughed, I murmured to her. It doesn't matter what
I murmured, it was the murmuring that counted, I
wanted to sit there in that darkness forever with my
daughter against me.*

As I sit back here in my own bed, writing, this is what I most want to say: To hell with tomorrow, to hell with fatigue, this is what really counts: the sibilance of the steam, the deep darkness, the fragile weight of my daughter against my own soft belly.

SACRED TIME

Sacred time: moments when the senses are acute, the heart open wide. Moments when we are opened both to the vastness of our existence and the intimacy of the present moment. Moments of being fully awake and receptive to what *is*, right now. These moments happen only when our hearts are open, soft, spacious. When the eye, like Kali's eye, is single: instead of being rigidly self-contained, we are "interbeing" (to borrow Thich Nhat Hanh's phrase):[17] no sharp divisions, no high walls, between ourselves and our feelings, our children, the world. Our brains still. Fully in our bodies. No struggle. Just an acute awareness of what is within us and around us at this moment.

The ancient Greeks had two words for time: *chronos* and *kairos*. Chronos is clock time, linear time, time marching relentlessly forward. Kairos is radically different. Kairos is time outside of time, life lived from the heart rather than from the clock. Kairos means living in the eternal now, the eternal present of saints, animals, children. We, as mothers, may reclaim kairos whenever we choose to open our hearts, breathe deeply, open ourselves to the multitudinous gifts our senses bring forward for us moment by moment. We may inhabit kairos while changing diapers, being with fussy children, driving a carpool. Any time may be sacred time.

We were raised in our culture to believe that some moments are more sacred then others, some times more special, according to certain set—albeit unspoken— rules. These special times become particularly holy if some important expert or priest pronounces them so. These "sacred" moments are usually confined to what- ever happens within church walls. Sunday services are "sacred time"; the rest of our life, and of everyone else's life, is "ordinary," non-sacred.

Now I see this differently: what if all moments are sacred moments? What if we are all priestesses of the present? What if all ground is holy? What if *all* bushes are burning, as well as trees, stones, creatures, our chil- dren, ourselves, and all the spaces between? What if the only thing keeping us from knowing all moments as sa- cred is our insistence on seeing ourselves and the world with two eyes instead of one, our determination to keep our hearts walled, guarded, safe?

What if all we have to do is remember this: to unshutter our single eye, spring open the gates of our hearts?

OPENING THE HEART

I began to understand that it was not my heart that was breaking, but rather the wall around my heart that I had erected, that I continued to try to make thicker, higher, stronger. The pain that I felt when my heart seemed to break was really the pain of that wall shattering into a million pieces. Hearts were not meant to live in such tight and constricted spaces as the one I had created for my own. Hearts were meant to be as big as trees, oceans, skies, worlds.

How much energy we use to guard our hearts! This energy, when released from defense work, can be channeled into more life-giving ways of being both mother and woman, for being open to new ways of touching, and being touched by, our children and the world. How immensely freeing to say no longer to life, "Yes, but . . . ," but now, simply, "Yes."

When we close our hearts and hunker down there is no space inside us for anything or anyone. We cannot selectively open the gates. We bar not only our own pain, our own anger, but also our own joys and celebrations. There is no room, either, for our own children with their ups and downs. When I resist myself I resist Eloise; when I shut myself out of my own heart my child is also left out in the cold. As I learn to cultivate gentleness and compassion, an open heart, toward myself and whatever I am experiencing, then I can let in my daughter too, make room for her no matter how she is feeling or behaving.

When we choose to open our hearts, to expand into rather than contract from the present moment, we need to do so with no holds barred. No conditions: "I'll open my heart to myself *if* I (stay calm and centered, do the "right thing" with my child, am a perfect mother . . .); "I'll open my heart to my child *if* she (stops screaming, does what I say, is "good" . . .).

Opening our hearts to our children does not always mean hugs and kisses. It can mean giving them loving space if that is what they need. It can mean saying "No," firmly, and sticking with it.

SAYING NO WITH AN OPEN HEART

Journal Entry
October 15, 1990

Eloise was in the bathtub this evening humming Happy Birthday, absorbed in orchestrating a birthday party among her plastic bath creatures. The timer for getting out of the bath rang, making her jump. She returned to serving her creatures bubble birthday cake. Our conversation then went something like this:

"Eloise, what is the timer for?"

"No, Mama, I don't want to get out yet. It's not time."

"Eloise, it is time. I know you'd like to stay in and keep playing, but the timer has rung to get out. Do you want to get out by yourself or do you want me to lift you out?"

"No, Mama, it's not time, it isn't."

I noticed that I had clutched my breath and my hands were clenched into tight balls. Frustration rose in me like fever. I remembered what I had been writing about these past months and took a deep, slow breath, centered myself. I let the energy of my anger course through me, crest, subside. I picked up the conversation, something like this:

"Eloise, one last time, do you want to get out of the bathtub by yourself or do you want me to carry you out?"

"No, Mama, I—"

I leaned over and lifted her out of the soapy water.

She looked at me briefly, surprised, and then began yelling and kicking. "Let me down! Stop it! I want my bath! LET GO!" She squirmed, slippery, in my arms.

"No, Eloise, it's time for you to get out and get ready for bed. It's your bedtime now." I am amazed by the calmness in my voice. My voice soothes me, centers me. I tell myself inside that saying no can be a sacred act. I see Kali smile.

"I want to go back to the tub! I don't like you." She kicks my knee, hard enough to hurt.

"All right, Eloise, that's enough. It's OK to be angry but it's not OK to kick me. Time for time out." I carried her, naked and wet, to her time-out chair in the living room, set her firmly on it. "Three minutes."

I left her crying in the chair, retreated to the relative sanctuary of the study. I sat down on the sofa, held my own hand, rubbed my right fingers over my left knuckles. The skin was rough and creased from gardening; the touch was reassuring. I heard my daughter crying in the next room and I consciously breathed, extended my heart to encompass her, her anger, her frustration.

I am finding that the more I can open to me, stay with myself no matter what, the more I can be present with Eloise, no matter what. Six months ago, a year ago, I would have been throwing my own interior temper tantrum while she raged on the outside. Tonight, though, it was really okay, I could breathe and open and be centered and present, present both to my daughter's anger and frustration and to my own "No." There is far more room in my own heart than I ever dreamed possible.

CHOICES

Opening our hearts can mean letting our children make their own mistakes and learn from them. Opening our hearts to our children can mean loving them and ourselves enough to set boundaries that as adults we know they are unprepared to set. Opening our hearts to our children can also mean celebrating them, nurturing them, being literally "in love" with them as we go through the day together. Opening our hearts to our children, with no conditions, does not mean we will always say "Yes" to what they do. It does mean that we will, to the best of our abilities, say "Yes" to who they are.

I was beginning to understand that to open my heart was always a choice for me, moment by moment. Each time I did open my heart I was healed, as mother and as woman, a little bit more. I had a choice, always, whether to contract into my old, small self or expand into the now, into grace, into new possibilities. A tight and constricted heart or a spacious one. The choice was, and is, always mine.

As we continue to make this choice to open our hearts, moment by moment, we learn how much energy we have spent resisting the present. When we have gotten frustrated and angry and tried to wall ourselves off from the "source" of our discomfort (our children!), we ended up feeling far more drained and lifeless than if we had simply chosen to open our hearts to the present moment, softened our bodies, and breathed.

Our spirituality may change in the process of opening. We find that sacredness does not lie in the past or the future, or in a particular place, or in what "should" be, but rather, simply and powerfully, in the present moment, in *kairos*. We find that as we open our hearts to whatever is happening at the time, not only does any difficulty become easier to deal with, but we also become reconnected to the Sacred, reconnected to the greater web of life that holds us all.

This is a time for learning important things about boundaries, for learning that "No" and "Yes" can happen at the same time. We find that we can set limits with our children, say "No" to them, and at the same time stay open, non-contracted, and soft, say "Yes" to the larger space that cradles us all. We learn that we need not become contracted and hard in order to say "No." We learn also that as we trust our ability to set limits, to say "No" to our children clearly and without guilt, and stay open at the same time, that we are able to say "Yes" to them, to ourselves, and to Life at even deeper and deeper levels.

CHAPTER
9

Beginner's Mind

I began to trust that I could really put into practice all that I had learned, that this new openness and softness was workable. As I practiced these learnings a new sort of simplicity entered my life.

This simplicity was connected with letting go and returning to the present. No matter how complex or frustrating a situation with Eloise got, I was beginning to be able to return to resting in my heart, allowing space to arise around and within the complexity and confusion. In fact, it was often by opening to my confusion, simply letting there be space for the turmoil within my heart, that I could return to simplicity. The simplicity and openness came not from resisting pain and confusion and struggle but from embracing them, opening my heart to whatever was going on in the present moment, whatever

I was feeling, whatever my daughter was feeling and doing.

Again, though, I had questions: Could I really trust that sort of simplicity? Was I too attached to dramas, the stress and excitement of having "problems" to worry over, try to solve? (After all, drama made great stories, and I loved to tell stories!) Was it possible to let go of "problems"? And if I did let go of "problems" what would take their place?

OPEN MIND, BEGINNER'S MIND

The partner of the open heart is the open mind, or "beginner's mind," as Shunryu Suzuki names it:

> The goal of practice is always to keep our beginner's mind. . . .Our "original mind" includes everything within itself. . . .That does not mean a closed mind, but actually an empty mind and a ready mind. If your mind is empty, it is always ready for anything; it is open to everything. In the beginner's mind there are many possibilities; in the expert's mind there are few. . . .The beginner's mind is the mind of compassion.[18]

When my heart is closed, my mind as well is shut firmly. I am sure I know the answers before I even ask the questions. Instead of asking myself, "What is really going on here between me and my child? Am I open or closed right now? Am I breathing? What are the possibilities here? What is this an opportunity for me to learn?" I respond to my daughter in a tight, reflexive way.

A shut mind has no room for surprise, for play, for learning, for grace. When our minds constrict around answers and solutions, mothering becomes a series of "problems" to solve instead of a dance to be danced between ourselves and our children.

Charlotte Joko Beck writes of such a mindset:

> When something really annoys us, irritates us, troubles us, we start to think. We worry, we drag up everything we can think of, and we think and we think and we think—because that's what we believe solves life's problems. In fact what solves life's problems is simply to experience the difficulty that's going on, and then to act out of that. . . .My action emerges from my experience.[19]

What a challenge and an opportunity for mothers: to give up "struggles" and "problems" and instead to simply be with what is happening, with ourselves and with our children.

NO PROBLEM

Journal Entry
November 2, 1990

Last night in the cabin Eloise didn't go to sleep until eleven. Every ten minutes or so after we put her down at nine the litany started from her room: "Mama, Daddy, don't leave me, don't go away." Then one of

us intoned our part: "We're here, Eloise, we haven't left, we aren't going anywhere. Go nightnight now."
The chanting continued back and forth for almost two hours.

Rodg and I went to bed, to sleep. We were awakened about twelve-thirty by her crying. I went into her room to reassure her, and we all went back to sleep. Then crying again at two. Then Eloise wanting to get out of her accursed bed for good at three-thirty, crying that she wanted to get up. We offered her our bed to come into, but she replied that she didn't want ANY bed, she just wanted to get up.

Terrified of her bed, refusing to come to ours. I was so tired and frustrated that after going in and comforting Eloise for the weary-eenth time, I returned to my own bed and sobbed. Eloise, hearing me cry, broke out into wails herself. Rodg, caught between the two of us, finally chose Eloise. As I cried I could hear him in the next room comforting her. I knew he was doing the right thing, but I wanted to kill him for going to her instead of me. I wanted to kill her, too, and then sleep for a long, long time in a very quiet room.

Rodg returned, rubbed my back. I lay there in the darkness searching for every possible explanation I could think of for Eloise's terror and unrest: Because I worked too much? Because I was home with her too much? Because Rodg and I fought? Because Rodg and I were too close and shut her out? Was there something terrible going on between Rodg and me that I was denying? Was there something organically wrong with Eloise that I was unaware of? Was she sick? Was she dying? Was I dying? Was she having a premonition of some future event that I wasn't aware of? Was I a bad par-

ent? Had I failed my child, somehow, miserably? The internal drama was interrupted by Eloise calling once again. . . .

Everything is jumbled in my mind after that. At least somewhere in my mind I knew I was hitting a bottom, although the bottom of what I had no idea, and some small part of me knew enough to keep with it, keep opening, that there was some gift for me at the end of the fall.

Finally about five A.M. *Rodg went in to Eloise's room, and, wrapped up in a yellow and black plaid blanket he found in her closet, lay down on the bare, cold fir floor beside her bed. Both my husband and child then went to sleep.*

I lay in my own bed for another hour or so, intermittently dozing (dreaming of going to see a therapist about this night, crying for the entire session, and finding the therapist had nothing, nothing useful for me at the end), and wrestling, falling, wrestling, falling.

At sunrise I felt the first bit of solid ground beneath me. I got up, put on slippers and robe, fixed a cup of strong coffee, and went out on the deck. I curled up in a weathered Adirondack chair and watched the waves breaking on the beach below me. The tide was going out, great masses of black boulders exposed by the retreating ocean, long stretches of grey grainy beach, dark green firs marking the curve of coastline, green hills modulating to blue in the distance under low grey skies, teal water breaking into foam in the cove beneath me. As I sat there I let both wind and wave wash over me, move through me, allowing myself to be baptized again by the sacraments of water and wind.

Only then could I let in the depths of Eloise's pain

and fear, allow myself to ease into the far reaches of her struggle. . . .

And then the gift appeared, unbidden: What if this, all of this night, wasn't a "problem" at all? What if, instead of being "a problem," that was just the cursed way my therapy profession and my culture might frame this night?

What if, instead, it was this, and only this: Eloise's fears and struggles that I, and Rodg, needed to open to and honor and do whatever we could in our power to ease? What if I was tired, very very tired, and that was that? What if beyond that I was helpless, truly helpless, and acknowledging this helplessness would be the greatest gift that I could give to my struggling child? What if I could give her the precious gift of being truly with her in each moment, no "problems," fully present to be with her in whatever way was best for that moment, unencumbered by theories and guilt and snatches from parenting books thrashing around in my restless brain?

BECOMING EMPOWERED

When we allow ourselves to go all the way down into the depths of our own experiences as mothers, we recover our soft hearts, our open minds. Once we hit bottom, we literally become grounded, grounded in our own bodies, grounded in our own feelings, grounded in our own lives. Our mothering then emerges from our own wisdom and understanding of whatever situation we are in with our children. We begin living our own mother-lives rather than one-dimensional imitations of them.

Until we are grounded in ourselves and the present moment, we are off balance. Anything or anyone can unseat us, knock the sacred wind and spirit out of us, because our feet are not firmly planted where we are right now. That is when difficulties arise. "Problems" are created the moment that we demand that life, our children, be different from the way they are right now. "Problems" are stories we tell ourselves in our own minds, not what we are really experiencing, not what is really happening "out there."

Trying to force our children, the situation, to be different, trying to control outcomes, limits our participation in life and mothering. Being ungrounded, contracting around problems, blocks learning, blocks the new and unexpected from life, blocks creativity and joy and grace.

As we surrender our demands of the way life *has* to be or the way our children *have* to be, we become empowered to deal with whatever difficulty is occurring, finding the right action that arises from what we have learned, from our own innate wisdom and love. We also then become open to the gifts and beauty that are always present in any situation with our children, gifts and beauty that we cannot see when we are blinded by our own demands of the way things have to be.

Beginner's Mind: simple, direct, compassionate. Letting go of fretting over "problems" the way a dog worries a bone. Being able to trust that the more we open our hearts and minds to the present the more we let go of having to be "in control" and knowing everything, the more our own innate wisdom can rise up and we can know what would be the best action to take in the present.

In the process, our sense of power, what it was and

how it is exercised, changes. Before my own shift, I had thought of power in terms of "power over": being in control, always knowing exactly what to do, getting my way, making my child bend to my will. All this changed. I understood the nature of "power within": the power to be present in my body, aware, awake, with an open heart and mind. Before, I had been afraid that if I wasn't always on top of things I would never get what I wanted. Now I understood that as I traded one sort of power for another, I was more whole than I had ever been, more contented. And, ironically, I was much more assured and fulfilled as a mother.

We find that as we loosen up, let go, find that power within, things become easier between ourselves and our children. We find that when things do get difficult, we know more easily what to do, and the turbulence passes more quickly, with little or no emotional hangover.

When we truly let go we also learn what takes the place of drama: the peace that passes all understanding. A sense of simplicity, and ease. A restful heart. A deep connection with life. We learn that, as we let go and practice beginner's mind, no matter how uncomfortable the situation we can still be cradled in this peace.

CHAPTER
10

Dancing on the Edge

*F*inally I could trust this new way of being with my child. I found that I could really be in this new space, be with my child in a way I had always hoped for.

I still had a lifetime of conditioning to deal with, though, as well as a healthy dose of my own humanness: I made mistakes with my child, had bad days, acted sometimes in ways with her that I regretted. I hadn't attained perfection. I learned, however, that perfection wasn't what this sort of mothering was about; perfection had been the name of the game for the Good Mother. Rather, this path was about aliveness, about flexibility, the way a cane of bamboo can bend rather than break in a strong wind.

An essential part of this path is remembering: remembering that there is a Center, an open and merciful heart in ourselves to return to; remembering that we always have choices; remembering that we are being cradled in a far more loving space that we can ever imagine, the greater web of life that always surrounds and upholds us, there always for us to relax into.

I discovered that I had characteristic ways of forgetting all of this. I knew that these might not be the same ways of forgetting that would hold true for all mothers, but that it was important to articulate and acknowledge my ways, just as it is for any mother.

Acknowledging that this is indeed a process rather than some static place of perfection actually enriches mothering. We can begin to think of mothering as movement, both internal and external, a wonderful sort of dance that we and our children are always engaging in, no matter what sort of music is playing.

THE RAZOR'S EDGE

As mothers we must learn to dance on a razor's edge with our children: the razor's edge of the open heart, the open mind, the single eye.

Off one side of this razor's edge is that muted country where we shut ourselves off from our own feelings and experiences. This is the life-denying territory of the Good Mother in Part I of this book. In this place we lose contact with our own life and heart; we focus only on being good; we try to numb anything else that comes up by eating too much, spending too much, being too busy. We listen to those voices, inner and outer, telling us and our children to be Good rather than Alive.

We not only lose contact with ourselves, we lose contact with our children. We cut off ourselves and our children from the dark and fertile territory of grief, anger, fear, helplessness. And when we deny access to these we deny ourselves access as well to joy, fun, love. When we shut out the dark from our lives there is no room, either, for the light.

Off the other side of the razor's edge lies a battlefield. When we contract, whether around painful feelings or rigid positions ("NO, Eloise, you can NEVER do that"), we tumble onto this battleground. We armor ourselves: our bodies tighten, our breathing constricts. Our focus narrows until all that we are aware of is our own pain, or whatever is "causing" that pain. As mothers, we know that the "cause" is usually our children.

This contracting and armoring is so painful that we lose sight of anything other than getting rid of the cause. I make Eloise the enemy. I then shout at her, make rigid demands of her, punish both overtly and covertly. I try in whatever way I can to force her to change so that I can feel better.

We lose our openness of both heart and mind, our softness, our flexibility. To use Martin Buber's phrase, we turn our children into Its, a bundle of those traits or behaviors that we are trying to force to change, rather than seeing our children as Thous, whole and complex beings in relationship with whole and complex mothers.

On this battleground we say things to our children that we later regret: "You'll be sorry if you . . ."; "Godammit, STOP IT"; "GET OUT OF HERE." When we pitch our tents on this battleground our children lose mothers and gain witches. The psychic wounds that we inflict on our children when we are contracted and battle-ready can take a long time to heal.

Both of the territories on either side of the razor's edge are literally dis-heartening. Off the first side we lose contact with our own hearts by numbing ourselves. Off the other side we contract so much, squeeze our own hearts so tight that all that remains is pain.

The third way, the middle way, the razor's edge itself, is the place of opening to life, to ourselves, to our children. To be on this edge takes courage, for it is about saying "Yes" to the unknown and unexpected. This is the place of unconditional "Yes" to myself, to my child, to life. In this place there is openness and space for it all: for my feelings, all of them; for my child's feelings and behaviors, all of them; for my own wisdom that arises when I slow down, let go, acknowledge what is, right now. This is the sacred place where life grows and love blooms.

RETURNING TO BALANCE

Journal Entry
December 3, 1990

This morning Eloise and I went to the Science Center. We immediately went to her favorite section, the small kids' section: tiny slides, water tables, tidepool, hatching chicks. Busloads of schoolchildren from outlying districts were there along with the usual moms with preschool kids.

Eloise tugged at my skirt, grabbed my hand, and led me over to a room with a child-size raft and a small dinghy. Recorded sounds of breaking waves lightly muf-

*fled the ambient roar of kids at play. Another mother
and child were in the room as well, the mother about
my own age, her little boy at the just-starting-to-walk
stage. She was strapping a blue and yellow and red life
vest onto him, preparing him to brave the choppy seas
while riding the dinghy. Several standard, plain orange
life vests were strewn about the floor as well.*

*Eloise pointed to the colorful life vest the little boy
was now wearing and announced to me in a loud voice
that* that *life vest was the one she wanted to wear. I
explained to her that the little boy was wearing it, and
that she could wear any of the ones discarded on the
floor. Eloise didn't, of course, want any of those; she
wanted* that *one, she said, glowering at the little boy,
now happily being rocked in the boat by his mom. I
smiled apologetically at her. The ensuing "conversation" with Eloise went something like this:*

*"You can have that one when he's finished with it.
These toys are for sharing, remember? You can have a
turn soon."*

*"NO. I want it NOW." She sat down emphatically
on the floor.*

*"I know you'd like it now, but he's using it. Your
turn will come soon. How about a flag?" I waved a
nautical blue and white flag, hoping that a sleight of
hand would do the trick.*

*"NNNNNNOOOOOOOO. I want it NNOOOOO-
OOOOWWWWWWWWWW." She rolled over on her
stomach and began to howl. I couldn't hear the waves
in the background any more.*

*With one more apologetic smile at the other mother, I
picked Eloise up, squirming and wailing, and carried
her out of the small room. I was sure every other*

mother in the big playroom we were then in must be looking up and shaking their heads. I looked around, briefly, trying to figure out what to do next, and was amazed to find that no one was paying any attention to us. I tried again:

"Eloise. Eloise, you have a choice: you can calm down and we can go back in the boat room and play with the boats or I'm going to have to carry you some place else. Which do you want?"

"I want it NNNNNNOOOOOOOOOOOOOOWWWW-WWWWWWW." This brought a new burst of kicking and wailing.

She was too heavy for this sort of thing. I looked around to find a place where I could put her down until I could figure out what Plan B was and execute it. The wall dividing the animal petting area from the play equipment was unoccupied. I hurried over before it was claimed by someone else, leaned over, and deposited Eloise on the brown carpet. Racing kids, unsteady toddlers, mothers carrying bright piles of jackets all eddied around us as I struggled to catch my breath and regain my composure. Eloise was curled up in a fetal position on the carpet and sobbing over and over, "I want it, I want it NOW."

I wanted her to shut up. I felt shamed (all those other mothers now saw what a lousy mother I really was). I felt resentful of Eloise (how dare she do this to me when we've planned this all week. . . .I even paid for parking today so we could have more time in the Center). I felt angry, contracted, tight.

My first unmitigated impulse was to pick her up and shake her until her teeth rattled. I breathed until the impulse passed. My next impulse, one that my muscles ac-

tually started to respond to (one that I've done in the past), was to lean over, pick her up firmly while explaining to her that she's made her choices and I'm making mine, and abort our Science Center trip by driving us home, fuming inwardly.

And then something happened inside me. As I leaned over, my body relaxed, I took a deep breath. I straightened up without her. My focus widened and softened: instead of just being aware of myself and Eloise and the pain she was "causing" me, I saw the crowded room around me, noticed that her crying was drowned out by the sounds of rambunctious kids all around us, saw that no one was paying the slightest bit of attention to us, much less judging us. . . . I understood that the drama was taking place principally in my mind and not "out there." The "difficulty" lay not in what Eloise was doing but in the way I was dealing with the situation in my own mind and heart.

I became aware that I had options I had not entertained while I was in such a contracted and hard state. As I opened and softened, my choices multiplied. I saw that this was not a grocery store, or a library, places that I would have immediately removed her from. The Science Center was particularly crowded and noisy this morning, and no one could hear Eloise more than a foot or two from where she was crying. She was disturbing no one except herself and me.

It was as if I had changed the channel. As I opened my mind and my heart to what was happening right there and then, rather than contract around what "should" happen or what I "should" do, everything changed. I almost laughed out loud with the joy and novelty of it: THERE WAS NO PROBLEM. I couldn't stop smiling. I looked up to see another mother smiling back at me across several children. She winked at me and turned her attention back to her two children playing at the water table.

My heart felt so big and wide and open. I felt dizzyingly grateful to Eloise, there crying on the floor: I wanted to thank her, I wasn't sure for what, but I wanted to tell her how grateful I was that this had happened. Instead, I stood and grinned while her sobs began to subside.

Finally, she looked up at me, wet mess all over her face, and in a high wavering voice told me she wanted to go see the baby chicks coming out of their shells.

I told her OK. I knelt on the carpet, stroked her snarled-up hair, pulled a muffin-crumbed napkin from my pocket and wiped her face. She stood up and I followed suit. I couldn't stop smiling at her.

She must have wondered what had happened to her mother, for after a moment, she grabbed my hand and said, "C'mon, Mama, C'MON, the baby chicks are GROWING."

What I decided to do with Eloise that day at the Science Center was almost irrelevant. There were any number of choices I could have made, dependent upon many different factors. What was important, though, was that I was able to return to center, breathe, back off from seeing my child as an It to be managed so I could feel better, and only then make a choice about what I wanted to do. Again, as mothers we will make different choices for discipline based upon our own values and circumstances. We all do, though, have the potential for making those choices out of a breathing body, open heart, and clear mind.

DANCING ON THE EDGE

The greatest gift we can give ourselves and our children is to keep returning to this razor's edge no matter how frequently we fall off.

When we tumble off into the numb country we need to wake up, open our eyes, and acknowledge what is truly happening both inside us and around us. We need at this point to let go of trying to be the Good Mother and rather let ourselves be alive, full of feelings both dark and light.

When we find ourselves off the other side of the razor's edge, contracted and battle-ready, we need to soften, breathe, open up both heart and mind, let go. Returning to the razor's edge, returning to our breath, returning to our hearts. Returning to ourselves and our children.

So easy, when we are tired or sick or stressed, to fall off this razor's edge. So easy, then, to be hard on our children and ourselves, to say "No" when "Yes" would be just as easy; to say "Yes" out of weariness, when "Yes" is a disfavor both to our children and to ourselves. So easy, when we fall off, to raise our voices at our children or turn away from them in numbness or spite.

And then, after we have committed some thoughtless act, large or small, directed at our children, so easy to shut ourselves out of our own hearts. It is then that the Good Mother rises from her grave, points a spectral finger at us, and intones once more, "You *should* have. . . ,"

"You *oughtn't* have. . . ," "How can you call yourself a mother, a Good Mother, after *that?*"

It is precisely then that we need our memory. We need to remember that this razor's edge is a Way, not a destination, that as we learn to balance we will inevitably fall off. And when we do fall off, the greatest gift we can give ourselves and our children is to remember to breathe, remember to dust ourselves off, soften, and let ourselves back into our own hearts. It is only then that we will be clear and open enough to know what reparations, if any, are needed. It is only then that we will be able, as well, to open once again to our children and rest ourselves in the greater love and grace that cradles us all.

Days, weeks may go by without a falling off. There are other days when we may spend most of our time, it seems, remembering, climbing back on, remembering, breathing, remembering, opening up once again. The important thing, the most important thing, is to return, return to the razor's edge, no matter what.

To be on this edge is to dance: to dance Kali's dark dance, to dance with life, to dance with the ineffable sweetness of our own children. The music will inevitably change: sometimes tender; sometimes intense. A lullaby, a dirge, a jig. Giving ourselves over completely to the dance, no matter what the steps, is what mothering at its dark and fertile heart is about. Charlotte Joko Beck writes:

If we surrender to the experiencing . . . for the first time we can clearly see. When we can see, we know what to do. And what we do will be lov-

ing and compassionate. The religious life can be
lived.[20]

And mothering can be released into what it is meant to
be, a deeply spirited and spiritual process.

NO MORE SECONDHAND MOTHERS!

Peter London, in a book called *No More Secondhand Art*
about finding the artist within us all, remembered some
words of Buckminster Fuller: "Why not meet God directly? Why take someone else's story about hearing
someone else's story as your own religious experience?"
In just this way, then writes, London,

> We can engage in the creative process with the
> awe and exhilaration of every new beginning. If
> we are to engage in the act of creation directly
> and fully, we must set aside all that is second-
> hand news and bear witness to our direct encoun-
> ter with the world as if for the first time.[21]

Just so with mothering: No more secondhand mothers!
No more secondhand mothering! No more secondhand
children!

There is, to be sure, a time and a place for learning
the how-to of parenting. The Dr. Spocks and Dr. Bra-
zeltons of childrearing have important things to say, and
much may be learned from them. But then it is time to
cast the books and advice aside, trusting that the learning
and our own wisdom will come to us as we need them,
trusting that as we open our hearts and minds to ourselves

and our children we may heal, no matter what is happening, into the sacredness of the present moment.

Let us so awaken each morning, each moment: new, vital, alive. Let us remember that the invitation to Kali's dark and fertile dance is always extended to us, that all we need is "Yes," each morning, each moment.

Let us be open-hearted with ourselves, our children, our lives. Let us reclaim the sacredness of Now.

Time now, and always, to be First Mothers with our First Children, Original, dancing together on that holy edge of love and open space.

AUTHOR'S NOTE: for help along the way, see the exercises described in the Resource section of this book, especially those under Stage 3: The Return.

CHAPTER

11

Roaring Redux

*N*othing, really, can be written about what followed for me, except that there were, and still are, days when wave after sweet wave of gratitude rolled through me. All my heart can say is thank you, thank you to Life for this ineffable, grace-full gift of mothering.

Journal Entry
December 1, 1990

Eloise is into roaring these days. Roaring dinosaurs. Roaring dragons. Roaring lions. Roaring monsters. She becomes a lion, she drops down on her hands and knees.
"Mama," she says, "I'm a lion named Brietta that

goes ROAR. Listen, Mama, listen!" And she roars.
Her eyebrows draw together in concentration, her back
arches, "RROOOOOOOAAAAAAARRRRRR! RRRR-
RROOOOOOOAAAAARRRRRRRR!"

She stops for a moment, silent, as if listening to some
far off echo of her own roar. I come to attention, alert,
awake: I want to hear it too, feel the walls reverberate
with my own daughter's potency. Morning sunlight,
rare in winter, streams onto the rug where she is poised
and whitens her blond hair. "RRRRRROOOOOOO-
AAAAAARRRRRRRR! Mama," she says, "come
roar with me!"

I drop from my lazyboy onto the floor, the stubbiness
of the old Kirghiz carpet scratching my bare knees. The
sun is so bright I turn away from the window, feel the
sun's warmth on my shoulders and back. Where is my
roar? I clear my throat, hmmhmmhmm, "roar." Not
much. Where is my roar?

"RRRRRRRRROOOOOOOOOOOOAAAAAAAAAA-
ARRRRRRRRRRR!" comes Eloise. If I crouch we
are almost eye to eye. All that I've been writing about
flashes dark, electric, through my body. Roar, roar
from the darkness. Roar from that place. Roar. I take
a deep breath, fill my belly, and "RRROOOOOAAAA-
AARRRRR!" I surprise myself.

I, too, stop for a moment. Yes, I can hear the
echoes, feel the reverberations. Again!
"RRRRRRROOOOOOOOAAAAAAARRRRRRR-
RRR!" My belly shakes, my womb hums, my body tin-
gles. Eloise rears up on her knees and roars back at
me, louder. There is now an added intensity to her
roar, dancing at the edge of something truly wild.

I let the wildness in me, new and alive, answer

back. We leapfrog our roars, playing together on that edge of something untamable and dark and utterly foreign, utterly ours. Something in me wants to hold back, protect my child from my wildness, but she is leading me in this. Such roars I've never roared, free, dark, potent: "RRRRROOOOOOOAAAAAAAARRRRRR-RRR! RRRRRRRRRRROOOOOOOOOOOOOO-AAAAAAAA*

RRRRRRRRRRRR! RRRRRRRROOOOOOOO-OOOAAAAAAAAAARRRRRRRR!"

I collapse on the flowered rug, spent. I roll over on my back, close my eyes against the sunshine, neon blue and orange and purple vibrating in the darkness behind my lids. My underarms are damp, and I feel a drop of sweat slide down the side of my forehead into my hair. I'm breathing hard, from deep down in my body. It is good. Eloise has also thrown herself down on the carpet, and I can hear her panting close by.

Everything is vivid: the warmth of the sun on my face, Eloise's panting beside me, the scratchy feel of the old rug under my fingertips. I hear the high, faint beepbeepbeep of a truck backing up. My own breathing slows, deepens; my heart, my chest, are spacious, tender, soft.

The roaring has broken me open once again. Old pieces of me lie scattered throughout the room. I don't need them anymore. Bits of me are all over the house, everywhere I've cried or despaired or raged or danced with a heart burst from joy. Pieces everywhere. As I lie here on this rug, in this room, on this winter's day, with this sunlight warming my eyelids, I am new landscape. My geography is different: big sky, fences down, no KEEP OUT signs. Open country.

All this graced from those moments, hours, days of darkness as a mother. Days of nowhere to go but down. Hours of nothing to do but die. There will be more, I know, in the future, but right now that doesn't matter. This is what matters, this, lying here on the rug and breathing with my daughter, warm, present, alive.

Thank you. Thank you.

Resources

Until one is committed there is hesitancy, the
chance to draw back, always ineffectiveness. Con-
cerning all acts of initiative (and creation) there
is one elemental truth: that the moment one defi-
nitely commits oneself, then Providence moves too.
—GOETHE

All well and good, you say, this book about staying in the present, about recognizing mothering as an emotional and spiritual transformative path, but how do you do it? (Or, at least that is what I might say after finishing the book!)

EXERCISES

These are some of the exercises that I, and the mothers in the classes and groups that I have taught, have found helpful. The first section includes helps that are applicable at any point in the process. The subsequent sections are ways applicable to specific stages. Try any of them, or none of them. Make up your own. (Let me know of any others you use; I'm always learning.) Trust your own wisdom in this. Trust your own heart.

All these practices are for you-as-mother, to learn to be more present with yourself and your child. As you practice these, however, you may be pleasantly surprised to learn that you have become more open to *all* of your life—a wonderful side effect! Practice whichever points you choose whenever you can: while folding laundry, sweeping floors, attending departmental meetings, driving on the freeway. The more you practice opening to yourself and whatever the present moment brings, the more you will be able to be open and alive with your child, no matter what the situation.

GENERAL HELPS

○ Cultivate an awareness of your own breathing: notice when you're breathing. Notice when you're not. (When you're not, stop whatever you're doing and take a deep breath.) Let your breathing come from deep within your belly, a soft and open belly.

○ Touch base with your body. Ask yourself, "What am I feeling right now in my body, and where?" The more you can practice this, and the more you can practice breathing, in everyday, non-stressful stiuations, the easier it will be for you to remain aware when you are in difficult situations with your child.

○ When you're feeling bored, numb, restless with your child, ask yourself, "What am I avoiding feeling/experiencing right now?" Then feel it. If you can't honestly answer the question, don't judge yourself for not knowing. Simply allow yourself to feel the boredom, numbness, restlessness as fully as you can.

○ Find or create a support group of like-minded mothers with whom you may speak the truth about your own mothering experiences, share the ups and downs of the journey, and give and receive support for mothering with an open heart. Even one other mother can be a valuable help.

○ If you are having trouble getting started on the journey or you feel overwhelmed even at the beginning, consider the possiblity of therapy. If you are feeling out of control, and are being emotional and/or physically abusive with your children, it would be wise to seek professional help. With a good and trusted therapist you can learn to open up to the present moment, to whatever you are feeling, and heal. Let the therapist know that this is what you want to do.

○ Cultivate gratitude. As you face difficult inner times, or frustrating moments, with your child, ask yourself: What is this an opportunity for me to remember, practice, learn? What is this an opportunity to be grateful for? What is the gift in this? See the significance of whatever presents itself to you. Brother David Steindl-Rast calls gratefulness "the heart of prayer."

○ Meditate. Find a type of meditation, such as vi-
passana, or insight meditation (see Recommended
Reading), designed to open you up more to the
sacredness of the present moment.

○ Read. There is a list of recommended books at
the back of this book. If you know any people
who have taken this or a similar journey, ask if
they have any favorite books about the process.

JOURNALING

I advocate keeping a journal, as you may have noticed
throughout the book. Journaling is a powerful tool for
enriching self-awareness and can be a helpful way to
deepen your practice of mothering with spirit. If you are
currently keeping a journal, or are thinking of doing so,
consider the following exercises (again, these are general
ones for the journey; exercises for more specific stages
may be found in the appropriate sections below).

○ Tell stories. Someone, I can't remember who,
once wrote that the universe is made not of atoms
but of stories. Tell stories, complete with dialogue, in your journal about your experiences
with your child. Telling stories is healing on
many different levels, and it may help you get a
new perspective on your mothering and where
you are in the process.

○ Try "timed writing" in your journal. Pick a topic,
such as "being a mother," and write for twenty
minutes without stopping or censoring. You will
be surprised at the depths to which this kind of

writing can take you. You might want to do this timed writing with another mother, and read your writing, without comment from either of you, to each other at the end of the time.

○ Record your dreams in your journal. Keep your journal and a pen by your bed so that you may write down the dreams as you awaken. After you've recorded a dream, ask yourself what this dream might be saying about the process that you're going through. If you wish, you may "incubate" a dream: just before you go to sleep, ask for a dream that will help you in this process. If you want more information on working with dreams, see the Recommended Reading at the end of this chapter.

○ Write about what the word "spirituality" means for you. If mothering is to be a spiritual path for you, what does that mean in your life and words? What is your vision of mothering as a spiritual path? How does the darker side, the "underbelly" of mothering (the inevitable griefs, fears, guilts, despairs, angers), fit into your vision?

○ Close your eyes, relax, and meditate on your sense of the connection between spirituality and mothering. Pay attention to physical sensations and emotional feelings as you do so. Allow an image, a symbol of the way mothering and spirituality are connected for you, to arise from deep within you. Observe the image in detail; experience its presence. Draw the image in your journal (experiment with drawing it with your non-domi-

nant hand). Let the image speak to you. Let
yourself respond. Ask yourself in the journal,
"What do I need in order to feel safe enough to
start this journey?"

○ What most gets in your way of practicing mothering as a spiritual path and as a doorway into
wholeness? What can you do about this?

○ Ask questions about mothering. Big questions. If
you don't have any, make them up. Don't worry
about the answers right now. Madeleine L'Engle
(at least, I believe it was she) once wrote, "God
doesn't ask us to know the answers. He asks us
to love the questions." Rainer Maria Rilke ad-
vised, "Live your questions now, and perhaps,
even without knowing it, you will live along some
distant day into your answers." Ingrid Bengis tells
us, "The real questions are the ones that obtrude
upon your consciousness whether you like it or
not. . . .The real questions refuse to be pla-
cated. . . .They are the questions answered most
inadequately, the ones that reveal their true na-
tures slowly, reluctantly, most often against your
will." We are by nature question-askers, but in
this culture we are discouraged from being so.
Try it. Allow yourself to ask questions about
mothering that you have never dared articulate.
Ask yourself this: what sorts of things am I not
supposed to question as a mother? Question
them. Try softening into the questions with an
open heart rather than closing down around some
answers.

○ Ask yourself in your journal, "Why do I want to take this journey? What do I see as the rewards, on both a personal and a more global level, for doing this?"

STAGE 1: NAMING

These exercises address the material covered in Part II of this book, from page 18 to page 42.

JOURNALING

○ Write a letter, one that you need never send, to your own mother. Tell her the ways she mothered you that you wish to copy with your children and the ways you do not wish to pass on. Acknowledge the ways she hurt you as a mother; acknowledge the ways she loved you. After letting the letter sit for a week or so, go back and reread it. Add anything to it you might have forgotten. Then write about the way everything you've written affects your own mothering practice.

○ What most gets in the way of your staying awake and aware when you are with your child? When do you go unconscious with your child? What can you do about it?

○ Notice when your internal Good Mother steps in and criticizes you. When does she do it? How does she say it? How do you respond, both internally and behaviorally, to her judgments?

○ How have this culture, your childhood religion, and your own mother, grandmothers, and aunts influenced, for better and for worse, the way you now are as a mother? What images, ideas, and ideals might you need to let go of in order to deepen your practice of mothering with an open heart?

STAGE 2: THE DESCENT

These exercises address the material covered in Part III of this book, from page 56 to page 85.

○ Identify sources of help and support for yourself. Who can listen, simply listen, to your pain, confusion, despair, without getting entangled in it? Who will honor your pain without trying to fix it? Who can hold the bigger picture for you, quietly, as you enter your own dark night?

○ Give yourself permission for more separateness and distance from your child for the time being, if you feel you need it. You need to figure out how to do this at a physical, practical level, and articulate this to your partner, if you have one. We, as women and mothers, are given very little permission by our culture to claim space for ourselves. This may be one of the times in your life when it is important to claim it, and make sure you get it, even if only in small ways.

○ Tell your child, in simple, developmentally appropriate language, that you are hurting inside and that *it is not your child's fault*. This is important, for children are very sensitive, and if they are not told what is going on they will usually feel responsible for it in some way. Let your child know you will feel better later and that you love him or her.

○ Tune in to your body. This is a good time to get a massage, or to begin having bodywork if you've been considering it. Find ways to lovingly connect to your own body. Warm, fragrant baths are great. Make a list of what's good for you.

○ Ground yourself and your pain. Bodywork is one way to do this. Simply being aware of the soles of your feet on the ground is another. Walking meditation is good. So is holding your own hands, giving yourself a hand or a foot massage.

○ Notice where in your body you carry different feelings. Practice staying aware of your body as you feel pain, anger, grief, despair, and so on.

○ On some days the feelings may be too intense to do anything but simply try to stay aware of your breathing. Go through the day one breath at a time.

○ Resist the temptation to think in terms of all or nothing—it's what you can do in small pieces that counts. There is no way to go through this stage perfectly; in fact, that's what this stage is about: letting go of internal demands for perfection.

○ Let go of thinking that you *have* to do something about the feelings. In a therapy-oriented society, there is subtle pressure to "do" something with our feelings whenever we feel them. Much of this second stage is deep, internal, vegetative work, where often simply experiencing the feelings, breathing through them as you might do with labor pains, is all that needs to be done. Sometimes we simply don't have all the pieces of the puzzle yet, and waiting for the next step is the most important thing to do.

○ If, however, you find the feelings are simply too scary to experience on your own or with a friend, or if you find yourself stuck deeply in them, don't hesitate to call a therapist (see general guidelines at the beginning of the Resources section of this book).

○ If you find yourself, at this point or any other point in this process, hurting yourself or your child, *get help*. In this situation, it's the greatest gift you could bestow either on yourself or on your child.

○ Give yourself permission to take a break from your feelings. This is not suppressing them, or shutting down, but getting some distance, lightening up. At some points this may not be possible, but at others times it is. Go see a funny movie with someone you care about. Read the comics. Play on a playground.

○ Take some time to get into nature: hike, camp, spend some time in a park, garden. This is important for two reasons: first, it grounds you; second, it is an opportunity to see the bigger picture, observe the bigger cycles of death and birth, decay and growth. Sit down against the trunk of a tree and let the tree nurture you and sustain you. Talk to your roses. Nature can be part of that larger, loving, holding space so deeply needed at this stage.

○ Making use of ritual at this stage can be very valuable (see Recommended Reading at the end of this chapter if you want help and ideas). Rituals around acknowledging the darker side, acknowledging the crossroads of the liminal stage, acknowledging one's grief, anger, despair, fear connected with mothering, or around letting go, around surrendering a past way of life or a past way of mothering, can be tremendously helpful and healing around this time.

JOURNALING

○ How have cultural and religious connotations of "darkness" influenced and affected you as you read this book? What are the negative and positive connotations of "darkness" that you are aware of? How might these various connotations hamper, or enhance, your journey of opening to your dark side?

○ How comfortable are you with the dark mother inside you? As you did with the question for Stage 1 connecting mothering with spirituality, go inside and allow an image of the dark mother to rise up from within you. If you wish, draw her in your journal. Then have a dialogue with her in your journal; you might try writing what she says to you with your non-dominant hand and responding to her with your dominant hand. Ask her questions, take a deep breath, let her answer you. You might ask her name and inquire why she is appearing to you. Tell her what you think and feel about her; if you are afraid of her, as most of us are, tell her so, and allow her to respond. Tell her what you want from her (assistance, wisdom, a gift); ask her what she wants from you and for you. Continue to converse with her for as long as you like. When you are done, thank her and release her. As you go through this process notice how this figure, and your relationship with her, changes.

○ Make a list of the ten things that disturb you the most about being a mother (for instance, "I don't have enough time for myself," "I'm afraid my child will die," "I'm afraid I will hurt my child somehow"). Pick one of the items on your list and write about it for twenty minutes from that place in yourself that feels it. Ask your inner censor to take a brief break, and then let the part of yourself that you picked write as honestly and unobstructedly as possible. (Thanks to Dr. Barbara Turner-Vesselago, teacher of Freefall Writing, for this suggestion.)

STAGE 3: THE RETURN

Use these ideas in connection with the material covered in Part IV of this book, from page 100 to page 131.

○ Learn the difference between hard focus and soft focus. Hard focus is contracted, tight, aware of only one or two elements in your own landscape. (This is different from relaxed concentration: in hard focus I am tense and contracted; in relaxed concentration I am open, breathing, "soft-bellied.") Hard focus promotes battle-readiness. In soft focus I am aware of the entire field: my body, my feelings, my child's feelings and behaviors, the cawing of a crow outside the window, and the way the sun coming through the window highlights the dust motes dancing above my child's head.

○ Try experiencing your feelings, especially the more difficult ones, as energy patterns in your body, rather than labeling them as "anger," "sadness," "joy," and so on.

○ Ask yourself, "What is going on *right now* (inside me, with my child, between the two of us)?

○ Try breathing at the same rate as your child when you are spending some time with him or her.

○ When you're experiencing a difficult feeling, try the following:

• Make space for it in your body; soften around its edges.

- Allow your heart to soften: open both to the pain and to yourself as the feeler of the pain.

○ When you find yourself in a difficult situation with your child:

- Take a breath!

- Ask yourself, "What hurts most right now? What am I most afraid of right now? What am I resisting most right now, either in myself or in my child? What is there for me to learn in this, right now?

- Be less concerned, for the moment, with what to *do* and focus more on softening your heart and your focus, opening your mind, and seeing what is truly happening right then.

○ Are you someone who tends to close off from joy, tenderness, gratitude, as well as other feelings? (I am.) Practice keeping your heart fully open to the more expansive, light feelings as well as the darker ones.

JOURNALING

○ What are your characteristic ways of forgetting, of falling off the razor's edge? How can you best remember and climb back on?

○ Write about a painful incident concerning yourself and your child in the past. If you hadn't already decided the experience was painful, how else might you have seen it? From your vantage point of the present, what did you learn from it? What in it can you now be grateful for?

○ Letting go:

- What does letting go mean in a spiritual context for you? How does that translate into the practicalities of mothering?

- What is it that you most need to let go of in order to enter more fully into being an alive, open mother with your child? What to let go of will be different for every mother. For one mother it might mean letting go of being rigid about certain things with her child; for another mother it might mean the opposite, letting go of giving in to her child in certain situations.

○ Struggling:

- Write about a time you stopped struggling with your child about something and the way the situation resolved itself. How does that connect with your response about the spiritual context of letting go?

- Think about a struggle you are currently having with your child in some aspect of your relationship. What if you stopped struggling, opened your heart and your mind to yourself and your child, trusted your own wisdom, and went from there? What are you afraid might happen? What might happen instead? What in this current struggle is there to be grateful for?

○ Notice how, as you stay more in the present with your child, a sense of wonder about mothering, wonder about your child and yourself and the holy spaces between, arises from within you. Write about a time, an "ordinary" time, when the wonder broke through. Writing about these times in your journal as they occur will increase your ability to notice wonder and stay with it.

○ What about being a mother are you thankful for?

Journal Pages

Notes

1. Louise Mahdi, Steven Foster, and Meredith Little, eds., *Betwixt and Between: Patterns of Masculine and Feminine Initiation* (La Salle, Ill.: Open Court, 1987), p. 5. The entire first essay in this collection, "The Liminal Period in Rites of Passage," by Victor Turner, is highly recommended as a way to understand the archetypal structure of all rites of passage.

2. *Ibid.*, p. 5.

3. *Ibid.*, p. 18.

4. Sy Safransky, ed., *Sunbeams: A Book of Quotations* (Berkeley: North Atlantic Books, 1990), p. 90. This book contains a lot of quotes. There's nothing I enjoy better than a well-placed, pithy quote, and as a result I have a lot of them rattling around in my head. Unfortunately for the reader, this means that I am often unable to give the source for the quote. My apologies.

5. Paula Caplan, *Don't Blame Mother: Mending the Mother-Daughter Relationship* (Harper and Row, 1989), p. 47, refers to a study documenting officially what I found in the library that dreary morning: that mental health workers of all occupations

"overwhelmingly indulged" in mother-blaming. In the 125 articles in major mental health journals that they studied, "mothers were blamed for 72 different kinds of problems in their offspring, ranging from bed-wetting to schizophrenia, . . . from learning problems to 'homicidal transsexualism.' "

6. Sibylle Birkhause-Oeri, *The Mother: Archetypal Image in Fairy Tales* (Toronto: Inner City Books, 1988), p. 32.

7. Kathie Carlson, *In Her Image: The Unhealed Daughter's Search for Her Mother* (Boston: Shambala, 1989), p. 9.

8. Joanna Macy, *Despair and Personal Power in the Nuclear Age* (Philadelphia: New Society), p. 4.

9. Fred Gustafson, *The Black Madonna* (Boston: Sigo Press, 1990), p. 86.

10. "Kali the Mad Mother," in *The Book of the Goddess*, Carl Olson, ed. (New York: Crossroad, 1990), p. 111. Kali, a goddess in the Hindu pantheon, is both creator and destroyer. She is typically portrayed as black, naked (free from all covering of illusion), and full-breasted (ceaselessly creating and nurturing as Mother). Kali represents "the vital principles of the visible universe which has many faces—gracious, cruel, creative, destructive, loving, indifferent—the endless possibility of the active energy at the heart of the world." Leonard Nathan and Clinton Seely, *Grace and Mercy in Her Wild Hair* (Boulder, CO: Great Eastern, 1982), pp. 62-63, in *Kali: the Feminine Force* (New York: Destiny Books, 1988).

11. Carlson, *op. cit.*, p. 85.

12. Barbara Hannah, *Encounters with the Soul: Active Imagination* (Boston: Sigo Press, 1981), p. 7.

13. *Ibid.*, p. 7.

14. Fritjof Capra, *Uncommon Wisdom* (New York: Simon and Schuster, 1988), p. 32.

15. *Sunbeams: A Book of Quotations*, p. 153.

16. "Untamed Goddesses of Village India," in *The Book of the Goddess*, p. 158.

17. Thich Nhat Hanh, *The Heart of Understanding* (Berkeley: Parallax, 1988), p.14.

18. Shunryu Suzuki, *Zen Mind, Beginner's Mind* (Tokyo: John Weatherhill, 1970), pp. 21-22.

19. Charlotte Joko Beck, *Everyday Zen: Love and Work* (San Francisco: Harper and Row, 1990), p. 165.

20. *Ibid.*, p. 172.

21. Peter London, *No More Secondhand Art* (Boston: Shambala, 1989), p. 5.

Recommended Reading

TRANSITIONS AND CHANGE

Karpinski, Gloria. *Where Two Worlds Touch: Spiritual Rites of Passage*. New York: Ballantine Books, 1990.
A wonderful book about ways to consciously use change as a spiritual rite of passage.

Mahdi, Louise, Steven Foster, and Meredith Little, eds. *Betwixt and Between: Patterns of Masculine and Feminine Initiation*. La Salle, Illinois: Open Court, 1987.
A collection of interdisciplinary essays describing transitions at significant stages of life around the world. See particularly Part Five, "Personal Initiation," for essays about the inner meanings of personal transformation.

MOTHERING

Berends, Polly Berrien. *Whole Child, Whole Parent*. New York: Harper and Row, 1987.
A classic work on seeing the deeper meaning of parenting. Full of both inspiration and practical advice.

Caplan, Paula. *Don't Blame Mother: Mending the Mother-Daughter Relationship*. New York: Harper and Row, 1990.
A book about replacing with understanding and respect the anger, guilt, disappointment, and mother-blame daughters often feel towards their own mothers.

Carlson, Kathie. *In Her Image: the Unhealed Daughter's Search for Her Mother*. Boston: Shambala, 1989.
An excellent book on healing our relationships with our own mothers through exploring three dimensions of the mother-daughter relationship: the purely personal, the feminist perspective, and the transpersonal perspective.

Gray, Elizabeth Dodson, ed. *Sacred Dimensions of Women's Experience*. Wellesley: Roundtable Press, 1988.
An anthology of women's writing concerning the integration of everyday life with the sacred. See especially the section entitled "Caregiving."

Rabuzzi, Kathryn Allen. *Motherself: A Mythic Analysis of Motherhood*. Bloomington: Indiana University Press, 1988.
An insightful book that proposes a female alternative to the hero's journey: the way of the mother, the goal of which Rabuzzi names as the achievement of "motherself."

Rich, Adrienne. *Of Woman Born: Motherhood as Experience and Institution*. New York: W.W. Norton, 1986.
A landmark book. Rich examines the cultural institution of motherhood from a feminist perspective.

INTEGRATING DARKNESS

Gustafson, Fred. *The Black Madonna*. Boston: Sigo Press, 1990.
A book about the integration of the dark feminine, using the Black Madonna of Einsiedeln as symbol.

Mookerjee, Ajit. *Kali: the Feminine Force*. New York: Destiny Books, 1988.
An entire book about Kali and her place in Hindu cosmology. Contains many helpful reproductions of statues and paintings.

Perera, Sylvia Brinton. *Descent to the Goddess: A Way of Initiation for Women*. Toronto: Inner City, 1981.
This important book presents the descent into darkness as a way of initiation for women, an initiation into one's own essential nature.

RELATIONSHIPS

Macy, Joanna. *Despair and Personal Power in the Nuclear Age*. Philadelphia: New Society, 1983.
I particularly recommend the first two chapters about the passage through darkness into the web of life.

Moss, Richard. *The Black Butterfly: An Invitation to Radical Aliveness*. Berkeley: Celestial Arts, 1987.
An inspiring book, in part about sacred relationships as a path to radical aliveness.

MEDITATION

Goldstein, Joseph. *The Experience of Insight*. Boston: Shambala, 1976.
———and Jack Kornfield. *Seeking the Heart of Wisdom*. Boston: Shambala, 1987.
Levine, Stephen. *A Gradual Awakening*. Garden City: Anchor Books, 1979.
Three outstanding books about the theory and practice of insight meditation.

RITUAL

Beck, Renee, and Sydney Merrick. *The Art of Ritual*. Berkeley: Celestial Arts, 1990.
How to create rituals to commemorate symbolic moments and assist in times of change. Gives sample rituals, as well as ritual guidelines and a worksheet to help in the creation of personal rituals.

Paladin, Linda. *Ceremonies for Change: Creating Personal Ritual to Heal Life's Hurts*. Walpole, New Hampshire: Stillpoint International, 1991.
A book to help readers create and celebrate personal ceremonies to mark important personal transitions. Included with the book are ritual cards to help with the process.

DREAMWORK

Baldwin, Christina. *Wisdom of the Heart: Working with Women's Dreams*. New York: Bantam, 1989.
Excellent guide to working with dreams, written especially for women and their issues.

Johnson, Robert. *Inner Work: Using Dreams and Active Imagination for Personal Growth* (San Francisco: HarperSanFrancisco, 1986).
Good introduction to the unconscious in the forms of dreams and active imagination. Includes theory and practice for both.

ACTIVE IMAGINATION/GUIDED IMAGERY

Hannah, Barbara. *Encounters with the Soul: Active Imagination*. Boston: Sigo, 1981.

A classic book on working with active imagination written by an analyst trained by Carl Jung. Contains illuminating case studies and deals in depth with the injured feminine.

Johnson, Robert. *Inner Work: Using Dreams and Active Imagination for Personal Growth.*
See section above on Dreamwork.

Murdock, Maureen. *Spinning Inward: Using Guided Imagery with Children.* Boston: Shambala, 1987.
Although this book was originally developed for teaching children ages 3-18 how to work with guided imagery, it is one of the best books available for adults as well. Contains many helpful exercises.

LIVING IN THE PRESENT

Beck, Charlotte Joko. *Everyday Zen: Love and Work.* San Francisco: Harper and Row, 1989.
A book about practicing awareness during the problems and challenges of everyday life.

Gendlin, Eugene. *Focusing.* New York: Bantam, 1981.
A useful guide for learning how to recognize and integrate feelings as they arise in the course of daily living.

Suzuki, Shunryu. *Zen Mind, Beginner's Mind.* Tokyo: Weatherhill, 1987.
Classic on the spiritual practice of living life with an open mind, a beginner's mind.

Melissa West is a writer, teacher, speaker, and therapist. She may be reached at:

Melissa West
9040 Evanston Ave. N.
Seattle, WA 98103-3816